THE
RATABAN
BETRAYAL

Also by Stephen Alter:

NONFICTION

FICTION

STEPHEN ALTER

THE RATABAN BETRAYAL

A Novel

Arcade Publishing • New York

First North American Edition

This is a work of fiction. Names, places, characters, and incidents are either the products of the author's imagination or are used fictitiously.

Arcade Publishing books may be purchased in bulk at special discounts for sales promotion, corporate gifts, fund-raising, or educational purposes. Special editions can also be created to specifications. For details, contact the Special Sales Department, Arcade Publishing, 307 West 36th Street, 11th Floor, New York, NY 10018 or arcade@skyhorsepublishing.com.

Arcade Publishing® is a registered trademark of Skyhorse Publishing, Inc.®, a Delaware corporation.

Visit our website at www.arcadepub.com.
Visit the author's site at www.stephenalter.net.

10 9 8 7 6 5 4 3 2 1

Library of Congress Cataloging-in-Publication Data

Alter, Stephen.
   The rataban betrayal / Stephen Alter.—First North American edition.
     pages; cm
   ISBN 978-1-62872-575-9 (hardback)—ISBN 978-1-62872-623-7 (ebook)
   I. Title.
   PS3551.L77R38 2016
   813'.54—dc23
                 2015028698

Cover design by Owen Corrigan
Cover photo: Shutterstock

Printed in the United States of America

The mind of another is a foreign land.
Himalayan proverb

Dedicated to
Friends and Neighbors in Mussoorie

Author's Note

This novel is a work of fiction. All of the characters are entirely imaginary and bear no likeness to any person, living or dead. While many of the historical and cultural references are based on reality, the narrative is not intended to be a factual rendering of events, political circumstances, or contextual details. The hill station of Mussoorie and many of the locations described in this novel do exist, but poetic liberties have been taken with the geography; many of the places described can be found only within the confines of this story. RAW is an acronym for the Research and Analysis Wing, India's foreign intelligence agency. The Intelligence Bureau, which is a separate agency, focuses primarily on domestic intelligence and security. Depiction of these agencies and their affiliates in this novel is entirely fictional. Finally, it must be emphasized that this book is written with the utmost admiration and respect for the Tibetan people, their cultural heritage, their religion, and their future.

THE
RATABAN
BETRAYAL

One

1969. Tibet. Behind them stood the high Himalayas, impenetrable barriers of rock and snow, buttressed with ice falls and glaciers. An avalanche broke loose on one of the snow peaks above the pass, a rumbling white cloud that poured down the vertical face of the mountain. To the north, in front of them, spread the Tibetan Plateau—arid, undulating steppes as far as the eye could see. Once the floor of a primordial ocean, the plateau now lay 14,000 feet above sea level. The wind felt brittle and raw, as if scarce molecules of oxygen had crystallized in the air, invisible particles that cut your lips and tongue before dissolving painfully in your lungs.

Jigme watched the quarreling cluster of men, huddled on a flat rock at the far edge of the pass. His face was stern and unemotional, though his eyes betrayed the fear and remorse that lingered in his mind. Six yaks were tethered nearby, standing so close to each other they looked like a single, large animal—a shaggy black beast with a dozen horns and restless hooves. On a slope below were the horses, heads lowered, searching for grass in the frozen soil. They would find no forage, nothing to graze on, until they descended two thousand feet below the pass.

The men were arguing, and their voices rose in anger. One of them lifted his hand in a threatening gesture as he was shoved aside. Another got to his feet, holding up a pair of leather climbing boots by the laces. Dressed in sheepskin coats draped across one shoulder and heavy woolen robes of several layers, all of the men were nomadic hunters from Western Tibet. As the rest of the party stood up, Jigme could just make out a corpse lying on the boulder. Stripped naked, the dead man was as white as the patches of snow amid the rocks. Each of the hunters had claimed his loot—a pocket knife, a compass, a pair of trousers torn at the knee. One carried a nylon parka stained with blood. Another had removed a watch from the dead man's wrist.

The pass was marked with several cairns of mani stones—inscriptions etched on granite, basalt, and schist. *Om Mani Padme Hum . . .* and other invocations honoring the divine elements and highland spirits who guarded this desolate region. Some of the stones were embedded with fossils, prehistoric mollusks and fish that once swam in the Tethys Sea, eons ago, before the Himalayas were formed. Piled on the cairns were bleached skulls of yak and bharal, wild sheep, as well as ibex. Tattered prayer flags trembled in the breeze, but most had been snapped by savage gales that blew across the pass. Strings of pennants lay on the ground, printed verses and images of wind horses and snow lions fading off the gauzy fabric.

Two of the hunters carried antique muskets with long barrels. The rest of the men were armed with modern weapons. Jigme was a Khampa, from Eastern Tibet. He stood apart from the group. These were not his people, and he barely understood their dialect. They had descended from warring clans of Shangshung, human predators as wild as their prey. For generations, their ancestors had been poachers and bandits, feared by travelers from Marco Polo to Sven Hedin. Even the Mongols had not subdued them, allowing these wandering brigands to pillage and plunder along the lower margins of the Silk Route. The hunters stuffed whatever clothes and other belongings they had stripped from the corpse into bundles loaded on their yaks.

The dead man was an American. He had fallen into a crevasse that morning while they were crossing a glacier. Jigme had been able to plunge his ice axe into the snow and anchor the rope, but when they'd pulled the American out of the crevasse, he knew the man would not survive. One leg was broken and there was a gash across his forehead where his skull had cracked. He was unconscious but breathing in shallow gasps. They had carried him this far, strapped to one of the yaks, knowing it was pointless. He had died an hour ago, as they were climbing up to the pass. Digging a grave in the frozen earth was impossible, and there was no fuel at this altitude, not even a juniper twig, with which to burn the body. Their only option was to consign the American's corpse to a sky burial, according to the practical and spiritual traditions of Tibet.

Glancing behind him, Jigme could see the second American standing fifty yards away, a solitary figure with a rifle slung across his shoulder. Like Jigme, he was dressed in a thick down parka, its fur-lined hood pulled over his head. He was facing away from the pass, scanning the distant horizon through a pair of binoculars. The American seemed untroubled by the loss of his companion and the scavenging of the hunters, who had joined them yesterday, after they crossed over the main bulwark of the Himalayas, leaving India behind. Jigme watched the lone figure with distrust. They had spent the last two months together, but the American had remained a stranger, aloof and secretive as a ghost.

The nomads began to whistle through their teeth, calling the horses as they untied their yaks. Four hours of daylight still remained, and they were eager to get down off the pass. As the American turned to join the others, hoisting a rucksack onto his back, Jigme saw two circling shapes in the sky. A pair of Himalayan griffons passed over-head, spiraling down on outstretched wings. They seemed to come from nowhere, out of the void of heaven. As the vultures soared past Jigme, he could hear the murmur of their feathers. Within a minute the huge raptors had landed on the corpse. By this time, the hunt-ers were already a hundred yards down the trail, still whistling at their animals. The American stopped and glanced back for a second, as the griffons began to feed. Jigme winced and mumbled a prayer for the dead, incoherent words catching in his throat and making him cough. The wind echoed his chanting with a solemn dirge, as it scoured the lifeless terrain.

Another vulture swooped in low and settled on a nearby cairn before opening its wings and strutting across to the pale figure on the granite slab. Soon, many more of these giant birds would join in the carrion feast. The grim ceremonies of nature commenced, and, before darkness fell, the sky burial had been consummated. As the sun disappeared behind the mountains and the wind grew still, the American's bones were picked clean of flesh and scattered on the barren slopes below the pass. Then, like winged phantoms, the vultures returned to the sky, carrying with them the dead man's spirit and dispersing it in the clouds.

Two

"Let goods and kindred go, this mortal life also;
The body they may kill: God's truth abideth still,
His kingdom is forever."

The closing verse of the final hymn, "A Mighty Fortress Is Our God," rose in a disparate chorus of voices scattered around the church. The pastor in his white cassock and scarlet stole led the singing with both arms raised, as the congregation joined together in the closing lines. The organist, an elderly woman in a green chiffon sari, pumped the treadles with both feet as her diligent fingers picked at the keys. Behind the altar was a triptych of stained glass windows depicting the Crucifixion, Resurrection, and Ascension. Tall brass candelabra stood on either side, amber flames flickering in their grasp.

Dexter Fallows bowed his head as the pastor began the benediction. His folded hands fidgeted and his shoe tapped lightly on the marble floor. He was in his late sixties, a gaunt, agitated man with a youthful face, despite his age. He was clean shaven, though he had missed a patch of bristle under his chin this morning, as he'd hurried to get ready for church. His hair was white and thin, parted to the left. Fallows closed his eyes when the prayer began, but they blinked open almost immediately, a watery blue color that startled people when they met him first. He sat alone in one of the pews toward the back. Most of the congregation was Indian, members of the protestant community in Landour, though there were a number of foreigners in their midst.

Surreptitiously, Fallows rotated his wrist so that he could see the face of his watch protruding from beneath his sleeve. 11:38.

The service had dragged on for more than an hour. Distracted by his own convoluted thoughts and worries, Fallows had not been able to pay attention to the sermon, as the pastor admonished his parishioners about forgiving their enemies. Leaning forward, he hunched his shoulders under the gray gabardine fabric of his suit. His whole body seemed to twitch as the pastor brought the service to a close with words of blessing and deliverance.

An old cantonment church, St. Paul's was consecrated in 1840, when Landour was first established as a convalescent retreat for colonial troops in North India. Landour was now part of the larger hill station of Mussoorie, though it remained a discreet area of the town, with scattered homes on a forested ridge, isolated from the main bazaar. Rows of notches were carved into the hard wooden pews at St. Paul's so that British "Tommies" could rest their rifles during worship. After 1857, when many of the British were slaughtered by rebellious sepoys, European soldiers in India were ordered to bear arms in church rather than stacking their weapons outside. Today, no Enfield rifles rested against the pews. Fallows reached up nervously and flipped open the wooden latch that once held a loaded firearm in place.

For more than fifty years, he had attended this church. There were other places of worship in Mussoorie, but Fallows preferred St. Paul's, which was walking distance from his house. He was at the end of his career as a missionary with the North India Bible Fellowship, administering several charities and Christian institutions funded by churches abroad, a paternalistic sinecure that gave him plenty of time for other pursuits. Fallows had grown up in Mussoorie, himself a child of missionaries. He had gone to school in Landour as a boy and returned here after college and seminary, to carry on his parents' calling but also because it was his home.

In another six months, Fallows would retire and go back to America. Though anxious and ambivalent about the move, he had already signed a lease on an apartment in Arlington, Virginia. His wife had died a decade ago, and she was buried in the cemetery on the north side of Landour. They had no children, and his only living relative was a half-brother in Milwaukee, but the long cold winters of Wisconsin held little appeal for someone who had spent all of his life in India. For a while, Fallows had considered staying on in Mussoorie, but this year he had decided it was time to move back, before he got any older and his health declined. As a life-long expatriate, Fallows still pledged allegiance to America, though he had lived outside its borders for so many years he hardly knew the country. From time to time, he had returned to the United States on short furloughs, but he had never lived there for more than three months at a stretch. Going back, he felt uneasy about becoming an exile in his own homeland.

"Amen!"

Exhaling a grateful sigh, Fallows echoed the pastor's exclamation and quickly rose to his feet. Fastening the uppermost button of his suit, he stepped into the aisle and rushed outside. Earlier that morning the sky had been overcast, but now the sun was breaking through the clouds. In the churchyard, a bed of scruffy dahlias were still blooming. The clear October air was scented with resin from the tall deodar trees that grew on either side of the church, their massive columns surrounding the red roof, yellow walls, and bell tower. Here in Landour, the architecture of nature overshadowed the sanctuaries of man.

Fallows hurried across the lawn, reaching for the inside pocket of his coat. Eagerly, his fingers closed around a packet of unfiltered Charminar and a box of matches. As soon as he was behind the largest deodar tree, he shook out a cigarette and tucked it between his lips. Furtively, he struck a match and cupped its flame in his palm, as he lit the roasted flakes of tobacco. A bittersweet fragrance soothed his restless nerves. As Fallows inhaled, his anxious thoughts seemed to ease. The tension between his shoulder blades was gently unknotted as the nicotine entered his lungs and dispersed through his veins.

Just then, a rifle shot rang out, but Fallows didn't hear it. A single bullet punctured his skull, an inch behind his left ear, knocking him forward against the trunk of the tree. He was dead before his body slumped to the ground. The cigarette lay smoldering in the grass until it was extinguished by a spreading pool of blood.

Three

Breathing hard and pumping his arms in a steady rhythm, Colonel Imtiaz Afridi propelled himself forward, keeping his eyes fixed on the corners ahead. His wheelchair was a racing model, made by a company in Switzerland that specialized in high-performance equipment for disabled athletes. Afridi's legs were folded under him in a mesh cradle, with a harness around his waist. The two rear wheels were positioned so that he got maximum thrust as he pushed himself forward with gloved hands. He looked like a swimmer doing the butterfly stroke, a repetitive crab-like motion. Never having been a man of caution, Afridi wore no helmet. As he came to a steep incline, his hands shifted to a steering mechanism connected to the single wheel in front. Leaning forward, he exhaled and let the wheelchair gather speed. The spokes whirred like propellers, and the breeze cooled the sweat on his face. At sixty-eight, Afridi was in better shape than most men half his age, though he'd lost the use of his legs in a mountaineering accident, nearly forty years ago.

The gradient lessened as Afridi took a sharp corner, almost colliding with a young couple holding hands. He had often thought of attaching a horn to his wheelchair so he could warn people of his silent approach. Hurtling down the road, his body was jarred by the rough surface, but he was used to physical punishment. The burning ache in his arms and shoulders made him feel he was fully alive. As he came around the next corner near St. Paul's Church, Afridi touched the brake just enough to slow his progress.

A curious crowd had gathered near the churchyard fence, watching a television crew interviewing two policemen at the scene of the crime. The cameraman was focusing on the ridge above, as if trying to locate the shooter. A group of journalists from the local papers were loitering nearby, cameras in hand. One of the police inspectors noticed Afridi and stiffened, giving him a sharp salute. Afridi acknowledged the policeman with a curt nod of his head but did not stop, his hands resuming their work as he gathered momentum again and passed the small market of Char Dukan beyond the church. Another kilometer and he would be home. Lowering his head, Afridi pumped the wheels like a steam engine, with the graceful symmetry of human locomotion. Two minutes later, he crossed an invisible line that marked the end of his workout. Throwing himself back in his chair, Afridi pressed the button on his stopwatch.

33:14. Good enough, though not his fastest time for three circuits of the Chukkar. As the wheelchair coasted up a ramp to Ivanhoe, his cottage, Afridi glanced over his shoulder with a defiant look at the Himalayan summits arranged against the northern horizon.

An aging Bhotia mastiff got to his feet and wagged his tail with a hoarse bark of greeting. Afridi reached out as the wheelchair came to a stop. He took the dog's head in his hands and stroked his ears affectionately.

"*Arrey, mera Bhotu*! Why are you barking?" The dog sniffed his hands and licked Afridi's sweating face.

Turning the chair around with a quick pirouette, Afridi entered the house in reverse. The ramp was positioned so that he could go straight into his gym, which was attached to the cottage. As he wheeled himself past a weight machine, Afridi paused beneath the climbing wall. The roof of the gym had been raised to accommodate thirty vertical feet of artificial rock with handholds at different heights.

Unbuckling his harness and grabbing two parallel rods bracketed to the wall, Afridi hoisted himself into a second wheelchair. Taking a towel from a rack, he wiped his arms and face. From the gym, he passed through double doors that opened into the rest of the cottage. His bedroom lay to one side, and ahead of him was the drawing room, a compact but comfortable home designed expressly for his needs. Afridi had always been a bachelor and proudly protected his independence and self-sufficiency.

Wheeling himself to the bar in one corner of the living room, he opened a small refrigerator and took out a bottle of water. Raising it to his lips, he drank slowly but steadily. As he drained the bottle, he heard a voice behind him.

"Colonel sahib, what race are you training for?" The question was asked in Hindi, and Afridi immediately recognized who it was.

"These days I only race against myself," he said, taking his time to turn around.

Seated in an overstuffed armchair on the opposite side of the room was a Tibetan man with weathered features. His long white hair was braided and coiled around his head. The clothes he wore were Western, a loose canvas jacket over a cotton shirt and trousers, neatly creased. His shoes were polished to a military shine. In one hand, he held a string of prayer beads that he fingered as he spoke.

"Did you hear?" Jigme asked. "There was a shooting behind the church."

Afridi nodded. "I didn't hear the gunshot, but news did reach me."

"Things have changed, Afridi sahib. Before, this never happened in Mussoorie . . . a killing in cold blood."

Afridi set the empty water bottle aside and wheeled himself toward Jigme.

"Still, it was a quick and painless death," he said. "Fallows never knew what hit him. I can think of worse ways to leave this life."

Jigme closed his eyes for a moment. "And enter the next," he added.

"It makes you wonder. . . . " Afridi mused. "We all have premonitions of our own mortality. Do you think that Fallows knew he would be shot?"

"*Kya patta?* Who can say?" said Jigme. "But his fate was decided long ago."

"Fate?" said Afridi. "Or is it the choices we make?"

"Colonel sahib, we can challenge our destiny," Jigme muttered, "but nobody escapes what's written."

As he spoke, the old man's eyes traveled over the walls, which were covered with framed photographs of mountaineering expeditions. His gaze was drawn to one picture—two men on a summit, holding the Indian flag. It was a photograph of Afridi and Jigme more than forty years ago on top of Trishul. Two ice axes were crossed above the fireplace. Between another set of pictures hung a pair of crampons attached to a carabiner. Next to this was a black-and-white photograph of a mountain at the head of a broad valley. In the white margin below the image he read the name:

RATABAN

6,166 MTS

"What can I offer you to drink, Jigme? *Kya piyogey?*" Afridi asked, gesturing toward the bar. "Brandy? Scotch?"

"No, thank you. I've stopped drinking during the day," came a gruff reply. "After sunset, I'll have a glass or two, maybe a whole bottle."

Jigme's eyes crossed to the other side of the room, where hunting trophies were displayed on the wall, a bharal ram and an ibex with arched horns almost three feet long. The glass eyes on the trophies stared back at Jigme unblinking.

"What's your theory?" Afridi asked. "Who shot him?"

"How should I know?" Jigme shrugged. "But amazing aim, from a range of more than three hundred meters! The American's head popped open like a coconut. *Thapaak!* Clean bowled."

Afridi studied him with cautious eyes, still wiping the sweat from his face. There was a time when Jigme could have out-climbed Afridi any day, but he had aged a lot in the past few years and his knees had stiffened with arthritis. As a young man, Jigme was tireless. Altitude never seemed to affect him. Now, he was often short of breath and spoke in choked bursts.

"Have you come here to give me cricket commentary or was there some other purpose?" Afridi asked, his voice impatient.

Jigme switched briefly to English. "Market report."

Afridi reacted with interest.

"Three weeks ago. On the tenth of last month, a shipment of raw *shahtoosh* arrived from Tibet. Fifteen kilos. The price was ten lakhs."

"Where was it sold?" Afridi asked.

"Pithoragarh," said Jigme. "From there it went straight to Kashmir."

Fifteen kilos . . . A million rupees. Afridi did the calculation in his head. "You're sure it's connected to the other shipments?"

"Definitely," Jigme replied.

"But we don't know, for sure, who smuggled it across the border . . . or how?"

"Not every pass in the Himalayas is guarded. This year there has been less snow," Jigme said, "which means more routes are open. For someone who knows his way through the mountains, it isn't difficult."

"Ten lakhs isn't a lot of money these days, considering the risks involved," Afridi said. "There must be other motives."

"Of course." Jigme reached into the voluminous pocket of his coat and produced an antique prayer wheel. "This came with it as well."

Afridi accepted the prayer wheel and spun it around with a thoughtful smile.

"Thank you, but I don't need your prayers."

"Open it, Afridi sahib. There's a voice inside."

Afridi kept spinning the wheel but raised his eyebrows.

"When did you start hearing voices?"

"Ever since people started invoking the name of Chairman Mao again," said Jigme. "Look at what's happening in Nepal, the Communists. Sir . . . I'm sure, one way or another, the Chinese had a hand in this shooting. Believe me," Jigme spoke with indignation, leaning forward in his chair, "this is not the last bullet to be fired. The Maoists have chosen their targets. Others will die as well."

"There are plenty of killers and plenty of victims," said Afridi, "but China isn't the only nation with blood on its hands."

Jigme shook his head and rose stiffly to his feet.

"Be careful, Afridi sahib," he said. "Both you and I know the American wasn't killed by accident."

"Why are you worried, Jigme? By now, most of our enemies are dead. We've outlived them all," Afridi chided him.

"I'm not so sure of that," Jigme replied.

"You've always been a pessimist."

"All right," Jigme said waving a hand in frustration. "If you're not going to take my warning, I'll be on my way. . . . *Khuddah Hafez.*"

Picking up his cane, he started to let himself out.

"*Khuddah Hafez,*" Afridi answered under his breath. "God go with you." Then, as Jigme was about to leave, Afridi called out. "By the way, how is Renzin?"

The old man grunted. "Which father understands his son? I never know what he's doing."

With that, he let the door close behind him. As the prayer wheel stopped spinning, Afridi studied it for a moment, the metal drum embossed with sacred lettering and designs. Setting it aside, he removed the gloves from his hands. A holster with a pistol was buckled to the side of his wheelchair and he touched it briefly. Then, cupping his right hand over the cylinder of the prayer wheel, Afridi pried it open. When he shook it lightly, a small flash drive, shaped like a lozenge, fell into his open palm.

Four

Moving carefully and deliberately from right to left, Noya Feldman's steady hand copied the verses with careful precision, graceful swirls and eddies of Urdu script flowing between the parallel lines of her notebook. As she finished writing the second stanza, Noya read the poet's words aloud:

> *"Koi ummeed bar naheen aatee*
> *Koi soorat nazar naheen aatee*
>
> *"Maut ka ek din mu'ayyan hai*
> *Neend kyun raat bhar naheen aatee"*

Noya's teacher, Salima, corrected her pronunciation in a quiet voice—*"mu'ayyan,"* an accent on the second syllable. Mirza Ghalib's couplets seemed so simple but layered with deeper meanings that left Noya with a troubling sense of premonition.

> "The one whom I await is not coming
> No familiar face appears before my eyes
>
> "When death will surely arrive one day
> Why am I unable to sleep tonight?"

Teacher and student sat together on a stone bench inside the *havaghar*, a small roadside pavilion near the Landour Language School. When the weather was pleasant, tutorials were held outdoors. Most of the students were beginners, studying Hindi, Urdu, Punjabi, and Nepali, but Noya had finished three years of Urdu already, completing a Masters degree in Oriental Languages at Tel Aviv University. Instead of focusing on grammar and vocabulary, as she would have done with her other students, who were beginners, Salima had chosen to study the poetry of Ghalib with Noya.

Wandering up the Chukkar Road to the crossing near the language school, Karan Chauhan could see clusters of teachers and pupils scattered in the sun and shade. It was a warm, autumn day, and he was dressed in jeans and a sweatshirt. An athletic man in his early thirties, Karan was clean shaven but with two days' stubble and lightly gelled hair. Around his neck was a Nikon D3X, with a zoom lens. Every few steps, he paused to take a picture. The main town of Mussoorie was spread out on the ridge to the west of Landour, and beyond that, the Doon valley four thousand feet below. Karan had arrived the day before and was still trying to figure out where he was, puzzled and intrigued by a place that seemed a part of India but was also removed from the crowded chaos of the plains.

Earlier in the morning, Karan had gone for a run around the Chukkar, the road looping about the top of the hill and joining up with itself in a broad figure eight. Karan had run two circuits, only four miles, though he could feel the altitude straining his lungs. His hotel was a small guesthouse called Rokeby Manor, which lay five minutes' walk from the language school, just above the Chukkar. In the other direction was the Char Dukan market and St. Paul's Church, where the shooting took place.

Karan had read about it in the newspapers, which still carried short articles about the missionary's death two days after he was shot. Nobody was certain why Dexter Fallows had been killed. The journalists quoted police sources, saying they were following several leads, including the possibility of a terrorist plot, though none of the usual suspects had claimed responsibility and Mussoorie seemed an unlikely place for a political assassination.

Karan had been surprised by the number of foreigners in Landour. Almost all of the language students were Europeans or Americans, as well as a few Koreans and Japanese, undergraduates on exchange programs, missionaries learning the language of prospective converts, foreign correspondents and scholars who wanted to understand the babel of voices around them. Karan had even considered enrolling in a tutorial, brushing up on his Hindi. Though he had learned the language as a child, from his parents, he had lived outside of India for most of his life.

In the twenty-four hours he'd been in Mussoorie, Karan had met several of the language students at the tea shops in Char Dukan, where they gathered for bun omelets, *paranthas*, and chai. The shooting didn't seem to have alarmed them, though the students laughed nervously when he asked if they were worried. A couple of embassies, including the Americans, had issued travel advisories after the shooting, but only a few of the foreigners seemed to have left because they were afraid of a terrorist threat.

Given the circumstances, Mussoorie wasn't exactly a destination he'd choose for a holiday, but Karan wasn't a tourist by nature. After spending the last three years working sixty-hour weeks without a vacation, he was still adjusting to the idea of hanging out. He hadn't wasted this much time doing nothing since he was in college. Enslaved by technology, Karan was so used to measuring each second in gigahertz and megabytes, it was difficult to accept the idle pleasures of a hill station, where everything moved at a slow, indifferent pace. When he normally traveled on work, it was always intense, requiring complete concentration and an awareness of every minute ticking away. Today, since breakfast, he hadn't even looked at his watch.

Karan spotted the teacher and her student framed inside the *havaghar*, with its slate cladding. He raised his camera and focused on the two women, taking a couple of pictures before zooming in on the girl with ginger blonde hair. Twenty-five or twenty-six, he guessed. Her face was not just beautiful but unique. The line from her forehead to her nose formed a strong profile but with a softness that belied the fierce concentration in her eyes. He guessed she was a European, maybe German or Dutch, though there was a Mediterranean fullness to her mouth and her complexion was naturally tanned. Karan clicked a couple of close-ups and lowered the camera just as Salima glared at him.

Pointing an accusing finger, she called out in Hindi, "*Arrey, Besharam*! Why are you taking photos without asking?"

Noya looked up, startled. Karan shrugged with a guilty smile. "I'm sorry. Forgive me," he answered in Hindi. "I wasn't taking pictures of you. I was photographing the mountains."

As if to prove his innocence, he lifted his camera once again and zoomed in on the white panorama of snow peaks visible through the branches of deodar trees that lay beyond the *havaghar*. The high Himalayas stood to the north of Landour like the battlements of a crystal fortress, a distant citadel of ice and rock. Their gleaming summits stood out against the clear October sky.

Five

The voice was low and indistinct, like someone mumbling into a keyhole. It was impossible to identify the accent, though the Urdu phrasing, with traces of Awadhi, suggested a Lucknow dialect. The speaker was certainly not Punjabi or Pathan, and probably not Kashmiri either. Most likely a Muhajir, a refugee who moved to Pakistan during Partition. The message contained an extended reference to *paan* leaves and betel nut— *supari*— as well as mention of *chuna*, or "lime." These were code words for a contract killing, but the fluid slang of violence was always changing and it could just as easily suggest the delivery of explosives or an illicit payment. The man was speaking on a mobile phone connected to a landline in Mumbai. His conversation took less than two minutes. From the noises in the background, it was obvious that he was on a railway platform. A hawker was selling tea, "Chai chai! Chai chai!" and there was the whistle of a train pulling out of a station. All of these sounds had been captured and separated, leaving only the enigmatic, muffled voice.

Tapping a command on the keyboard, Anna adjusted her headphones and replayed the first ten seconds. A name was mentioned in the greeting, but it was incoherent. *"Salaam aley kum . . . _____sahib, khairiyat?"* Two garbled syllables. Mushtaq? Rafaat? Ulfat? It was impossible to know for sure. Slowing the speech down and playing each phrase at half its speed, Anna tried to pick consonants from the slurred greeting. Intelligence Bureau had traced the Mumbai number to a flat near Chor Bazaar belonging to a man named Raza Siddiqui, who had links to minor mafia figures, a courier who would communicate the message to others.

Anna rubbed her eyes with exhaustion. She had been staring at the screen for more than three hours without a break. The vacillating graph of voice imprints was like a mountain range that went on forever. Anna had established a possible match with a known terrorist and ISI operative, Rafiq Mohammed, better known as Karachi Bhai, but the quality of the recording was too poor for her to confirm it was him. The message itself, though, was worrying, with cryptic references to *Banarasi patta* and *ilaichi*—innocuous words for *paan* leaves and cardamom, but in the lexicon of terror they suggested an attack was being planned somewhere in Mumbai. Anna had noted down every word she recognized, like clues that refused to fit into the tidy boxes of a crossword puzzle.

Noticing the pulsing light on her mobile phone, Anna removed her headphones. The ringtone sounded shrill and insistent after the mumbled conversation. She didn't recognize the caller's number.

"Hello. Yes?"

"Annapurna Tagore?" A coarse, male voice on the phone.

"Yes, this is Anna."

"What'll you eat? Veg? Non-veg?"

"Who is this?" she asked, irritated, ready to hang up. "*Kaun hai?*"

"*Arrey, batah dey,* darling," the man continued in crude Hindi. "Tell me. What do you want for lunch? Mughlai? Chinese? Udupi?"

She finally recognized who it was and smiled with annoyance.

"Chinese."

"Chowmein Palace. One o'clock."

Anna glanced at the time on her phone. It was just past noon. She put on her headphones and adjusted the cursor with her mouse, clicking the Play button once again. The unintelligible voice repeated itself. By now she had heard the message a hundred times, but only half the words made sense. It was like overhearing a conversation in a crowded market, fragments of speech that refused to fit together.

In the end, no matter how clever or precise the technology, there was no way to decipher the ambiguities of a human tongue.

‰

Being one of the great catastrophes of urban planning, Nehru Place towers above South Delhi like an elaborate set for a disaster film. It is the perfect target for a flaming asteroid from outer space or a tsunami of sand blowing in across the deserts of Rajasthan. An earthquake would topple the skyscrapers like dominoes of reinforced concrete. And if a giant ape were to climb the buildings they would crumble in his paws, scattering air-conditioners and satellite dishes on terrified victims fleeing below.

Anna dreaded the elevator to and from her office on the ninth floor. More than once she had taken the stairwell, but that was even worse, full of pigeon shit and *paan* stains, as well as fused bulbs on the landings and the bitter stench of bidi smoke. The elevator was always crowded. Inevitably, one of the men would sandwich himself against her hip with a faraway look in his eye. She used her elbows and knees to discourage them, putting on her most intimidating scowl, but there was no escaping the claustrophobic intimacy of the elevator as it descended to the ground floor.

Outside in the plaza was the usual bedlam of hawkers selling cheap clothes and factory seconds, T-shirts emblazoned with unknown brands, denim jeans in uneven sizes, and enormous brassieres like twin Taj Mahals of starched white lace. Slipping on her dark glasses as she stepped into the glare of sunlight, Anna brushed past a tout selling pirated CDs.

"*Panch so key teen! Panch so key teen!*" he croaked. "Five hundred for three!"

Sleek corporate signboards advertising Hewlett Packard, Microsoft, and Sony contrasted with the black-market chaos of the plaza. One man, squatting over a cardboard box on the pavement, was refilling printer cartridges with a syringe full of ink, while another was peddling mobile phone rechargers and cheap reprints of software manuals. Anna hated the grotesque functionality of the towers and the cluttered warrens of shops on their lower floors. She had been working here for sixteen months, at a company called Megadot, which provided a convenient cover for the Research and Analysis Wing's audio surveillance project. At twenty-eight, Anna was a senior acoustical engineer, specializing in cyberlinguistics and speech analysis, all of which were fancy names for keeping an ear to the ground and listening in on dangerous voices.

Across the plaza, between two shops selling an identical range of computer accessories, Anna could see the sign for Chowmein Palace, one of many restaurants that fed the insatiable yet frugal appetites of salesmen, customers, and office workers in Nehru Place.

Pushing open the door, which had a brass handle shaped like a dragon having an epileptic seizure, Anna entered the restaurant. Even after she took off her glasses, the interior was dark. Stagnant air bore the stale smells of cabbage, vinegar, and garlic. Six booths were arranged along one wall with vases sprouting plastic chrysanthemums. The waiters were dressed in shabby uniforms, buttons missing. As her eyes adjusted to the shadows, Anna spotted Manav Shinde seated in one of the booths, near an aquarium.

Manav was dressed as always in a rumpled *khadi kurta*, looking like a CPI(M) party worker or a social activist for a rural NGO. He cultivated a simple, Gandhian style, even though he held the senior rank of joint secretary. A short man, in his indeterminate fifties, he wore old-fashioned spectacles that punctuated his ascetic demeanor. He was known as one of the shrewdest intelligence officers in RAW. Manav was especially adept at navigating the treacherous terrain of Indian intelligence agencies, each with its own competing agenda. RAW focused on foreign threats while the Intelligence Bureau directed its attention to domestic operations, but the two constantly overlapped and had to maneuver around Defence Intelligence, which had its own chain of command and operational protocols. When it came to keeping his eye on the target while juggling complex priorities and reaching contentious compromises, Manav Shinde was a master of the covert game. Folding his hands in greeting, he gestured for Anna to take a seat opposite him. A pot of jasmine tea was already on the table.

"What'll you drink, *madamji*?" Manav asked, continuing in Hindi with the same exaggerated banter. "*Nimboo pani?* Soda? Sweet *ya* Salt?"

"Nothing, just tea, thank you," said Anna, shaking her head.

The waiter slid a dog-eared menu in front of her. It looked as if someone had worried the corners in a fit of anxiety when faced with too many choices. The endless list of dishes included enigmatic variations such as "chilly chicken," "chicken with chilly," and "chillie chicken with/without cashews."

"You insisted on Chinese," Manav said, still teasing. "But I was in the mood for Mughlai, or maybe Continental."

"Too late, you should have said something earlier," Anna replied. Though Shinde was her superior, they had been friends for several years. He winked at her, then switched from Hindi to English, his accent flawlessly cosmopolitan.

"I would have thought you'd be more patriotic, choosing South Indian at the very least. This is enemy territory." He pretended to be conspiratorial, glancing at the waiters hovering near the cashier's counter.

"China isn't our enemy anymore," Anna said, scanning the menu. "They're our competition. Besides, this place is owned by a *Mallu* and the waiters are all from Darjeeling."

"Competition? Is that what it's called these days?" Manav eyed her with amusement. "Whatever it is, the Chinese are winning."

Anna snapped back at him in Hindi. "Now, who's being unpatriotic? If you talk like that, I'll have to report you."

Manav laughed softly. "What are you going to do? Have my phone tapped?"

Ignoring him, Anna turned the page of the menu. "Burnt Garlic Prawns. Do you think they're fresh?"

As she said this, two of the goldfish in the aquarium darted out of sight. Another tropical species, like a miniature shark, swam into view. Manav eyed it with a thoughtful expression. Anna could tell by the way he laced his fingers together that the pleasantries would soon be over. After the waiter took their order, Manav's voice became businesslike and he spoke in a quiet, professional manner, explaining the reason for their meeting.

A week ago there had been an incident along the border in the mountains of Kumaon, near the Milam Glacier. Two *jawans* of the Indo-Tibetan Border Police, who were manning an observation post at 5,000 meters above sea level, had been shot and killed. It wasn't clear how many infiltrators there were or where they had gone. The only evidence IB had gathered was a discarded mountaineering jacket, which had been found by a goat herder on the *bugiyal* meadows above Munsiari. Manav showed Anna a photograph of the military arm patch on the jacket. Below a line of Chinese characters was a snarling visage of ferocity and cunning.

"Snow Leopard Unit. 12th Squadron," Manav explained.

"Chinese special forces," said Anna. "But aren't they an antiterrorism unit?"

"It looks as if they've expanded their mandate."

Half an hour later their plates were empty. Using his chopsticks, Manav plucked the last prawn from a nest of crispy noodles.

"So, my dear . . . you're going on a holiday," he said, glancing up with a wistful smile.

"Not possible," said Anna. "I'm in the middle of this project. I can't leave everything. We've got the voice signatures almost ready."

"Then think of it as a honeymoon."

"No way! We're at a crucial point!" Anna shook her head defiantly, though she knew that Shinde wasn't going to give her a choice.

"You haven't even asked me where you're going," he said, twirling a toothpick between his fingers.

"I don't care, Manav. It's important we don't lose momentum!"

"This is more important," he said, then paused for several seconds. "Mussoorie."

Anna made a face, not hiding her disappointment.

"Mussoorie?"

Six

"Situated at an invigorating 7,000 feet above sea level in the bucolic foothills of the Himalayas, Mussoorie is popularly known as 'Queen of Hills,' a title bestowed upon her modest yet seductive demeanor by generations of besotted admirers. With its salubrious climate and stupendous snow views, Mussoorie is a quaint and glorious haven for lovers of rustic, unspoiled nature. This pleasant, welcoming town is spread out along the crest of a meandering ridge, with comfortable hotels and charming cottages that offer incomparable delights for those who relish the quiet pleasures of a secluded alpine retreat—"

Karan had walked into the center of town to try and find a guidebook on Mussoorie. Browsing the shelves at the Cambridge Book Depot, this was the first he had opened, skimming the pages impatiently. Titled *Majestic Mussoorie,* it was written in an overblown style that seemed to use more adjectives than nouns and verbs combined. According to the blurb on the back, the author was Mr. Dharam Paul Khosla, a retired advertising executive and graduate of St. Stephen's College and the prestigious Doon School, who made his home in Mussoorie. But beneath the florid style, the text was devoid of any useful information. Rather than provide helpful details and directions for a first-time visitor, Khosla seemed to want to do nothing more than "acquaint my dear readers with the poetic nuances of this hilly region."

Setting this book aside, Karan picked another guide from the shelf—*Mussoorie Then and Now*. It looked more reliable, with the cover displaying an old photograph of the bandstand at Library Bazaar, with rickshaws and horses passing along the Mall Road. This book was written by an Englishman named Phythian Barnes, who lived in Dorset but visited India regularly. His only claim to authority was that his great grandfather had been a deputy commissioner in the 1920s. He seemed to have a collection of family photographs and letters written about Mussoorie, from which he quoted regularly and at length. Though the title of the book suggested some contemporary relevance, Barnes included very little about Mussoorie today, except for passing remarks about the town's disfigurement and ruination, which he believed had followed Independence.

"It is safe, yet sad, to say," he wrote in the introduction, "that Mussoorie's best years are behind her. Where dandies, rickshaws, and coolies once trotted up the mossy paths, there is nothing but badly poured concrete. The Mall Road used to describe a gentle parabola around Gun Hill. Amorous couples could always find a moment of privacy in a shadowy corner of Camel's Back Road, which is now overwhelmed by the worst kind of modern architecture, robbed of any aesthetic charms, an abysmal clutter of windows, balconies, fuse boxes and laundry lines. Even the quiet side streets of Mussoorie are overrun with boisterous, ill-mannered throngs of middle-class tourists. . . . "

Much of this book focused on colonial history. Phythian Barnes had obviously spent his time wandering through the graveyards of the hill station, where he had disinterred the stories of East India Company officers and social secretaries to the Maharajahs, a nostalgic ramble amid the moldering remains of the British Raj. Though a few of the pictures were interesting, including an old photograph from 1898 of Rokeby, the hotel where Karan was staying, he found himself irritated by the writer's obsession with the past and his condescending prose.

"Mussoorie began as a humble potato patch, once farmed by Captain Young, a gallant Irish officer who survived the Ghurka wars and built the first shooting lodge in Landour, in 1826, at the top of what is now Mullingar Hill. It must have been a perfect spot to enjoy the brisk mountain air and set off on *shikar* in the surrounding hills, hunting panthers and mountain goats. Unfortunately, Captain Young's estate is now a crumbling tenement slum, filled with Tibetan refugees and other castaways. . . ."

Karan stuffed the book back on the shelf, wondering why the British still felt any sense of entitlement in India.

The third guidebook showed little promise. All Karan really wanted was a succinct history of the town and plenty of useful facts, but he was beginning to wonder if Mussoorie was a place that inspired hyperbole and little else. The third guidebook was cheaply printed at a local press and thinner by half than the other two. The image on the cover was a blurred picture of the clock tower; and its title was simply *Mussoorie and Landour*. There was no copyright date or publisher's imprint. Even the author was anonymous, though the opening sentences of the book were written in the first person.

"When most visitors come to Mussoorie these days, invariably the first question they ask is whether they can buy a small cottage somewhere on the hillside, a mountain hideaway where they can escape their urban discontent. I've learned to answer this question with a patient smile and a helpless shrug. Mussoorie has few homes for sale and those of us who live here prefer to keep the neighbours we know. Tourists are welcome, but we'd rather not have them stay too long."

Karan wondered who the writer was, a venerable crank with a sarcastic sense of privacy. The book seemed to be written to keep tourists away, though it was full of detailed information: 1) Where to buy whole wheat bread? ("from Burre Khan the baker who delivers to your door"); 2) What to do with your laundry? ("Fancy Drycleaners in Landour Bazaar and Dhobi Ghat in the valley"); 3) How to buy a ticket to leave Mussoorie? ("at the Railway Outagency near the main Post Office in Kulri Bazaar, which opens at 9:00 a.m. but closes for lunch between 1:00 and 2:00 p.m., no matter how many people are waiting in the queue. Please note: There is no Ladies' Queue but senior citizens are allowed to buck the line. Several elderly touts are always loitering nearby, happy to expedite the purchase of your ticket for a reasonable fee.")

Basic facts about the town were listed in a series of charts.

Population: 26,342 (winter) 41,235 (summer)
Distances: Mussoorie–Delhi 298 kms
            Mussoorie–Dehradun 31 kms

One chapter of the book provided advice on hotels in town, with plenty of critical reviews: "More rats and cockroaches than staff" or "You'll need to purchase extra newspapers to stuff between the cracks in the windows." Taxi services up and down the hill to Dehradun were subject to the same kind of advice: "Most of the drivers employed by this company get drunk after 8 p.m. Safer to walk home." The author described the different areas of the hill station, from Jharipani and Barlowganj to Happy Valley, where the Tibetan Homes Foundation shared a portion of the hill with the Lal Bahadur Shashtri Academy of Administration. This invited another barbed remark from the anonymous author ("Where successive cadre of India's esteemed administrative service learn to prevaricate and procrastinate over government files, offering grudging 'No Objection Certificates,' rather than whole-hearted approval.")

The book emphasized the number of boarding schools in Mussoorie, an important feature of the town. A list of these was included in the guidebook, and the author provided a frank assessment of each. "Educationally sound, but shabby facilities and a tendency to raise fees without warning," was one of the remarks. "On the cutting edge of mediocrity." "Very good at marching during athletic competitions." "When a student gets expelled from other schools, this is where they end up," and finally: "Irish Brothers, need I say more?"

Landour was given a separate chapter in the book, and here the writer became more guarded, praising the silence and seclusion of the hillside, while directing tourists to other sites. "For most visitors, Landour will offer very little in the way of entertainment or distraction, unless you enjoy a quiet stroll around the Chukkar, with nothing better to do than count lampposts along the way. For amusements of a racier kind try Dhanaulti or Kempty Falls.

"The Landour Hillside is equally divided between military establishments and missionary endeavors. Churches and barracks are the two main features, as well as a number of cottages that used to belong to mission societies, where women and children were sent up to the hills in summer. The population of missionaries has dwindled and many of the homes have been bought by wealthy entrepreneurs from Delhi and Mumbai, raising property values to absurdly exaggerated levels. Building restrictions, both in the cantonment and municipality, have kept new development at bay and inflated the value per square foot well beyond the price of luxury flats in Juhu or Malabar Hill."

Karan found the guidebook amusing because it was intentionally off-putting, though its author expressed a genuine love for the place, especially the Chukkar in Landour, which he described as, "a former bridle path that circles the three summits of the hill and offers a quiet respite from the town, a mostly level road that leads nowhere but back into itself."

Deciding to buy a copy, Karan handed over two hundred rupees to the proprietor of the store, who gave him back thirty as change. The book was only a third of the price of the other two and certainly much better value.

"Do you know who the author is?" Karan asked the bookseller.

The man smiled, as if it were a well-known secret. "Yes, he's a longtime resident of Mussoorie."

"Why didn't he put his name on the book?"

"He's a very private man," said the owner of the shop. "But nobody knows this town better than him. He's lived here for more than thirty years and researched the history carefully. He knows everything about Mussoorie, and about the Himalayas as well."

"Who is he?"

The proprietor hesitated. "A retired mountaineer and army officer. He has a cottage in Landour but doesn't like to be disturbed."

Seven

The all-seeing eyes of the Buddha, painted on the lower wall of a chorten, gazed out across the temple courtyard with unblinking omniscience. A group of acolytes, ten to fourteen years of age, with their heads shaved and wearing maroon robes, were playing a game of cricket to one side of the chorten. An empty cardboard box served as the wickets. They had only one bat, its handle cracked and taped together.

The bowler, nearly tripping on his robes, hurled a scuffed rubber ball at the batsman, who stepped confidently forward and took an aggressive swing, missing completely. As the ball struck the cardboard stumps with a hollow thud, the fielders raised their arms in a cheer of victory. The ball then rolled across the slate flagstones to the other side of the chorten.

Seated there, on a low plinth, was Noya Feldman, dressed in a loose cotton kurta and baggy *salwar*. She had her legs tucked under her in a lotus position and her hands folded in her lap in a *dhyana mudra*. Her eyes were closed and her back was straight, mind and body focused in transcendental contemplation. The young acolytes, chasing after their ball, came to a sudden halt and studied her with amusement and curiosity, jostling each other and snickering among themselves.

After a few moments, one of the younger boys, no more than ten, got up the nerve to reach out and pull at Noya's sleeve. She opened her eyes abruptly, staring at the group, who were grinning at her.

"Hello . . . What is your name?" said the oldest boy, using the little English he knew.

She looked at him and smiled.

"Noya."

"Which country, please?" asked another.

Noya heard the sound of a motorcycle arriving outside the gate of the monastery.

"Israel," she answered. "Do you know where that is?"

The boys looked puzzled and began to laugh as Noya unfolded her legs and got to her feet, rolling up the yoga mat on which she had been sitting.

Dzogchen Gompa lay in the upper reaches of the Rohru Valley, beyond Chakrata, bordering the district of Kinnaur, nine hours' drive northwest of Mussoorie. This cloistered spiritual retreat was home to seventy Tibetan monks who preserved the religious traditions of their culture along with the expectation that, someday, they would be able to travel back across the mountains and reclaim their ancestral homeland. As the crow flies, Tibet was hardly fifty kilometers away, but it might as well have been a hundred times that distance, separated by a vast, impassable barricade of rock and ice.

The Himalayas rose above the yellow roofs and colorful facade of the monastery, so close it felt as if you could step across the ridges and set foot on their snow-covered slopes. The border was now sealed but the main road that passed below the monastery used to be known as the Hindustan-Tibet Highway. At one time, Bhotia traders crossed back and forth over the high passes in summer, carrying salt, tea, and butter. But now there was no commerce through these mountains, and military forces blocked access on either side. Silhouetted against the snow peaks, Dzogchen Gompa appeared to be the last outpost of exile, where the monks conducted their rituals and prayers in the dwindling hope of returning home.

For all of the political tragedy it represented, the monastery was a cheerful place, the buildings brightly painted with traditional pigments and designs. Prayer flags rustled in the breeze, their rainbow colors providing a bright contrast to the variegated foliage of the surrounding forest and the porcelain blue of the sky. In the main courtyard of the temple stood several chortens. Two monks were slathering the white dome of the largest chorten with a fresh coat of lime wash, while a third was polishing the gleaming brass spire, topped with an emblem of the sun and moon.

Noya could see Renzin coming across the courtyard with his helmet in one hand. Renzin had a wisp of a mustache on his upper lip and long black hair pulled back in a loose ponytail. He was dressed in a brown leather jacket and jeans, walking with a casual swagger. Noya waved to him as he approached. When the acolytes saw him coming, they moved aside and fell silent. Noya folded her hands to say goodbye to the curious circle of boys.

"Are you ready?" Renzin asked.

"I want to see the mandala one more time . . . before we go," she said, pointing toward the temple.

They had arrived the day before, driving through the mountains and camping overnight along the way. It was a long, exhausting drive on the motorcycle, over rough, winding roads full of potholes because of the monsoon. Today, they would return by another route, circling down onto the plains through Chandigarh and reaching Mussoorie by tomorrow. Noya had insisted on the trip, after Renzin told her about the monastery and the sand mandala.

She and Renzin walked across to the entrance of the temple, which was guarded by two fierce-looking painted figures on either side of the main door. The central shrine was dimly lit, with rows of butter lamps glimmering in front of a gilded Maitreya Buddha, the future one, whose arrival would bring eternal peace to the world and an end to suffering. A life-size idol of the goddess Tara, symbol of feminine power and creative energy, was seated to one side of the sanctuary, also in an attitude of meditative repose. The chapel was draped with dozens of *thanka* paintings, some of which had been brought from Tibet, others copied from ancient artworks. All around the room were tiny shrines, a reliquary of sacred objects and totem images lit by dozens of burning wicks. In front of the idols were offerings of sacred cakes made of barley and butter, kneaded and pinched into decorative shapes. Amid these objects was a recent portrait of the Dalai Lama, a simple photograph in a plain, unornamented frame.

After entering the temple, Noya led Renzin to an adjacent room next to the main sanctuary. Four middle-aged monks were crouched in the center of the floor, their heads bowed, as if paying obeisance to each other. The monks took no notice of Noya and Renzin circling around them. The concentric lines of an elaborate mandala were taking shape, as the monks trickled colored sand on a smooth platform, elevated off the floor. Using tiny funnels that spilled one grain at a time, they constructed the mandala from memory, an intricate wheel of time that represented cosmic order and illusion.

"It's so detailed, so precise," Noya whispered. "When will it be ready?"

"By the time His Holiness comes here next week."

"And afterwards . . . it just gets swept away?" Noya's voice was full of disbelief. "It seems like such a waste."

The monks who had worked so patiently to create the mandala would brush it up with their hands after the ceremonies were over, collecting the sand like the ashes of the dead and immersing them in a river or a stream.

"It's a symbol of impermanence. All that we experience and imagine in this world. But in the end, it is erased. It vanishes, like everything else around us," Renzin explained, his voice hushed, not wanting to disturb the monks in their creative contemplation.

As Noya circled the mandala, the patterns seemed to rotate with her, wheels turning within wheels, like the cogs and gears of a celestial clock of many colors.

"Has the Dalai Lama ever visited here before?" she asked.

"Only once. His last visit was twenty-five years ago," said Renzin, "when I was seven."

"Did you meet him?" Noya asked.

"Yes, my father brought me here to receive his blessing. In those days we had to walk the last ten kilometers up to the monastery. We came by bus from Mussoorie, and it seemed to take forever. My father wanted me to join the monastery and become a monk."

Noya looked surprised. "Why didn't you?"

"I refused. I didn't want to have my head shaved and be locked away in here forever. I wanted to wear blue jeans, not ochre robes. My father tried to persuade me, but I told him that I would run away. I was still upset and angry because of my mother's death. It was difficult for my father to look after me on his own. He was away from home for most of the year. I suppose he thought the monastery was a good solution."

They both looked across at the young boys playing cricket near the chorten.

"So, what happened?"

"We went back to Mussoorie, and I stayed in a foster home. It wasn't the happiest childhood, but I could never have become a monk."

Noya smiled. "Did you see your father often, growing up?"

"Only once or twice a year. After a while it was like meeting a stranger. I blamed him for abandoning me, but later I understood."

"I know what you mean. I never knew my father, as a child," said Noya.

Leaving the temple, they walked back across the flagstone courtyard toward Renzin's yellow Kawasaki, but halfway there he guided Noya to one side of the monastery. They approached a black granite monument more than eight feet high. Compared to the brightly colored ornamentation of the temple, it looked grim and somber. Shaped like a chorten, the monument had very little carving, only a stylized image of clouds and conch shells as well as an inscription in Tibetan characters. At the base of the monument was a small eternal flame in a blackened brazier. As Renzin and Noya circled the memorial in a clockwise direction, he explained.

"This is a memorial shrine for members of the Tibetan resistance. Next week will be the fiftieth anniversary of the Paryang massacre . . .

when our freedom fighters were slaughtered by the Chinese. His Holiness will offer prayers in their honor."

As they moved away from the memorial, Renzin took a pack of cigarettes from his pocket and lit one.

"How many of them were killed?" Noya asked.

He stared at her impatiently, then said with bitterness, "Does that really matter?"

Noya looked away toward the gate of the temple and the line of prayer wheels along one wall. The roof of the temple was gilded by the mid-morning sun. In the background rose the snow peaks, their summits more than 20,000 feet above sea level. The tiny flame burning in front of the memorial was dwarfed by the immensity of the mountains, but it seemed to glow with an inextinguishable fire as if drawn up from deep within the earth.

"Maybe not," she said.

"These were unknown soldiers," Renzin continued. "Fighting for a forgotten cause . . . They had muzzle-loading muskets and bolt-action rifles, no automatic weapons. The Chinese finished them off with fighter jets and bombs."

Renzin drew deeply on his cigarette.

"Why is the memorial here?" Noya asked.

"One of the survivors built it. . . . He was a monk who took up arms against the Communists—a guerrilla fighter and a saint. My father fought beside him at Paryang. Only sixteen of them survived."

"I thought Buddhists weren't supposed to commit acts of violence," Noya said. "Isn't it a sin to kill someone?"

"If the end result is peace, any actions are permitted, even if they cause harm to others." Renzin turned to spit. "Especially if they are Chinese."

"Would you go and fight the Chinese?"

Renzin rolled his eyes.

"Those days are over," he said. "It's hopeless now."

"But there are still protestors on the streets of Lhasa, people fighting against the Communists. Monks have immolated themselves."

"It's pointless," said Renzin. "Beijing has filled Tibet with outsiders. There is little anyone can do. We have become a minority in our own country. And the rest of the world seems content to leave things as they are. Tibet has been forgotten," Renzin said. "We will remain refugees forever."

Tossing away his cigarette, he pulled on his helmet and threw one leg over the seat of his bike, which was loaded with their tent and other gear. Noya was about to climb on behind him, then put her hand on his shoulder.

"Let me drive," she said.

Renzin glanced at her before stepping off the bike. Taking his place and gripping the throttle, Noya kicked the engine to life. Renzin climbed on behind her, removing his helmet and holding it in one hand, as Noya accelerated out of the temple gate. They headed down a narrow driveway to an outer gate, where the motor road circled around the ridge before turning eastward. In the other direction, the winding road led back into the mountains, toward the borders of Tibet.

"Two hundred and thirty-two!" Renzin shouted, over the roar of the Kawasaki.

"What's that?" Noya asked.

"The number of men who died at Paryang."

Eight

Anna's red convertible took the corners with engineered ease, its pistons throbbing to the muffled pulse of internal combustion. Shifting down as she swung the BMW Roadster around a series of hairpin bends, Anna could see a bus ahead belching clouds of black exhaust. On the highway up from Delhi, she had kept the canopy raised and used the air-conditioning, but now that she was on the hill road, the top was down and she was glad to be breathing fresh mountain air—at least, until now. The noxious plume of diesel smoke made her grimace, as she pressed the horn several times and accelerated past the lumbering vehicle on one of the few straight stretches of the road. Leaving the bus behind, she took a deep breath to clear her lungs.

Doggerel on the road signs warned her, SPEED THRILLS BUT KILLS! Anna ignored the message, her foot firmly pressing down on the accelerator. THE MORE YOU HURRY, THE MORE YOU WORRY! She wondered who had come up with all of these absurd slogans, probably some frustrated poet condemned to government service because of his dreadful rhymes and metaphors. DEATH LAYS ITS ICY FINGERS ON SPEED DEMONS! I'M CURVACEOUS. BE SLOW!

Anna had never imagined that she herself would ever become a government employee. It was the last thing on her mind when she had finished her degree in acoustical engineering at IIT Kharagpur. After that she had been given a Fulbright scholarship to pursue a master's degree in the United States. Her professors at Texas A&M had tried to persuade her to complete a PhD, but she had come back to India, unwilling to remain abroad. Her father was an industrialist in Kolkata, and he could have paid for her to follow any career she wanted, or married her off to the highest bidder, but Anna had always been independent. Besides, becoming an intelligence agent had held the allure of unpredictability for her.

Anna enjoyed the open road and was looking forward to a break from the office. Though she had been reluctant to abandon her audio surveillance project, being in the mountains would be a welcome change. It had taken her six hours to drive from Delhi with only one stop along the way. Mussoorie was another fifteen kilometers on ahead. Anna had been here once before, as a girl of thirteen, when her parents had tried to put her in school at Waverly Convent. Under the strict supervision of the nuns, she lasted four days, rebelling against the regimented routines and protective rules, as well as the bland food in the dining hall. On the third night, Anna had broken out of the dormitory and climbed down a rain gutter, escaping into the town with a couple of her friends to eat *chaat* and pastries on the Mall Road. By this time, she was already in trouble for laughing at one of the sisters who had scolded Anna because her skirt was too short. Summoned in front of the Mother Superior after the *chowkidars* caught her sneaking back into the dormitory, she failed to show the kind of contrition that might have let her off with a stern warning. Her friends had wept and pleaded, but Anna held up her chin and refused to apologize for the adventure. The end result was exactly what she had hoped for. Her parents arrived and took her back home to Kolkata.

Even at an early age, Anna Tagore knew how to get her way.

Returning to Mussoorie, sixteen years later, she felt a sense of mischief at the memory of her standoff with the nuns. She remembered the Waverly uniform they'd forced her to wear and wondered what the Mother Superior would think of her jeans and polo shirt, not to mention the wraparound sunglasses that shielded her eyes.

After that first experience, Anna had sworn that she would never come back, yet here she was.

A few kilometers on ahead, she turned a corner of the road and saw the town spread out above her on the ridge. As a girl, Anna had thought that Mussoorie looked like a train wreck on top of the mountain, the red and rusting metal roofs scattered about like derailed carriages, piled on top of each other. The town still had a chaotic, accidental appearance, but Anna was surprised to see how much it had grown, spilling down the ridge in different directions. As her car sped along the twisting road toward the hill station, she felt a plunging sense of disappointment.

It only grew worse as she entered the town, maneuvering through the crowded taxi stand and passing along the Mall Road. Instead of the satisfied rumble of the BMW's engine, the car seemed to complain, muttering impatiently as she crept forward through swarms of tourists and motorcycles. As she entered Landour bazaar, just beyond the clock tower, there was a traffic jam. An overloaded jeep was coming from the wrong direction along a one-way road. The truck in front of her had BAJAA HORAN, NIKAL PHOREN! painted on the tailgate, as well as HORN BLOW PLEASE. When Anna pressed her horn in frustration, the other drivers leered at her and laughed.

Coming from the opposite direction, Karan Chauhan spotted Anna as he was making his way through the snarled traffic. He was on foot, squeezing past the vehicles wedged bumper to bumper in the narrow bazaar. The red convertible caught Karan's eye, even before he noticed the young woman behind the wheel. His opinion of Mussoorie suddenly went up a notch—this town had more to offer than just snow views and colonial history! As he approached Anna, she blew the horn again. Karan gave her an appreciative look.

"There's no point blowing your horn," he said, coming up beside the car and smiling. He spoke in Hindi, though Anna couldn't identify his accent. "You're going to be stuck for a while. There must be twenty vehicles on ahead."

Anna looked away, trying to ignore him. She wasn't in the mood for making conversation with a stranger, no matter who it was. Although she tried not to make eye contact with him, her first impression wasn't entirely negative. He was better dressed and better looking than most of the men who tried to chat her up. Anna noticed he was wearing an MIT sweatshirt and guessed he must be visiting from abroad, though he could just as easily have been from Delhi University or, more likely, some rural post-graduate college in Haryana. Anna had a practiced ear for languages and prided herself on being able to locate where someone came from, but she couldn't place him, though his Hindi had an awkward tone, as if he hadn't spoken the language for several years. She tried to ignore him, but he persisted.

"You shouldn't be driving in Mussoorie," Karan said, with an endearing grin. "You should be walking."

"Mind your own business," Anna snapped back, as she eyed the steel buckle on his belt. She knew his type, young, brash, and happily unemployed, with eyes that remained focused on her chest. One of the problems with driving a convertible, with the top down, was that anyone and everyone felt entitled to stop and flirt.

Karan gave her a hurt expression. "Forgive me. What have I done wrong?"

"Nothing," she said. "Just go away."

He held up both hands defensively and switched to English.

"Hey, no offense! Just admiring your car."

Moments later, the truck in front of Anna started to move. She quickly shifted out of neutral and released the clutch, almost running over Karan's foot. As she drove off, he watched her with an amused expression, wondering why she was alone and where she was headed.

෴

Eventually, after half an hour of being stuck in traffic, Anna made her way up the corkscrew bends of Mullingar Hill to the top of Landour ridge. Manav Shinde had given her directions, but just to be sure, she had plotted her route with the help of a GPS and satellite maps that showed every twist and turn of the road. By the time she reached the top of the hill, her car sounded more content despite the steep gradient. Anna was relieved to have escaped the confined streets of the bazaar as well as the lecherous eyes peering into her car and down the front of her shirt. The air was sharp and clean, redolent with the fragrance of cedars and oaks. As she drove along the Chukkar Road, which appeared like a twisted noose on the satellite map, she caught glimpses of the Doon Valley out of which she'd climbed, a distant patchwork of forest and fields. Anna felt as if she was on top of the world.

Five minutes later, she reached the main gate of the Himalayan Research Institute. Signs warned her that this was a PROHIBITED AREA. Unauthorized visitors were not allowed entry. NO PHOTOGRAPHY PERMITTED. Seeing her car, the guards opened the gate and saluted, as Anna passed through without having to brake. The main building was unimpressive, a sagging bungalow with broad verandahs, wisteria vines climbing up the trellises. It looked like a colonial club that had seen better days. The gardens were overgrown because of the recent monsoon, which had ended a few weeks ago; gladioli and nasturtiums were poking out from amid a tangle of green foliage. But the vision that caught Anna's eye as she pulled up in front of the institute was something quite different.

Through the arched branches of deodar trees, she could see the Himalayas arrayed to the north. The October air was as clear as a magnifying glass and the mountains stood out, as white as chiseled marble, jagged profiles rising above the layered strata of hills below. Anna sat for a moment and stared at the peaks in silent awe. As she got out of her car and went across to the edge of the garden, she stretched both arms above her head. The disappointment she'd felt driving up to Mussoorie had suddenly evaporated with the view.

"Takes your breath away . . . doesn't it?"

Anna turned to see Afridi sitting in his wheelchair at the edge of the verandah. He smiled as she walked toward him.

"Colonel Afridi . . . Sir."

Despite his disability, he had a commanding presence. They had met once before, and she remembered the strength of his grip as they shook hands.

"Welcome. You must be exhausted. We could have flown you up from Delhi, or sent a car," Afridi said, holding Anna's hand for a few moments.

"I prefer to drive myself," she said.

Afridi glanced over at the sports car. "I can see why," he said. "Government servants must be getting paid a lot more these days."

Anna smiled. "My father helped me buy it. It's my only indulgence."

Afridi raised his eyebrows.

"Of course. Your suite is in the annex." He pointed to the right. A block of guestrooms lay beyond the main building.

"Do you live here?" she asked.

"No, I have a cottage about a kilometer away, on the north side of the hill. It's called Invanhoe," he said. "But my office is here. . . . Once you've had a chance to freshen up, please come over. I'll be waiting for you."

The guards had already taken the suitcases from the back of Anna's car, and they led her across the compound. Her rooms were on the ground floor, with a view of the Tehri Hills to the east. Anna recognized the contours of the mountains from the satellite maps, steep cliffs dropping away below the HRI, its buildings clustered on a knoll at the far end of Landour ridge. As Anna stood at the window of her room, a hawk flew by, its wings almost brushing the square panes of glass. Far off, in the distance, she could see the Gangetic Plain spreading southward until it disappeared into a blurred horizon. She still didn't know exactly why she was here. Manav Shinde had insisted that it was an urgent matter of national security related to the border incident at Milam, but he'd told her that Colonel Afridi would explain the details when she got here. Despite misgivings, she was beginning to look forward to whatever lay ahead.

Nine

"What the hell are you afraid of? Dying? Shit! That's nothing, compared to living like this . . . no country, no home, the fucking Communists taking over your property, murdering your brothers, raping your sisters, destroying your temples. Now's the time to act! The only way to change the world is blow it up . . . blow it up in their goddamn faces. Don't forget what happened at Norbulingka. It can happen again!"

The voice was clear, each word enunciated in an angry American accent. Afridi leaned forward in his wheelchair and turned up the volume, though he already recognized whose voice it was. The flash drive that Jigme had given him was plugged into the computer, and a light flickered on and off, as if in rhythm with the words.

Afridi's office was paneled with polished cedar. One wall was occupied with bookcases, a collection of mountaineering books, first editions of Herzog's *Annapurna* and Heinrich Harrer's *Seven Years in Tibet*, Tenzing Norgay's *Tiger of the Snows* as well as other Himalayan classics by the Duke of the Abruzzi and Sir Edmund Hillary. There were novels too, mostly British and Russian authors and books on military history, the kind of masculine library that one would expect to find in a regimental mess. Several mountaineering photographs were displayed on the walls, as well as a series of watercolor paintings of Himalayan wildflowers. Kashmiri carpets lay on the parquet floor, and the fireplace was neatly stacked with logs. Afridi's tastes were refined and traditional, reflected in the furnishing and decor.

Anna took all this in as Afridi replayed the final few words: ". . . Don't forget what happened at Norbulingka. It can happen again!"

Seeing her, he switched off the recording and turned his wheelchair around.

"I'm sorry. I interrupted you," Anna apologized.

"Not to worry," said Afridi, waving dismissively at the computer. "Let me show you around."

"Who was that?" Anna asked, curious about the American voice.

"Later," said Afridi, with a frown. "Please come with me."

Anna had expected a briefing, but Afridi seemed in no hurry to explain why he had summoned her to Mussoorie. Though she had heard about him from the first day she joined RAW, Anna had met Afridi only once before, at a security conference in Chennai. He was both a legend and an enigma within the intelligence community, keeping himself apart from the politics and intrigue of Delhi while running the Himalayan Research Institute like his own private eagle's nest in Mussoorie, a secret window on India's northern frontier. As a young man, Afridi had served in the Kumaon Rifles. He had been promoted rapidly and rose to command the Special Frontier Force, also known as Establishment 22, a paramilitary unit based in Chakrata, fifty kilometers west of Mussoorie. Most of this force was made up of Tibetan guerrillas who were trained in mountain warfare and survival.

Afridi had been one of the most fearless mountaineers of his generation until he was injured in an accident and lost the use of both legs to spinal injuries and frostbite. Since then he had devoted himself to understanding the mountains that crippled him and ensuring the security of the nation that depended on these high ramparts of snow and ice. Officially, Afridi was retired and no longer held any post, but he continued to maintain his office at the HRI, and when it came to strategic matters in the Himalayas, everyone still took orders from him.

The door opened automatically as Afridi wheeled himself past Anna and out onto the verandah. By now the sun was going down, and the snow peaks were turning mauve and amber in the last flush of daylight. Without pausing, Afridi passed through another door, which slid open when he pressed a button on the arm of his chair.

As they went inside again, Anna was startled by the contrast. Afridi's office and the exterior of the HRI looked like any ordinary hill station bungalow, but the rooms they entered were like something between an R&D laboratory at a high-tech corporation and a multimedia communications studio. The three main rooms had no windows and were separated by sliding glass partitions, an open, interconnected space that seemed cold and sterile after the comfortable warmth of Afridi's office. The rooms were filled with all kinds of electronic wizardry, banks of computers and a dozen high-definition screens displaying satellite maps and live images of mountain passes —a Pakistani artillery battery on the Siachen Glacier, a roadblock near the Line of Control in Kashmir, and another CCTV feed of what Anna recognized as the Nathu La pass from Sikkim into Tibet. Indian sentries guarded the border. A dozen technicians and analysts, all wearing uniforms, were seated at consoles, monitoring the screens. Afridi had recruited them himself, an elite team of military and civilian experts, with the highest levels of security clearance.

The Himalayan Research Institute was operated by Army Intelligence, though they collaborated closely with RAW and the Indo-Tibetan Border Police. Anna had heard rumors about the facility, though she had never imagined a place like this. Afridi had founded the institute more than thirty years ago, and the Defence Ministry seemed to have an unlimited budget for anything he required. While others had to beg and borrow hardware, Afridi could get whatever he asked for, and no ministers or secretaries refused him. This led to obvious resentment in other departments and agencies, but his integrity and patriotism had never been questioned. Nobody knew the Himalayas as thoroughly as Afridi, even if he remained an outsider within the corridors of power. Nevertheless, it was significant that in the North Block of Delhi's Central Secretariat, where many of the government ministers and chief bureaucrats had their headquarters, a special ramp had been installed on the steps leading up to the defence secretary's office, providing unobstructed wheelchair access for Afridi.

Two young officers were studying a satellite image of the Siachen Glacier, with enemy positions marked in red and the Indian observation posts identified by blue icons. As soon as the officers saw Afridi, they saluted. Anna noticed that despite so much technology and hardware, the rooms were silent, except for the hushed murmur of air-conditioning and an occasional *beep* or the whirring of computer fans.

"Impressive," said Anna, once she'd taken it all in.

Afridi spoke with quiet satisfaction. "We can watch every inch of our borders," he explained, "as well as our neighbors. If a yak crosses into Sikkim, we know about it. If a mobile phone switches on in Kashmir . . . we're listening. These are our eyes and ears."

He gestured to one of the technicians, who came across and demonstrated a program that simulated the landscape on the other side of the Niti Pass, beyond the border between India and Tibet. A satellite map was transformed into a ground-level view of rugged terrain, as if seen from a helicopter flying low over barren slopes.

"This is sixty kilometers north of us," said Afridi. "If you follow a straight line beyond Gangotri, up the Jad Ganga valley."

The technician manipulated the image so that it felt as if they were flying off the edge of a cliff, the valley dropping away a thousand feet to the river below.

In the distance, Anna could make out a cluster of buildings partly hidden behind a low escarpment. Seconds later, they were hovering over this complex, and she could see it was a military installation with an airstrip. Several transport planes were parked on the apron along with a couple of fighter jets, preparing to take off.

Afridi explained that the Chinese had upgraded this complex a year ago, and they were building a new road from the installation

47

leading up to a pass that overlooked Indian territory. Their fighters had been flying reconnaissance sorties near the border at least twice a week, and several times they had entered Indian airspace. This was part of the constant provocation that Chinese forces routinely engaged in along the border, all the way from Ladakh to the northeast.

At a signal from Afridi, the technician rotated the image on the screen, so that they were facing the Himalayas to the south. Anna could see the road under construction, with large earth-moving vehicles and lines of trucks. As the perspective changed, they seemed to be gliding slowly toward the mountains, about three hundred feet above the ground.

"Wait," said Afridi, under his breath.

Pausing the imagery with a touch of his finger, the technician zoomed in on a tiny shape. It was a bird of prey with outstretched wings, soaring above the valley.

"A Lammergeier. *Gypaetus barbatus*," Afridi said, almost speaking to himself. "Also known as the bearded vulture. Notice the tapered shape of its tail. They have a wingspan of more than three meters."

The technician pressed another button and the huge raptor soared off the screen. In its place, Anna could see an open landscape of rolling grasslands, with a lake in the distance rimmed by snow peaks.

"Over there," said Afridi, directing the technician, "to the right."

A small herd of animals came into focus, their tawny coats blending into the muted colors of the steppe. Most of them were females, but Anna could see the horns on two of the grazing males.

"Beautiful," she said. It felt as if they were only a hundred meters away.

"Tibetan Antelope," said Afridi. "Also known as Chiru—"

"*Pantholops hodgsonii*," Anna added. "Critically endangered."

Afridi acknowledged her expertise with a raised eyebrow.

"Yet the poaching continues," he said with quiet finality.

Guiding Anna through the institute, Afridi pointed out the various features, listening devices with antennae so sensitive they could pick up conversations in Pakistani foxholes across the Indus, near Kargil, or cameras mounted near remote passes in Arunachal Pradesh, where the slightest encroachment by Chinese troops set off an alarm that could be relayed to army headquarters in Delhi. The entire system was encrypted with several layers of firewalls that made it impossible to detect.

"As far as the outside world is concerned, there's nothing here except for a couple of laptops checking email," Afridi said. "We've got independent servers that are protected from any kind of cyber surveillance, a closed system that can't be hacked."

After the tour of the facility, Anna followed Afridi onto a terrace behind the institute. By now it was growing dark, and they could see the lights of Dehradun and Mussoorie flickering below. Just beyond the terrace lay a helipad with a small, unmarked chopper.

"My only indulgence," said Afridi, smiling at Anna.

She admired the sleek, aerodynamic profile of the helicopter, like a streamlined dragonfly ready to take flight at the slightest hint of warning.

"Virtually invisible," Afridi boasted. "Shielded from radar. She's a specially modified Aerospatiale SA 315B Lama, equipped to fly above six thousand meters."

"How often do you use it?" Anna asked.

"As often as necessary," Afridi replied. "I can circle the summit of Nanda Devi within half an hour from here, stop for tea with the ITBP Commander in Mana, then be back home for dinner . . . and nobody would know where I've been."

"Not even the Americans?" Anna asked.

Afridi gave her a warning glance.

"The Americans know far less than they would like us to think!" he replied.

Ten

Noya rolled off of Renzin and lay on her back, breathing hard and staring up at the wavering shadows on the ceiling. The only light in the room came from a couple of candles burning on the dressing table amid a miniature pantheon of gods and goddesses, who had looked on in silence while they were making love. Renzin reached up to brush his hair away from his face with a contented expression of spent pleasure, while Noya's eyes searched the darkness, showing uneasy satisfaction.

"What language was that?" he asked. "Hebrew?"

Noya looked across at him, puzzled.

"What do you mean?"

"You kept saying something. . . . I couldn't understand you."

She laughed. "Yiddish. My grandmother's tongue."

"Very sexy," he said, rolling his eyes. "What were you saying?"

Lifting herself up on one elbow, she leaned over and bit his shoulder lightly, her teeth leaving a mark on his skin. Noya's eyes now carried a hint of mischief.

"Do you really want to know?" she asked.

He nodded.

"It means. 'If you stop, I'll kill you!'"

He grinned and pulled her against him, their bodies reuniting in a gentle embrace. During sex she seemed possessed, overcome by an untamed spirit that seemed determined to possess him too. Noya was quieter now, her limbs draped over his with the lassitude of physical fulfillment, her lips open in the slightest suggestion of a smile. Only her eyes were restless.

Renzin wondered what she was thinking. They had returned from the Dzogchen Gompa this afternoon. Her mind seemed far away, as if on another continent, perhaps in some other century. Sometimes he felt the need to protect Noya. At other times she frightened him. He ran a finger down her neck, between her breasts, to the polished stud that pierced her navel like a silver rivet at the center of her body.

"Did it hurt, when they did this?" he asked.

Noya glanced down, her fingers playing with the stud.

"A little. Not as much as I thought it would. But afterwards it took a month to heal."

"I don't think I could ever get my body pierced," he said.

"Why not?" she said. "I'll do it for you."

He laughed.

"I'm not kidding," she said, pinching his earlobe. "First, I'll put a ring in this ear. Then I'll do your tongue. I think a steel spike, maybe in the shape of a tiger's claw."

Noya's fingers played with his lips.

"Forget it," Renzin said.

"And then we'll put two safety pins right here." Her hand brushed against his nipples and started to move down his body.

Renzin shuddered and sat up. "No thanks!" he said. "Just thinking about it makes my skin crawl."

Noya lay back and laughed, while Renzin got up from bed and found his clothes among the jumbled pile they'd dropped on the floor. As he pulled a T-shirt over his head, Noya reached under her pillow and took out a folded wad of dollars. When Renzin turned toward her, she held it out for him to take.

He looked confused, not touching the money.

"Take it," she said.

Renzin pulled on his jeans and buttoned them at the waist.

"What for?" he said.

Noya kept a straight face, though her eyes betrayed amusement.

"Come on, I'm paying for your services," she said.

The lighthearted banter of their earlier conversation was suddenly over. Renzin studied her with a puzzled expression, stepping into his boots and reaching for his jacket, as if in a rush to leave. She kept her arm extended, turning the dollars over in her fingers, as if to tempt him. Noya laughed when he gave her a hurt expression.

"You're crazy," he said.

She hid her face in the pillow for a moment, muffling her laughter, then turning to look at him again.

"Hey," she said. "Don't get upset. I just need you to change this for me. Two hundred dollars. Can you get me rupees by tomorrow?"

Renzin held back for a moment, then took the money, shaking his head in irritation as he left the room.

After he was gone, Noya got out of bed. An assortment of deities occupied the dressing table, including images from almost every faith. There was even a picture of the Ka'bah surrounded by throngs of Muslim pilgrims, framed by a border of Arabic calligraphy. Ganesh with his coiled trunk and broken tusk sat beside a porcelain Madonna, her head lowered in demure divinity. Next to her was the goddess Durga with her many arms and necklace of skulls. Most of the images were Buddhist idols, Shakyamuni, Avalokitesvara, Maitreya Buddha, as well as female figures—Dolma, the White Tara. Noya had also included a couple of Bon deities, recent copies of ancient images—Drenpa Namka, the eighth-century magus of western Tibet, in sexual congress with his consort, Oden Barma. Burnt sticks of incense had left powdery ash on the dresser, and two candles had melted down into knuckled stubs of discolored wax.

Noya had collected these votive figures over the years, her own private pantheon, which she carried with her on her travels like silent companions accompanying her on a constant quest for the truth. From the Dzogchen Monastery she had brought back a tiny image of Milarepa, given to her by one of the monks.

Since childhood, she had been seeking some larger meaning in her life—a faith, a cause, a passion that she might embrace completely, something she could believe in with absolute certainty. Raised within a secular Jewish family, she had been troubled by her grandmother and mother's non-observance. With friends in school, she had dabbled in Kabbalah and other mystical traditions. She had read everything from Khalil Gibran to Osho, experimenting with Zen, TM, even Scientology. Her interest in Oriental languages, which she studied in college, came from a search for answers in the poetry of Sufi masters, wanting to read Jelaluddin Rumi and Hafez in their original Farsi. But instead of answers, she always seemed to find a new path to follow, yet another unexplored direction for her personal pilgrimage.

Five years ago, when Noya had been conscripted into the Israeli Army for her compulsory military service, she'd approached it as another avenue toward truth, training herself in martial arts, strengthening and toning her body, focusing her mind to overcome fear and weakness through an inner core of discipline. Though she grew to appreciate the regimented teamwork of her unit and the strict authority of her commanding officers as well as the nationalistic purpose of defending Israel against her enemies, there remained a discontentment and the roaming urge to carry on her search. Sometimes it felt as if she were undertaking a quest that began in a previous life, long before this birth.

After her mother's death, she had bought an English translation of *Bardo Thodol: The Tibetan Book of the Dead*. Though it was confusing and filled with obscure references that made no sense to her, she found the book strangely comforting, like a puzzle that she returned to, again and again, deciphering each of the esoteric classifications and metaphors, until she felt as if she could follow her mother's passage through the afterlife. Isabella Feldman had been an atheist, even at the end, when cancer ravaged her body. She'd dismissed her daughter's religious pursuit as naive immaturity, but Noya had prayed for her mother's soul, seeking her release from the physical torment of this world and a painless escape into the next.

This was Noya's second trip to India. Ignoring the places she had visited before, she had come directly to the mountains. Hinduism intrigued her, and she took from it what she wanted, but Buddhist teachings were more appealing—purity attained through suffering, erasing duality, and overcoming illusion, tantric rituals that probed the final mystery of death. She had studied Farsi and Urdu at the university, and her classes at the language school allowed her to refresh her memory. Salima, her teacher, had insisted on her studying Ghalib. Noya had found most of his poetry too matter-of-fact, entirely of this world, even romantic at times. She preferred the verses of the Sufi poets, whose language took them beyond the present and into the outer realms of the infinite unknown.

Like many of the language students, Noya had rented a small room in a guest house, walking distance from the Landour Language School. Doma's Inn was a simple, comfortable place to stay. Tibetan murals decorated the walls, brightly painted dragons and snow lions, as well as elaborate mandalas in vivid colors. She had been here for two weeks already and had become used to her routines, an hour of Urdu every day with Salima, a run around the Chukkar, lunch at one of the outdoor restaurants at Char Dukan and dinner at Doma's or one of the other hotels in town. Her visa was valid for 180 days, and she had enough money to keep her going like this for several months, though she wasn't sure how long she'd stay in Mussoorie.

Noya sometimes had lunch with other language students, but mostly she kept to herself. Renzin was the only person she had grown close to so far. He didn't ask too many questions. She liked his quiet, brooding manner, and he was patient about ferrying her around on his motorcycle. Though Noya had been involved with several men before, none of the relationships had lasted more than a month or two. Love wasn't something she was searching for.

Undressing in the bathroom, she turned the water on for a shower and studied herself in the mirror. Sometimes she thought her body looked more like a man's than a woman's, her shoulders squared and the muscles in her arms clearly defined. She was tall, 5'10" but with a firm, athletic build. On her right forearm she had a yin and yang tattooed. Her breasts were small, the areola barely a shade darker than the rest of her skin, though her arms and legs were tanned. Her stomach was firm and her hips compact. In school she had played basketball, but Noya preferred solitary sports, running and swimming, competing against herself as much as against others.

After showering and dressing, she sat on the side of her bed and picked up a photograph in a silver frame. Noya carried this picture wherever she went, along with her other deities. Her mother had died three years ago. The photograph had been taken several years earlier, before the cancer had started. Her hair was just going gray, and she had a look of impatient affection on her face. Noya brushed her fingers over the design of lilies on one side of the frame and the star of David embossed at the top. She turned the picture toward the light, and she could almost hear her mother's voice, admonishing her. "You'll never find what you're searching for. Be satisfied with the life you've been given. Don't worry about what happens next."

On the bedside table beside the picture lay a copy of the *Tibetan Book of the Dead*. Noya turned to the last page she had been reading:

(The Third Method of Closing the Womb-Door)
Still, if it be not closed even by that, and thou findest thyself ready to enter the womb, the third method of repelling attachment and repulsion is hereby shown unto thee:

There are four kinds of birth: birth by egg, birth by womb, supernormal birth, and birth by heat and moisture. Amongst these four, birth by egg and birth by womb agree in character.

As above said, the visions of males and females in union will appear. If, at that time, one entereth into the womb through the feelings of attachment and repulsion, one may be born either as a horse, a fowl, a dog, or a human being.

If (about) to be born as a male, the feeling of itself being a male dawneth upon the Knower, and a feeling of intense hatred towards the father and of jealousy and attraction towards the mother is begotten. If (about) to be born as a female, the feeling of itself being a female dawneth upon the Knower, and an intense hatred towards the mother and of intense attraction and fondness towards the father is begotten. Through this secondary cause—(when) entering upon the path of ether, just at the moment when the sperm and the ovum are about to unite—the Knower experienceth the bliss of the simultaneously-born state, during which state it fainteth away into unconsciousness.

Eleven

Seated at his desk, with half-rimmed reading glasses perched on his prominent nose, Colonel Afridi was studying a contour map of the Garhwal Himalayas. Despite the array of sophisticated equipment, computer-generated images, and satellite telemetry that the Himalayan Research Institute possessed, he still preferred an old fashioned Survey of India map, the kind that unfolded to reveal a carefully measured grid, on a scale of one inch to two miles. His finger slid up the creased paper to the head of Milam Glacier, noticing the names of the mountains nearby. Nanda Devi. Changabang. Nanda Ghunti. Trishul. He traced across the contours toward Longstaff Col, remembering how he'd stood there as a young cadet on his first mountaineering expedition. The view into the Nanda Devi sanctuary was one of the most spectacular panoramas he'd ever encountered, and the surrounding ring of peaks had made him want to keep climbing, higher and farther . . . ascending forever.

Drawing himself back into the present, Afridi moved his finger across to the border post above Milam, where the two ITBP jawans had been killed. He then traced a line to Munsiari, down the Gauri Ganga valley, where the mountaineering jacket was found. From there he moved his finger to the town of Pithoragarh and then southwest to Nainital before following the twisting line of a motor road back up toward Milam. Though Afridi tried to connect the dots, it didn't make sense. He found his mind sliding back into the past, as his finger was pulled instinctively toward another point on the map. The name was printed in faint red ink: Bhyunder Valley (Valley of Flowers) and the name and altitude of the peak: Rataban 20,236 ft.

Pushing back his wheelchair with an impulsive thrust of one hand, he moved across the parquet floor to a bookcase that stood against the wall. Opening it, his hand brushed the spines of hardbound volumes before he found what he was searching for.

LOST HORIZON
James Hilton

The dust jacket was torn at a couple of places, and one corner of the cover was foxed. Otherwise the book was in good condition. Afridi had watched the movie years ago, starring Ronald Coleman, though he preferred the novel, even if it was an overblown romance, full of colonial fantasies. The book was a first edition, 1933. It had belonged to an uncle of his, and he had read it first as a teenager. He could still remember how the name Shangri-La conjured up all kinds of images in his impressionable mind, the magical secrets of the Himalayas. Replacing the novel, Afridi ran his fingers over the other volumes, until he pulled another book from the shelf.

THE VALLEY OF FLOWERS
Frank Smythe

This was also a first edition that Afridi had bought from a bookseller in London, off Great Russell Street. The dust jacket was missing, but the book itself was in mint condition. Opening to the title page, Afridi glanced at the publication date: 1938. He then flipped ahead to a chapter, "Rataban." The British had a habit of misspelling Indian names. It should have been transliterated as *Rakht'baan*, which meant "Arrow of Blood." Afridi had read this book several times, remembering that Smythe and his Sherpas had tried to climb Rataban but were forced to turn back below the summit, because of bad weather.

Tucked between the pages was a newspaper clipping, yellowed and brittle with age. Afridi opened it carefully. *Times of India,* September 6, 1969. It was a short article, about three column inches, with a headline that took up as much space as the story.

FOUR CLIMBERS KILLED ON RATABAN
Indo-US Expedition Ends in Tragedy

༄

The mountains were in Afridi's blood. His ancestors originally came from the borderlands of the Hindu Kush, near the Khyber Pass, along the Northwest Frontier Province. Afridis were a Pathan tribe, one of the "martial races," as the British called them. His great, great grandfather had worked as an assistant surveyor with Colonel Algernon Durand, when he'd mapped the high Karakoram in the 1890s. His father had served in the Indian Army, fighting with colonial regiments in the First and Second World Wars, eventually settling in Delhi. Though parts of his family had moved to Pakistan at the time of Partition, Afridi's parents had remained in India and he had always considered himself an Indian. After finishing school, he had joined the Indian Military Academy, preparing for an army career.

In 1962, four months after he was commissioned in the Kumaon Rifles, India and China went to war over their Himalayan borders, a sudden, brutal conflict that took the country unaware and unprepared. The Chinese swept in across the McMahon Line, which demarcated the boundary between India and Tibet. Though Indian troops fought back bravely, they were ill-equipped for unprovoked aggression and high-altitude warfare. Before a ceasefire was declared, the Chinese occupied large sections of disputed territory.

As a junior officer, Afridi had just been posted to Ladakh. Unaware of the hostilities to come, he was looking forward to climbing some of the unsummitted mountains in that region, when he suddenly found himself defending an unnamed ridge, near Rezang La. One hundred nine out of 123 soldiers at the border post had been killed, including the commanding officer, Major Shaitan Singh. When the Chinese attacked, Afridi had been out on a reconnaissance expedition. He and his company of twelve jawans and a fellow lieutenant, who was only a few months senior to him, fought off a flanking attack. They held their ground on an exposed spur at 5,500 meters, in bitterly cold conditions, armed with nothing more than .303 rifles and service revolvers. Afridi had been wounded in his left arm. The other officer was killed, along with eight of their men, but they had frustrated the Chinese assault. The battle of Rezang La was one of the most heroic stands of the regiment, and Afridi was decorated for his gallantry.

Yet, the horror and savagery of that battle had sickened him; to think that men should have to sacrifice their lives in such an unforgiving environment. Survival in those mountains was difficult enough without having to fight off an enemy that outnumbered you ten to one. After he recovered from his injuries, Afridi became increasingly obsessed with the mountains, dedicated to giving the men he commanded the best training in mountain survival. At the same time, he took solace in challenging the summits of Himalayan peaks, where danger lay only in the terrain itself, not enemy bullets. Here in the mountains, courage and teamwork overcame the obstacles of nature rather than the violent incursions of man.

After the humiliation of 1962, Indian military officers were encouraged to lead mountaineering expeditions as part of their training. Afridi gained a reputation as one of the most daring climbers, pushing his body to the limit, risking his life to conquer all of the major peaks that remained within the borders of India.

A few years later, when Pakistan and India went to war in 1965, Afridi had fought in the mountains of Kashmir. After the war ended, he was awarded a Vir Chakra for leading an attack against an artillery battery across the Indus near Kargil. Scaling a 1,500-foot cliff with ropes, Afridi and two of his men had taken the Pakistanis by surprise, destroying the guns that threatened the main road between Srinagar and Leh.

After this, he was promoted to Major and assigned to the Special Frontier Force in Chakrata. Afridi's obsession with the Himalayas continued. Though he led several large scale expeditions, he preferred climbing alpine style, with a minimum of porters and equipment, breaking new routes and overcoming technical challenges on his own.

In 1966, the Americans approached Indian intelligence to help plant a listening device on Nanda Devi so they could monitor Chinese nuclear tests and missile installations in Tibet. Originally, Afridi had been selected to be part of this covert expedition, but he fractured his arm in a skiing accident and had to withdraw from the team at the last minute. The Nanda Devi expedition failed to accomplish its mission and the plutonium-powered transponder was abandoned in bad weather, then lost in an avalanche. Afridi was recruited the following year to help search for the device. The entire operation had been cloaked in secrecy, and it was only several years later that rumors got into the press and questions were raised in parliament. Covert collaboration between the CIA and Intelligence Bureau, as well as fears that radioactivity from the plutonium might pollute the headwaters of the Ganga, created a political storm.

Afridi spent more than a month on Nanda Devi, scouring glaciers with Geiger counters and rappelling into crevasses to try and retrieve the device. Nothing was found, but the next season, the Americans teamed up with them again, this time to climb Rataban, which was forty kilometers east of Nanda Devi and less difficult to climb. Afridi had been part of the summit party, along with two Americans. They succeeded in planting a monitoring device on the summit, but disaster struck as they were coming down off the mountain.

The accident on Rataban cut short Afridi's mountaineering career. Though the newspapers initially reported that he was one of four climbers killed, Afridi had survived against all odds. The Himalayas extracted their revenge for the many risks he'd taken and the peaks he'd conquered, leaving him paralyzed below the waist. Even then, he did not blame the mountains for his disability. His enmity was reserved for human adversaries.

Twelve

Approaching the gate, an uneasy tension plucked at the nerves between his shoulder blades. Renzin had spent seven years inside this compound, almost half his childhood. He lifted the latch and entered, the hinges shrieking. Nothing had changed. Tennyson Lodge always looked as if it had sunk into its foundations, the roof coming down to within five feet of the ground and the windows at waist level. Behind the house, on the other side of the yard, stood the dormitory block, an L-shaped building with a kitchen and dining room on one side and two floors of rooms. Upstairs for girls. Downstairs for boys. A balcony ran the length of the upper floor, opening off a narrow staircase that Renzin had been forbidden to climb. Above the kitchen and dining hall was a small apartment on the second floor, where the matrons used to live, Miss Carter and Miss Arnette, a pair of spinsters who shared three rooms and never seemed to sleep. Mr. and Mrs. Fallows lived in the main house, which the children entered only on Sunday evenings, when they were given slices of lemon cake and plastic mugs of lukewarm Bournvita.

Between the buildings lay an outdoor basketball court. One of the backboards was broken, the twisted hoop hanging down like a derelict gallows. The concrete surface was cracked and pitted.

A dog began to bark near the servant's quarters, which were off to one side, built up against the slope of the hill. Nobody seemed to be around, and the grass had not been cut for a while. Renzin took out a cigarette and lit it, though he felt a guilty sense of hesitation when he struck the match, remembering how they had sneaked behind the dorm to smoke when he was a boy. There wasn't anyone to stop him now. Walking across the basketball court, he could see traces of painted lines, broken up by veins of moss growing along the cracks. A tall fence stood at one end, to keep the balls from going down the *khud*. The dormitory had been closed since 1998, when the last few children were sent off to a boarding school in Dehradun. By then, Miss Carter and Miss Arnette had already retired. Even when Renzin had been here, in the 1980s, the dorms were never full. He was one of eight boys and there were only seven girls.

"The Beulah Spank Memorial Children's Home," according to the cornerstone, had been opened in 1959, when the first waves of refugees came across the border. There were other institutions for refugee children, including the Tibetan Homes Foundation on the other side of Mussoorie, in Happy Valley. This home was operated by the North India Bible Fellowship. In the beginning there were sixty children and half a dozen missionaries working here.

Renzin had hated this place, though it was the only home he'd known when he was growing up. He was suspended twice and finally thrown out, soon after turning fifteen. Miss Carter had tried to save his soul and prayed over him many times, clutching his hands in hers so that he could feel the perspiration on her palms and the tremor in her fingers. He refused to repent. The missionaries never failed to remind the children that they were fortunate to be here and recounted the suffering, persecution, and atrocities committed by the Communists in Tibet, as if that justified the tasteless porridge and mildewed quilts, cold baths and punishments that ranged from detentions to copying passages of scripture until your knuckles ached.

It was only much later that Renzin realized the reason for his father's absence. As a boy, he hadn't understood that Jigme was a resistance fighter or that Mr. Fallows and some of the other missionaries probably worked for the CIA. All of this Renzin had learned years afterwards, though he remembered hearing rumors about guerrilla units in Tibet and stories about older boys from the children's home who had been killed while fighting the Communists. One of them had died because his parachute didn't open.

Walking through the grounds of the orphanage, Renzin felt a lonely sense of estrangement, recalling the atmosphere of abandonment and exile in the dorms. Though he was told that Tibet was his homeland, there seemed to be no reason to go back. He imagined himself plunging from the sky toward a vast plateau, the earth coming up to meet him in a fatal embrace. A few of the orphans had been adopted and sent away to other countries, but most went on to study or work in other parts of India. Hardly anyone returned to visit the children's home, and when they did, there was a look of wounded sadness on their faces, as if they had surrendered their innocence here within the shadows of these whitewashed walls.

Renzin remembered Mr. Fallows as a quiet, awkward man who ran a boy scout troop, teaching him different kinds of knots and how to carve a toy boat out of wood. After he was finally expelled, Fallows helped arrange for Renzin to stay with another Tibetan family in town until Jigme returned to Mussoorie the following year. Though he had never been close to Fallows, Renzin would greet him whenever they met in town. And now, hearing that the old man had been killed, he felt almost sorry for him.

Crossing behind the dormitory, Renzin found the old stone staircase at the back, leading up the hill. It was choked with stinging nettle. He broke a branch off an apricot tree at the edge of the yard, and slashed at the weeds until he cleared a path. Nobody was around, except for the dog, who had stopped barking by this time. At the top of the stairs he followed a steep trail that led around an elbow of the ridge to a flat area, about 150 meters from the dormitory, sheltered by trees. Built against the hill was a squat, square structure without any windows. The walls were concrete, and it was set into the mountain like a bunker, with a heavy steel door in the center.

Renzin heard a whistle from the trees to his right. He knew there was another path that descended from above, but the upper section had washed out several years ago, so that you had to scramble over a landslide to get down. The young man who came across to greet him smiled anxiously as they clasped hands.

"You're late. I almost left," he said.

Lobsang was nine years younger than Renzin and several inches shorter, slightly built. He had a boyish face, with dark, naive eyes and short, spiked hair. Renzin offered him a cigarette, but Lobsang shook his head.

"I haven't been here for years," said Renzin, stepping across to the door of the building. Layers of paint were peeling off, and patches of rust were visible where the steel sheets had been riveted and welded together. Somebody had scratched their initials on the plaster outside, but otherwise no markings could be seen.

"It's open," said Lobsang, as Renzin tried the metal handle, which resisted for a moment and then creaked loudly. The door swung outward with a metallic groan. Throwing away the remains of his cigarette, Renzin stepped inside.

There was no light except what entered through the door, but he could see all the way to the back, where the bunker extended into the mountain like a concrete cave. It was a rectangular room, thirty feet long and twenty feet wide, with a low ceiling, no more than a foot above Renzin's head. Two light sockets were fixed to the roof, but there were no bulbs. A few pieces of old furniture lay inside, a steel cabinet with a missing door and a couple of broken chairs and cots. Renzin could see that most of what used to be here had been removed. In one corner was a large air filter with a vent going up through the roof. A musty, animal smell filled the room, as if a wild creature had been living here.

Renzin could see a torn mattress lying next to the cabinet and a couple of empty bottles, old newspapers, and rags.

The fallout shelter had been built by missionaries in the '50s. There were three of them on the hillside, but this was the only one that hadn't been destroyed. The reinforced concrete walls were three feet thick. Renzin remembered coming here for bomb drills when he was a boy, the matrons blowing their whistles and the children trooping up the steps and hurrying along the trails. After Mr. Fallows unlocked the door, they would file inside and sit against the walls, boys on one side, girls on the other. In those days there were at least six cabinets stocked with food, water, and bedding. The matrons had explained that as long as they remained inside, the radiation couldn't reach them and they would be safe. Renzin remembered the sound of the steel door closing and their faces lit up by the dim glow from the overhead lights, a sense of claustrophobia and fear that they might never escape. Before returning to the dorm, Miss Carter and Miss Arnette led them in prayer, asking Jesus to protect them from the Communists.

"Somebody's been staying here," Lobsang said.

Renzin nodded as he kicked the mattress aside.

"Who?" he asked.

"I don't know. He must have moved out a week ago." Lobsang picked up one of the newspapers and showed it Renzin. "The last date on these is October 6."

Near the mattress was a candle stub fixed to the concrete floor with a congealed lump of wax. Renzin took out his matches and set it alight, the flame blooming slowly and casting a yellow aura around the room. Graffiti decorated the walls, from long ago. Someone had drawn a woman with enormous, lopsided breasts and names were scrawled in charcoal and chalk. Two years after Renzin entered the foster home, they stopped holding drills, though the cabinets remained full of supplies and Fallows kept the key on a ring clipped to his belt. Later, somebody had broken the lock, and it became a place where hillside kids hung out to smoke and drink. After the cabinets were vandalized a new lock was installed and the shelter had been sealed ever since, until now.

"Look there," said Lobsang, pointing above them.

Renzin glanced up to see something written in black lettering on the ceiling.

༈ རྣོར་བུ་གླིང་ཀ ༈

It was a single word in Tibetan characters: Norbulingka. On either side were two swastikas, awkwardly drawn with the same black lines. The writing looked much more recent than the other graffiti on the walls. Once again, Renzin felt an uncomfortable sensation, as if there was another presence in the room, an invisible observer watching them.

"How would he have written it up there?" Lobsang asked.

Renzin stared at the lettering for a moment, then reached down and pried the candle off the floor. Raising it above him, he held the flame close to the concrete surface overhead. Carefully, he traced over one of the swastikas, drawing with the candle flame and leaving a black trail of soot on the ceiling.

"When did you discover this?" he asked.

"Four days ago, after the shooting," said Lobsang. "I heard that a motorcycle was parked behind the garbage incinerator on the Chukkar. When I checked it was gone, but I could see that someone had been using the upper path, and when I came down here the lock had been opened."

"Any idea who it was?"

"No, but I don't think he's coming back."

Renzin looked up at the swastikas again and noticed that they were reversed in a counter-clockwise direction.

"Is this the only reason you called me here?" he asked.

Lobsang shook his head, then reached into the pocket of his jacket and took out a cheap, compact camera. Switching it on, he handed the camera to Renzin, as the screen lit up.

Thirteen

The *dargah*, a sufi's tomb, lay at the base of a twisted oak. This ancient tree had grown over a boulder, wrapping the huge stone in a gnarled embrace as its roots extended into the soil on either side. The tomb itself was much more recent, covered with green porcelain tiles and surrounded by a rectangular mausoleum of painted screens and a sloping tin roof, all of which enclosed the moss-covered trunk of the tree.

Anna was intrigued by this shrine at the side of the Chukkar, a small, untidy structure. As she approached the tomb, she smelled the cloying odor of incense and saw blue and green scarves, fringed with tinsel, tied to the screens.

Someone was kneeling in front of the entrance. Anna waited patiently, not wanting to disturb their devotion. Only when the figure stood up, did she realize it was the same man who had spoken to her the day before, when she was stuck in traffic.

Karan had been taking photographs of the tomb. As a gesture of respect he had covered his head with a handkerchief. Removing this, he rose to his feet and caught sight of the woman watching him. For a moment, he didn't recognize her. Then it struck him—the red convertible.

"*Arrey, aap?*" he said in Hindi. "Good morning. Where's your car?"

"I decided to walk today," she said.

Anna studied him for a moment. He looked harmless, and the smile on his face was reassuring, though Anna remained guarded.

"Whose *dargah* is this?" she asked in Hindi.

Karan glanced across at the marble plaque on the wall of the shrine, inscribed in Urdu and English.

"Hazrat Barkat Ali Shah," he said, pretending as if he'd known this all along.

"Who's that?" Anna asked.

Karan shrugged.

"*Kya patta?* Some sufi . . . *koi fakir.*"

Anna went around to the front of the tomb and glanced inside, seeing the exposed roots of the tree blackened with incense smoke. Pink rose petals had been sprinkled on a green muslin shroud, embroidered with gold thread. Karan watched her as she crouched down to examine the interior of the shrine. There was something mysterious about this tomb at the side of the road and the boulder locked in the roots of an oak.

"Are you from Mussoorie?" Anna asked, turning around and speaking in English.

Karan stepped back to let her pass.

"No," he said. "I'm just a tourist . . . visiting the Himalayas." He gestured toward his camera. As Anna began to walk away, Karan quickly caught up with her.

"Why come to Mussoorie?" she asked. "You could have gone somewhere more exciting. Kashmir. Kathmandu."

"I'm not that sort of tourist," he said. "I enjoy the kinds of places other people ignore, destinations off the beaten track."

"You sound like an American," she said.

"That's because I am an American," he said.

Anna slowed down to look him over once again.

"You've got a Boston accent," she said.

"Very good! How did you . . . ?" He was surprised. She'd caught him off guard.

"I have an ear for languages," said Anna. "And what do you do when you're not a tourist?"

"I'm a software engineer. A month ago, I lost my job." Karan made a helpless gesture. "I needed a break, so I've come back to India to reconnect with my roots." He put out his hand to shake. "Karan."

Anna took his hand in hers, just long enough to feel the confidence in his grip.

"Annapurna," she said.

"You're named after the mountain?"

She shook her head. "No. The goddess. Most people call me Anna."

"So, Anna . . . What brings you to Mussoorie?" he asked.

"Visiting an old friend," she replied.

Something in the way she said it made him disbelieve her, the answer coming too quickly and too easily, as if rehearsed. Continuing around a bend in the road, they arrived in front of the Landour Language School, clusters of students and teachers sitting in the sun poring over their lessons. Karan scanned the crowd. The girl he'd photographed wasn't in sight, but her teacher was sitting with another student in the *havaghar*.

"What are all these foreigners doing here?" Anna asked.

"Learning Hindi. And Urdu, Punjabi. Nepali. This is the Landour Language School. For a hundred years foreigners have been studying Indian languages here. Most of them are college students on a semester abroad." Karan paused for a moment, switching back to Hindi, before adding. "*Yaad rakhna.* Remember, I'm a foreigner too."

Anna gave him a sidelong glance, then looked away. The road in front of them forked in two directions, one sloping down the south side of the ridge, the other heading along the north, facing the snow peaks.

"Which way into town?" Anna asked.

Karan pointed to the left, toward the south fork of the road, which would eventually take her into the bazaar. Without saying goodbye, Anna set off. For almost a minute, Karan watched her heading down the road. He raised his camera and zoomed in on Anna until she finally turned around, as he knew she would, glancing back over her shoulder to see if he was still there. Karan waved and started walking in the other direction, around the north side of the hill.

Fourteen

Three low-resolution images were displayed together on the flat screen monitor, hurried photographs taken on a cheap digital camera with an inadequate zoom. The technician had enhanced them as best he could, but they remained blurred and indistinct, the colors muddy. Nevertheless, Afridi could see enough to understand their significance. In two of the pictures, the front end of a motorcycle was visible and he could tell it was a Royal Enfield Bullet, an older model—probably early '80s, judging from the mudguard—350 cc, a dull green color with a dent in the petrol tank. The rider was more difficult to discern, for the motorcycle had been moving when the photographs were taken and the light was poor. Blotches of shadows from the surrounding trees and a midday glare erased any details. Wearing a helmet with a full-face visor and some sort of camouflage jacket, the motorcyclist was impossible to identify. It could have been almost anyone. By themselves the first two photographs were of little value.

But it was the third picture that gave them relevance.

"Can you make it any sharper?" Afridi asked. "Try to read the license number."

"Sorry, sir," the technician replied. "If I magnify it any more, we'll lose all definition. And if I increase the contrast, the shadows will be too dark. This is the best we can do."

Afridi glanced across at the figure leaning against the doorframe.

"Why can't these journalists use decent cameras?" Afridi complained. "It looks as if they were taken on a mobile phone."

"He's a freelancer," said Renzin, stepping forward and stooping down to study the screen. "It's all he can afford, an old Olympus that belonged to his uncle."

"What's his name, again?" Afridi asked.

"Lobsang Bhotia. Most of the time he covers news in town for the *Free Tibet Journal*, as well as local editions of the Hindi papers, *Dainik Jagran*, *Amar Ujala*, anyone who will buy his stories about Mussoorie events, town politics, illegal construction. . . . He's just starting as a journalist, but very persistent. I've known him since he was a kid."

"Did you pay him for the pictures? I want to make sure that none of these get printed in the newspapers."

"They won't," Renzin assured him. "I made him give me the memory chip before he could download anything. These are the only copies."

"How did he know to contact you?" Afridi watched Renzin intently.

"I've used him before. A reliable source. Lobsang knows when to keep his mouth shut."

Afridi frowned and moved his wheelchair a couple of inches closer to the screen. In the third image, the motorcycle was rounding a bend, the driver leaning into the curve. Unlike in the first two photos, there were no shadows. The license plate on the back was unreadable because of the angle, but across the rider's back, a rifle was clearly visible. It was easy to make out the shape of the barrel and the stock, as well as the outline of the telescopic sight. Afridi would have the image analyzed, but he already knew it was a Chinese weapon, Type 88.

"When did he take this?"

"A week ago. Sunday morning, just before noon. 11:56 a.m.," said Renzin. "The date and time are recorded with the images."

"Fifteen minutes after Fallows was shot," Afridi said.

Renzin nodded, his right hand cradling a packet of cigarettes in his pocket.

"And where, exactly, were these pictures taken?"

"Beyond the hospital, heading east, sir." Renzin paused. "Lobsang told me that he was walking back from visiting a friend who was sick with typhoid. He saw the driver on the Bullet going past and spotted the rifle. By the time he was able to get a picture, the motorcycle was already across the valley."

"I'm sure your freelancer must have told everyone by now. Why did he wait so long to give you this?" Afridi demanded.

"He was trying to get something more. The pictures are poor quality and he was hoping to find out where the motorcyclist was hiding. He knew the story was worth much more than the two rupees a word he gets from the *Free Tibet Journal*," Renzin explained. "There were a couple of leads that he was following."

"Such as?" Afridi asked.

"He didn't tell me. All he said was that he had a suspicion the shooter was camped out nearby, after leaving the fallout shelter near Fallows's house."

"Show me the writing again," Afridi said.

Pressing a key, the technician changed the image on the screen. This time it was a picture Renzin had taken of the ceiling in the shelter. Afridi studied it in silence, his eyes tracing the two swastikas and the Tibetan letters spelling out the word *Norbulingka*.

"He was stalking Fallows," Afridi said. "Maybe he even contacted him. Maybe Fallows knew that he was staying in the shelter. The lock on the fallout shelter wasn't broken, was it?"

"No," said Renzin. "But if he was in touch with Fallows, then why would he kill him?"

"Because Fallows refused to cooperate. Maybe he threatened to expose him. There could be any number of reasons." Afridi paused a moment. "I'd like to speak to your journalist friend."

Renzin hesitated. "Lobsang was supposed to meet me again, but he's disappeared."

Afridi looked at him sharply, then waved a hand at the technician. "Get these analyzed. I want Subhash and Ravi working on it, everything they can tell me: what make of helmet he's wearing, his clothing, approximate height, confirm the model of the bike, and all specifications for the rifle."

Turning his chair around abruptly, he pushed past Renzin and went outside onto the verandah. The afternoon sun was filtering through the branches on the deodars, a clear but fractured light.

"What do you mean, he disappeared?" Afridi snapped at Renzin, without looking directly at him.

"Gone, sir." Renzin held up both palms in a gesture of frustration. "I met Lobsang yesterday morning, when he gave me the pictures. We arranged to meet again, last evening. I went to his house, but his family said he hadn't come home. His sister had a call from him around noon. He said he was working on a story and might be late. After that, he vanished. No sign of him."

"Has this been reported to the police?"

Renzin shrugged. "Yes, but they haven't registered a case. They're saying he must have run off with a girl. The family have no idea where he's gone."

"He didn't say anything to you about where he was planning to search for the shooter?"

"No, sir." Renzin shook his head. "He may have thought that if he got more information, it would earn him a little extra—"

"Why didn't you bring this to me yesterday?" Afridi asked.

"I was hoping that Lobsang would deliver something more. Some kind of confirmation," Renzin said, then looked away. "Besides, I've been preoccupied."

Afridi glanced up at him.

"Yes, of course, the Israeli girl. How's that going?"

"Fine."

"Nothing more to report? She's still studying Urdu?" Afridi brushed his hands lightly over the wheels on his chair. "Nothing suspicious?"

"No, sir."

Afridi sat silent for a minute or two, his face turned aside.

75

"Thank you. I don't want any of this leaking out in the press. You're sure that Lobsang didn't talk to anyone else?"

"Yes, sir. I made it clear he wouldn't get paid if anything was published."

Nodding, Afridi put a hand on Renzin's arm.

"Did you tell your father about the photographs?"

Renzin shook his head. "No."

"It's probably best to leave it that way. Last time we talked, he seemed upset. I wouldn't want to alarm him any further." He shifted forward in his chair. "But, keep me informed."

Afridi began to wheel himself toward his office, then spoke over his shoulder, without looking back.

"Renzin . . . be careful."

Fifteen

An ominous committee of grimacing masks, with bulging eyes and flared nostrils, some with horns and others with fangs, glowered down from the wall above. The narrow space was crammed full of artifacts and antiques, stacks of brass bowls and other vessels, *khukri* knives large enough to sever a buffalo's neck and small, slender daggers, their scabbards decorated with turquoise and other semi-precious stones. Beneath the masks was a collection of *thanka* paintings, depicting Tibetan saints and demons, as well tantric deities knotted together in erotic contortions. A single, 60-watt bulb was suspended from the ceiling, casting a yellow sphere of light that barely reached the corners of the room.

On dusty shelves were images of Bodhisattvas in all shapes and sizes, as well as metal ornaments and ancient trumpets with gaping mouths like dragons. Glass cases were filled with jewelry, necklaces, and amulets of tarnished silver, rings set with semi-precious stones—moss agate, jade, and turquoise.

Jigme sat motionless in one corner of his shop, except for the prayer beads that slipped through his fingers, one by one. His face was grooved with lines, and his features showed little expression, except for his eyes, which reflected a tragic sense of sorrow and loss. On the wall behind him, draped with a white scarf, was a framed photograph of the Dalai Lama.

Entering the shop, Anna brushed aside the strings of beads that formed a curtain near the entrance. A musty smell emanated from the walls inside, of mildewed fabric, leather, and soot. The sign outside had caught Anna's eye: POTALA ANTIQUES. At Afridi's suggestion, she had taken the morning off to explore Mussoorie, wandering through the bazaar and window shopping. Except for a few general comments about the border incident and audio recordings that he wanted her to analyze, Colonel Afridi had not explained the purpose of her visit, though he had promised to brief her completely tomorrow. After having been summoned on short notice, Anna was puzzled by the apparent lack of urgency.

Browsing through the shelves, she picked up a copper bowl and examined it. Anna hadn't noticed Jigme at first, but when she looked up, his eyes were watching her.

"*Namaste*," she said, startled by his presence.

"*Namaskar*," he replied, without moving.

Holding up the bowl, Anna asked how much it was.

"Don't worry, *madamji*," Jigme answered. "I'll make a special price for you."

"Is it antique?" she asked, examining the patterns on its surface. The lip of the bowl was dented.

"Everything in this shop is antique," said Jigme. "Even the shop-keeper."

Anna smiled at the old man, moving across to another jewelry case and studying the jumble of silver bracelets set with coral, tiger's eye cuff links, and amethyst earrings. She glanced toward the ceiling where the top shelves were stacked with dusty objects, tea pots and butter churns. Several strings of prayer flags were suspended across one corner of the shop. Anna knew that most of the items were cheap curios and imitations of antiques, but there was a feeling that hidden under the clutter and bric-a-brac lay something of value, something ancient and mysterious. Turning back to the jewelry, she noticed a necklace of amber and silver beads. When she pointed it out, Jigme opened the case and took it out. He watched, unblinking, as Anna held the necklace up to the light.

"And how much is this?" she asked.

"Twelve hundred."

"Eight," she said.

"You can have it for a thousand."

The bargaining took place without hesitation and Anna smiled as she counted the money in her purse, handing the notes to Jigme. Clasping the necklace around her throat, Anna let her eyes travel up to the ceiling again.

"What's that?" she asked, pointing.

Jigme got up slowly, trying to figure out what she wanted.

"In the corner, behind the copper jug," said Anna.

Jigme had to get a step stool to reach the object, climbing slowly onto the precarious perch while bracing himself against one of the shelves. He moved stiffly, and Anna was afraid he might fall as his hand reached out and took down an old bow and a quiver of arrows. Before handing these to Anna, he dusted them off with an oily rag. She watched him carefully, trying to guess his age.

"This is very old," he said. "More than a hundred years."

Anna drew one of the arrows out of the quiver. The shaft felt so brittle, she thought it might snap between her fingers. When she pressed her thumb against the arrowhead, it was still sharp, though the metal was badly rusted.

"Lethal," she said.

"Yes, it can kill your enemies." Jigme nodded, then added under his breath, "Rataban."

"Rataban?" Anna asked.

"Haven't you read the Mahabharata?" Jigme asked. "A single arrow from Karna's bow slaughtered thousands of soldiers."

As Anna picked up the unstrung bow and balanced it in her hand, Jigme gestured toward the wall beside him. Next to the framed photograph of the Dalai Lama was a snapshot of a mountain at the head of a broad valley.

"This is Rataban," he said. "A beautiful mountain . . . They say that Karna's arrow flew straight toward the Himalayas after destroying the Pandava armies and scattering their blood on the battlefield at Kurukshetra. It was a weapon from the gods, capable of annihilating everything in its path. Karna's arrow cut through the mountains and carved this valley before it finally came to rest in the glacier below the peak. That's how the mountain gets its name. Rataban. At sunset, its snow is stained with blood."

"*Rakht' baan*," said Anna, pronouncing the Sanskrit correctly, as she slid the shaft back into its quiver.

From the street outside came the sound of a motorcycle pulling up.

"*Udta teer, kabhi vapas nahin aata,*" said Jigme. "Once an arrow is released, it never returns."

Before he could say any more, a young man entered the shop, removing his helmet. Catching sight of Anna, he looked her up and down, without speaking. She observed him with caution, as she handed the bow and arrows back to Jigme.

"Give me the key to the house," the young man said.

Anna started to leave, as Jigme pulled out a key ring from his pocket and handed it to his son.

Outside, the sunlight was almost blinding as Anna stepped into the street. She slipped on her dark glasses and paused for a moment, watching the streams of tourists promenading along the Mall Road. A yellow Kawasaki was parked next to the shop, leaning on its side stand. Across the street, music was playing over loudspeakers at a small amusement park. Children were riding a merry-go-round. She paused to watch a cable car pass overhead, ascending to the top of the hill, while a second gondola was coming down toward her. Anna touched the necklace she had bought as she headed back up the crowded street, wondering about the trajectory of Karna's arrow.

Sixteen

Running can be a form of meditation, clearing the mind and focusing the senses. Your body finds its natural rhythm, each step leading on to the next, each breath, each beat of the heart, each contraction of the muscles in your legs. Whenever Karan ran, he imagined that he was being chased, not by a threatening creature like a wolf but by a protective human figure, loping a few steps behind, encouraging him to keep going. Often, it felt as if there was more than just a shadow following at his heels, a double image of himself, both a competitor and a companion. Occasionally, the figure seemed to overtake him and he imagined that he was chasing himself, struggling to keep up. He often felt this sense of physical dislocation, as if he had outdistanced himself.

While running around the Chukkar, Karan had repeatedly passed the Christian cemetery on every circuit, but this was the first time he had stopped. Entering the gate, he switched off his iPod and removed the earphones. Except for birdcalls, the mournful cries of Himalayan barbets wailing in the valley, there was total silence. The tall deodars and cypresses cast long shadows over the terraces, which were lined with graves. Most of these contained the remains of British soldiers who had died of malaria and cholera more than a century ago. Stone crosses and angels with broken wings rose out of the weeds, the headstones overgrown and neglected. Retaining walls for each of the terraces were covered in moss and ferns, though most of these were turning brown, now that the monsoon had ended.

Karan avoided cemeteries as a rule. He found them disturbing. The gravestones had a kind of eerie anonymity that made him feel unsettled. Though the names and dates on the tombs bore witness to the lives of those who were buried here, and the Bible verses inscribed in stone invoked reassuring messages of salvation and redemption, there was still a melancholy finality about the graves.

On one of the upper terraces, Karan could see a figure partly shrouded by the branches of an oak. He headed slowly up the path, still breathing hard from his run. When he reached the stone steps leading up to the terrace, he could see an elderly man with a white beard and a lace skull cap. He had a dog on a leash, a black and white cocker spaniel. Facing away from Karan, the man seemed to be praying with his palms held out in front of him.

As Karan approached, the dog noticed him and growled. Stopping, Karan waited for the man to finish his prayer. In front of him, he could see a fresh grave, a mound of reddish dirt covered with wilted bouquets of flowers. When the man finally turned, Karan greeted him politely.

"*Salaam aley kum.*"

"*Aley kum salaam,*" the old man replied, eyeing him with suspicion.

"Is this Mr. Fallows's grave?" Karan asked, speaking in Hindi.

"Yes," said the man, pulling the dog toward him on the leash. "The burial was four days ago, but I wasn't permitted to attend. The police had kept me in the *thaana.*"

"*Aap?*" Karan asked, not sure who he was.

"I am the sahib's cook. Muhammed Tasleem. For forty years I was true to his salt," he said, with sudden bitterness, "*Chalees saal sey unka namak khaiya.* But, even then, those bastard cops thought that I would kill him."

Muhammed Tasleem wiped his hands over his face to brush away the tears of anger and remorse. The dog sniffed at Karan's running shoes, now wagging the stub of its tail.

"And this is his dog?"

"Yes, poor thing," said Muhammed Tasleem. "For the past five days he's been crying, even if I leave him alone for five minutes."

Karan reached down to pet the spaniel.

"What's his name?" he asked.

"Nixon."

The old cook pronounced the dog's name with an accent on the second syllable. He didn't seem to understand the irony. Muhammed Tasleem headed slowly toward the path and started down the steps before stopping to turn and look back at Karan.

"Did you know the sahib?"

"No," Karan answered, glancing at the grave.

"His memsahib is buried next to him. She died ten years ago."

Karan noticed the gravestone beside the mound of earth, and he could just make out the name: Enid Fallows.

"It was a terrible thing..." Muhammed Tasleem's voice was choked with emotion. "*Khuddah jaaney* . . . God knows who shot him!"

"Which house did Mr. Fallows live in?" Karan asked.

"Tennyson Lodge . . . above the mission school, in the same compound as the orphanage."

"Is anyone from his family coming here?"

"No. He had no children. No other relatives."

As the old man continued slowly down the path, the wailing calls of the barbets from the valley below seemed to grow louder and more persistent, like a chorus of grief, echoing up the forested slopes.

Karan walked across to the grave and stared down at the mound of earth, the wilted gladioli and tuberoses. He felt an uneasy premonition, as if someone was watching him through the trees. He could almost feel a set of crosshairs aimed at the back of his skull. Ever since he'd come to Mussoorie, Karan had felt as if he was being followed, not by a protective shadow, but by a dangerous, invisible presence, hidden somewhere in the trees.

Moments later, he heard a pumping sound, as if a generator had been started, or some kind of compressor engine. Karan looked around, but there were only silent lines of graves buried amid the weeds. He realized the sound was coming from above, like the beating of wings but more mechanical, a thudding noise that grew steadily louder. Suddenly, through the branches of the deodars, he saw a helicopter passing overhead. It was a small, sleek aircraft with a glass cabin, and he could see two people inside, the pilot and one passenger. Turning away from the hill, its engine no more than a murmur now, the helicopter headed toward the higher mountains. The last glimpse Karan had was a glint of sunlight reflecting off the rotor blades, a momentary flash before the helicopter disappeared.

Seventeen

As they flew out of the Bhagirathi valley and began to climb over Panwali ridge, toward Kedarnath, turbulent air currents shook the helicopter like a shaman's rattle. Though the sky was perfectly clear, strong updrafts and crosswinds made flying treacherous, especially when they followed the ridgelines, where the wind threw up invisible waves like heavy surf breaking over a reef. Afridi was strapped into the passenger seat. He had removed his helmet, watching the terrain passing below, as the pilot took them above 4,000 meters, circling eastward, then due north along the Alakananda. Far below, he could see the tributaries of the Ganga, the confluence and temples at Rudraprayag, but mostly villages with terraced fields, forests, and cliffs.

From the air, the mountains looked different, their extended contours visible instead of simple profiles. The snow peaks grew larger, and the helicopter was like a tiny insect flitting into oblivion. Their flight path avoided the main towns and highways. As they swept over a bugiyal meadow, Afridi could see Gujjar herdsmen below, buffaloes grazing on high pastures and the thatched domes of their seasonal huts.

Within ten minutes they dropped down into the Vishnu Ganga gorge below Joshimath, flying between walls of eroded rock, where the river had carved a tortured passage through the mountains. The helicopter shuddered and swung from side to side, the air currents as violent as the white water rapids below. At points, it felt as if they would be picked up and tossed against the cliffs, but the pilot knew exactly what he was doing. He had flown this route many times before. Emerging from the gorge beyond Joshimath, the chopper began to climb again, rising up the main thrust of the Himalayas. Afridi caught sight of Nanda Devi to his right and Trishul beyond. Ahead of them, the granite mass of Kamet appeared, as well as the sharp white spire of Nilkanth. They were now above the central arc of the Zanskar Range, and it felt as if an invisible hand was raising them to a level with the surrounding summits. Though the cabin was pressurized, Afridi felt his ears pop as they passed above Gangaria, 5,000 meters and climbing. On the ridge below, he could see pilgrims trudging up the trail to Hemkund Sahib. Some of them caught sight of the helicopter and waved, but within seconds they were beyond the last settlements and temples, entering the Bhyunder Valley.

Neither the pilot nor Afridi spoke. They had flown together hundreds of times, in far worse conditions. Though the Lama was intended for border surveillance, more than once it had rescued climbers from the mountains, responding to emergencies. A special set of brackets were fitted to the undercarriage, between the struts, where a stretcher could be attached. They had carried injured mountaineers off glaciers and near-vertical snow fields, airlifted dying soldiers from remote border posts, and saved earthquake survivors who needed to be carried to hospitals on the plains. The mountains were not only beautiful but dangerous. Afridi knew the risks involved.

Along one flank of the Bhyunder Valley, a dozen waterfalls, like braided strands of liquid glass, were dangling from the crags. The birch trees, with their white bark and yellow leaves, shimmered in the afternoon light. Shadows climbed the rocks. Afridi scanned the vegetation below, trying to spot any trace of movement, but the landscape seemed deserted and they were high above the valley, heading straight for the mountain.

Rataban stood in front of them, a broad, triangular peak, skirted with glaciers. There were other mountains on either side, but Afridi had his eyes fixed on only one summit. The vibrations in the helicopter seemed to increase the higher they went, though flying was smoother now and there was only a light headwind that slowed their progress. Once again the pilot began to climb, edging his way over the glacier, which was scarred with crevasses and seracs, a mangled terrain of fractured ice.

As they reached the snowfields of the col, Bhyunder Khal, to the west of the peak, they were barely fifty feet above the surface of the mountain and the drumbeat of the rotor blades seemed to echo off its slopes. Afridi studied the smooth, unblemished contours of the col, as if searching for footprints on the vast expanse of white. They began to circle now, a broad spiral that took them up to 6,000 meters. Afridi had memorized every feature of this mountain, and he could trace dozens of different routes over rock and ice. As they swung past the summit, he could see a snow plume billowing up. For a second, the helicopter seemed to drop, but the pilot controlled it with precision, coming in at an angle. Now it was the breeze from the rotor blades that was kicking up the snow. Afridi's face was pressed against the glass, and he could feel his heart pumping in time with the engine. Suddenly, he felt cold and exposed, almost afraid, until a surge of anger overcame his fears.

The pilot did not touch down, but merely brushed one skid across the summit, leaving a slash mark in the snow. Afridi felt a momentary sensation of connecting with the mountain before they passed over Rataban. He could see what lay beyond, several ranges of snow peaks and, in the distance, Tibet. As they wheeled westward, he looked back over his shoulder at the mountain that had nearly claimed his life, burnished by an evening glow. The helicopter now flew westward into the setting sun, like an arrow returning to its bow.

Half an hour later, they were home.

Eighteen

The smoke had an evil smell. At first, Karan thought it might be a forest fire, woolly gray clouds funneling up a steep ravine and spilling across the Chukkar road. But instead of the odor of burning bark and leaves, there was a synthetic stench, as if an old sneaker had been tossed into a campfire, poisoning the air with fumes of melting rubber and plastic. Maybe someone was burning garbage. He looked down over the railing, but all he could see was a whorl of soot and shadows spiraling up through the dark limbs of oaks.

A building must have caught fire somewhere on the hillside below. Shouts of panic and alarm carried up with the smoke. Karan hurried around the bend, where a narrow, unpaved driveway cut down the side of the ridge. The wind was blowing the smoke in the opposite direction, and from here the only sign of the fire was a gray smudge spreading against the sky. A man was rushing up the hill, out of breath. He pointed over his shoulder as he passed.

"We need water. The pipes are dry," he said.

The driveway angled to the right, descending below a rocky slope overhung with trees, from where Karan could finally see the flames. In the afternoon light, they looked artificial, like amber gels used to illuminate a stage. But the crackling sound made it clear how real the fire actually was. The gate was open, and several dozen people were gathered in the front yard. One of them was holding a garden hose from which a trickle of water emerged, not even enough to reach the nearest flames. The heat was intense, and everyone stood back fifty feet.

Again, Karan was conscious of the toxic smell of the fire. The building itself was a long, single-story structure with a line of small, square windows. It looked like some kind of warehouse or industrial shed. Electric wires were sparking near a fuse box on a narrow verandah facing the gate. Karan could see the corrugated metal sheets on the roof, buckling at the joints. Talons of fire were working their way under the wooden beams. A window frame was aglow, the glass panes having shattered; a grid of wooden struts flared up before collapsing into ash. It was obvious the building would burn down to its foundations. By now, the fire had reached every room and there was a deep, volcanic roar inside, as if the core of the building had become a furnace.

Turning to a couple of men standing beside him, Karan asked, "Is anyone inside?"

They shook their heads, and one of them answered. "This building hasn't been occupied for ten years."

Karan could see a bolted door at the back, sealed with a brass padlock. The green paint had blistered with the heat. Smoke was seeping out from under the sill and through cracks in the wood. Most of the people standing around looked as if they were neighbors or employees from other houses nearby. The only foreigner was the girl. She stood by herself to one side of the building, watching with a serious, distracted expression. On her shoulders, she carried a light backpack and looked as if she was about to set off on a trek. Her reddish blonde hair was pulled back in a braid, and she was wearing jeans and an olive green T-shirt. Karan remembered her immediately from the day he'd taken her photograph outside the Language School, but when she looked across at him, the young woman stared through him without recognition.

One of the wooden pillars on the verandah collapsed, bringing down a shower of plaster and sparks. Immediately, the smoke blew in their direction and everyone moved farther back, choking and coughing. The man with the garden hose brushed past Karan and wiped his eyes, the rubber pipe dribbling pathetically.

"Why isn't there any water pressure?" Karan asked.

The man shrugged, blinking because of the smoke.

"It's been turned off."

"Can't someone turn it on?" Karan said.

"The chowkidar has gone to open the valve at the top of the hill, but it will take time. The linesman is off duty, probably drinking in town." The man spoke with resignation, knowing it was already too late.

Landour's water supply came from reservoirs positioned at the highest point on the ridge, where it was pumped up, two thousand feet, from a stream in the valley. The manager at Karan's hotel had explained that there was a chronic water shortage, telling him how the city supply was released for only an hour or two each day, flowing by gravity to the hillside homes. It was an outdated, inefficient system that depended mostly on the linesman's wrench to release airlocks and rusted valves. The reservoirs at the top of the hill were six huge tanks, known as Chey Tanki. These were filled each day, then drained within a couple of hours through a labyrinth of half-inch pipes that supplied the hillside.

More people were arriving to gawk at the fire, and an elderly gentleman in a frayed tweed cap walked over and spoke to the man with the hose, asking how the fire had started.

"I have no idea," said the other. "Two hours ago, when I came by, there was no sign of anything wrong. And then, a little while ago, I heard someone shouting from above. The flames were already coming through the windows."

"Was it electrical?" Karan asked. "A short circuit?"

The man with the hose shrugged. "Who knows? The building has been locked for years. Why would it start all of a sudden?"

"Who does the house belong to?" Karan asked.

"Foreigners," said the man in the tweed cap. "It's the old mission press, where they printed Bibles and other literature."

He gestured toward a sign that Karan hadn't noticed before because it was half hidden behind an overgrown hedge.

THE NORTH INDIA BIBLE FELLOWSHIP
CHRISTIAN PRINTERS AND PUBLISHERS
"IN THE BEGINNING WAS THE WORD,
AND THE WORD WAS WITH GOD,
AND THE WORD WAS GOD." JOHN 1.1

"They closed it down about ten years ago," the man continued, "but the presses are still inside. Nobody uses those kinds of machines anymore. Everything is computerized now."

The front half of the building had mostly burned down, the roof having fallen in upon itself and charred timbers sticking up at awkward angles. Karan could just make out the remains of a press in the wreckage, a large, hulking shape with rollers and gears. He could also see a clutter of shattered jars, boxes, and canisters blackened by the fire that must have contained ink and printing fluids, which were giving off the fumes.

The red-haired girl had climbed onto a ledge by herself, above a retaining wall that looked as if it might have been a terraced garden, once. She had her arms wrapped about her knees and the backpack made her look like a grasshopper waiting to leap into the fire, though she didn't move, as if hypnotized by the flames and smoke. Karan eyed her, wondering why she had come down here. Probably for the same reason he had been drawn to the fire, out of a sense of curiosity and fascination, witnessing a catastrophe that couldn't be stopped.

By the time water began to flow through the pipes, most of the roof had caved in and even the masonry walls had collapsed except for the far corner of the building, which had been spared. Finally, the hose began to sputter and spewed out a concentrated stream, but there was very little to save. The man who was holding the nozzle sprayed a heap of glowing embers, as if he were watering a bed of smoldering petunias. A large crowd had gathered since Karan's arrival. Several policemen showed up, but instead of moving people back, they pushed their way to the front and stared at the fire, with their arms crossed.

A little while later, a fire truck arrived on the Chukkar above, its bell ringing insistently, as a couple of firefighters in khaki uniforms came running down the drive. They too, made little effort to control the blaze beyond commandeering the hose and dousing the gutted remains of a cupboard stacked full of books. As the water extinguished the last of the flames, Karan could see they were Bibles, with hard black covers and gilt lettering on the spines.

Within an hour it was over. The interior of the main building had been gutted, though there were some metal shelves that survived, stacked with reams of charred paper and binding materials. A few scraps of paper had blown into the yard, and Karan picked one up. It was printed in Hindi, a series of Bible verses, with a line drawing of Jesus standing alone in a fishing boat, like a castaway at sea.

More than a hundred people were now blocking the driveway, looking down at the fire. Karan stepped past a cluster of men who had dragged a steamer trunk out of the wreckage and were guarding it, as if it contained some salvaged treasure. Circling around the rear wall of the building, he came to the only section that was still standing.

Surveying the blackened remains, Karan felt certain the fire wasn't an accident. As his eyes explored the wreckage, he imagined an arsonist spilling petrol or kerosene on the stacks of paper inside the press, then setting it alight with a match, the fire spreading quickly to the inks and solvents, glue and paper. The fire had destroyed almost everything except for the larger pieces of machinery, which had survived, along with several cabinets along one wall that were fitted with narrow drawers and a composing table with a slanted surface.

Moments later, Karan was aware that the girl had climbed down from her perch. She walked past him, as if he wasn't there, and crouched down to study something on the ground next to one of the cabinets, which had toppled over on its side. As Karan went nearer, he could see hundreds of tiny pieces of lead type scattered on the ground. Some of them had melted and then congealed into gray, misshapen puddles, but others had survived. The drawers in the cabinet were filled with more of the same letters, scrambled alphabets and punctuation marks.

The girl had picked up a Bible from among the scattered papers, a thick black volume. The edges of the pages were singled and yellowed from the fire.

"What language is that?" Karan asked.

She turned abruptly, looking up at him with a defensive expression.

"Sorry," he said, "I didn't mean to startle you. Is that Tibetan script?"

"Yes," said the girl, flipping through the brittle pages.

"Can you read it?" he asked.

She shook her head.

The Tibetan characters had an ornate quality, each letter shaped like a decorative pattern, as if embroidered in black ink upon the yellowing page.

The girl said nothing as Karan stepped over to examine the cabinet and composing table. Picking up a handful of lead type from one of the drawers, he recognized the same Tibetan script, each letter tightly curled and knotted in upon itself. He held them out to show the girl, and when she cupped her hand he let the lead type fall into her palm.

"It seems so pointless," she said.

"What do you mean?" Karan asked.

"Translating the Bible into Tibetan." She pinched one of the letters between her fingers and held it up like a tiny gem. "That's the last thing they need."

"So, you're not a missionary, are you?" he said.

She looked at him with a guarded expression, then shook her head. After a moment, Karan held out his hand.

"I'm Karan," he said.

She poured the lead type onto the ground before shaking hands.

"Noya," she said, then glanced at the burnt-out shell of the house and added, "It's finished."

Karan wasn't sure if she meant the building or the fire. The mangled remains of the presses were like the wreckage of old steam engines covered in soot, while the rest of the building looked as if a bomb had fallen on it. Though the fire had taken a couple of hours to burn out, the devastation appeared to have happened in an instant, the result of a sudden explosion rather than a slow conflagration.

The girl had let go of his hand, but Karan was aware that she was staring at him now, with a look of sudden intensity.

"What's that on your arm?" she said.

Karan's shirt was rolled up a couple inches above his wrist, exposing the lower section of his forearm. Before he could stop her, the girl reached out and tugged the sleeve up to his elbow, revealing dark blue lines, a flowing tattoo in Arabic script, that looked like a faded bruise against the pale brown pigment of his skin.

"*Bismillah al Rahman al Rahim*," Noya read the phrase. "In the name of God, the most gracious, and most merciful."

She looked at him with a quizzical expression, both suspicious and intrigued. Karan withdrew his arm and was about to explain, when the girl turned abruptly and walked away, circling past the burned-out building and then pushing her way through the curious throng of people near the gate.

Nineteen

After leaving the fire, Karan made his way back to Rokeby Manor. The old, two-story building had been recently renovated into a small but comfortable hotel. The guard saluted as Karan reached the stone portico, which was framed by massive oak trees draped in ferns. The mist had come in during the afternoon, and there was a gloomy atmosphere that seemed to evoke the haunted moors of Scotland. Like many of the colonial homes in Landour, Rokeby took its name from a book-length poem by Sir Walter Scott, a bestseller during the days when the house was built.

Inside the lobby, he collected his key at the reception desk. High ceilings and exposed stonework on the walls gave the hotel a rustic elegance. Karan went up the wooden staircase to his room. A large window opposite his bed looked out over the town of Mussoorie. Through the arched branches of the oaks, he could see a jumbled mosaic of corrugated tin rooftops following the contours of the ridge. The mist had parted for a moment but then swept in again on a sudden breeze.

Kicking off his running shoes, Karan threw himself on the bed, exhaling with a combination of exhaustion and frustration. He had been killing time in Mussoorie for four days now and was eager for some hint of what lay ahead. Just then, he heard the evening call to prayer coming up from the mosque in town. An amplified voice, hoarse with static, summoned the faithful to worship.

"Allah ho Akbar! Allah ho Akbar!"

The muezzin's cry took Karan back to another evening, two years ago, when he had heard the same *azaan* outside a village in Afghanistan. He had just entered the outskirts of the settlement, which appeared deserted except for the repeated call from a crumbling minaret. It was a small roadside hamlet in a dusty, fly-bitten valley between Kabul and Kandahar. Evidence of warfare was everywhere, a burned-out tank at the western edge of the village, several craters where bombs or IEDs had exploded. The cracked mud walls of the buildings were the same tawny brown as the surrounding hills, pocked with bullet holes and shrapnel. These drab exteriors seemed to shelter only tragedies within. At the edge of the village they had passed a graveyard with a few slate headstones, the rest no more than humble mounds of sandy earth decorated with strands of tinsel.

Karan was accompanied by two Afghans, all three of them dressed in loose *salwar kameez* with quilted vests. He wore a woolen Chitrali hat on his head. Each of them was armed with an AK-47, and they looked like any ordinary trio of mujahedin strolling into the village at dusk. A passing truck had dropped them at the turning outside the village.

For the last three weeks, Karan had been living at a training facility run by a Chechen jihadi aligned to a local Taliban cell. He had crossed over from Pakistan by way of Peshawar and the Khyber Pass, traveling by bus and lorry. After entering Afghanistan, Karan had lost contact with the outside world, no cell phones or computers. All electronic devices were banned in the camp. Most of the mujahedin were foreigners like himself, Yemenis, Egyptians, Pakistanis, even an Indonesian, who spoke a language nobody could understand, though he had tattooed a "Bismillah" on each of their arms. They lived together as brothers in a bombed-out village hidden away in the mountains. Twice already they had been attacked, and their training consisted mostly of building bunkers beneath the rubble of ruined homes.

As the call to prayer ended, the three men turned into a side street, which was narrower, with an open drain running down the middle. Ahead of them was a flock of sheep and goats tended by a young boy with a prosthetic leg. Karan noticed the pink color of the artificial limb as they walked past the boy, the animals parting in front of them. The rank odor of goats and sheep was overpowering. On ahead, a car was parked at an angle, blocking most of the lane. All of its wheels were missing and the body was covered in dust, the steel carcass of a vehicle that would never move again.

Like so many villages in Afghanistan, this wayside settlement was littered with the relics of war. The burned-out wrecks of Russian tanks and American Humvees lay side by side along the roads, and the scorched earth of this region seemed inured to the presence of invaders. If you dug deep enough in the soil, there would be the remains of earlier battles, from British muskets to Macedonian swords. The barren landscape seemed hardly worth the conflicts it had fostered, a wasteland of human brutality and suffering.

Karan was alert to any hint of ambush. They were going to meet a man who claimed he had access to the Taliban commander for this region.

As they passed the car, Karan noticed it was a Chevrolet Impala. For no specific reason, a warning switch went off in his mind, a sixth sense that signaled danger. He lifted his hand to the trigger guard on the Kalishnakov, feeling the hairs on his arms begin to bristle. Seconds later, the first shot was fired.

The man on his left collapsed to his knees and fell, face-down in the dust, as bullets whistled by. Karan threw himself onto the ground, instinctively. Rolling over, he saw his other companion thrown backwards, hit twice in the chest. It happened so quickly, he couldn't tell where the shots were coming from, but Karan crawled toward the old Chevy, the only cover he could find.

As he scrambled behind the front fender, he felt a bullet catch him in the shoulder, below the ball and socket. It felt as if someone had elbowed him in the chest. For a few seconds he couldn't breathe. The windshield of the Chevy exploded into myriad crystals of glass. Karan could see his own blood in the dust, brighter red than

97

he expected. With his uninjured arm, he struggled to raise his rifle, though he didn't return fire. The shooting continued for another minute, loud bursts of gunfire followed by silence. Karan crouched beside the rusted lug nuts on the hub of the car's rear wheel, bracing himself for another attack.

Down the street, he could see the flock of sheep and goats heading away from him, the crippled boy staring over his shoulder impassively as if this were a daily event. Then, he heard a shout. Lifting his weapon, Karan tried to calculate where the shooters were hiding. By now, he could feel nothing in his wounded shoulder. Blood was seeping through his vest and running down the inner seam of his sleeve.

Again there was a cry, a call for surrender. Karan recognized it was an American voice.

Setting his rifle aside, he raised his good hand and waved. No bullets were fired. Karan stumbled to his feet, holding one arm over his head. The other hung limply by his side, dripping blood on the shattered glass. He expected more shots, but as he stepped away from the wrecked car, a crouching figure moved from one doorway to another. The helmet and camouflage convinced him that he was right, as did the shouts in English.

"Get down! Get the fuck down!"

Karan dropped to his knees as he saw two soldiers break cover to his right. They ran toward him, yelling as they tackled him, knocking him to the ground. For the first time, he felt a searing pain in his shoulder and ribs. Karan cried out, and it took a moment before he could speak as the soldiers cuffed his hands behind his back.

"Whoah!" he said. "Take it easy, man. We're on the same side!"

The soldiers hesitated, confused by his accent. There was blood and dust in his mouth, but Karan spoke slowly, deliberately.

"I'm an American. I work for the US government."

Twenty

Guantanamo Bay. The last front line of the Cold War and the first redoubt of America's struggle against terror. Seagulls kited and planed over tangled coils of razor wire that barred access to the beach. A setting sun like the soft-boiled yolk of a cosmic egg oozed into the Caribbean Sea. Hemingway's Cuba was a distant memory on this lonely, benighted patch of American sand. Instead of frozen daiquiris with miniature parasols and maraschino cherries, the only sundowners at Gitmo were served with a waterboard.

A bearded prisoner sat alone in the interrogation room, his face expressionless. Fluorescent lights, recessed into the ceiling, cast a harsh, clinical aura around the vacant walls. Two folding chairs and a table stood in the middle of the uncarpeted floor. The only other object in the room was a large TV positioned in one corner. It sat on a trolley with a DVD player attached and wires plugged into a socket in the cinderblock wall. The screen was a blur of silent static.

Handcuffed and shackled, the prisoner was wearing an orange jumpsuit, which was the only color in the room, a livid, synthetic hue. It was hard to tell the man's age from his rugged features— at least thirty, no more than forty. His beard was flecked with gray, and he had a scar across his face that ran from his left eyebrow to the corner of his lip, pulling up the side of his mouth in a constant sneer. But there was no arrogance or hostility in his eyes, and his hands were perfectly still as they rested together on the table. His name was Yusuf Badrawi, an Egyptian from Zagazig, who had been a schoolteacher for several years before he had joined the mujahedin, fighting the Russians in Afghanistan. He had told his story several times, how he had been wounded in a rocket attack and sent home to recover in 1988. Six years later, when he was well enough to fight again, he volunteered a second time. By now, the enemy had changed—Americans, NATO. He had killed five Canadians in an ambush near Istalif before he was captured. There was nothing to hide. Yusuf was prepared to tell his story again.

Without warning, the television came on, the screen turning blue and strains of music filtering out of the speakers. Yusuf recognized the song, from a film he'd watched as a boy before he'd renounced the pleasures and temptations of cinema. It was a popular Egyptian production that played for several months in Zagazig. The lilting chords of music from an oud touched a nerve inside of him, a feeling of separation and loss. But Yusuf was a man of strong character and strict principles. He resisted the pull of the music. A belly dancer performed on the screen—a nightclub act. In the film she was seducing a young man from the village who had come to Cairo in search of his lost brother. As the belly dancer swayed in time to the music, Yusuf remembered the squeamish excitement he had felt watching the movie with an older cousin. Averting his eyes, he stared at the door. Yusuf could not understand why his captors were showing him this film.

The door opened. An interrogator entered, dressed in fatigues, a black leather bag in one hand. Only when she turned around did Yusuf realize it was a woman, her tawny hair tucked beneath a cap. Her name, Vinson, was stitched above the pocket of her shirt. She greeted him in Arabic.

"*Sabah al kheer.*" Her voice was firm yet friendly.

Yusuf nodded but said nothing as he watched her open the bag and remove a syringe and three small vials. With medical efficiency, the interrogator pulled on a pair of purple surgical gloves before preparing the injection. Yusuf did not resist as she took his hand in hers and turned his forearm so that she could find a vein, just above the steel handcuffs. He felt only a slight burning sensation as the needle went in and released its venom.

The song on the television was almost over, the dancer gyrating wildly in front of a lecherous crowd of men who were drinking wine and laughing. The hero of the film was seated among them. His eyes were full of noble innocence and restrained desire. Yusuf felt as if he was watching himself, from twenty years ago, projected on the screen.

Soon the questions began, the woman's voice soft but insistent. By this time, the television had been switched off, but the melody and lyrics kept running through his mind as the serum worked its evil in his brain. Yusuf imagined his interrogator swaying to the rhythm of the drums, her voice crooning in his ear. He could picture her breasts jostling inside the rough fabric of her uniform, her hips unhinged by the music. She asked him about his cousin, who had been killed in Kandahar the day that Yusuf was captured. Her Arabic was clumsy but proficient, with a Lebanese accent. She knew the names of his companions and asked about them, as if they were all together in the same room, watching her perform. He could not stop himself from speaking, her lyrical whispers prying answers from his tongue, the persuasive drugs creating an erotic hallucination in his mind.

Yusuf had so far avoided the woman's eyes, but now he stared into the bright blue irises, hypnotized by a chemical fantasy. Her purple hands caressed his face. A wave of hair curled about one ear, which was pierced and held a tiny stone that caught his eye—a diamond, glinting like a tear. He watched her moist lips moving as she spoke, the flashing whiteness of her teeth, forming questions that he was eager to answer. He wanted to please this woman with his replies. Yusuf told her everything he knew, singing like a caged bird, his voice unleashed, accompanying the lyrics of her song.

ﻉ

A thousand miles away, three flat-screen monitors displayed the interrogation room from different angles, each hidden camera positioned in a separate corner of the ceiling. There was no music, and the interrogator's voice was clear and steady, like a school teacher prompting a reluctant pupil. Lieutenant Vinson was still wearing her purple gloves, but she stood across the table from the Egyptian, speaking with firm insistence, demanding that he tell her the names of mujahedin he'd fought with and the whereabouts of a man named Salah al Badri. The prisoner's face was contorted with emotions. Karan recognized fear in his features, as well as anger and defiance. One minute he was laughing wildly, then, suddenly, he burst into tears. The prisoner spoke like a child, babbling out his answers, terrified yet eager to please and anxious for praise.

Karan zoomed in on his face, grabbing a sequence of images, one after the other. He used a remote control device to adjust the cameras, catching the prisoner's profile. Another set of images cascaded onto his computer screen. The questions and answers didn't matter, it was the man's features and expressions he was after. Someone else would record and analyze what the man was saying. Karan cared only about the visual data, capturing every facial contortion, as the prisoner struggled to answer the questions, even as his mind was melting into delirium.

Quickly, typing commands, Karan filed away each set of images. Focusing on the man's eyes, he tried to record every furtive glance and averted gaze, as well as the subtle expressions that revealed much more than his words, the tightening of muscles around his eyes, the lines on his forehead, a twitch of his nose.

Seated in Cambridge, Massachusetts, on the ninth floor of a building near Kendall Square, Karan examined the prisoner's face, as if it were a cryptic puzzle to be decoded. His computer shuffled the array of images and processed every line and contour, even the ragged scar that curled the man's lip into an insolent grin. It was all a mask, and Karan was peeling away layers to discover the truth. Using a simple facial recognition platform, augmented by customized software developed by the team of programmers who shared his office, Karan would be able to map the prisoner's features and compare them to other terrorists.

The fundamental problem was to scan a thousand faces at an airport, a shopping mall, or a political rally and be able to spot the terrorists among them. Instead of metal detectors and body scans, someday there would be a system that identified suspects through a simple CCTV feed, picking up faces in a crowd who could be recognized as potential threats.

This was the next generation of security systems, replacing human error, prejudice, and guesswork with digitized probability. When people today complained about racial profiling, they didn't understand that anonymity would soon be a thing of the past. Karan had been working on the project for a year, creating profiles of arrested terrorists and prisoners of war, men like Yusuf Badrawi. His real name was Salah al Badri, one of Al Qaeda's top lieutenants. As the serum dispersed through his veins and the capillaries of his brain, he confessed his true identity and the names of men he'd recruited in Egypt and Yemen, Bahrain and London, Amsterdam and Toronto. All of this was vital information, the kind of first-hand intel that helped solve problems today, but Karan was less interested in the immediate value of this prisoner's confession. It was the future that mattered, how to spot a person with violence embedded in his mind, before he acted on those dangerous thoughts. Karan liked to think of it as psychic programming, employing the clairvoyance of computers. Millions of dollars had been spent already and the project wasn't scheduled to produce any measurable results for another twenty-eight months. Yet, as he pulled each image from the live feed at Guantanamo Bay, Karan already had a feeling of excitement and anticipation. This was a new digital frontier, the whetted-edge of virtual identities, unmasking the face of terror.

A hand squeezed Karan's shoulder, and he nearly leapt out of his chair. Looking up, he saw one of his coworkers, Ivana, standing behind him.

"Shit!" he said. "Don't ever do that . . ."

Ivana laughed. She spoke with a Russian accent, "Sorry, you should take a break."

Karan massaged his temples. He was dressed in a T-shirt and shorts. His running shoes lay under his desk. Ivana's hands still rested on his shoulders, kneading the tense muscles in his neck. Aside from typing code, her fingers were equally adept at accessing his erogenous zones.

"I need to get this done," he said. "The images still have to be compressed and collated."

Thirty years ago, Ivana would have been working for the KGB in Moscow. But today, the CIA Branch Office in Cambridge was like a committee of the United Nations—East Europeans, Cubans, Lebanese, Angolans, Chinese, and Koreans working together in a maze of cubicles—an elite team of programmers who would have been trying to hack each other's computers a generation ago, now together under one roof, united in an effort to fight the same elusive enemy rather than the paper tigers and polemics of the Cold War.

"Someone's here to see you," said Ivana, gesturing toward the elevators.

Karan glanced over and saw two men in their late thirties watching him from across the room. Both were dressed in sweat suits and running shoes. He didn't need a face recognition program to tell him who they were. Pushing back his chair, Karan walked across to meet them.

"Karen Chowen?" said the first man, butchering his name. He had a toothbrush mustache, the bristles trimmed to the same length as his close-cropped hair.

Karan corrected him. "Karan Chauhan . . . Yes?" He studied them warily.

The second man was thinner, with restless eyes.

"Let's go for a run," he said, his voice half an octave higher than the other's.

"It's midnight, man. . . . Who are you?" Karan looked at his watch.

"Jim Burger," said the mustache. He put out his hand to shake. "And this is Dan Yankowitz. We need to speak with you. How 'bout a 10K loop down by the Charles? Talk while we run."

"Look, it's a real pleasure to meet you guys, but I don't know who the hell you are and I went for a run already." Karan knew exactly who they were. Nobody could have entered this room without the highest security clearance.

"We've come up from Langley," said Burger. "You can call Caleb if you want."

Karan's expression didn't change, but his eyes acknowledged what he heard.

Yankowitz piped up. "Hey, c'mon. You're not going to qualify for the Boston Marathon unless you put more miles on those feet."

Karan looked down at his toes and knew he didn't have a choice.

Fifteen minutes later they cut through the MIT campus, past the Strata Center that looked like something out of Dr. Seuss and the more sedate but equally impressive Brain and Cognitive Sciences Centre. When Karan was an undergraduate at MIT, neither of these facilities were here. He remembered the old Building 20, built during World War II, where radar was invented. It was gone, the windowless office up a flight of rickety stairs, where his advisor had welcomed him on the first day of classes back in 1995. Three years later, it was demolished to make way for new buildings. Whenever Karan ran through campus, he felt as if he was stepping back into his freshman year, the competitive synergy of young minds released into an exciting world of unsolved problems and big ideas for the future.

Memorial Drive was deserted. Leaving the MIT dome behind them, they jogged across to the concrete sidewalk that ran along the river. The glimmering skyline of Boston lay across the water. Burger and Yankowitz ran smoothly, setting an aggressive pace, one on either side of him, their shoulders even, moving with a predatory rhythm. Their breathing was strained, but they spoke clearly and succinctly, outlining the purpose of their visit, informing Karan that he would have to leave for India immediately. He tried to protest, insisting that he had work that couldn't wait, another set of facial profiles to unmask. But Burger and Yankowitz made it clear that his assignment had a higher purpose.

Eight years ago, when he first joined the CIA, Karan had signed up to be an analyst, but more than once he'd been drawn into covert ops by Caleb Holstrom, who'd recruited him during his senior year at MIT. There was an undeniable excitement to the work, the lure of danger, being a secret agent instead of a computer hack, going undercover rather than sifting data, holding a pistol in your hand instead of a mouse, a clip of bullets replacing a hard drive.

"Think of it as background research," said Burger. "Fieldwork."

He hawked and spat as they passed the marina, sailboats bobbing on the dark water with the lights of Longfellow Bridge ahead of them, a gothic span with heavy pylons. Beyond this lay the newer Zakim Bridge, its cables lit up like a celestial harp. In the darkness, the Charles was black as oil, its sluggish current seeping into the sea.

"We need an Indian, or somebody who looks like one," Burger went on.

Any other time, Karan might have challenged him, but he let the comment pass.

"Who are we after?" he asked.

Yankowitz eased forward, a step ahead of him as they ran up the ramp to cross the Longfellow Bridge. "Don't worry about it," he whined. "You'll get a briefing in Delhi. Just keep your head down . . . blend in with the billions."

Karan was born and raised in Boston. This city was his home. His ancestral origins may have been South Asia, but he had never thought of himself as anything but American. It didn't matter what he looked like; he was born in the USA. The three runners fell silent for a while and only spoke again after another half mile, when they had reached the other side of the bridge and turned toward the Hatch Shell, past the statue of General Patton. A police cruiser was racing down Storrow Drive, lights flashing, its siren screaming.

"I don't know anybody in India," Karan said.

"It's better that way," said Burger. "Your flight's at six a.m. The ticket's been sent to your inbox. Get home. Get packed. You've got four hours to get to the airport."

Ten minutes later, they reached Mass. Avenue. Over the tops of the brownstones, Karan could see the blinking Citgo sign in Kenmore Square. It was 1:00 a.m., but the lights of Boston were still burning as they paused a moment to shake hands before Yankowitz and Burger disappeared into the city and Karan headed back across the bridge, toward Cambridge, a lone runner silhouetted against the skyline.

Twenty-One

Proving his identity had always been a challenge. As Karan took his passport out of his pocket, he saw the American eagle on the cover, holding an olive branch in one of its talons and a quiver of arrows in the other, symbolizing peace and military might. In its beak the bird of freedom held a banner emblazoned with the national motto: *E Pluribus Unum.* Flipping open the passport, Karan saw his photograph and name. For once, he wasn't traveling with false documents or using an alias, which made him feel suddenly exposed.

Karan had been to India only twice before, both family visits with his parents, when he was a boy. For him, India had always been a country that he approached with ambivalent feelings. As a child, he had enjoyed visiting relatives and experiencing life in cities like Delhi, for a couple of weeks, but each time, he was glad to fly back home to the familiar comforts of New England.

As he passed through air-conditioned corridors, along moving walkways, Karan braced himself for what lay outside. Though the airport was new and flashy, he expected the crush of taxis and waiting families, the swarming, muggy chaos of arrival that he remembered from his earlier visits—the smells, the shouts, the heat and perspiration.

But this time, it seemed different. Filling out the landing card on the plane, he had been conscious of obscuring the truth, even though all of his personal details were correct. For "purpose of visit," he had ticked "Tourism." As he studied the faces in the arrivals hall, lines of disheveled passengers queuing up at the immigration counters, he asked himself how many of these people were hiding their true identities. Karan wondered if he himself would be flagged as a threat by the facial profiles they were developing, matching the features of potential terrorists to anonymous faces in a crowd. As the immigration officer stamped his entry on the page, he felt a sense of relief at not having to answer any questions.

Beyond Baggage Claim and Customs, a line of drivers stood silently behind the metal barrier. Karan scanned the signs until he spotted a placard with his name.

MR. KARAN CHAUHAN
HIMALAYAN GETAWAYS

Somebody had a sense of humor, he thought, though he wasn't entirely sure if it was a joke or not. The driver, an elderly Sikh with a lopsided turban, greeted him and took charge of his luggage trolley. They said nothing as they headed across to the parking garage. It was warm in Delhi, and the air was perfumed with diesel exhaust and a smell of dry earth that evoked memories for Karan of the last visit he had made to his grandfather's village in Rajasthan. The new airport gleamed in the artificial light, concrete, steel, and glass.

Inside the garage, they came to a dark gray Ambassador, its dumpy, outdated profile virtually unchanged from the cars he had ridden in in the past, though he could tell the vehicle was practically new. Karan gave the driver a skeptical look. The windows were tinted, and he noticed a Delhi license plate. The time was 10:30 p.m. His flight had been delayed for an hour and a half.

Flying in over Afghanistan, Karan had tried to imagine the topography below. Through his window, there was only darkness until the moon came up over the Karakoram, bathing the snow-clad peaks in a fragile light. The man in the seat in front of him had reclined fully, so that the tiny video screen was only inches from Karan's face.

He had watched the moving map for several hours, the icon of the airplane like a fly trapped against a window pane, progressing slowly across the earth below. The names on the map kept changing as they approached India. Samarkhand. Kabul. The Tibetan Plateau. Peshawar. Lahore. Srinagar. Chandigarh. Delhi.

As the driver opened the back door for him before stowing his luggage in the Ambassador's trunk, Karan was conscious of a figure inside. He hesitated before getting into the car. The only thing he knew about his handler was his name, Bogart, and he felt sure it was another joke . . . perhaps.

"Long flight?" said Bogart, putting out his hand to shake.

"Yeah," said Karan. "Painful. You could have put me in business class."

Bogart gave him an elastic smile that revealed no amusement. He was a dark-haired man with unexpressive eyes that betrayed nothing but a cynical look of exhaustion. His skin was sallow and showed his age, somewhere beyond fifty.

"Sorry," said Bogart. "It's part of your cover, a techie who's lost his job . . . coming back home to find himself."

The car began to move as the driver headed toward the exit of the parking garage. They didn't speak until they were outside on the airport highway. Bogart gave the driver directions in Hindi.

"Go by way of Dhaula Kuan, then along Ring Road to the hotel. *Koi jaldee nahin hai. Dheeray chalaana.* There's no rush. Drive slowly."

Karan glanced over at Bogart, who reminded him of an older version of Johnny Damon, the Red Sox outfielder traded to the Yankees in 2005. Definitely older but with the same square chin and jaw.

"Your Hindi's good," said Karan. "How long have you been here?"

"Long enough," said Bogart, with an evasive cough. "How's yours?"

"*Bol leta hun, thodi bhot,*" Karan replied. "Just well enough to make myself understood." His mother had insisted he speak Hindi as a child.

Bogart stared at the lights passing outside the tinted windows, which made the night seem even darker than it was.

"You're heading into a fluid situation," he said. "I can't predict what's going to happen."

"I understand," said Karan.

"No, you don't," Bogart replied brusquely. "This could be the last time I speak with you, so listen carefully. This case is sensitive. Once you get out of this car you're on your own. Don't try to call the embassy or email anyone. Don't access your computer in Cambridge. Nobody will help you, no matter what."

"That's reassuring," Karan said.

Bogart reached across and handed Karan a padded envelope with something heavy inside. As Karan opened it, his handler took out a packet of gum and slipped a stick into his mouth. Juicy Fruit. Karan recognized the cloying smell as he unwrapped the pistol and examined it. There were three extra clips of ammunition, which he stowed in his computer bag, along with the handgun.

"It's what you asked for," said Bogart. "Glock 17 with a laser sight."

Karan noticed they were on an overpass now, driving on a level with the upper stories of buildings along the highway, lighted billboards on the rooftops. Eighteen years had passed since his last visit to Delhi, and he didn't recognize the city any more. Bogart chewed his gum for a moment then started speaking, slowly, methodically.

"Day before yesterday one of our senior operatives was shot in Mussoorie. His name was Dexter Fallows. He'd been working undercover as a missionary nearly fifty years. Fallows was going to retire next month."

"Who shot him?" Karan asked.

Bogart pressed a button on the armrest between them. The back of the front seat slid open to reveal a video screen. *Not my grandfather's Ambassador*, Karan thought. As Bogart spoke, he uploaded images on the screen. First there was a black and white image of Dexter Fallows in Srinagar thirty years ago, with a Kashmiri man. Both of them were seated in a *shikara* on Dal Lake, smoking cigarettes. There were a dozen other pictures, like a tourist's snapshots of

Kashmir—Shalimar Gardens, carpet shops along the Bund, playing golf in Gulmarg, Nedou's Hotel.

These were followed by a short clip of Fallows on horseback in the mountains near Pahalgam. The whole time he was showing these to Karan, Bogart kept up a terse commentary, explaining how Fallows had worked undercover with Kashmiri agents who moved back and forth between India and Pakistan. Some of them were members of the Jammu Kashmir Liberation Front—JKLF. Pictures of Mussoorie appeared, the Savoy Hotel, hill station bungalows. There was a photograph of Fallows holding a rifle and posing with a snow leopard he'd shot, the dead animal stretched out in front of him.

"We're not sure who killed Fallows," Bogart said, "aside from the usual suspects. It could be his old friends from Kashmir. Jihadis. ISI. Lashkar-e-Taiba. Fallows kept in touch with his contacts from the eighties, the usual courtesy calls on former informants."

"Why now? At the end of his career?" Karan asked.

Bogart shrugged, then opened the window for a moment, spitting out his gum. The rush of air and the smell of dry grass and neem trees entered the car.

"It looks as if there might be a religious angle," said Bogart, ". . . shooting him outside the church."

"Has anyone claimed responsibility?"

"Nothing credible," said Bogart.

He pressed another button on the console between them, and a photograph came up on the screen, a bearded Muslim, his features slightly out of focus.

"Right now, we're guessing it could be this man," Bogart said. "Mohammed Mustafa, better known as Haji Yaqub. He's a Kashmiri separatist from Baramulla who trained as a sniper in Pakistan. Yaqub's been linked to assassinations in Srinagar and Kathmandu."

A second photograph of the same man appeared. In this one, Haji Yaqub was aiming a rifle at a target. He was dressed in a loose *salwar kameez*, with a white cap on his head.

"So, what am I supposed to do?" Karan said.

Bogart handed Karan a CD case, containing two unlabeled discs.

"For the moment . . . nothing. Just do your homework. Study these files. We've got you a room at a comfortable hotel in Mussoorie. Settle in. Keep your eyes open and wait for our instructions. . . . Learn whatever you can but keep a low profile and maintain your cover. If we need you, someone will be in touch. If we don't, you can think of it as a paid vacation."

Bogart didn't smile as he said this. The final photograph of Haji Yaqub appeared on the screen, this time without a beard. He was wearing an open-collared shirt with a sweater vest. It looked like a passport picture, stiffly posed. Pressing the remote control, Bogart switched off the screen and the back of the Ambassador's front seat closed up again. Outside, the lights of Delhi slid past the tinted windows, like phosphorescent creatures, jelly fish and Portuguese men o' war, glowing in the dark. Karan felt as if he was under water. The round, padded roof of the car and the convex windshield were like being inside an old-fashioned bathysphere, submerged beneath the surface of the night.

Twenty-Two

"Does it bother you?" he asked, as her fingers traced the crooked lines.

She looked at him with an aggrieved expression, though her voice was calm and controlled.

"Of course, it bothers me," she said. "Any Jew would hate this symbol, but I've learned to understand how much older it is than the Holocaust. Hitler and the Nazis corrupted and perverted it. But the swastika goes back centuries before any of our histories were written. Whether you're Buddhist, Jain, or Hindu, it's a symbol of creative energy and good luck, not death and persecution."

"It represents the sun and the wind," said Renzin.

The swastika, or *yungdrung*, was turned in a counterclockwise direction, arms twisted to the left. It appeared at each of the four corners of the *thanka* painting. The pigments were dark, and it was difficult to make out the shapes on the fabric scroll, which was coated with a grimy shellac, having hung for years within a temple sanctuary, collecting dust and soot from butter lamps.

"How old is this?" Noya asked.

Renzin shrugged. "Two hundred years, at least. Three hundred, maybe."

He had waited until his father was away from the shop before showing Noya the *thanka*. Potala Antiques was filled with Tibetan handicrafts and souvenirs, almost all of them cheap imitations of traditional artifacts—brass thunderbolts, wooden masks, and prayer wheels, produced for the tourist trade.

The *thanka* was kept in a room behind the shop, locked away in a cupboard. It was rolled up inside a copper cylinder, which was even older than the painting itself, engraved with sacred symbols and characters. Renzin had taken the *thanka* out and carefully unfurled it on a table under a light suspended from the ceiling, so that the images and colors seemed to glow beneath the accretions on its surface.

"Is this for sale?" Noya asked.

"No," said Renzin, his voice on edge. "Not everything has a price."

At the center of the *thanka* sat an austere figure in a teaching posture, one hand raised, the other holding a small scepter, each end of which was decorated with a yungdrung, identical to those that appeared at the four corners of the *thanka*. The figure was surrounded by a rainbow, its colors faded but clearly visible. Outside of this was a concentric ring of fire, the flames like clusters of tiny orange leaves. Beyond the central image lay a diagram of sacred geography, a schematic map of an idyllic valley encircled by mountains. The dark patina of the painting was cracked and damaged at places. Noya could make out geometric shapes and lines, walls within walls. There were houses and temples, trees, lakes, and rivers as well as miniature figures on horseback or seated in worship. Some of their garments and jewelry were outlined in gold paint that glinted like precious ore. Near the top of the painting was a stylized image of a single mountain, more prominent than the rest. Noya recognized the shape.

"That's Mount Kailash, isn't it?" she said. Beneath the snow peak was a wild-looking figure riding a white yak, a mountain deity with glaring eyes.

"Yes, but here it is called Mount Tise," said Renzin. "The seven-storied swastika mountain."

"Is this a Bon *thanka*?" said Noya.

Renzin nodded. "A forbidden mandala. Some consider it a form of heresy."

Though the painting looked as if it contained traditional Buddhist symbols and motifs, there were subtle differences. The figure in the center bore a strong resemblance to Shakyamuni, the great teacher, but the iconography came from a different religious heritage altogether. The counterclockwise swastika, the rainbow and ring of fire, all of these were hints of an older, more mysterious faith.

"The monks who painted this *thanka* faced persecution long before the Communists took over Tibet. This painting would have been burned by Buddhist lamas who believed it was a kind of blasphemy, part of an impure tradition," Renzin explained.

"But it looks as if it could be Buddhist," Noya said.

"Sometimes, to preserve an endangered tradition you must disguise it behind the masks of your oppressors," Renzin said. "The artist who painted this mandala hid apocryphal symbols inside a familiar landscape."

"It's like a secret map," said Noya.

"That leads to a place which no longer exists," Renzin added.

The painting was filled with layers upon layers of meaning, a complex cartography of myth and legend. Each of the tiny figures represented a story, an episode in the lives of saints, hunters, and warriors. Though the *thanka* measured only twenty inches by eighteen inches, it contained an infinite epic within its brocade margins, a narrative without a beginning or an end.

"Is this Shangri-La?" Noya asked, her finger circling the ring of mountains, tracing a path through the geometric labyrinth of lines.

"Everything in this painting has more than one name," Renzin told her. "Shangri-La. Shambala. But for the Bon, this is the land of Olmo Lungring, the birthplace of Tonpa Shenrab, the founder of their religion."

"I suppose every culture and people believe in a place like this, an Eden out of which their ancestors were exiled," said Noya.

"The promised land," said Renzin.

But Noya was no longer listening, her eyes fixed on the obscure shapes and images of the *thanka*, as if searching for something hidden beneath the shadowy layers of paint and soot.

She was a strange girl. Renzin hadn't figured her out—a tangle of contradictions. Her questions were persistent, and she never seemed satisfied with his answers. She was interested in all things spiritual, from every religion, especially Tibetan Buddhism and tantric ritual. Sometimes Noya could talk without interruption for an hour or more. Then, suddenly, she would fall silent, and he could get no response from her except a sullen nod of the head, or a whispered "yes" or "no." Her face was like a mask. Her personality was a paradox as well, independent and distant for much of the time, then suddenly eager for company, insisting that he stay with her. Often, she seemed insecure, almost wounded. At other moments she was hard and unyielding as stone. Without warning, she would demand that he leave her alone, only to call back an hour later and ask Renzin to pick her up and take her somewhere.

"Where did this come from?" Noya asked, after she had studied the *thanka* for several minutes.

"It was smuggled out of Tibet by my father, in 1970. The shaman who gave it to him made him promise to preserve it. His monastery in Guge had been destroyed during the Cultural Revolution. The Chinese smashed all of the images and burned the library, desecrating both Bon and Buddhist shrines. This *thanka* had been buried once before, to hide it from the lamas. The shaman had discovered it as *terma*, hidden wisdom. Now he had buried it again, to protect it from the Communists.

"When my father met the shaman, he was living in a cave near the source of the Indus. At first, he appeared to be a Buddhist monk, but then he revealed himself as a Bonpo mystic. He told my father where he had buried the *thanka*, in a gorge nearby, and asked him to retrieve it. The shaman was almost a hundred years old, sick and dying, weak with hunger, but he recounted all of the stories in this painting and told my father the secrets it contained, the names of each of the figures and the sacred landscape of Olmo Lungring, as well as the abstract meaning of the mandala, a magical diagram of origins that holds everything in place.

"My father promised the shaman that he would conceal and protect the painting. Returning to India, he carried it with him. Ever since then, he has kept it safely. When I was a boy, he used to take it out and tell me the stories, how the mountain god, Machen Pomra, guards Mount Tise and rides on a white yak, the spirits of the sky and earth, and the legend of the horned eagle who carries Tonpa Shenrab on his back. It's all here in this painting like a memory that goes back thousands of years."

"This should be in a museum," Noya said, looking up at Renzin, as if the spell that held her had been broken.

He shook his head and began to roll up the *thanka*.

"Many people, scholars and art collectors, have offered to buy this *thanka*, but my father refuses to sell it. He says that someday it will return to Tibet, so that the painting can hang in a temple once again, where it belongs."

Before Renzin had finished rolling up the scroll, they heard the front door of the shop open and a rustling sound of someone entering through the beaded curtains. Moments later, the tapping of a cane on the concrete floor made Renzin stiffen, as Jigme shuffled into the room. He stopped immediately when he saw his son and Noya, though his eyes betrayed no obvious surprise. For several seconds he stared at them before his gaze was lowered to the *thanka* on the table.

Noya had met Jigme a couple times before, though they had never spoken and he had always ignored her. But now, the old man glanced up at her with disapproval and suspicion. When he finally spoke it was in Tibetan.

"Put it away," he said to Renzin, though he kept his eyes fixed on Noya. "Why did you show it to her?"

Renzin did not reply as he slid the painting into the copper cylinder.

"It's very beautiful," said Noya, trying to ease the tension.

Jigme answered her in English, his voice polite but stern.

"Please go," he said. "There is nothing more for you to see."

Twenty-Three

Serving tea was a ritual for Afridi, one that he performed with care and conviction whenever he had a guest in his home. As a lifelong bachelor, he was fastidious about things that mattered: the knots he tied were always perfectly dressed, the framed photographs on his walls were never crooked, his pistol was cleaned and oiled each week, his dog was well groomed, and he poured his tea through a silver strainer that was never allowed to tarnish. The tea service, carried in on a lacquer tray by his servant, was English bone china, which he had bought several years ago when he had gone to present a lecture on survival training at Sandhurst. The tea leaves were a carefully balanced blend of Darjeeling (for flavor and bouquet) and Assam (for strength and color). Each came from a different estate where he knew the owner and received a monthly package, custom dried and never more than three weeks off the bush.

Anna watched Afridi remove the embroidered Kashmiri tea cozy, as he explained that the water was just as important as the leaves. He had a slate-lined tank behind his house, where he collected rainwater off the roof, especially for making tea.

"Milk?" the Colonel asked. "Sugar?"

"Just a little milk," she replied.

As Afridi poured her tea, Anna studied the photographs on the walls of his sitting room and the memorabilia above the fireplace.

The two ice axes were crossed precisely, and she could see his initials carved in the wooden shafts. She recognized Afridi in one of the photographs, even though he would have been no more than twenty-five when he posed on the summit, and his face was masked by glacier glasses and a balaclava. He had a lean, athletic build and looked taller than she expected. In a wheelchair, it was difficult to gauge a man's stature. But something in the confident smile on his face and the way he held up a defiant fist made her sure it was him in the picture. As he passed her the cup of tea, Afridi's hand was steady.

Anna wondered how he had reconciled himself to this life, after so many adventures and risks on the mountains, a man of action hobbled by his injuries. Her thoughts were somewhere else, as she heard him begin to speak.

"The man who was shot outside the church was an American named Dexter Fallows. He worked for the CIA," said Afridi, catching Anna's eye as she focused on what he was telling her. "We knew it, of course. He was watching us. One of our analysts posed as an informer, giving him just enough of the truth to be convincing . . . a convenient means of learning how much the Americans knew."

"Why was he shot?" Anna asked, setting her teacup on the table beside her.

"That's the puzzle," Afridi answered. "He was hardly a threat. Sixty-nine years old, almost seventy. Ready to go back to a peaceful retirement in Virginia. He was the kind of spy who just fades away. . . . Biscuit?"

As she took one from the plate he offered her, the old dog who was lying across the room lifted his head. Until now, he hadn't moved. Afridi chose one of the Marie biscuits and tossed it across to him. The dog didn't even rise to his feet, taking the biscuit between his jowls and chewing quietly for a moment before returning to his nap.

"Fallows operated undercover, as a missionary, with the North India Bible Fellowship. For a while he was based in Kashmir, but most of their work focused on Tibetan refugees, rehabilitation programs, health, and education. NIBF had a Christian publishing house, here in Landour, that printed Tibetan translations of the Bible and evangelical literature. . . ."

"The building that burned down yesterday?" Anna said.

Afridi confirmed with a nod of his head.

"Do you think it's connected to the shooting?" she asked.

"Of course, but it's still not clear exactly what the connection is." Afridi lifted his cup and took a sip of tea before continuing. "For a while, they used to publish anticommunist leaflets, along with gospel tracts that were distributed in Tibet. Along with the press, Fallows used to run a foster home for Tibetan refugees. He and his wife looked after them, with a couple of other missionaries. Most of the children were orphans. Others had been separated from their parents, for one reason or another. A number of them went on to become resistance fighters. In the early days, during the late fifties and sixties, as soon as they turned eighteen, he sent them off to America to be trained in guerrilla warfare and surveillance, so they could be parachuted into Tibet. Back then, we were cooperating with the CIA, a reciprocal arrangement. We even recruited a few of his boys for the Special Frontier Force."

"Did he convert them to Christianity too?" Anna sounded skeptical.

"Some," said Afridi. "For Dexter Fallows, the lines between proselytizing and his clandestine activities were always blurred. For a while, he ran an operation smuggling Bibles into Tibet, while sending some of his boys across the border to keep an eye on military installations. He believed in fighting Communism with the word of God. The Chinese finally shut that down."

"Who would have wanted to kill him?" Anna asked.

Afridi broke a biscuit in half and dipped it in his tea before eating it.

"The bullet that killed Fallows was a 5.8 mm, fired from a Type 88 sniper rifle," said Afridi after taking a swallow of tea.

Anna looked up at him, startled.

"The same weapon that killed the ITBP jawans in Milam?" she asked.

"Same ballistics but fired at a range of three hundred and fifty meters instead of point blank."

"Do you think it could be a Chinese commando?"

"That's what it looks like," said Afridi, though he didn't sound convinced. "All we know is that someone crossed the border three weeks ago, killing two sentries. We haven't picked up any communication with the Chinese, but there's other evidence . . . the mountaineering jacket with the snow leopard patch. Also, a money changer in Nainital bought ten thousand yuan from a man who claims he sold a motorcycle to somebody he never met."

Anna picked up her cup and saucer as if she were holding something so fragile it would break in her hands. The flavor of the tea was strong but not bitter, fragrant without being flowery. Anna scanned the mountaineering pictures, tents pitched on a snow-covered ridge that looked barely wide enough for a man to stand on. In the foreground were two figures roped together, facing the camera with expressions of weary determination. She wondered how many days it had taken to climb so high and imagined the cold wind that swept across the exposed ridge. Afridi was staring at her intently.

"That's a beautiful necklace you're wearing," he added, almost as an afterthought.

She fingered the amber beads self-consciously.

"Thank you. I bought it in the market yesterday," Anna replied.

Afridi gave her a knowing smile, then reached across to the table beside him and handed her a packet, wrapped in brown paper.

"You've got good taste, Miss Tagore," he said. "Now, tell me what you make of this."

Anna looked puzzled as she opened the packet. Inside was a Kashmiri shawl, embroidered with paisley patterns. It seemed to weigh almost nothing at all, as light and soft as feathers. Anna gave Afridi a questioning look, not sure if this was a gift.

"Put it on," he insisted.

Anna felt uneasy as he watched her stand up, his eyes following every move she made as she unfolded the woolen fabric. Then, cautiously, she wrapped the shawl around her shoulders, realizing what it was.

"*Shahtoosh*?" she asked, feeling the delicacy of the weave between her fingers.

"Correct," said Afridi. "Confiscated by Customs in Delhi six months ago, along with twenty other shawls. A shipment to Copenhagen."

"Must be worth a lot," said Anna, admiring the paisley patterns and rich colors, reds and umbers, as well as a black border with gold *chinar* leaves.

"Seventy-five thousand rupees," said Afridi. "Four antelope were killed to make that shawl."

Anna slipped it off her shoulders with a look of dismay.

"May I have your ring?" Afridi asked, as he took the shawl from her.

Still confused, Anna removed the ring from her right hand. Afridi threaded one corner of the shawl through the ring, then pulled the entire length of fabric through, with a grand gesture, like a magician performing a sleight of hand.

Anna reacted with a grim smile.

"The fibers are six times thinner than a human hair and worth two hundred and fifty thousand rupees a kilo, combed and carded," he said, returning the ring. "Fifteen kilos of *shahtoosh* arrived from Tibet a week ago. It's the third shipment in a month. Altogether, since June, we've tracked more than one hundred and fifty kilos coming across the border, enough to finance a terrorist plot."

"Who sold it?" Anna asked.

Reaching into his jacket pocket, Afridi took out the flash drive that Jigme had given him and passed it to Anna.

"What's this?" she asked.

"Do you believe in ghosts?" Afridi replied.

Anna turned the flash drive over in her hand, as if it were a fetish object, a riddle without a punch line.

"I want you to analyze the voice on these recordings," Afridi said, pouring her a second cup of tea.

He then handed her an old cassette with a battered plastic case. It had Chinese characters on its label and a picture from a patriotic opera, a woman in her Mao jacket and cap with a red star above her breast. Flags were waving in the background and dancers with billowing scarves. But the tape inside bore no connection to the cover. It only had the initials, "H.S. 1982" written with a felt pen that was going dry.

"This recording was made thirty years ago," Afridi muttered. "Not the best quality, but see if there's a match."

"Whose voice is it?" Anna asked, replacing the tape in its scratched case and slipping both the flash drive and the cassette into her jacket pocket.

"I'm not certain," Afridi answered. "It could be . . . someone I climbed a mountain with, back in 1969."

Anna followed his gaze to one of the framed pictures on the wall. The photograph was a blurred image of two men atop a peak—a hurried picture of triumph on the summit, with clouds closing in. She wasn't sure, but one of the men looked like Afridi. They were holding flags, the Indian tricolor and the American stars and stripes.

"Rataban?" Anna asked.

With a flinch of his eyes, Afridi expressed surprise that she knew the name of the mountain, then nodded.

"Not the highest peak I've climbed," he said, examining the calluses on his right hand, "but certainly the most treacherous."

Twenty-Four

Renzin watched his father moving along the line of prayer wheels, rotating each of them as he made his way around the shrine in a clockwise direction. In his left hand, Jigme held his cane, though he didn't use it, shuffling forward with unsteady determination. The old man seemed to be propelled by the momentum of the prayer wheels, even as he made them move with the touch of his hands.

Though it was only 8:00 a.m., a dozen elderly Tibetans were circling the prayer wheels at the Shedup Choepelling Temple in Happy Valley, at the western end of Mussoorie. Each of them was lost in their own thoughts and memories. Having completed his circumambulations, Jigme moved toward the main temple, where he climbed a flight of shallow steps and entered through the brightly painted portico. Inside the temple stood a cardboard cutout of His Holiness that always took Renzin by surprise, it looked so lifelike. The Dalai Lama was wearing yellow robes and an abbot's hat, seated cross-legged, with a beneficent smile on his face.

Jigme prostrated himself in front of the image, lowering himself stiffly to his knees and then slowly pressing his forehead to the floor of the temple. His cane was placed beside him, and after several minutes Renzin helped his father get to his feet. Neither of them spoke, as Jigme folded his hands and prayed in front of the gilded Buddha in a glass case, his lips moving slowly and a guttural chanting rising out of his throat, a sound of reverence and resignation. Renzin had said a silent prayer when they entered the temple, but he did not prostrate himself, watching his father patiently, as he completed the rituals he performed each week. They had already lit butter lamps in the annex of the temple, setting the cotton wicks aflame.

Though he had always been a man of action rather than contemplation, descended from a proud clan of Khampa warriors, a mountaineer, a soldier, and a spy, there was a spiritual side to Jigme, a quiet sense of awe for the mysteries of this life and the next. The older he grew, the more devout he had become, believing that whatever he had experienced or accomplished during this birth was meaningless in the larger pattern of faith and fate.

In his youth, Jigme had had been one of the Chushi Gangdruk resistance fighters who helped His Holiness escape from Tibet in 1959. Back then, he had been a brash young militant, several years younger than Renzin was today. Jigme remembered when he had seen the Dalai Lama for the first time after he fled from Lhasa, a young monk about his own age, disguised as a nomad. They had been ordered not to show His Holiness any obvious deference on the journey, and certainly not to prostrate themselves in front of him, for Chinese informers would be watching. Each of them had sworn to give his life for their spiritual leader. Though they were full of grief to see the Dalai Lama escaping into exile, Jigme and his companions were honored to serve as his bodyguards. For part of the route out of Tibet, Jigme had ridden beside His Holiness, and he remembered stopping once at a stream, where they let the horses drink. He had helped His Holiness dismount and in a furtive gesture of respect, Jigme had touched his forehead to the Dalai Lama's hand. Later, once they were safely across into India, he had been given an opportunity to pay obeisance. In those days, there had been such despair in their minds as they helped their leader flee, and yet a sense of conviction and hope that they would be able to reclaim their homeland from the Communist invaders. Today, he had reconciled himself to the failed promise of their struggle, realizing that Tibet itself, that distant homeland, was nothing but a nation of illusion, a mandala of politics and persecution.

Stepping outside the temple, Jigme shaded his eyes in the bright sunlight, feeling a sense of calm. Next week, he would go to the Dzogchen Monastery, where he would meet His Holiness for the last time and pay his respects at the shrine to the martyrs of Paryang, his comrades and compatriots who had been slaughtered by the Chinese. The Dalai Lama would honor them all with his prayers and ceremonies, those who had died in the struggle and those who had survived. Jigme's eyes clouded with tears, remembering the devastation and horror of Paryang. More than three hundred resistance fighters had gathered to launch an attack against a Chinese garrison thirty miles away, but that morning they had received a message over the radio.

He could still hear the earnest, youthful voice, speaking in their own language, ordering them to retreat, the words garbled with static. Jigme had always carried a photograph of His Holiness, tucked into the folds of his coat, an image that sustained and motivated him during their struggle, helping him to overcome hardship and loneliness. The Americans who had trained them were now betraying their promises of support. The US president had gone to Beijing, shaking hands with the enemy, raising a toast with Chou En-Lai, posing for photographs with Chairman Mao. The pictures had been published in Indian newspapers, and it had burned a scar on his soul. Jigme remembered the voice on the radio calling them back across the border.

Many of the fighters at Paryang had refused to believe that this was His Holiness's voice being broadcast. They argued, saying it was a trick. They did not trust the radio, which had been parachuted in across the border, a crackling metal box with wavering eyes that spoke like an oracle. The Americans and Indians had forced the message upon them, said some of the resistance fighters, refusing to pack up their weapons. They would stand firm and ignore the order to retreat. How could His Holiness ask them to surrender? This was not his voice. There was no proof. But Jigme had recognized the gentle manner in his leader's speech, as well as the firmness of his command. He understood that their struggle would continue, but this was a tactical retreat. They were being called back across the border because of politics, not destiny.

In the end, of course, it didn't matter whether they had been ordered to give up their position at Paryang, because the Chinese jets arrived two hours later. The bullets and bombs had fallen like a hailstorm bursting out of a cloudless sky.

Jigme recalled the sudden violence of that attack and their helplessness on the ground. The resistance fighters were camped on the outskirts of Paryang, beside the upper reaches of the Tsang Po River. Most of the structures at Paryang had already been destroyed and offered little cover or protection. He had thrown himself behind the ruins of a mud wall. As the fighter jet flew past, Jigme emptied his rifle at the ruthless iron bird. It screamed overhead like some kind of demon with wings of steel and claws of fire. All around him, he had seen men falling under the stuttering bullets, strafing the sand like a swarm of dust devils. In the end, Jigme was only one of a dozen fighters who were still alive and able to obey the Dalai Lama's command. The rest lay dead or dying on the banks of the Tsang Po. After that day, as he crossed back over the mountains and made his way into India, Jigme had often wondered why he had survived when so many others had died.

Later, he had returned to Tibet on several occasions, slipping back across the border on secret missions, part of the Special Frontier Force, spying for the Indians and the Americans but always in the hope that he could, someday, avenge the death of his comrades and help the Dalai Lama return to the Potala Palace in Lhasa.

Now that he was nearly four times his age at the time of massacre, Jigme looked forward to a peaceful death, a quiet escape from the suffering and illusion of this body and this world.

As he climbed onto the back of Renzin's motorcycle, his arthritic legs aching with the simple act of mounting the seat, he remembered how he had found one of the few horses that hadn't been shot by Chinese guns. He had kicked his boot into the stirrup and thrown his leg easily over the saddle, galloping away from the carnage with his tears dried by the wind.

Twenty-Five

On August 28, 1969, the Indo-American Rataban expedition had been flagged off in New Delhi by the US ambassador and India's home secretary. It was a private ceremony, and members of the press had not been invited. Because of America's support for Pakistan and India's criticism of US military action in Vietnam, relations between the two countries were tense, but the climbers were hailed as a "friendship mission," an opportunity to set aside political differences and work together toward a common goal. The truth couldn't have been farther from the false bonhomie and rhetoric on the lawns in Chanakyapuri, where Afridi stood sweating in his dress uniform, listening to diplomats and bureaucrats deliver meaningless speeches about heroism and courage.

Two weeks later, they reached the road head at Govindghat, after driving through monsoon downpours and being delayed for twelve hours above Rudraprayag because of a landslide that blocked the road. They hadn't even set foot on the mountain, and Afridi already had misgivings. He had picked his team of climbers carefully, including Jigme, with whom he had climbed six peaks already. But it was the Americans who worried him. They had spent ten days together in Mussoorie preparing for the expedition, planning their route and training for the mission. Most of them were friendly in a patronizing kind of way, though he could tell that the younger men were inexperienced and nervous. Their leader, his counterpart, was a man named Hayden Sayles who kept to himself most of the time. Despite their joint command, Sayles had made it clear to Afridi, from the start, that he considered himself in charge of this mission. He was a major in the US special forces, having served in Vietnam as an Army Ranger. Afridi carried the same rank but had not challenged him directly, knowing that the mountain itself would determine the true hierarchies in their team.

After a wet trek to Gangaria, they'd entered the Bhyunder Valley the following day, with thirty mules and twenty-five porters. Afridi had been here once before but only in late spring. He was eager to see the valley in its optimal season. The Valley of Flowers had been given its name by Frank Smythe, one of Britain's greatest mountain-eers, who had wandered into the Bhyunder watershed after conquer-ing Kamet and several other prominent peaks in 1931. Smythe had described the unspoiled beauty of the valley, descending out of the snow and mist into a vast rock garden of monsoon flowers.

Afridi was not a botanist, but he appreciated the array of bloom-ing plants, from white anemones to blood-red potentilla, delicate fritallaries with nodding heads, golden fields of ferns and rhododen-drons of every shade from white and pink to violet. Several of the Americans had brought cameras and spent every minute, when it wasn't raining, taking photos of the flowers. Afridi had showed them the grave of Joan Margaret Legge, a Scottish botanist who had come to the valley to collect specimens to take back to Edinburgh. While climbing the nearby cliffs to collect rare plants, she'd slipped and fallen to her death on the rocks below.

Rataban stood at the northern end of valley, a mountain shaped like a massive arrowhead. Much of the time it was cloaked in clouds, but in the evenings these mists parted and the peak turned red at sunset, as if dipped in mythic gore. On their first night, by a camp-fire of birch logs perfumed with juniper twigs, Afridi recounted the episode of the Mahabharata from which the mountain took its name. The Americans had listened in silence as he described the great battles between the Pandava and Kaurava clans—cousins pitted against each other in an apocalyptic conflict that threatened to destroy the world. Karna, a half-brother raised by foster parents who were untouchables, was one of the greatest warriors on the battlefield of Kurukshetra. As his chariot advanced upon the enemy, he strung his bow, then fitted his arrow, drawing it taut. *Rakht'baan*, the arrow of blood, killed thousands in its path, slaughtering Karna's kinsmen as it flew toward the Himalayas. It finally landed here at the foot of this mountain that now bore its name, carving a gorge and leaving its stain on the snow.

Sayles had listened to the story with a bored expression. He had no time for the physical beauty of the valley or the colorful metaphors of Hindu mythology. He was eager to get up on the mountain and impatient with the acclimatization that Afridi insisted was necessary. The Americans had all been living at sea level and needed to let their bodies adjust to the altitude. Base Camp was established near the snout of the Rataban Glacier, out of which the Bhyunder Ganga flowed, a murky stream clouded with snow melt. After the mules and porters had departed, they were a group of nine climbers and six high-altitude porters. The expedition had the valley to themselves, except for a Hindu mendicant who lived in a cave across the river from their camp, a solitary sadhu in saffron robes, who appeared at a distance, hailing them with a wave of his arm but making no attempt to cross.

On their third day in Base Camp, Jigme took three of the Americans across the glacier to visit the sadhu, carrying with them several kilos of rice and lentils as a gift. When they returned, they said the mendicant was a friendly, cheerful man, though he had taken a vow of silence and could tell them nothing about himself.

Soon enough, the team began ferrying loads up the glacier, establishing a route through a frozen labyrinth of ice. It was slow work and each day the glacier moved enough to make their progress unpredictable, opening up new obstacles in their path. Afridi oversaw the setting up of an advance base camp and organized the climbers and porters into ropes of four men, hauling supplies over treacherous ice. Sayles remained aloof. He and one of the others in his team, Russell Tanner, had brought rifles with them and they went hunting on the crags above base camp, returning with wild sheep for dinner. The sound of their rifles echoed off the cliffs like thunder. When they ferried their rifles up to Camp 1, Afridi told them there wasn't going to be any game on the mountain, though Sayles had seen signs of bear and snow leopard prints. He was eager to claim a trophy.

As with most mountaineering expeditions organized by the Indian Army, they brought with them "meat on the hoof," a euphemism for live goats that were slaughtered to feed the climbers as they advanced up the mountain. These were procured by the quartermaster from shepherds in the Bhyunder Valley and were part of their standard rations up to Advanced Base Camp. Afridi recalled how the meat got tougher the farther the goats had to walk. On the Rataban expedition, there was a strange and disturbing incident involving Sayles. One day, instead of letting the cooks kill the goats, he insisted that the climbers should do it themselves. He taunted a couple of Afridi's men, after they refused.

It was one of those minor events on a climb that could have led to an ugly confrontation and divided the group. Sayles himself had slaughtered the first goat, slitting its throat with a commando knife that he carried strapped to his leg. Afridi remembered the swift, ruthless manner in which he had grabbed the animal by one horn and twisted its neck to the side. The blade had opened the arteries in its throat, spraying blood onto the snow in a bright red arc.

After that, Sayles had challenged the Indians to do the same, but nobody stepped forward and the Americans began to laugh among themselves as the cooks dragged the carcass away to be butchered.

"Come on," said Sayles. "If a Chink soldier comes across that ridge, are you going to be afraid to cut his throat?"

The warm blood had melted the snow and soaked in, as if the mountain itself had been wounded. Sayles was still holding his knife unsheathed. For the first time, Afridi could see a crazed, psychotic look in his eyes. Sayles began to pick on one of the junior officers under Afridi's command.

"What are you, Singh, a fucking vegetarian or something?" Sayles said.

Afridi had no choice but to intervene. Without saying anything, he stepped forward and took the commando knife from Sayles's hand. Then, without hesitation, he caught a second goat by the rope tether around its neck. With a quick slice of the knife, he cut open its throat but instead of spattering the blood in a wide circle, he let it drain into the snow, as the goat shivered in his grip and then went limp. In a gesture of contempt, he tossed the knife at Sayles's feet and walked away to his tent.

After they were acclimatized, the climbers established a second camp on a broad col overlooking the glacier. This was the pass through which Smythe had crossed into the valley in 1931. Beyond it lay the final bulwark of the Himalayas before Tibet. By now, there were only four climbers in the advance party, Afridi, Jigme, Sayles, and Tanner. A fifth member of the assault team, an American named Osgood, was suffering from the first symptoms of pulmonary edema and had to be sent down to base camp three days before the summit attempt. Sayles and Afridi had negotiated a grudging truce. They knew that the stakes were high and understood what none of the other climbers had been told.

Two of the loads brought up to Camp 2 by their high-altitude porters included a pair of aluminum canisters, weighing thirty pounds each. The one contained a sensor device, with a small radio transmitter and an antenna. Assembled, it was about the size of a portable television set. The second canister, which was wider and sealed with a rubber collar filled with lead, contained a plutonium power source.

Afridi, Sayles, and Tanner had been instructed on the assembly of this device, how to connect the sensor to the power pack and align the antenna so it could collect the information required. Nobody else on the expedition had been told what the canisters contained or the clandestine purpose assigned to the summit party.

Above Camp 2, the western ridge of Rataban ascended to an exposed flank, where the wind had sculpted shelves of ice overhanging the glacier. The altitude here was 5,700 meters. Afridi estimated they were about three hours below the summit, a relatively easy climb if the weather held. He and Jigme had scouted the site and set up two tents to prepare for the final push. So far, the weather had been unpredictable, as it always was at the end of the monsoon, clear mornings followed by clouds at noon and snow flurries until dusk. The nights were brilliantly clear, as soon as the temperature dropped. Afridi had stood outside his tent with Jigme, looking up at the vast mirrorwork of stars. Spotting a satellite orbiting overhead, he had pointed it out with his gloved hand, mentioning that the Americans were looking down on them.

The next morning all four men were planning to push for the summit, but at the last minute Sayles insisted that Jigme stay behind with the radio. He was adamant, though Afridi argued with him, before giving in. Carrying the canisters in their packs for the final climb, the three mountaineers set off at daybreak. The wind obliterated their footprints almost as soon as they crossed the snow field beyond the tents. Roped together, they moved slowly up a ridge of mixed rock and ice, where cornices leaned out over the southern face of the mountain. There was a risk of avalanches breaking loose. Jigme had watched them leave with uneasiness and disappointment, though he had accepted his supporting role in the team.

Four hours later, after a methodical ascent that included two technical pitches but mostly a steady slog up the mountain, the three men dragged themselves to the summit. Afridi was the first to arrive and dropped his pack in the snow. Before the others reached, he had a few minutes to appreciate the view from the summit of Rataban, looking north toward Tibet and southward at Ghodi and Hathi Parbat, the "horse" and "elephant" peaks, which were difficult to recognize from this angle. But mostly there were clouds, quilted layers of moisture rising out of the valleys, delivering snow and rain on the slopes below.

As soon as the others made it to the top, they unpacked the canisters and set to work without speaking. There was no moment of jubilation, no handshakes or bear hugs, only a rehearsed process of assembling the sensor. Afridi had to remove his gloves to attach the wires to the power pack. As he did this, his fingers began to freeze, sticking to the metal, a numbness seeping into his knuckles. He wondered if it might be a symptom of radioactivity rather than the first signs of frostbite. When he finally finished, he clapped his hands together to restore the circulation. They had placed the device on a natural platform just below the summit to the west, an area six feet in diameter that seemed solid and partially sheltered from the wind. Before they began their descent, Tanner took a photograph of Afridi and Sayles, holding their countries' flags, a quick snapshot to please the speechmakers in Delhi. Stuffing the camera into his empty pack, Afridi led the way down, his rope snaking back to Sayles and Tanner.

Almost as soon as they began heading down to camp, the clouds folded in over the ridge, like a frothy white tide. They had fixed ropes on two difficult sections of rock, which made it quicker for them to descend, but with visibility diminishing they had to move cautiously for fear of breaking through a cornice.

An hour after leaving the summit, it began to snow and a blizzard swept in. Afridi was leading, but when he glanced behind, he could see nobody following. Only the sluggish tension on the rope established the presence of his fellow climbers. Moving through white-out conditions and exhausted from the climb, Afridi tried to focus on the route they'd followed. It was mapped out in his mind, though he could not see the contours of the mountain, a circuitous path through uncharted snow.

Sayles had seemed strong enough when they reached the summit, but Afridi was worried about Tanner. He had a delirious look in his eyes, and the sloppiness of his movements showed that he was suffering from altitude sickness. Several times on the descent, they had stopped and huddled together to gather strength for the ordeal ahead. Each time, they had to force Tanner to get on his feet and keep moving. Afridi guessed they had another hour to walk before they reached the tents, but the roar of the wind was too loud for them to speak to each other. He continued to lead, putting one foot in front of the other, hoping each step would not be his last.

Eventually, they reached an icefall that was almost perpendicular, with a sheer drop below. On the way up, they had cut steps, and Afridi had even considered fixing ropes across the 80-degree slope, a distance of no more than fifty feet, but in his rush to reach the summit, he had ignored his instincts and better judgment. Now, they would have to traverse this exposed stretch of ice in the storm. Even with their crampons, it was difficult to keep from slipping. The footholds they had cut a few hours earlier were frozen slick, and their axes barely penetrated the hard surface. Yet, Afridi knew he had to lead the others across.

What happened next was a sequence of events that had played out in his mind a thousand times over since then. Afridi remembered it as a terrifying blur, yet he could recall every movement he'd made within the swirling white chaos of the storm, experiencing a weird kind of vertigo . . . as if he were suddenly standing sideways, struggling to keep his grip on the mountain, which was pitching up like the deck of a ship riding a tall wave . . . the severed rope . . . his fear and alarm . . . a helpless sense of betrayal . . .

Seconds later, he'd found himself tumbling into the void.

෴

At the camp below, Jigme was waiting anxiously. The storm had eased, and he could see thirty meters up the snowfield, as the stumbling figures approached. Rushing from the vestibule of his tent, Jigme hurried to help his teammates back into camp. As soon as he realized there were only two men, he halted for a moment, trying to recognize who was missing.

Dragging Sayles into the tent, Jigme shouted over the moaning of the wind, but his voice was swallowed by the storm. Tanner kneeled in one corner, his head lowered as if in prayer, though he was retching. Jigme took a last look outside, peering through the circular doorway, before drawing the zipper taut. Sayles pulled off his goggles. Ice caked his beard and mustache. His eyes were expressionless, but he gestured with one hand, indicating that Afridi had fallen. Jigme tried to question the men, but they were too exhausted to speak, even after he had given them mugs of hot tea to drink. As they slept, he stayed awake throughout the night, waiting for Afridi to return. Having seen the frayed end of Sayles's rope, however, he knew it was a futile vigil.

Twenty-Six

A troupe of langur monkeys watched Anna from the chestnut trees along the Chukkar, their wizened black faces and silver hair giving them the appearance of somber dignity, though the younger ones somersaulted from branch to branch. Anna stopped to watch them for a moment, their long tails hanging down like dangling ropes. The expressions on their faces looked almost human. It seemed as if they could speak, and Anna was tempted to ask them a question.

After tea at Ivanhoe, she was puzzled and subdued by her conversation with Afridi, wondering if he really understood the situation or whether he was just living in the past, fighting enemies long since defeated. This morning, she had called Manav Shinde and told him that she felt she was wasting her time. The shooting of an elderly CIA agent may have rung alarm bells in Delhi or Washington, but this assassination didn't seem to have the fingerprints of any known terrorist group. Besides, there was little that she could bring to the case, even if it was a Chinese operation. Manav had persuaded her to be patient, saying that Afridi wouldn't have summoned her to Mussoorie unless he had a serious purpose in mind. Anna felt sure there were things she hadn't been told, crucial elements that might explain Afridi's purpose in calling her here.

Reaching into the pocket of her vest, Anna took out the cassette tape and flash drive, as if to remind herself that there was work to be done. But after hearing the account of the Rataban expedition, she had her doubts. Those events had occurred forty years ago, a decade before she was born; the old animosities had little to do with contemporary threats. How could they have any relevance today? On top of this, Afridi had seemed guarded and unwilling to tell her the entire story, holding back details of the truth. The only interesting thing she had learned was that the owner of Potala Antiques had climbed Rataban with Afridi—a coincidence that pointed to other secrets beneath the surface of Mussoorie's unprepossessing facade. And yet, in a world of suicide bombers and weapons of mass destruction, none of it seemed to add up to a major priority.

When Anna had asked Afridi why he had chosen her in particular to handle this project, he had given her a wary look.

"You've got a reputation," he said.

"Good or bad?" Anna asked.

"It depends on who I talk with," Afridi said. "Nobody disputes your skills in audio-surveillance, but when it comes to accepting the authority of your superiors, questions have been raised."

Anna nodded, knowing what he meant.

"I need your help with voice recognition and analysis," Afridi said, "but I also want someone who shows initiative in solving problems, someone who isn't afraid to take risks when necessary."

She met his eyes with a look of understanding, though she wished he would be more specific and give her details about her assignment.

"You're probably the only person in RAW who's received both a commendation and a reprimand for the same action," said Afridi. "That's a rare distinction, Ms. Tagore, and well deserved, on both counts, if you ask my opinion."

"I had no intention—" Anna began to explain but he cut her short.

"You don't need to make excuses to me," said Afridi. "I know how frustrating it can be when senior officers fail to act on urgent information. For what it's worth, I believe you had every reason to conduct yourself as you did. But you're lucky to be alive."

A year ago, Anna had identified a Lashkar-e-Taiba plot to place explosives on the Rajdhani Express, from Delhi to Kolkata. When she alerted her superiors, they had refused to take it seriously. Anna had made every effort to convince them that the threat was serious, but when they ignored her warnings, she took matters into her own hands and boarded the train herself, minutes before it departed. Against all standard operating procedures and in defiance of any chain of command, she located the terrorists herself, before they could carry out the bombing. When they resisted arrest, one of them was killed outright and the other was shot through the kneecap. The train was stopped at Kanpur and passengers were evacuated. An explosives team discovered enough RDX to blow up three carriages. Disaster had been averted, but Anna still had to face a disciplinary hearing. If it weren't for Manav Shinde's help and direct intervention from the home secretary himself, she would have lost her job.

"I admire your courage," Afridi said. "But more than that, it's your instincts that impress me and your willingness to act on them."

"Okay. But what about now? Can you tell me what you expect of me?" said Anna. "I'm not sure why you've called me here to Mussoorie. . . . Sir."

Afridi smiled and put his fingers together in a steeple. "Patience, Ms. Tagore. There is a time for action and a time for waiting. You'll understand everything soon enough."

As she approached Sisters' Bazaar, a small market halfway between Afridi's cottage and the HRI, Anna noticed half a dozen rhesus monkeys scavenging at an overturned garbage can. With their disheveled red fur and mangy tails, they had none of the dignity of the langurs and looked like a pack of miscreants digging through vegetable peels and plastic wrappers. As she passed them, one of the larger male monkeys met her eye with a menacing stare, then bared his teeth in a threatening grimace. Anna wondered which species of primate was closer to humans in the evolutionary chain. Though she would have liked to think it was the noble, black-faced langurs, it was more likely the belligerent rhesus macaques with their ruddy features and pale, ugly eyes.

Anna had passed Sisters' Bazaar several times already, but she hadn't entered any of the shops until now. From outside, A. Prakash & Sons didn't look as if it would carry anything that she would want to purchase (HOMEMADE JAM AND CHEESE, the sign announced), but she decided to have a look anyway.

On first glance, the interior seemed even less promising: cluttered shelves and display cases with an array of foodstuffs and other items that one might need in a hill station—umbrellas, flashlights, peanut butter, chocolate bars, detergent, and cough drops. Anna wasn't planning on staying any longer than necessary. The proprietor was seated in one corner, at a desk piled high with bills and receipts. He nodded in greeting, then returned to his accounts. Anna crossed the room to a set of shelves full of imported jams and cookies. She knew that she would be working late this evening, and the kitchen at HRI closed promptly at 9:00 p.m. after dinner was served. Sometimes it felt as if she was back in boarding school. Anna decided she would need something to keep her going tonight.

Her back was turned to the main door of the shop when it opened a minute later and Karan stepped in. He didn't notice Anna at first, as he went over to the refrigerator and took out a bottle of water. As Karan stepped toward the counter to pay, Anna turned around with a carton of orange juice and a packet of Oreos in her hands.

"Hey!" Karan reacted with surprise.

Anna nodded and smiled, awkwardly.

"We keep running into each other," she said.

"I promise, I'm not stalking you," Karan replied, holding up both hands in mock surrender. "Landour is a small place. All the paths circle back together."

Glancing at the bottle in Karan's hand, she said, "You're wise to be drinking that. Never trust the water in India. Foreigners get sick all the time."

He grinned at her. "It usually doesn't bother me, but I don't want to take any chances. Besides, the water up here has a funky taste."

Anna put her purchases on the counter as the proprietor extricated himself from his calculations and came across to serve them.

Karan reached over and turned the packet of Oreos around to look at the label.

"American cookies?"

"These days you get everything in India," Anna said, then took the packet away from him and spoke to the shopkeeper. "Just these. How much?"

Lying between them on the counter was a strange object, like a small tennis racket but with a fine mesh of copper wires instead of strings. Karan saw the writing on the plastic shaft.

"Made in China," he said.

"What is it?" Anna asked.

"A battery-operated flyswatter."

Anna laughed as she handed over three hundred rupees. "Ridiculous," she said. "What's the point of that?"

Karan swung the flyswatter, pretending to return a backhanded shot.

"The Chinese are making everything these days . . . whether we need it or not," he said. "They're going to take over the world with useless merchandise."

"Well, somebody has to be willing to buy what they sell," Anna said.

"I suppose you're right." Karan eyed the flyswatter thoughtfully. "But I still don't trust the Chinese."

"That's because you're an American," Anna said. "It feeds your paranoia."

As Anna picked up her change and started to leave, Karan turned toward her.

"How long are you here?" he asked.

"I'm not sure," she answered. "Another week."

"Then maybe our paths will cross again."

Pushing open the door of the shop, Anna glanced back at him and smiled. Though she didn't say anything, her expression suggested she wouldn't mind that possibility.

After he paid for his water, Karan stepped out the door and glanced in the direction Anna had gone. The band of rhesus monkeys was clambering over the roofs and hanging from the wires like acrobats. Two of them were vandalizing a TV antenna above the shops, while another was trying to pry open a window. Anna was already out of sight, but as Karan made his way quickly beyond the line of buildings, he could see her walking ahead. He followed cautiously until he saw her enter the gate of the Himalayan Research Institute. Karan had passed this way several times before and seen the signs: PROHIBITED AREA—TRESPASSERS FORBIDDEN.

Twenty-Seven

For the past two days, Afridi had noticed that the water in the taps had a strange odor. At first it was barely discernible, a faintly stagnant scent and a flat taste when he brushed his teeth. By that evening it was stronger, distinctly muddy, though it still ran clear. He thought the smell might be coming up from the drain, but when he scooped water into his cupped hand and held it to his nose, there was a mild stench of something like rotting leaves or the stems of flowers left too long in a vase. His servant had noticed it as well and brought him two jugs of filtered water to wash up that night. Next morning, there was no mistaking the fetid odor. Even the menthol fragrance in his shaving cream could not disguise the smell. Opening all of the taps, he let them run for several minutes, but the stench only grew stronger. After that he told his servant to use nothing but rain water, which was collected in a cistern behind the cottage.

When Afridi reached his office, the guards confirmed that the water at the HRI was also tainted. He told his secretary to telephone the chief engineer of the water department as soon as their offices opened, but before he could make the call, there was a message from Renzin, asking Afridi to come across to Chey Tanki.

By the time Afridi's jeep arrived, the police were fishing out the body. It had been dumped in one of the tanks, and, because the water level had dropped halfway, they had to run the pumps and fill the tank so the corpse rose to the top. Two policemen with hooked rods were finally able drag it out. A steel ladder ascended one side of the tank with a small platform at the top, barely a meter wide, which made it awkward to maneuver the corpse. On the ground below stood a dozen policemen and employees of the water department, each of them calling up and giving instructions. The constables who were extracting the body had handkerchiefs tied across their faces. Afridi watched from the open window of his jeep as they lowered the body on a rope, sodden clothes sticking to the bloated flesh. About halfway down, one of the arms to which the rope was tied separated at the shoulder, and the remains dropped the rest of the way to the ground, falling in a heap at the foot of the tank. Somebody shouted and the group of men scattered as the corpse nearly landed on top of them.

Afridi spotted Renzin ducking aside, one hand covering his nose and mouth. A few minutes later, he came across to the HRI jeep, his features contorted with revulsion and dismay. He spat a couple of times before he was able to speak, and Afridi could see the nausea in his eyes.

"Who is it?" he asked.

"Lobsang Bhotia . . . the journalist who took those photographs."

"He disappeared four days ago . . ." Afridi began to calculate.

"Five days, sir," said Renzin. "The body is decomposed. His skin is gray, and his face is so swollen I hardly recognized him, though I knew it was him from his clothes. The police will make a formal identification, but I'm sure it's Lobsang."

"How did he die? Not drowning, I'm sure."

"His throat has been cut," said Renzin. "I'm surprised the head didn't fall off."

"Aren't the tanks sealed?" Afridi said.

"Whoever dumped the body inside broke the lock. The linesmen only discovered that the lid on the tank was open this morning, when investigating the stench," Renzin said.

"I hope someone gets sacked for this," Afridi said, looking away in disgust.

Three hours later, five minutes past noon, Manav Shinde arrived in Mussoorie. Afridi had sent his helicopter to fetch him from Delhi. As usual, Shinde looked as if he had just risen from bed, his khadi kurta wrinkled and his eyes bleary behind the wire-rimmed spectacles that made him look like a nocturnal creature unaccustomed to being out in the daylight. He met with Afridi alone in his office for half an hour before Anna joined them. Manav greeted her with folded hands.

"*Namaskar*, my dear. How are you enjoying your holiday in Mussoorie?"

"It's actually nice to be away from Delhi," Anna said.

Manav gave her a look of disappointed amusement.

"We miss you," he said. "I hope Colonel Afridi isn't going to insist that you stay here forever in his mountaintop chalet."

Both men studied Anna across the table. They obviously knew each other well but couldn't have been more different from each other. The one was rumpled and austere, with a look of intellectual indolence in his eyes, slumped in a conference chair, fingers laced together and pressed against his chin. The other sat erect, every crease in his clothing ironed to precision and his gaze alert. Though he was limited in his movements, Afridi seemed poised for action.

Shinde explained that, regrettably, he could only stay for an hour.

"We've made two arrests. Members of a sleeper cell here in Mussoorie," he said.

"Jihadis?" Anna asked.

Manav shook his head. "No. Tibetans," he said. "We've had our eye on them for some time, part of an extremist group with links to foreign networks. I've been interrogating them in Delhi."

"Were they the shooters?" she asked.

"Not so far as we can tell," Manav said, and Anna could see from his expression that he did not want her to interrupt him again. She looked across at Afridi, whose eyes were fixed on Shinde, as he continued in a quiet, offhand tone that Anna recognized as the voice he used when he briefed cabinet ministers. It was almost as if he were reading from a confidential file, though she knew that none of this had ever been written down. The only dossiers Shinde maintained were locked away inside his brain.

"During the late 1970s, there was a power struggle within the Tibetan government in exile. The older leaders of the Kashag, the Dalai Lama's cabinet, were being challenged by a younger, more impatient generation. Limited forms of armed resistance had continued throughout the sixties and seventies, but it was hardly effective—occasional attacks by guerrillas along the highways in Western Tibet. We used members of the Special Frontier Force to carry out hit-and-run sorties but mostly for intelligence gathering. Some of the younger activists began advocating for a more violent approach. In those days, Yasser Arafat and the PLO were in the headlines for their terrorist attacks, hijackings, and bombings. There were fringe groups and radical factions among the Tibetans who wanted to draw attention to their cause by doing the same sort of things. A loosely knit alliance was formed who called themselves the Norbulingka Brigade, commemorating an uprising at the summer palace in Lhasa just before the Dalai Lama escaped from Tibet. They modeled themselves on the Red Brigades in Europe, small, fiercely committed teams of renegade fighters. Some of them were based in Kathmandu, and some in India.

"The Dalai Lama and his government condemned this approach and refused to endorse any form of terrorism. They preferred to follow a peaceful, nonviolent struggle. But the Norbulingka Brigade decided to carry out several attacks against Chinese targets. In Nepal there was an attempt to sabotage the Freedom Bridge, which was being built across the Bhote Kosi River connecting Kathmandu with Lhasa. The explosives failed to detonate, and three men were arrested. Later, two members of a Chinese trade delegation were kidnapped in Calcutta and held hostage for a month. Eventually, their dismembered bodies were found in trunks at Howrah Station. The Norbulingka Brigade claimed responsibility. They also burned a couple of cars belonging to the Chinese embassy in Delhi. It was nothing spectacular or particularly effective, but we were determined to put an end to it, and within a year most of these terrorists were rounded up. In the process, we discovered that they were receiving support from abroad. Some of the money was coming from Tibetan exiles living in Europe and the United States, but there were also ties to several right-wing American extremist groups dedicated to fighting Communism.

"Matters came to a head in 1989. We'd been keeping our eye on a couple of suspects within the Tibetan community at Majnu ka Tila, student radicals associated with the Norbulingka Brigade. It turned out that they were planning to hijack a China Airways flight from Delhi to Beijing, a desperate attempt to gain credibility for their cause, and they almost pulled it off. There were three hijackers, two of whom made it onto the plane with an improvised bomb and a homemade pistol. The third man checked in after them, and a knife was discovered in his briefcase. After he was apprehended, he panicked and confessed. They were planning to divert the flight to Kabul and demand the release of dissidents held prisoner in China. Fortunately, after a standoff on the tarmac, the other two Tibetans surrendered. When they were interrogated, we learned about an Irish conspirator who had helped them obtain the explosives and was planning to coordinate negotiations in Kabul. We started tracking him, but by this time he had already left the country.

"After the failed hijacking, we were able to break up the Norbulingka Brigade, and several of their cells were exposed. Two of the leaders committed suicide, and the movement seemed to have been destroyed. Over the years, though, there have been rumors that the brigade was reorganizing itself with new recruits. Earlier this year, a Tibetan activist was arrested in Mysore with half a dozen unlicensed pistols. There was also an explosion at a carpet factory where traces of Semtex were discovered in the wreckage. We've been monitoring communications within the Tibetan diaspora. Two separate websites claim to represent the Norbulingka Brigade. Recently, they've posted a call to arms, threatening to take revenge for betrayal of the Tibetan cause. It's a lot of angry rhetoric dissipating into cyberspace, but we didn't have any indication of a serious threat until last month. The problem has been that we don't know who or where the threat is coming from, but all of the evidence that we've been able to gather suggests there is an effort underway to regenerate the Norbulingka Brigade.

"We suspect that there are other members here in Mussoorie, aside from the men we've arrested, but it's hard to know exactly how many there are and what resources they have. The two men we have in custody aren't being particularly talkative. It's very possible that they could be Chinese agents. Part of the difficulty has been the infiltration of Chinese operatives into the Tibetan community. These are ethnic Tibetans who are Communist agents posing as refugees. Some of them have penetrated Tibetan institutions and hold positions of authority. The Norbulingka Brigade wants to capitalize on the suspicion and uncertainty, creating fear, disrupting relations between India and China, as well as the Tibetan government in exile. The primary motive is to destabilize the situation and overturn the status quo, so that more radical factions can emerge."

Afridi listened silently to Shinde, his head lowered in concentration. Anna guessed that he already knew most of what was being said, though she could see his eyes registering some of the facts with special interest.

"How do you know it was an Irishman who was conspiring with them during the hijacking?" he asked.

"We don't know that for sure," said Shinde. "The Tibetans claimed he was Irish and that was the passport he used when he registered at his hotel, but we later found that it was forged."

"So, he could have been anyone—European, American?" Afridi continued.

Shinde made a gesture with both hands to indicate that there were unlimited possibilities.

"Are you suggesting that the man who was found in the water tanks this morning was a member of the Norbulingka Brigade?" Anna asked.

"Possible. But it's not likely. He probably stumbled on something that put others at risk. Whoever killed him wanted him silenced," Shinde replied.

"But then, why dump him in the city water supply? Wouldn't it have been better to just get rid of the body discreetly?" Both men had their eyes on Anna as she spoke, and she felt uncomfortable.

"It's a statement and a warning," Afridi answered. "Just like Fallows's assassination."

Picking up the thread, Shinde concluded: "These are minor detonations, if you will," he said. "Most terrorists preface a major attack with something smaller, almost insignificant. For example, a low-intensity bomb goes off in a market and draws a crowd before the real explosion happens, killing dozens of curious bystanders. Or, perhaps, the opposite strategy: somebody fires shots at random, and security forces scramble to investigate, leaving the primary target unguarded and exposed. These killings could be a simple act of diversion."

"You're saying these incidents are just a prelude to something worse?" Anna responded, wondering which part of the truth she was or wasn't being told.

"Exactly," Shinde said, glancing at his watch. "But we can only guess what happens next. And now, if you'll excuse me, I have a meeting with the French *Ministre de la Défense et des Anciens combattants*, who's visiting Delhi, a complete waste of time but protocol must be observed."

As they accompanied him to the helipad, Shinde looked out at the high Himalayas that stood behind them and shook his head in disbelief.

"You know, Afridi sahib, those peaks are magnificent, but I've never understood the lure of mountains. They're cold and inhospitable, dangerous and lonely. Why would anyone choose to go there?" He waved his hand toward the snows dismissively.

Anna was surprised when Afridi laughed.

"Of course, you wouldn't understand," he said. "Because there's no such thing as protocol in the Himalayas."

Instead of replying, Manav folded his hands, then boarded the Alouette.

Twenty-Eight

Noya dissected a *momo* with her fork. The steamed dumpling was glutinous, its texture rubbery. A smear of hot sauce brightened her plate, fiery red chilies that burned Noya's tongue. The meat inside the momo was gray, and she wondered what animal it came from, buffalo, pig, or goat. The waiter had been noncommittal when she asked. Noya wasn't particular about her food. It might even be chicken, minced with onions and garlic, plenty of oil. According to Renzin, the best momos were those you ate with your fingers and the grease dribbled down to your elbow before you could stuff it all in your mouth. Noya broke off a piece of dough and put the morsel in her mouth, then washed it down with beer.

Renzin ate in silence, while Noya spoke. She was rambling on about rebirth and the transmigration of the soul, theories she had read about in a book by a Norwegian scholar of Tibetan Buddhism who had lived as a monk in Dharamshala for fifteen years before giving it up to become a professor of philosophy in Oslo. His writing was the kind of spiritual synthesis that seemed to appeal to Europeans, a little bit of this, a little bit of that. Renzin often wondered whether Westerners were really interested in Tibetan culture or whether it was just an exotic disguise that they could put on or take off to make themselves seem different. Noya sounded so full of conviction, but Renzin wasn't sure whether she was just playing a part, pretending that she believed in things she barely understood.

"I must have been born in Tibet in an earlier life," she said, her voice sincere but with a note of naive condescension.

Renzin found himself growing irritated when she spoke like this, as if she were trying to force him to agree with her.

"How can you tell?" he asked.

"It just feels as if that's where I belong," said Noya, waving her hand in the direction of an imaginary horizon. "Somewhere beyond the Himalayas."

Pouring the last of the beer into his glass, Renzin shook his head.

"But you're Israeli . . . from the Promised Land," he said.

Noya didn't smile, her face tense.

"Yes, that's what my grandmother used to tell me. She came from Antwerp. I was born in Jerusalem. . . . But, don't you think all of us are refugees from earlier incarnations?"

Renzin shrugged. "I don't know."

Noya's momo had been cut into a dozen pieces, the meat separated from the dough. It looked unappetizing, though she had eaten six already and forked a piece of gristle into her mouth, trying to taste for the flavor of beef or mutton. Most of the time, she was vegetarian, because it was safer on her stomach, not because of any ethical considerations or a fear of bad karma.

"I keep thinking we have so much in common," Noya said. "Israel and Tibet. We are the same."

Renzin swallowed his beer with a skeptical look across the table.

"Bullshit," he said.

"No, I really mean it. Our history is the same. Persecution. Displacement."

Noya was in one of her philosophical moods, the way she usually got after they had sex. Renzin never knew what to expect from her. Most of the time, she was silent and unresponsive. Other times, like this, she could talk forever, going on about politics, poetry, or some tantric ritual she had read about in a magazine or book.

During sex, she hardly made a sound, though Noya was always the aggressor. Renzin had never slept with a woman like her before, the way she pinned him down as if she was afraid he would escape her grasp, restraining him while letting herself go. When Noya had kissed him, he had been surprised by the sudden pressure of her lips, the way her tongue forced open his teeth.

The first time they made love was the day after they met. Renzin hadn't expected to have sex with her so quickly, even though he'd felt her hands on the inside of his thighs as they were riding back through the bazaar on his bike. She had given him no other indication of desire, but when he dropped her back at the hotel, Noya had taken him by the hand and led him to her room. Locking the door behind them, she unzipped his leather jacket and slid her arms inside, pulling him against her. Her kisses were an impatient prelude, no sentimentality or romance. As soon as she stepped back, Noya began to undress herself with an urgency that startled him, stripping off her underwear with her jeans and yanking her T-shirt over her head in a quick swipe of her arm.

This evening it had been the same, though he had known what to expect, the demanding look in her eyes, the taut smile on her lips. She was two inches taller than him, and her hands were strong, slipping behind his neck and grabbing his hair in a fist. There was nothing gentle about her touch, even though she often had a look of vulnerability about her. Noya didn't speak, her body demanding his compliance the way her thighs gripped him, her knees digging into his hips. All of the other women Renzin had slept with expected him to take the initiative, pretending they were surrendering themselves against their will. But Noya had none of their reticence or false modesty. She knew what she wanted, and she took it from him. Renzin felt as if there was no emotion in her embrace, only a need to satisfy a feral urge.

Now, as he looked at her across the table, talking about reincarnation and refugees, he remembered the determined, almost harsh expression in her eyes, an hour ago as she pushed him down upon the bed. Her fingernails had dug into his wrist, and when she lay against him, he could feel her muscles contract, like a runner crouching at the start of a race. Renzin had found it hard to control himself, both alarmed and aroused by her desire.

At first, he let her take the lead, but as soon as he tried to roll on top of her, it became a struggle. He was surprised how strong she was, though her body was thin and she weighed no more than him. As Renzin fought back, it only seemed to make her more intent on forcing him into submission. And when she finally came, her orgasm was a kind of tortured pleasure, her eyes squinted tightly shut, as if in pain. He followed her a moment later and his groans were like cries of surrender, allowing her to win this carnal combat. The only sound she'd made was labored breathing and a choked gasp of triumph.

A minute later, when she opened her eyes, Noya looked at Renzin as if she couldn't remember who he was. By then, her face was calm again and her hair fell over her forehead, the way it did right now, as if she had reassembled her disguise.

Noya continued talking, almost as if speaking to herself.

"Tibet and Israel have a lot in common," she said.

Renzin was hardly listening, but this time he challenged her.

"There's one small difference," he said. "The Americans have always supported Israel, given you money, arms. . . . With Tibet, they conveniently ignored us."

"That's just politics," Noya said, as the waiter cleared their plates.

"Everything is politics," Renzin replied, then asked. "Do you want another beer?"

She shook her head impatiently.

"Don't you ever want to go back?" Noya's question startled him.

Annoyed, he answered. "Back where? I was born here, in India."

"But Tibet is your homeland," Noya insisted. He recognized the same combative look she had when they were in bed, refusing to give in.

"My father's homeland," he corrected her.

"Whatever . . . same thing," Noya waved her hand dismissively. "Someday, Tibet will be free. I know it. You'll get your country back."

Renzin had pushed his chair away from the table. The frustration that had been growing in him suddenly boiled to the surface.

"Bullshit," he said. "It's never going to happen. Never!"

Rising to his feet, he started to walk out of the restaurant, then stopped himself and turned to face her.

"The truth is, we're more like Palestinians than Israelis," he said, an accusing look of bitterness in his eyes.

Noya watched him leave, his anger bringing a defensive smile to her colorless lips. She held her knuckles to her mouth for a moment as if hurt by Renzin's remark, but there was a look of victory in her eyes. A few seconds later, she heard the roar of his motorcycle departing and saw the headlight weave away in the darkness.

Twenty-Nine

The pulsing sound of a mountain scops owl's call punctuated the darkness, a single, chiming note that repeated itself indefinitely, steady and persistent as a metronome. There were no lights along this path, and the distant glow of streetlamps on the Chukkar above did not reach this far. Even the stars had vanished behind a blanket of clouds. Karan turned on his headlamp for a few seconds and lit up the winding trail as well as the roots and branches of oaks that formed a tunnel of overarching limbs, bearded with moss and dying ferns.

Switching off the lamp, he moved as silently as he could, remembering the contours of the path ahead, though his eyes were momentarily blinded by the glare. He kept one hand outstretched, touching the rough *pushta* wall to reassure himself that he wasn't going to step off the edge. In daylight, this path had taken him five minutes to walk, but now it seemed to go on forever as he crept forward. Karan could just make out a faint glimmer of light through the trees and knew it must be the house. Soon he reached the gate, opening it cautiously and wincing as the hinges creaked. In the darkness, he could barely make out the lettering on the sign:

TENNYSON LODGE
D. FALLOWS

The servant's quarters were at the back, a line of rooms built against the hill, and further back was the dark silhouette of the dormitory. A lone bulb was burning on the landing of the quarters. It was cold tonight and mist was filtering through the trees, diffusing the electric glow. The main house lay in darkness, no lights inside the black windows. Karan slipped around the corner of the building, where a rain gutter marked the edge of the verandah. He found the wooden pillars with his hand and stepped up onto the porch, pausing to listen for a moment.

Taking a pair of gloves from his pocket, he pulled them on and moved across to where he could feel the latch on the outer screen door. It opened easily. With his gloved fist, he punched the lowest window pane on the inner door, a square of glass that broke easily with a muted, shattering sound. Again, he listened for a minute. Only the owl was calling, like the ticking of a clock.

Reaching through the broken window, Karan fumbled with the knob. As it turned, he let himself inside. The house was hardly secure, with several points of entry. Stepping over the shards of glass, Karan switched on his headlamp. Immediately, he had a sense of the man who had lived here, the personality of the room and Dexter Fallows, who had occupied it for a lifetime. The sofa was low and dented, upholstered in corduroy fabric. Copies of *National Geographic* lay on the coffee table. A standard lamp leaned over an arm of the sofa, where Fallows must have sat to read in the evenings. The carpet was chewed at one corner. Three overstuffed chairs were arranged in a semicircle, two that matched the sofa and a third with wingbacks, the piping frayed along the edges. Karan could smell the odor of stale cigarette smoke. A cut glass ashtray sat on the coffee table. The unfiltered butts, crushed together, had not been emptied, as if out of respect for the dead.

The blue aura of the headlamp picked up the cast iron stove in one corner and hunting trophies on the walls, a cheetal stag, shoulder mounted, the branching tines of its antlers almost touching the ceiling, and a snow leopard skin tacked up against the opposite wall, its mottled rosettes like a dull pattern of soot and ash. The big cat's head was mounted with its jaws open in a snarl. The yellow glass eyes stared fiercely at Karan as he stepped past.

Moving through the sitting room, he entered an adjoining office, which had been ransacked. Someone, probably the local CID inspectors, had searched the room for documents. Papers were strewn on the floor, cardboard files disgorging receipts and letters, torn envelopes. When Karan kneeled down he saw an old carbon copy of a letter to a mission society in Illinois, Fallows's name was typed above the return address. The letter was dated 1976. The bookshelves had been searched, and drawers on the desk were open. Karan knew it was pointless to search the desk and filing cabinets. Fallows had worked undercover for too long. He would never have left confidential papers in his office. The only evidence of espionage was a stack of Graham Greene novels on the floor beside the rifled book shelf—*Our Man in Havana* and *The Quiet American*—paperbacks that hadn't been read for years, yet saved because of the few brief hours of pleasure and distraction they must have provided.

Karan stepped over these and entered the bedroom, which had been searched as well, the closets flung open and clothes hangers shoved aside, a disorderly queue of shirts and jackets waiting to be worn. Two suitcases had been pulled from under the bed, the contents disgorged. Karan felt sure the police had found nothing. Fallows couldn't have lived here all these years without taking precautions. He was old school, the kind of operative who knew how to cover his tracks. They weren't going to find his secrets hidden under the bed, though Karan could see that someone had moved the mattress. Instead of searching in the obvious places, he kept his eye out for something the others would have missed.

The sour stench of cigarettes was overpowering, and there was another ashtray on the bedside table. On the dresser in the bedroom were several photographs in frames. One of them was a picture of a woman with curled brown hair and glasses. This must have been Fallows's wife, who had preceded him in death. In the photograph, she wasn't smiling, her face turned to one side, holding a cocker spaniel in her arms. There was a second photograph, of both of them, husband and wife, standing outside a houseboat in Kashmir.

Karan entered two more rooms and a kitchen. All of the cupboards and chests of drawers had been turned upside down, and he could sense the growing frustration of the men who had searched the house. Even after his death, Fallows had preserved his anonymity. They must have known he was a spy, but there was nothing to incriminate him in the house, no evidence of his association with the CIA. Karan could picture the old cook, Ghulam Russool, watching as the inspectors carried out their investigation, the violation of a dead man's home.

In the dining room was a framed needlepoint embroidery on the wall, which he guessed must have been done by Fallows's wife. It read:

> *Christ is the head of this house,*
> *the unseen guest at every meal,*
> *the ever-present listener to every conversation.*

The house had an atmosphere of death. Karan remembered reading somewhere how thieves often targeted the homes of those who had recently died, spotting obituaries and funeral notices in the paper and waiting until the family had gone to the cemetery, then breaking in and stealing the belongings of the person who was being laid to rest. Several years ago, he had attended the funeral of a friends' widowed mother in a small town in western Massachusetts, and he was surprised to learn that one of the cousins stayed in her house to make sure it wasn't burgled. Tonight, he felt like a thief, preying on the dead, a grave robber like those who raided the pharaohs' tombs, searching for secret passages and hidden vaults within the unlit chambers of the dead.

Back in the living room, his headlamp picked up the black and white keys on the piano, which stood against one wall. On one of the side tables, he spotted a Bible and opened it carefully, the thin pages like tissue paper rustling between his fingers. As he turned, the headlamp caught the pattern of spots on the leopard's coat. Karan remembered one of the photographs Bogart had given him, of Fallows posing with the animal he had shot, the rifle nestled in the crook of his arm, the dead predator stretched out with a bloodstain on its flank. *It must be the same animal*, Karan thought. He stepped forward to see if he could locate the mark where Fallows's bullet had entered, but the taxidermist had done a careful job of repairing the damage, though the fur was brittle with age and moth-eaten at places. Instinctively, Karan reached up and pulled the skin aside. It was tacked to the wall but came loose easily. The paws were preserved with the claws intact, and there was a dark blue fringe of felt and canvas backing.

Behind the snow leopard skin was a safe, a small square door recessed into the wall with a single keyhole. Karan knew it would be easy enough for him to open. His steel probe worked its way inside with practiced ease, feeling the tumblers fall in place. Karan was like a surgeon performing an appendectomy with his eyes blindfolded. Ninety seconds later the door of the safe swung open.

Several unmarked files were stacked inside, containing documents and old photographs. As Karan flipped through the papers, he saw a photograph of Fallows with another man, both of them in shorts, standing on a ridge overlooking a gorge, with snow peaks in the background. There were a few more pictures, but Karan didn't study them as he quickly slipped the papers into a satchel slung across his shoulder. He was about to turn away, when the headlamp illuminated a small object in the locker. Reaching inside, Karan's fingers closed around a flash drive hardly an inch long, with a nylon tether and retractable port.

As he put the flash drive in his pocket, he heard a dog bark—a sharp yelp of alarm. Karan immediately switched off his lamp and moved away from the safe. He heard the dog again as he crept around the sofa toward the bedroom door. By now, a flashlight was waving about, illuminating the window panes in the kitchen. He heard a voice call out.

"*Kaun hai?*" The cook sounded frightened and uncertain. "Who's there?"

By the time the light caught the jagged edges of broken glass, Karan had slipped through the bedroom on the other side of the house and was already unlatching the outer door of the bathroom. He moved quickly and silently. Within a minute, he was outside in the garden, stealing through the open gate and up the path down which he'd come.

Thirty

A small herd of antelope, two males, three females, and a pair of calves, graze on sparse grasslands along the upper reaches of the Indus, which flows from the Lion's mouth, Senge Khambab, near the sacred mountain Kailash. Before it enters the gorges that drain into Ladakh, the Indus is a shallow, meandering stream that brings a narrow ribbon of life to the high deserts of Western Tibet. To the north are the burning wastelands of Taklamakan. Here chiru and gazelle, wild yak and kiang find summer pastures and struggle through the long winters. As the antelope cross over a low hill and descend to water, three shots erupt in quick succession. The two males stumble and fall, as well as the largest female, mother of the calves. The others bolt in terror as more shots are fired. A second female is wounded and struggles to escape, while the calves race away on clumsy legs. The youngest antelope have survived the hunters' ambush, but, soon enough, without the protective instincts of the adults, they will be killed by wolves.

Western Tibet defies geography; maps become meaningless and borders are nothing but errant lines drawn in the shifting sand. From here to Afghanistan lies a no-man's-land, claimed by many but governed by none. The Himalayas and the Karakoram establish a natural boundary over which lie difficult passes, some marked but many unknown or undisclosed. Each year the glaciers redraw their approaches, receding and fissured by crevasses. Only the most determined or desperate travelers would attempt a crossing through this forbidding frontier.

Beyond Mount Kailash, the rivers Indus and Sutlej flow through the canyons of Guge, with its caves and chasms. This region is known as Shangshung. Though the Chinese military have made inroads here, it has never been an easy territory to administer. Remnants of lost kingdoms and monasteries can be seen crumbling into the barren landscape. For some, particularly those who have never visited Guge, this could be Shangri-La, and they believe that here in the trans-Himalayas lies a forgotten paradise surrounded by seven rings of mountains, a land of hardy, everlasting youth. But anyone who has actually seen this terrain knows it is a place of death and desolation, not an idyllic cradle of life. Centuries ago, before Buddhist missionaries came from India, it harbored the magical traditions of the Bonpo religion, blending animism and sorcery. Here, fantastic stories are told—tales of a heroic prince who was conceived when a hailstone fell in a cup of butter tea, or the legend of a demon king who summoned a virgin every night to comb his hair, to brush and braid his long tresses and hide the horns on his head. After performing these duties, each girl was killed lest she reveal the terrible secret of the tyrant's horns.

The famous monasteries of Toling and Tsaparang lie at the center of Guge, evidence of a civilization that existed long before European explorers breached the Himalaya. Today, one looks southward over the shattered rooftops of ruined cities toward the great summits of Gurla Mandhata and Kamet, the northern ramparts of India. In 1966, Mao's Cultural Revolution destroyed what remained of the monasteries. Only the most remote and unknown *gompas* were spared this godless violation. Everywhere else the chapels were looted, their libraries burned and idols desecrated by the Communists.

And yet, traditions survive. One of the monasteries that remains untouched by the ravages of the People's Liberation Army, though violated by the elements—droughts, flash floods, and freezing dust storms—is the Tamdrin Gompa, which lies in a precipitous valley between the harsh embrace of two ridgelines that converge in a deep trench. The name of the valley means "cloven hoof," and it is a place where only wild goats and determined monks would dare to climb. At a distance, it is almost impossible to delineate the monastery's profile amid the conflicting contours of rock and eroded mud. Rough-hewn stones merge with the canyon walls, and the staircases that climb its perpendicular approach are likened to the fossilized vertebrae of a gigantic serpent whose tail extends into the hellish depths of the gorge, while its bleached skull and fangs are lost in the clouds. From the frescoes on its walls, the monastery appears to have been a Bon sanctuary, but the primary images are Bodisattvas and their attendant demigods. The monks in this monastery have an eclectic tradition, circumambulating both to the right and to the left while following the Buddha's teachings as well as the occult practices of ancient oracles and wizards like Tonpa Shenrab.

Over the years, rumors have attached themselves to the Tamdrin Gompa, stories of a violent warlord who inhabits its sacred precincts, both a patron and a predator. They say he is a white man who crosses borders with impunity, like a phantom hunter. He travels with a band of marauders—Bhotias, Kaffirs, and Muslims—his own personal militia. They hunt for chiru and gazelle, as well as ibex and bharal. His garments are those of the high plateau—sheepskin cloaks and heavy felt boots. The man is known as the pale demon, the mask of Alexander. Monks of the Tamdrin Gompa perform their devil dances when he appears and prepare a private room for him in the uppermost floor of the monastery. They treat him as their guardian as well as an aggressor, celebrating his departure with as much enthusiasm as his arrival. Even the most dogmatic Communists are afraid of him, and he is known to have tortured and disfigured Chinese scouts and frontier guards.

Few officials in Lhasa or Beijing give credence to his existence but the farther west one travels the more his stories are told. The Rimpoche of Tamdrin Gompa collects tribute on his behalf, taxing travelers and pilgrims who venture into the twisted ravines of Guge. Nobody within a hundred kilometers of Tamdrin denies his presence, and many people, shepherds and bandits, carry the spent brass casing from his rifle as totem objects. Few have seen him, with his long white hair and beard and fierce eyes that shine with madness like beads of fiery ice. Many believe he is an emanation of Tamdrin himself, the guardian deity whose ferocious aspect stands over the gompa and protects it from attack and depredation. Others claim he is descended from Greek satraps of Bactria, his royal lineage corrupted over generations.

He rides a gray stallion the color of smoke, and he seldom speaks, except to himself. His fighters are ruthless and undisciplined, like the packs of wild dogs that follow at their heels. When villagers see them coming, women escape into the wilderness and hide, while men leave their yaks and horses untethered, hoping they will elude the killers' blades. They murder and pillage with impunity, leaving devastation in their wake.

Thirty-One

"Tibet could have been the next Vietnam . . . without the fucking jungle!"

His voice was merciless, like a steel blade scraping against bone.

"We betrayed them . . . all of us . . . the goddamn CIA, the Indians. If only we'd given them the firepower they needed. . . ."

Male. Late fifties or early sixties. The accent was American, midwestern, like someone speaking with gravel in his throat. Occasionally, he coughed, as if he were smoking—the tobacco fumes choking his words as he exhaled. Anna could picture the old man's tongue forming consonants on his palate, aspirating vowels behind a broken line of yellow teeth. The recording was poor but clear enough, probably made on a hand-held Dictaphone or a cassette player. There was hardly any background noise, except for the whistling of wind, possibly through a crack in a window. Maybe he wasn't smoking, just sitting by a smoldering hearth, crouched beside a yak dung fire, the flames providing light as well as warmth.

"We hung them out to dry. They could have been victors instead of victims!"

It was impossible to know who this man was speaking to—his intended audience. The words were a rant, like some tin-pot dictator haranguing his subjects over the radio. It sounded like a shortwave broadcast, except there was a confiding tone to his voice, the brooding intimacy of madness, echoes of survival in each ragged breath. More than likely, there was nobody else in the room, just the speaker, alone with his microphone.

Anna could sense a loneliness in his delivery, the silence beyond his pauses, as if it were somebody who had no one to talk to but felt a need to deliver his message to the world—defiant statements tainted with bitterness and hatred as well as a feverish belief in a lost cause. Whoever it was, it sounded as if he hadn't spoken in years.

"We can still free Tibet. All it takes is a match to light the god-damn fuse. Just give those sons o' bitches the weapons they need. They'll kill every Communist from Lhasa to Kathmandu. Turn it back into fucking Shangri-La!"

Anna chewed the inside of her cheek as she listened, leaning forward over her laptop. The voice profile on her screen was like the teeth on a saw, serrated lines that rasped across the grain. Most of the recording was in English, but there were also sections in Tibetan that Anna couldn't understand. She'd played the recording three times now, pressing the buttons on the old Walkman rigged up with a USB port that connected to her computer. Anna then switched to the flash drive, opening the file in a separate window. It took a moment for the voice to be heard.

"What the hell are you afraid of? Dying? Shit! That's nothing, compared to living like this . . . no country, no home."

Definitely the same person. Anna didn't need to look at the voice signature to know this, though the lines matched perfectly—an identical profile. The only difference was that he sounded older, now, in his seventies. A weakened voice, more sand than gravel, and wheezing with a hoarse whisper of age. Only the word "Shit!" had the same brutality, as if he saved his breath for the expletives and mumbled the rest. This time, though, Anna's instincts told her he wasn't alone. The "you" that he was speaking to might have been someone in the same room, but it sounded more like a phone call, a threat delivered from an untraceable number. She had no sense of how it had been recorded. There was some static and a few clicks and pauses that made it seem as if the voice on the flash drive had been edited. Someone else was listening.

"Company bastards promised everything but never delivered. As usual, the Americans were shit scared. And the Indians were just worried they'd piss off the Soviets. Covering their own asses. Fucking cowards! We could'a done it. We could'a given the Tibetans what they deserved . . . a little bit of Uncle Sam needs you!"

Pausing and then replaying the first recording again, Anna slowed the voice down until it was a deep groan. On the screen, she could see the matching lines on two separate tracks, like one range of mountains rising above the next.

Anna had lost all awareness of time. The stark white lights and flickering screens made it impossible to tell what hour of day it was until she glanced at her watch and saw it was past ten o'clock. She had listened to the recordings with growing uneasiness, the crude rantings of a mad American, an insane soliloquy of vengeance.

More than the words, it was the voice that haunted her, the coarse syllables hawked up like phlegm, a throaty snarl. She didn't have a name, but Anna had constructed a face in her mind to fit the speech. He was seventy or seventy-five, she guessed. When he coughed, she could see him lifting the back of his grizzled hand to his chapped lips. She imagined he had a white beard and uncombed hair that fell in tangled strands to the frayed collar on his plaid shirt. Anna always made a mental picture of her subjects, the soft-spoken terrorists who whispered into a mobile phone, their clean shaven features like boys she'd known in college, hopelessly romantic yet spouting an ideology of evil, or the mumbling informants revealing unreliable truths, weak men with a stammer in their voice, a note of suppressed desire, immorality, and impotence.

Most of the voices Anna studied were men. She had often thought how different it would be to analyze a woman's voice. Female speech was far more difficult to read, with hidden nuances and less obvious hints of character or motive. Or maybe, it was just her own ears that were attuned to male voices. Listening to an audio recording was almost like looking at a photograph, offering her a portrait, an acoustical profile of perverted masculinity.

But this man frightened her, more than any other voice she'd heard before, the sustained anger in his speech, the vehemence of his opinions, the hoarse savagery of a septic larynx. Anna could almost see his eyes, bloodshot but with unclouded irises, a marksman's eyes despite the years of squinting at the sun, his pupils like tiny peppercorns.

"Fucking cowards . . . We turned them into piss-ass pacifists . . . chicken shits!"

Closing down her laptop, Anna unplugged the cassette player and the flash drive. The main room of the institute operated twenty-four hours a day, on eight-hour shifts. Half a dozen analysts were studying screens or typing notes. None of them looked up as Anna passed through the glass doors and onto the verandah.

The clear, dark air outside was a relief after the bright stillness in the room. A wind was blowing through the deodars, and Anna shivered for a moment, hugging her laptop to her chest. She was still unsettled by the American's voice, as if he had singled her out and was speaking to her. Over the past four years she had listened in on the conversations of dangerous men who had killed dozens of people, suicide bombers delivering their own elegies of martyrdom, political harangues by true believers and psychopaths. But this one was different. It was like hearing a voice of unrestrained hatred, stripped of any morals or humanity, yet strangely persuasive in its loathing, with a hypnotic tone of vengeance that was almost seductive.

Anna stepped off the verandah and was about to go to her room when she noticed that the light in Afridi's office was still on. She hesitated, then went across to the unmarked door. The curtains were drawn, but a warm, yellow light filtered through the cotton fabric printed with a geometric handblock pattern.

Knocking firmly, Anna waited until she heard Afridi answer. "Come in."

He was seated behind his desk, reading a file that looked as if it had passed through the hands of a dozen bureaucrats, the kind of well-thumbed sheaf of paper produced in Delhi purporting to out-line security risks—more speculation than hard facts.

"Miss Tagore, you're working late." Afridi closed the file, grateful to be disturbed and gesturing toward a chair across from him.

"So are you," she said.

Removing his reading glasses, Afridi shook his head.

"I'm supposed to be retired, but they keep sending me these damned reports for my comments. If I were to give my true opinions, I'd write 'Bloody Rubbish!' across each page."

He interrupted himself and glanced at Anna, who held up the flash drive with a questioning glance.

"Who is he?" she asked.

Afridi looked aside for a moment, as if trying to recall the man's face before replying.

"Hayden Sayles."

Anna waited for him to say more, but Afridi seemed to have lost his train of thought. Then, after several seconds, he continued.

"An American but born in China and raised right here in Mus-soorie, from the age of eight. You wouldn't know it from the language he uses, but his parents were missionaries. After the communists threw them out of Nanjing, they were assigned to India. Sayles was educated in Mussoorie, at the mission school. His parents worked for the North India Bible Fellowship and ran a rehabilitation center for Tibetan refugees in a town called Neelganj, about sixty kilometers to the east, in the foothills of the Terai. They were also involved in set-ting up the mission press in Mussoorie, publishing gospel literature in Himalayan languages.

"Sayles learned Tibetan as a boy, growing up among children of refugees. His parents instilled in him a lifelong hatred for the Com-munists after the atrocities they'd witnessed and the persecution of Christians in Nanjing. But he rebelled against the conservative pieties of his missionary upbringing. He had no time for Christian virtues of forgiveness and tolerance. Even at an early age, there was a psychopathic aggression in him. He had a fascination for guns and weapons. In his senior year, Sayles was suspected of firebombing one of the dormitories at the mission school, though it was never proved he did it. One of his schoolmates was Dexter Fallows. He was a few years younger, but they grew up together in these mountains, hunting and trekking. When Sayles graduated from school, he went back to America and joined the army. . . ."

Afridi seemed to have the whole story committed to memory, a complete resume filed away in his mind. As he spoke about Sayles, Anna could hear the suppressed anger in Afridi's voice, the way he described his background.

"An Army Ranger in Vietnam, he was decorated for bravery. But halfway through his second tour of duty he got picked up for a covert CIA operation, training Tibetan guerrillas. Because he spoke the language and had some knowledge of the Himalayas, he was a natural choice, a specialist in mountain warfare and survival."

Afridi paused, then wheeled himself over to the display of photographs and memorabilia on the wall, near the bookshelves. Anna thought he was going to show her a picture of Sayles, but instead, he glanced up at a length of climbing rope coiled into a loose shank and tied to an old carabiner. One end was frayed, the nylon fibers unraveling like a ragged paintbrush.

"Do you think Sayles is our shooter?" Anna asked.

"Very likely," said Afridi. "Were you able to match the two recordings I gave you?"

"Yes," she said. "But you knew that already, didn't you?"

"It's essential to confirm the truth, no matter how obvious it seems. That's the first rule of good intelligence. Never take anything for granted."

Afridi turned his wheelchair.

"I first met Sayles in 1969, when we were assigned to the Rataban expedition. At first, he didn't tell me who he was, but when we came up to Mussoorie for our briefing, he seemed to know everything about the town and I learned it was his childhood home. He never told me much about himself, but I got a few hints about of his past, how he learned Tibetan dialects and his hatred for the 'Red Chinese,' as he called them. Sayles has an almost messianic sense of purpose to drive them out of Tibet. Off and on, since the 1970s, he's set himself up in Western Tibet, operating along the borders of Ladakh, Afghanistan, moving back and forth across frontiers. Much of the region is disputed territory and he takes advantage of international ambiguities."

Afridi paused again, as if trying to decide how much he needed to reveal.

"After Rataban, I never saw him again, but I've learned a great deal more about Hayden Sayles since then, enough to know he's a dangerous man, capable of anything."

Thirty-Two

It was impossible to tell how old the photographs might be, but most of them looked as if they had been taken half a century ago. Many of the pictures were black-and-white snapshots of Mussoorie, scenic panoramas of the mountains and photos of young boys climbing trees and swimming in a stream, the kind of images that suggest an innocent childhood spent outdoors. There were school pictures too, groups of students lined up with their teacher, mostly scrubbed white faces, a few Indians in their midst. Names were penciled on the back, and Karan found Fallows in the front row of two photographs, a thin, gawky boy with glasses and hair cut so close to his scalp he looked almost bald. Though the resolution was poor, most of the pictures were clear enough to study the faces. Karan had laid these out on the bed in his room, to try and piece together some sort of sequence or chronology.

One set of pictures was of Tibetan children, from the age of five or six to eighteen, standing together as a choir and singing. In front of them was a white woman in a plaid dress with her hands raised to direct them, though it seemed as if she was trying to catch something flying about in the air, a moth or a bird. Other photographs showed the Tibetan boys wearing scouting uniforms, khaki shirts and shorts, scarves around their necks, standing at attention. With them were a couple of white boys, one of whom Karan recognized as Fallows, holding himself erect, shoulders squared, hands pressed to his sides. In a second picture, the boys were saluting, two fingers raised and held to their foreheads. There was an older, Caucasian boy in several pictures, his hair standing up in a cowlick and with freckles on his face.

One of the files contained a yearbook from the mission school in Mussoorie, a thin hardcover volume with a motif of pine cones on the front and the year 1960 written in roman numerals. As Karan flipped through the glossy pages, he recognized shots of Landour, snow peaks seen from the Chukkar, the clock tower in the bazaar. He turned to the senior class pages with individual photographs of bright-eyed young women with their hair bobbed and curled, chaste smiles on their lips. All of them seemed to be wearing the same cashmere sweater and an identical string of pearls around their throats. The boys, too, had a look of innocent maturity. Most of them had shrugged off their adolescence and seemed eager for adulthood, though the camera caught hints of fear and uncertainty in their expressions. Karan thought it could have been any high school in small-town America, except for three Indian students and a couple of Tibetans whose photographs seemed out of place, though they stared back at the camera with youthful nonchalance.

Each of the seniors had their name and a motto or saying beneath their picture. Most of these were Bible verses. There was also a list of activities and accomplishments, as well as a phrase that began "Most likely to . . . ," and Class Wills, leaving something behind for their juniors at school.

As he turned to the end of the senior pages, Karan recognized a face. It was the same boy from the scouting photographs, but six or seven years older. He was wearing a sports coat and tie and looked uncomfortable inside the stiff, buttoned-down collars, his head turned to one side. The freckles were still visible, blurring into acne on his clean-shaven cheeks. His hair was combed flat, except for the cowlick that defied even the most generous application of Brylcream. Of all the seniors in the yearbook, he had a maturity that made him look a year or two older than his peers, an intensity in his eyes that set him apart.

Karan held the yearbook open to this page and turned it toward the light, examining the face and the text beneath.

Hayden Sayles

"Something hidden. Go and find it. Go and look behind the Ranges—Something lost behind the Ranges. Lost and waiting for you. Go!" Rudyard Kipling

Basketball 9–12, Soccer 10–12, Swimming 10–12, Track & Field 9–12 (School Record in the Mile: 4:32), Cross-Country (School Record 16:24) Student Government 10–11, Boy Scout 8–10, Eagle Scout 11–12.

Most likely to become the first man on the moon!

Class Will: I solemnly leave my Bowie knife to Dexter Fallows.

Underneath, in a casual scrawl, was a handwritten message in blue ink: "Hey Dexie, don't forget the swell times we had and never give up the good fight. Yr pal, Hayden"

Karan flipped back to the earlier classes and found Dexter Fallows as a sophomore. His hair had grown out a little, but he still looked like the awkward kid in the front row, a dazed expression behind the blurred lenses of his glasses.

In one of the other files was an official military portrait of Hayden Sayles as a young soldier wearing the red beret and insignia of an Army Ranger. He looked as if he'd just been recruited, not yet twenty, but with a humorless arrogance in the way he stared at the camera, a cocky, unflinching stare. This was the last printed photograph in the file, though there was a slim yellow box of Kodachrome slides wrapped shut with a rubber band. Karan opened it and held each slide up to the light, squinting at the tiny, colored squares.

The first few shots were of landscapes in Tibet, broad vistas of grassy steppes with snow peaks in the distance. Yaks grazing by a stream, on the other side of which were nomad's yurts, domed tents of gray and black felt. In a couple of the slides, Karan could make out a group of men standing together in front of their horses. It was impossible to see their faces clearly, but one of them looked like Sayles. His beard was badly trimmed, a ragged tuft on his chin with thinner patches on his cheeks. His head was covered in a woolen cap. The rest of his clothes were Tibetan, a sheepskin coat draped over one shoulder and coarse woolen robes beneath, with a bandolier around his waist. His right hand emerged from the loose sleeve, holding a rifle with a telescopic sight. Only part of the rifle was visible, but it looked like an old M21, from the sixties.

In another slide, the same man was seated on a rock. In front of him was an antelope he had killed, the horns sticking up like crooked tines on a fork. In the background was a tent pitched on the shoulder of a low hill, clouds in the sky. The rest of the slides were pictures of a monastery with a flagpole, fluttering with colored pennants.

The file contained several notes and clippings, including a report from the World Wildlife Fund about the conservation of Tibetan antelopes. One section of the text, which reported international gangs of poachers operating in Western Tibet and Kyrgistan, had been highlighted with a yellow marker. It spoke of the international trade in animal parts—*shahtoosh* wool and the scent glands from musk deer, as well as leopard and tiger bones. There was also a short note written in cursive script, with what looked like a bank account number and a cryptic line of letters and symbols. The only words that Karan could decipher were Hotel Greenways, Peshawar. Monday 18 Sept. Arr. 4:00 pm.

Studying the photographs again, Karan could not recognize any of the faces from the images he'd been given by Bogart. He went back to his desk and plugged the flash drive into his computer. A warning came up detecting viruses, and he filtered these out before opening the first of two files. It seemed to be an audio recording. Seconds later, Karan heard a voice coming out of the speakers.

"Fallows, you fucking asshole . . . You betrayed me. You and all those company bastards. I should have known I couldn't trust you.

You betrayed the cause of freedom! I'm warning you, Fallows. You're going to pay for this. I know where you are. . . . I know exactly where to find you."

The message continued, but Karan paused the recording, holding up the slide of Sayles with the dead antelope. He was sure it had to be this man's voice on the flash drive. Something about the menacing tone, the words spat out like mucous from this throat, made him certain this was the sniper who had killed Dexter Fallows, even if they had been childhood friends. Those eyes stared at Karan from the color transparency, gray and heartless as lead.

Thirty-Three

After sharpening his knife on a whetstone that had been worn down with daily use, the butcher cut a foreleg off the carcass hanging in the front window of his shop. The blade sliced through the flesh with surgical efficiency, neatly separating the shoulder at the joint.

"You're sure it's fresh?" Jigme asked.

"Killed this morning," said the butcher. "*Subhey kaata.*"

"And it's definitely goat, not sheep?"

The butcher showed him the hoof at the end of the leg.

"Would I lie to you?" he said, defensively.

"Make it half a kilo of *keema,* properly minced. I can't chew these days. My teeth are coming loose."

The butcher, who was the same age as Jigme, with a white beard that fell over his chest, laughed at the remark. They had known each other for years and repeated this conversation every time Jigme came to the shop.

Renzin stood outside, watching his father examining the carcass. Jigme had insisted that his son bring him here to buy meat at the butcher shop near the mosque. Renzin had tried to persuade him to buy it later, but the old man said he wanted fresh mutton for dinner tonight. He would cook it himself.

Two freshly slaughtered goats hung from their hooves in the window of Rashid Ahmed's shop, their skin and heads removed. The sign

179

above the shop was written in English, Hindi, and Urdu, proclaiming HALAL MUTTON, CHICKEN AND FISH, with a picture of each.

"Do you have brain?" Jigme asked.

The butcher nodded, as he fed chunks of meat into a grinder, then poked two bare wires into a socket in the wall. The grinder roared as it chewed up the meat, spilling mangled flesh out of the perforated extruder. Gathering it up with his hands, the butcher ran it through the grinder one more time, then filled it into a plastic bag that he put on the weighing scale.

"Six hundred grams," he said.

"And one brain," Jigme said. "At least I won't have to chew on that."

Setting the goat's head on a chopping block, the butcher picked up a cleaver that lay near his feet. Renzin could see the dead animal's clouded eyes and a trickle of blood oozing from its nostrils. A few hours ago, this goat would have been tethered behind the shop, eating its last meal of straw. The cleaver came down sharply between the horns and split the skull in half. The butcher cracked it open with both hands and scooped out the soft, gray mass, as easily as removing a walnut from its shell. Slipping it into a second plastic bag, he weighed the brain quickly—150 grams—then bundled the meat together into a neat package. Jigme paid the butcher and carried the plastic bag in one hand, his other holding the cane. Renzin's motorcycle was parked at the top of an uneven staircase, which they climbed, slowly, painfully. By the time they reached the top, Jigme was breathing hard, and they rested for a moment before heading off on the bike.

⌁

The ATV started with the press of a button, its engine humming, a throaty chuckle of pistons and valves. Two of these vehicles were parked at Rokeby Manor for guests to explore off-road in the nearby hills. Karan had ridden the ATV around the Chukkar and out along the ridges, to the east, over unpaved forest tracks. Today, he had planned to walk into town but at the last minute decided to take the ATV instead. Some of the pictures in the files were of a shop in the bazaar, Potala Antiques. Karan had passed it once and remembered seeing the sign, but now he wanted to go inside and learn what connection there might be with Fallows and this man named Sayles.

As Karan swung the ATV around the corners on the road, letting the engine brake on the steep incline, he wondered how much longer he was going to be stuck up here. There had been no communication from Bogart, no instructions or information. Karan had taken the initiative to search Fallows's house and was glad to have more leads, though none of it added up to anything that made sense. More than once, he had wondered if he was wasting his time. "Think of it as a paid vacation," Bogart had told him. Having been in Mussoorie for more than a week, Karan was restless and ready to leave. There was only so much he could do to distract himself, and he kept thinking of all the work he'd left behind. Cut off completely, he couldn't even log onto the servers back in Cambridge to see how the face recognition project was moving ahead. He had thought of phoning Ivana but remembered Bogart's warning and knew they would track the call back here.

After a half mile, he came to a crossing at the top of Mullingar Hill. Instead of turning left to follow the road back into the mountains, he turned right toward the bazaar. The steep descent forced him to use the hand brake on the ATV. He blew the horn on the corners, but it was still early in the morning and the traffic jams had not begun. Karan eased the ATV through a crowd of schoolchildren, all of them in uniform, with book bags on their backs. Shops were just beginning to open as he made his way around the tight corners. Mussoorie had only one main street, which ran from east to west. In Landour bazaar it was barely wide enough for two cars to pass. Farther on, the Mall Road opened up, though it was always crowded with pedestrians and cars parked along the sides. As he drove slowly past sweet shops and provision stores, Karan could smell the morning fragrances of charcoal smoke, soap scum, and sewage.

It didn't take him long to reach the toll barrier where he paid a hundred rupees to an old man who ignored his request for a receipt. The Picture Palace cinema stood here, its entrance locked, the dilapidated facade boarded shut. On ahead, past a police station, he drove up Kulri Hill, a steep climb but without the tight corners that made Mullingar so treacherous. He passed the State Bank of India and the main post office, then took the upper fork in the road. Just ahead, he could see the cable car, which carried tourists up to Gun Hill. In the guidebooks, he'd read that there used to be a noon gun, fired every day, a single, booming expletive of time. The noon cannon was discontinued in the 1930s, when the clock tower was built, but the high summit with its limestone crags overlooking the town was still known as Gun Hill.

Karan slowed down as he spotted the sign for Potala Antiques. The grilled shutters were locked, though the shops on either side were open. In a park, on ahead, music was playing, a Bollywood soundtrack with a disco beat. Children were lining up to get on a Ferris wheel, and vendors were erecting their stalls along the side of the road, one man selling roasted peanuts, another cotton candy that was a poisonous pink. *Chaat wallahs* were setting up stands and lighting kerosene stoves. Several fruit sellers had constructed pyramids of apples, guavas, pomegranates, and oranges. A sweeper with a wicker basket on his back was clearing litter from the day before. The cable car descended into an open shed. Tourists were queued up at the ticket window.

Pulling over to the side of the road, where several motorcycles were parked, Karan turned off the engine on the ATV. He checked his watch. 10:15 a.m. The carnival atmosphere on the Mall Road was just beginning. A line of rickshaw pullers were waiting for passengers. Saddle ponies were nibbling at marigolds in beds along the fence of the park. As Karan got off the ATV, he looked around, watching the passersby, then leaned against the concrete railing to wait for Potala Antiques to open.

Weaving through the promenading crowds on the Mall Road, Renzin blew the horn on his bike impatiently. He and Noya hadn't spoken since their argument in the restaurant, but he planned to go and see her later in the morning. As they approached the shop, Jigme looked up at the cable car descending from Gun Hill. Several children had their faces pressed to the windows and waved at the crowds below.

"Stop here," said Jigme.

"What is it now?" Renzin asked him, annoyed.

"I want some fruit." Jigme said, gesturing toward one of the vendors at the side of the road.

"I'll get it for you later," Renzin said. "Just tell me what you want."

"No," his father insisted. "I'll choose the fruit myself."

As they pulled over, Jigme dismounted slowly and handed Renzin the meat. He then walked slowly across to the nearest vendor, his cart piled high with apples, guavas, and papaya.

Karan had been waiting for a quarter of an hour, and he was about to give up as he watched the cable car descending with another load of tourists. Among the motorcycles parked beside him was an old Royal Enfield Bullet 350 cc. It was battered and leaking oil, a rough-looking bike painted dark green, beneath a coating of mud and grime. The music was playing loudly in the park, an old Mohamed Rafi tune, badly remixed. The cotton candy vendor was doing good business, spinning out pink candy floss. Tourists were riding ponies and rickshaws along the Mall Road.

Suddenly, Karan heard a snapping sound, like the crack of a whip but much louder. Despite all of the noises on the street, he immediately recognized the sharp report of a rifle. At the same moment, he saw an elderly man, next to the fruit vendors, fall forward, scattering a carefully arranged display. This happened all at once, and Karan took a moment to connect the sound of the rifle to the man lying face down on the side of the road amid scattered oranges and guavas, a hundred feet away. Someone screamed, and Karan could see people running forward. Immediately, he headed toward the fallen man. The music continued playing while one of the ponies panicked, galloping off down the road, nearly trampling tourists in its path.

A young Tibetan man in a leather jacket was kneeling beside the body. Karan could tell the victim was dead, blood streaming onto the pavement. The young man lifted the body slowly and rolled him over, so that Karan could see the exit wound on the old man's forehead. The upper half of his face was blown away. One of the papayas had split open and was lying in a pool of blood, next to a couple of guavas and apples, a macabre still life. By now a crowd was gathering, people running past Karan, brushing against his shoulders, craning their necks to see what had happened.

As Renzin glanced up, he met Karan's stare with a look of panic and horror. Their eyes locked for an instant, both of them realizing what had occurred. Moments later, Karan heard another sound he recognized, a motorbike being started somewhere behind him, the thumping beat of a Royal Enfield Bullet. Turning, he saw a figure in black leather, wearing a helmet with a tinted visor and carrying something that looked like a rifle slung across his back. Instinctively, Karan began to run back toward the ATV. Before he reached the vehicle, he saw the rider drive off, almost colliding with a man pushing a baby carriage.

As Karan threw himself onto the ATV and fumbled with the key, he glanced behind him and saw Renzin running toward his motorcycle. They didn't know each other and hadn't spoken, but a silent, unconscious signal had passed between them when their eyes connected. Within seconds they were chasing the Royal Enfield down the Mall Road. Karan gunned the ATV's engine, trying desperately to keep the rider in sight as they raced around the corners. Though the street was relatively broad, it was full of obstructions. A man carrying a bundle of newspapers was nearly hit, tossing the *Times of India* in all directions. Behind him, Karan could hear the other motorcycle accelerating and catching up.

Realizing that the shooter was escaping, Renzin had left his father's lifeless body by the side of the road. At this moment, he felt nothing at all, only a desperate impulse to try and catch the rider on the Bullet. He had seen the other man giving chase and knew the helmeted driver must be Jigme's killer. It had taken him no more than a couple of seconds to understand what he must do. Instead of braking on Kulri Hill, he twisted the throttle and raced ahead of the ATV. A car was coming up the slope and Renzin swerved around it, gaining on the Bullet. The shops and signs on either side were a passing blur, cries of panic and alarm.

At Picture Palace, the toll barrier was just coming down as the rider on the Royal Enfield raced under it and ploughed through a crowd of men, knocking two of them to the ground. A policeman blew a whistle, but the shrill sound had no effect. Renzin pulled up short in front of the toll barrier and shouted at the attendant to let him through, waving an arm to emphasize it was an emergency. At the same moment, Karan roared past on the ATV and smashed the barrier without stopping, skidding as he made the turn, and heading up the hill toward the clock tower. Renzin popped his clutch and followed. For almost a minute the Enfield was out of sight, but as they came to an open stretch of the Mall Road, they caught sight of the rider several bends ahead, crouched over the handlebars.

As soon as they entered Landour Bazaar, Karan could see the Enfield had been forced to stop. Two vehicles were squeezing past each other, a car and a scooter going in opposite directions. Once the road was open, the motorcycle shot through the gap, sending a pair of schoolboys leaping into a nearby shop. The delay had given Karan and Renzin a chance to catch up. Renzin kept his thumb pressed to the horn, adding a shrieking wail to the gnashing growl of engines. The three vehicles were now within forty meters of each other, moving as fast as they could. A porter carrying a gunnysack of vegetables was knocked aside. Even the rhesus monkeys watching from the rooftops darted for cover. Karan felt a jolt as he ran over something. For a moment, he thought he'd hit a pedestrian, but looking back over his shoulder, he saw it was the sack of vegetables dropped in the middle of the road.

Outside a hardware store, a group of men had gathered around a carom board. The black-and-white disks were clustered in the middle, and the shooter was fired with a flick of a finger, shattering the neat arrangement and sending caroms in all directions. A second player picked up the shooter and took aim, leaning to one side as he calculated the angle of his shot, but before he could fire there was an ear-splitting roar as the lead driver came bulldozing around the corner. The players jumped for cover, and the board tipped over, scattering caroms across the street.

Renzin had driven this road a thousand times. He knew every bottleneck and corner. So far, there had been no traffic coming from the opposite direction. He saw the Bullet skid as the helmeted driver swerved to avoid a parked jeep. For a moment it looked as if the shooter was going down, but then the Enfield righted itself and regained traction. Another hundred yards, and they would be next to the Gurdwara at the foot of Mullingar Hill. For the first time in his life, Renzin was glad to see a traffic jam ahead. A long line of cars and jeeps were stalled on the steep slope. Farther on, a taxi had broken down, and the driver was standing with the hood raised, steam gushing out of the radiator.

The helmeted rider seemed to hesitate for a moment, seeing the blockage ahead. Karan also eased back on the throttle, preparing to stop. But just as he did, he saw the Enfield accelerate again and go around the last car in the line, then weave past a minivan and the vehicle ahead. There was just enough room to squeeze by and then take the first sharp turn, past a tailor's shop. Renzin followed and Karan held his breath, not sure that his ATV would make it through. But he was able to drive over the front steps of a dry goods store, toppling sacks of rice and lentils as well as a bag full of red chilies that were crushed under his tires. On ahead, he saw the Bullet disappear up a narrow lane that turned off the main road.

Still blowing his horn, Renzin threaded his way through the gaps between the cars and shot up the alley, his motorcycle lurching wildly as it bumped up a flight of steps before emerging into an open courtyard. Two women were hanging laundry on a line, and they flattened themselves against the walls as the motorcycles burst through.

The Enfield crossed to the other side and crashed into a doorway that opened onto the glassed-in porch of a hotel. At the other end, the Enfield smashed into a second door and careened down a series of steps and a narrow gulley that descended back down to the main road, above the point where the taxi had broken down. The shooter's bike jumped an open drain and just missed the bumper of a car before spinning around and heading up the steep incline. Renzin followed, scraping his leg guards against the walls, as Karan came to a sudden halt, the gulley too narrow for his ATV.

Jumping off, he followed on foot, just in time to see the two motorcycles, only a few feet away from each other, maneuvering past a heavily loaded truck. Seconds later, a tractor appeared around the corner, its brakes squealing as it negotiated the turn. It was pulling a trailer loaded with a large tank of water. Once again, the Enfield accelerated just in time to squeeze through the gap between the railing and the trailer. By the time Renzin tried to follow, however, there wasn't enough space as the trailer jackknifed behind the tractor, its water tank wedged against an electric pole. Renzin was only able to watch as the helmeted driver raced away toward the top of Mullingar Hill and disappeared. A few seconds later, Karan caught up with him, out of breath. He shouted at the tractor driver to reverse, but he already knew it was too late. By now, the Enfield was out of sight, escaping eastward along the Tehri Road and back into the hills.

Thirty-Four

Coils of smoke unraveled out of the valley, loose gray strands spiraling into the cloudless sky. Flames rose to the height of a man, pale and liquid in the mid-morning sunlight. The stacked pile of logs was burning by the side of a stream, which tumbled over polished stones and boulders. The crackle of the burning pyre mingled with the gurgle of the water, a sad, incoherent harmony of elements that consumed Jigme's mortal remains.

Renzin stood apart from the others near a shallow pool of clear water that drained through a funnel in the rocks. He wished the flames would burn more quickly, even as he mourned his father and hated to let him go. The heat from the pyre warped the air like a mirage so that the cluster of men who were seated on the rocks across from him had blurred into an anonymous crowd of strangers. Renzin knew them all, old friends and acquaintances of his father who had embraced him and offered condolences, but at this moment he wanted only to be alone. Two Buddhist monks were chanting prayers and burning incense, seated cross-legged on a patch of sand. Their mumbled incantations meant nothing to Renzin, and he resisted an urge to walk away and turn his back on the cremation.

In his mind, he kept replaying the moment when his father died. Renzin had been watching Jigme as he haggled with the fruit seller, leaning forward to inspect the apples, holding one in his hand, its color red and green. Then, all at once, he fell forward, as if he'd lost his balance, dropping his cane and colliding with the vendor's cart, scattering the fruit. Renzin hadn't heard the rifle shot. He had only seen his father drop to the ground.

By the time he got to Jigme's side, his father was already dead, the bullet having passed through his skull. When Renzin turned him over, he could hardly recognize the shattered features. Jigme's blood had soaked his sleeve and jeans. In his horror, he released his grip on his father's shoulders, letting him fall back onto the ground, the old man's head lolling to one side. In his right hand, Jigme still held an apple, his fingers clenched in death, as if the nerves had contracted from the sudden impact of the bullet. Even at that moment, Renzin could not comprehend what was happening. It was only when he heard the motorcycle starting and saw the stranger, their eyes meeting for an instant, that he had realized his father had been shot.

As the breeze changed direction, smoke blew low across the water, flowing in the same direction, like a shadow of the stream, carrying with it the odor of charred flesh and bones. The stranger, who had chased the shooter with Renzin, was now standing at the edge of a group of mourners. For a moment, their eyes locked again. Renzin didn't even know his name. They had spoken briefly after the motorcycle escaped on Mullingar Hill. Seeing the blood on Renzin's arm, the man had asked if he was hurt. Renzin had shaken his head and rushed back immediately, driving through the town again until he reached the cable car shed, where hundreds of people had gathered. The police had arrived, and he had gone with them to the hospital, where his father's body was carried into the morgue. The police asked him to identify Jigme and Renzin had nodded, though he could barely recognize his father's mutilated face.

Across the stream, where a path came down from the motor road, Renzin could see Colonel Afridi in his wheelchair. Two uniformed soldiers stood on either side of him, and there was a woman whom Renzin didn't know. He looked away as the logs in the pyre collapsed, sending up a shower of sparks.

Half an hour later, Afridi and Anna sat in the backseat of the jeep. The two guards had carried his wheelchair up to the motor road from the stream. The path was narrow and uneven. Anna had resisted an urge to try and help. As Afridi was hoisted through the door of the vehicle, his useless legs hanging beneath him, Anna tried not to look, seeing him helpless and injured for the first time. The indignity of being assisted like this, lifted and settled in his seat, could only frustrate a man who was used to being in control of himself and others. She waited until the guards closed his door before climbing into the jeep beside Afridi. He was staring straight ahead, one hand gripping the seat in front of him. For the cremation, he had put on his uniform with a regimental cravat, as well as his military ribbons and medals. Before the pyre was lit, he had raised his hand in a final salute.

As the guard who was driving turned the jeep around, they took one last look at the burning pyre. Afridi's eyes were focused on the dwindling flames in the valley below.

"Who was he?" Anna asked.

Afridi waited a few moments before he answered.

"A warrior and a mountaineer. We climbed half a dozen peaks together."

"Sherpa?" she asked.

"No. Khampa," said Afridi, as the jeep drove off. "A Tibetan resistance fighter. He served with me as part of the Special Frontier Force. Jigme blew up Chinese convoys single-handed. He was fearless, but bitter in the end."

"Why?"

"He trusted us and we betrayed him."

"But it was a losing battle," Anna said. "The Tibetans were outnumbered a thousand to one. They could never have defeated the Chinese."

"When you're fighting for your homeland you never stop to do the math," Afridi answered, staring out the window of the moving jeep at the forests of pine trees covering the slope of the ridge.

"Why would Sayles have killed him?" Anna asked.

"Jigme had promised to recruit men for Sayles, to help him fight the Communists in Western Tibet. For a while, they worked together, but when he saw what Sayles was actually doing, functioning more like a feudal warlord than a liberator, he stopped supporting him. Sayles accused him of being a traitor and a coward. He even tried to kill him once before, blaming Jigme when some of his fighters abandoned him."

Anna waited for him to continue, but Afridi had fallen silent, his eyes focused on the winding road ahead.

"What really happened on Rataban?" she asked.

Afridi made an ambiguous gesture with one hand, suggesting resignation.

"I learned the meaning of survival."

Thirty-Five

His voice changed as he told the story. Anna could hear an echo of anguish in Afridi's words. He explained again about the early warning device, the failed mission to Nanda Devi, and the decision to work with the Americans, to place a plutonium-powered sensor on the summit of Rataban. All of this he recounted quickly, his memory methodical and precise, recalling dates and names. However, once he began describing how they reached the summit of Rataban and their descent, Afridi's tone grew less decisive, almost hesitant. He spoke slowly, as the jeep circled up the switchbacks on the road, an hour's drive to Landour. Anna could tell that he had never talked of this before.

"By the time we had attached the wires and secured the device, the wind was blowing hard and we had a thousand meters to descend to our summit camp. My fingers were already numb from having taken off my gloves to assemble the sensor. A simple task at sea level becomes a terrible challenge above six thousand meters. Sayles and Tanner worked with me, and by the time we had finished, the clouds were spilling in around us. The only summits we could see were Ghori and Hathi Parbat to the southeast of us, and Mana and Kamet to the northwest. I remember, just before we headed down, Sayles pointed beyond those peaks and gestured to Tanner. I couldn't hear what he said, but I imagine he was telling him that on the other side of those ridges lay Tibet.

"I was leading as we descended, followed by the Americans. We were roped together, moving much more slowly than I would have liked, for I knew the worst was still to come and we needed to get off the mountain as quickly as possible.

"Most of it was a steady slog down the shoulder of a ridge, the snow coming up to our thighs at places. I tried to follow the steps we'd made on our ascent, but the wind had drifted loose snow over the route and most of it had been erased. There were cornices along the ridge and I kept clear of them as much as possible. The snow was brittle and sugary, with a crust of ice that broke beneath our boots. After half an hour, fresh flakes began to settle on us as the clouds closed in. Instead of falling snow, it was more as if the crystals of ice were forming in the air around us, clouds condensing into a blizzard that grew thicker and heavier the lower we went. At one point, I wondered if the air itself would harden into a solid mass, encasing us in freezing vapor. Altitude plays tricks with your mind, and I began to feel a sense of claustrophobia, as if we'd suffocate in the storm.

"The sluggish pull of the rope at my waist reminded me that the Americans were struggling behind. We reached a difficult section, where a chimney between two cliffs led down onto an icefall, which we had to traverse, moving laterally across the rim of another cliff that dropped five hundred meters below us. Of course, I could see only a foot or two ahead of me, but I had memorized this section on our ascent, knowing that we would have to negotiate the ice on our return.

"I was exhausted and thought of asking Sayles to take the lead, but both he and Tanner seemed to be having trouble keeping up and I was worried that we would get stalled on the mountain. There should have been another three hours of daylight left, but inside the freezing clouds it was already growing dark, like a dense white shadow. I know that doesn't make sense—but it's the only way I can describe it, like being trapped inside the negative of a photograph, where black is white and white is black. My feet were already beginning to freeze, and they felt like stumps of wood, as if the bones in my legs had turned to stone."

Anna could see the pain in Afridi's eyes as he spoke.

"We made it down the chimney, somehow, though Tanner lost his ice axe in the process. It came crashing past me and went over the edge, a momentary flash of steel, spinning into the thick emptiness below. I remember thinking, if I fall, he's not going to be able to hold me anymore. Our reflexes were too slow by this time to respond in an emergency. If I took a wrong step, all of us would be gone.

"Because we'd carried the device with us, we hadn't brought anything for a bivouac, no tent or sleeping bags. Otherwise, we might have dug in and waited for the storm to pass, but I knew that we would freeze to death before we excavated a cave in the snow. The only hope we had was getting down to our tents, where Jigme was waiting. He had wanted to come with us, but Sayles insisted he stay behind. It was a strange decision and I regretted it, for I could have used a strong second climber as we began the traverse. We had cut steps on our way up and I had thought of fixing a rope, but in our haste to reach the top, we hadn't taken the obvious precautions. Now we had to cross about forty feet of ice at an angle of eighty degrees, the kind of slope that's treacherous even when it's clear. From where we crossed, the angle grew steeper, until the mountain dropped away to a hanging glacier. But all of that was hidden now, and I could see nothing but the swirling core of the storm, so close to my face I felt as if I was trapped in a whirling cyclone of ice. The only consolation was that beyond this point the route was simple, a relatively easy descent to our camp, which was about five hundred meters below. That was when I felt the rope tighten.

"I was already most of the way across. Instinctively, I dug my axe into the snow as an anchor and braced for the plunge but nothing happened. A few seconds later the rope went slack. I pulled it toward me and the loose end snaked down the slope until I retrieved the last few feet and saw that it was cut, a frayed limp end, caked with ice. In my confusion, I thought Sayles had fallen and the rope had snapped, but it made no sense at all.

"A minute later, a figure came through the blinding snow, close behind me. It was Sayles, though I could barely recognize him. I waved my arm, relieved but baffled by what was taking place. Lifting my axe out of the snow, I tried to move aside to let him pass, thinking he was going to take the lead. Within the howling wind, we couldn't hear each other speak, even though we were inches apart. As I turned, I felt the first blow against my shoulders and I stumbled, struggling to keep my balance. He hit me once again, this time across my lower back, which knocked me forward down the slope. I lost hold of my axe but it wouldn't have saved me, for I was already tumbling down the mountain. My last thought was that Sayles had planned this all along, though I had no chance of speculating on his reasons. After that, my mind went blank."

As Afridi fell silent, Anna could imagine the sudden terror of that moment, his climbing companions turning against him, the severed rope on which their lives had depended, and the white turbulence of the storm. She wanted him to continue the story and tell her how he had survived, but instead Afridi began to talk of Sayles. The bitterness was evident in his voice, but he spoke with analytical detachment that made it seem even worse, because the tragedy had been premeditated, part of a larger, grotesque plan.

"Hayden Sayles was the coldest man I've ever met," Afridi said. "We spent three weeks together on Rataban, but he remained a stranger to the end."

The driver of the jeep blew his horn as they approached a blind corner on the road, and Afridi paused until they had taken the turn.

"Sayles had this apocalyptic vision. He was going to use the Tibetans to destroy Communism. They were going to attack the missile base at Lop Nor, capture it, and hold the Chinese hostage with their own nuclear weapons. It was madness, but he insisted it was possible, ranting on about democracy, as if he were the chosen prophet of freedom. He tried to convince me several times, while we were acclimatizing in the Bhyunder valley and working our way up the mountain. At first I thought he was joking. When I realized he was serious, I tried to reason with him, but he refused to understand the absurdity of his ambitions. After that, he treated me with disdain and distrust. Sayles was convinced that he could change the course of history, and if I didn't believe him, I became his enemy. When he talked like this, he became irrational, a depraved zealot obsessed with his own convictions. As far as he was concerned, it was pure and simple American logic: 'If you aren't with us, you're against us.' He called me a coward when I told him he was insane."

Anna could see Afridi's finger tracing an invisible figure eight on the armrest of the jeep, as if he were tying a knot in his mind. She glanced at the rows of ribbons and medals on his chest, emblems of courage that represented far more than the cloth and metal out of which they were made.

"After Sayles pushed me off the mountain, he and Tanner returned to our summit camp. They told Jigme that I had fallen, an accident in the storm. The next morning, after the weather cleared, they announced their plans had changed. Instead of going back down to Base Camp, they would cross the col and head toward Tibet. They insisted that Jigme go with them. When he protested, Sayles threatened him and told him that this was an order, his only chance to fight for his homeland. On their way up, they had left a cache of supplies, including their rifles, on the col at a place where they could cut across to the north face of Rataban and descend along a series of ridges to the east of the Niti Pass.

"Jigme never forgave himself for leaving me, but he believed that I was dead. In his desperation he decided to follow the Americans into Tibet. He should have known that they were lying, but he went along with their deceit, abandoning camp and making it appear as if we'd all been killed on the mountain."

"What about you?" Anna asked. "How did you survive?"

Afridi smiled for the first time, almost as if the question were irrelevant.

"Sometimes the greatest danger saves us in the end," he said. "Though I had imagined the precipice below me was perpendicular, it fell away less steeply than I thought, particularly at the point where Sayles attacked me. After the initial fall of fifty meters, as I was rolling through the snow, there were some rocks and then another hundred meters of steep ice that funneled into a couloir that came up from the glacier. I don't have any memory of what happened, but I must have struck those rocks, then slid from there, for when I came around, I was lying in a narrow trench, where the snow had drifted into a bank. This protected me from the wind, and as I faded in and out of consciousness, I was aware that the storm had eased. By morning, the sun was out.

"My legs were gone, partly from frostbite but also because of a spinal injury during the fall. At the time, all I knew was that I had no sensation or movement below my thighs. Slowly, I began to drag myself out into the open, so that I could see where I was. It seemed hopeless, but then I realized that I was on the main glacier, below our summit camp. If I could cross the upper edge of the glacier, I could reach the moraine on the other side and get off the mountain. My mind was playing games with me, but I understood what I needed to do. Of course, I was afraid of what I would find if I survived. Sayles had tried to kill me once, and he would probably finish me off, unless I got there before him and alerted the others. I shouted for Jigme, but nobody answered. Using both arms, I hauled myself forward, a few inches at a time. Fortunately, most of it was a gradual, downhill slope, so that I could slide and crawl, dragging my injured body like a sled. At several points, I lost consciousness, but each time I came around and told myself to keep on going.

"It took most of the day and the rest of the next night to get off the glacier. Only then did I realize that I was on the opposite side of the river from our base camp. When I reached the rocks and moraine, it was much more difficult for me to pull myself forward, as I had done on the ice. Unable to use my legs, I could barely move a few feet in the space of an hour. I felt as if I had escaped from the peak only to die in the valley. By then, I was delirious, exhausted, and dehydrated. My face was badly burned and my mouth was so dry, I could barely shout. My hands were numb with frostbite. But something in the larger scheme of things had determined that I should live."

He looked at Anna, then smiled again, this time without any bitterness.

"A sadhu found me. Bhyunder Baba's cave was only a hundred meters from the glacier, and he heard me crying out and spotted the bright blue color of my jacket. I don't have any memory of being carried to his cave, but I do remember the twig fire burning in his hearth and the warm, sweet liquid that he forced between my lips. After that, he alerted our men at Base Camp, across the river. They came and lifted me onto a stretcher, and radioed for a helicopter. By that evening, I was in a military hospital in Bareilly. If it weren't for Bhyunder Baba, I would be dead. I survived, but my legs were gone."

The jeep was now climbing the road to the top of Landour hill. After an awkward silence, Anna asked, "And the Americans?"

"They crossed an unguarded pass into Tibet. Tanner died on the way, but Sayles survived. At the border they met up with a group of resistance fighters, hunters, and bandits, whom the Americans had armed and funded. These men accompanied Sayles across Western Tibet, toward Taklamakan and Lop Nor, though I have no idea if he ever reached his objective or finally understood the madness of his plan. Jigme remained with Sayles for almost a year but became suspicious of his motives and finally escaped, returning to India by another route, through Guge, into Lahaul Spiti. It was never clear whether the CIA had approved the mission. Later, the Americans claimed Sayles was dead and denied any knowledge of his plan to enter Tibet. They said he was a rogue agent, acting on his own. Whether that's true or not, it's impossible to say."

Thirty-Six

The face was a composite image, grabbed from several different photographs in the file that Karan had taken from Fallows's safe. These included the yearbook picture and the portrait of Hayden Sayles as an Army Ranger. The beret and uniform had been removed, as well as the backdrop of the American flag, but he still had a military bearing, the way he held his head: cocked to one side, with his chin tilted up. Karan studied the features, noticing the flat cheekbones and sharply sculpted lines of his jaw. Some women probably found him handsome, though Sayles's eyes had an unattractive intensity accentuated by the heavy eyebrows and a low forehead. His hair was combed to one side as in his senior picture, and he looked about twenty years old, full of youthful arrogance and an absolute sense of his own invincibility.

Karan had enhanced the image so that the grainy, indistinct texture of the original photographs had been replaced with high definition contrasts and details. The face remained a true likeness, but he had filled in missing elements from the original prints, using a computer program that cloned the absent features. In this case, the photographs were relatively clear, but the program could even reconstruct a face out of a blurred image in a mirror or a TV news broadcast, picking up faces in a crowd. This technology was originally developed for FBI forensics, and the CIA had adapted it to meet their surveillance needs.

Tapping the keys on his laptop, Karan created a three-dimensional version of the face so that he could rotate the image, making Sayles look right, then left, capturing the profile of his face from either side. The expression didn't change—the hard, unsmiling lips, the tightness of the muscles in his jaw, as if his teeth were clenched.

Leaning back in his chair, Karan wondered if the face recognition program would identify this man as a terrorist. Probably not. Even though there was blatant hostility in his eyes, more than likely the FRP would pass him over as an innocuous threat. Pressing two more keys, Karan clicked on a menu tab that popped up in one corner of his screen. Slowly, the face began to change, aging at the rate of one year every ten seconds. Karan watched his subject grow older, imperceptibly at first, then with a relentless inevitability. The skin began to slacken and the hair became thinner. The shadows under his eyes grew darker, though his eyebrows faded and the mouth was creased with lines on either side, like a pair of crooked parentheses, bracketing an expressionless mouth. His hair changed from brown to gray and finally to white. By now his forehead was broader and higher, etched with lines. The nose was larger too and less defined. Karan paused the program at the age of seventy.

As he saved the image onto an external hard drive, there was a knock at the door. It was still light outside, though he could see a rusty hue in the sky over the purple line of the horizon. Lowering the lid on his laptop, Karan reached into a drawer of the bedside table and took out his Glock. Holding it behind his back, he unlatched the door.

One of the bellboys was standing there.

"Sir, there's someone here to meet you, in the lobby."

"Who?" Karan asked.

"Somebody from the bazaar."

Karan looked puzzled. He nodded, then told the bellboy he'd be down in a minute. Closing the door, he pulled on a jacket and tucked his pistol into an inner pocket. When he went outside, he locked his room carefully and descended the wooden staircase to the lobby.

He recognized Renzin immediately and smiled, though the only response he got was a suspicious stare.

"Who are you?" Renzin asked in Hindi, without any greeting.

Karan put out his hand to shake.

"Karan Chauhan," he introduced himself, then added. "I'm sorry about your father."

Renzin hesitated before he clasped hands with Karan, though his voice remained guarded.

"Why are you here?"

It took Karan several minutes before he was able to convince Renzin to continue their conversation over coffee in the restaurant upstairs. After the waiter had taken their order, Karan finally answered Renzin's question, still speaking in Hindi.

"I'm here on holiday for one or two weeks."

Renzin was less belligerent but still cautious. "What do you do in America?"

"I'm a software engineer. *Market down ho gaya. Naukri chut gayi.* I lost my job, so I thought, let me go back to India. . . . Decide what I'll do next."

Interrupting him, Renzin leaned forward across the table, his hands clenched together.

"The man who shot my father. . . . Why did you follow him?"

Karan switched to English. "Instinct," he said. "Nothing more. I saw what happened and couldn't let him get away."

Renzin leaned back, and Karan could tell that he was trying to decide if he should believe him, his eyes full of doubt.

"But he got away. From both of us," Renzin's voice was edged with anger.

When the coffee arrived, they fell silent. Karan could see the grief on Renzin's face as he spooned sugar into his cup.

"Do you have any idea who it was that shot your father?" Karan asked.

"No." Renzin shook his head. "Probably, the same person who killed the American at the church last week."

"Random targets?"

"I don't think so," Renzin replied. "My father was convinced the Chinese were after him. He claimed their agents were working with Maoists in Nepal. He said they had infiltrated across the border and were targeting Tibetan refugees."

"Did you believe him?"

Renzin shrugged. "I was never sure about anything my father told me."

Letting his words hang there for a moment, Karan took a sip of coffee. He waited patiently until Renzin continued.

"My father was a guerilla fighter, part of the Chushi Gangdruk Resistance Force, who opposed the Chinese fifty years ago. He lived in the past, fighting enemies that no longer exist."

"Do you think he told you everything about his past?" Karan asked.

Renzin met his gaze with a look of suspicion. "No. Of course not."

"The man in the wheelchair, at the cremation . . . Who was he?" Karan asked.

This time, Renzin looked away. "Colonel Afridi. He and my father climbed together before he was injured."

Karan watched Renzin closely, trying to read how much he was hiding. A young man who had just lost his father, he seemed innocent enough, trying to uncover the truth behind a personal tragedy. Yet, Karan knew there was always another angle to every story, always two answers to every question.

"*Aur larki?*" Karan asked. "What about the girl?"

"Which girl?" Renzin asked.

"The one who rides around with you on the motorcycle?"

"Noya?" Renzin said, looking away self-consciously. "She's just a friend. I met her when she came to our shop. I've been showing her around . . . that's all."

Thirty-Seven

"Before the Rataban expedition, we spent three weeks in Mussoorie during the summer of 1969, preparing for our climb with technical briefings and training sessions. The Americans joined us in the second week, Hayden Sayles, Russell Tanner, and three others. There was also a man from the embassy in Delhi, a liaison officer with the CIA. In those days, the Himalayan Research Institute didn't exist, but the Ministry of Defence had an officer's training center in the same facility. The entire operation was supposed to be kept under cover, but the Americans came up from Delhi in a Buick station wagon and it got stuck on Mullingar Hill. They weren't supposed to be seen, but in the end they had to get out of the car and push. The Americans brought all kinds of food with them, steaks and hamburgers as well as whiskey and beer, even potato chips flown all the way from America. We had a barbeque almost every night. None of the other Indians in our team would eat beef, but Jigme and I didn't hold back. In those days Mussoorie was a quieter place. This road wasn't even paved."

Anna and Afridi were out on the Chukkar, walking his dog. Afridi realized that he hadn't spoken about Rataban for years, not even with Jigme. He was conscious that Anna's presence made him talkative, though he told her only what she needed to know. It was all written down, of course, in his reports, a confidential file that somebody with the appropriate security clearance could access if they really wanted, probably buried in some steel cabinet in the archives at RAW. Like so many other reports, nobody would ever read it again and the file would remain forgotten until it was eventually eaten by silverfish and worms.

"Though Sayles kept apart from us and the other Americans, refusing to join in the drinking and stories each evening, I soon discovered that he spoke Hindi fluently as well as Tibetan. He even knew the Khampa dialect and could talk with Jigme in his own language. Nevertheless, there was something about Sayles that made me distrust him . . . perhaps the fact that he didn't trust us."

Anna was leading the dog on a leash. Afridi had suggested they go for a walk, a chance to get some fresh air after they'd been working in the office all day. The old dog moved stiffly, sniffing at the parapet walls along the edge of the Chukkar, picking up scents in the dirt and dry leaves. As they walked past the sufi's tomb, the sun was beginning to go down over the valley, glowing a brilliant orange.

Anna read the name on the marble plaque. "Who was Hazrat Barkat Ali Shah?"

Afridi smiled. "Nobody knows for sure. . . . There are different stories."

A woman and two small children were praying at the tomb. A Muslim fakir was sitting outside, dressed in a green kurta, black vest, and checkered *lungi*, with a white turban and bristling beard. He had a wand of peacock feathers with which he tapped the younger child on the head. Both Hindus and Muslims, even a few Christians, prayed at this shrine—anyone who needed some form of divine intervention.

"This *mazaar* was built only twenty years ago," said Afridi. "Before that, there was just the rock and the tree . . . a natural phenomenon, no grave or shrine. According to one version of the story, somebody saw a ghost at this spot. It kept appearing night after night until people were too afraid to walk past here after dark. Finally, someone built a tomb, and the apparition was never seen again. It's the only way to get rid of ghosts. You prepare a grave for them, and they disappear, quite happy to settle down and rest in peace."

Afridi kept a straight face as Anna gave him a skeptical glance.

"Did you trek all the way from Mussoorie to Rataban?" Anna asked.

"No," said Afridi, wheeling himself forward. "Because it was a covert mission, we traveled separately by road. The Americans weren't supposed to be seen with us, and the whole expedition was top secret except at the highest levels of government. It was only afterwards, when Sayles and Tanner disappeared and I was rescued, that the newspapers carried articles about the climb, reporting the accident. But the true purpose of our expedition was never revealed."

As they passed under a tunnel of deodar branches, Anna saw several langur monkeys leaping from tree to tree. The dog reacted immediately, barking and straining at the leash. She struggled to control him until the monkeys ran off down the hill.

"Twelve years old, but still ready to pick a fight," said Afridi.

Growling, the dog wagged his curled tail as Afridi patted him on the back.

"What breed is he?" Anna asked.

"Tibetan mastiff."

The dog settled back down to a slow, arthritic pace, the three of them moving along the north side of the Chukkar. They had passed a couple of other people, but the road felt deserted. Clouds were covering most of the snow peaks, though several of the summits were visible, tinted with an evening glow.

"Is someone else going to get killed?" Anna asked.

Afridi glanced up at her with a fatalistic gesture of one hand. "More than likely."

"This man, Hayden Sayles. He must be ancient," Anna said. "Even if he is alive, he'd be a toothless old man."

Afridi smiled without humor this time. "He'd be seventy-two. Three years older than me."

Anna caught herself. "Sorry."

"No offense taken," Afridi replied. "Sayles has survived this long in some of the most hostile conditions you can imagine. He may not be as strong or agile as he was when we climbed Rataban together, but you can be sure he's still capable of enduring almost anything for his cause."

"But what about the Chinese?" Anna argued. "The ITBP guards who were killed above Milam . . . the Type 88 rifle . . . It all points to a Snow Leopard Commando. There's even the jacket we found."

Afridi shook his head. "I've never accepted that theory, though it was the obvious answer . . . too obvious. Somebody wanted us to think it was the Chinese . . . an inscrutable killer. Our enemies to the north."

"So, you're saying that Sayles came all the way from Tibet disguised as a Chinese agent?" Anna asked, still not convinced.

"He moves across the border often enough, smuggling shatoosh into Kashmir and Pakistan. I'm sure he has access to Chinese weapons and he planted the jacket, knowing it would be found."

"I don't believe it," said Anna. "All of this, just to kill two men he hasn't seen in forty years . . . And why would he try to blame it on the Chinese?"

"Sayles feels that both of them betrayed him. . . . He had threatened them, all sorts of accusations and recrimination, for promises he imagined they hadn't fulfilled. After Rataban, Fallows was one of the few people Sayles kept in touch with on a regular basis over the years, but eventually they had a falling out. Fallows was supposed to supply him with arms and explosives through the CIA, but when Langley refused, he sent him a shipment of Bibles instead. Around the same time, Sayles contacted Jigme, asking him to recruit fighters who would help him carve out his own frontier fiefdom in the disputed regions of Shangshung. We encouraged Jigme to talk with him, but in the end, of course, he didn't deliver the men that Sayles expected." Afridi paused to look at Anna. "Both men died because they . . . *we* underestimated Sayles, not just his ruthless sense of destiny but the calculating fury of his madness. He killed them because they ignored him . . . but neither of those men were his ultimate target."

"Who is?" Anna asked.

Afridi maneuvered himself over a bump in the road and pulled up for a moment, his fingers strumming the spokes on his wheelchair.

"Come on, Anna. You're a clever girl," he said, with a chiding voice. "You've listened to Sayles ranting. All that talk of freedom and violence. If you wanted to create chaos in this part of the world, who would you kill?"

Anna paused for several beats, then shook her head, confused.

Afridi continued. "If you were an embittered old man, who realized that his mission in life had failed . . . If you were convinced, with a twisted passion, that nonviolence and passive resistance were a mistake for the people of Tibet, a sign of weakness and misguided fatalism, who would you blame?"

After a few more seconds, Anna realized whom he meant.

"That's impossible!" she said.

Afridi began to move on again.

"Four days from now His Holiness is visiting the Dzogchen Monastery, two hundred and thirty kilometers west of here. He's going to conduct a memorial ceremony for Tibetan Freedom Fighters who died in the Paryang massacre fifty years ago." Afridi spoke softly but without hesitation. "He's a perfect target. Everything a terrorist could want. High profile. Maximum effect. It's exactly as Sayles put it: this will be the match that lights the fuse."

Still trying to comprehend what she'd been told, Anna replied, "But if Sayles really wants to help the Tibetans, surely, he wouldn't assassinate the Dalai Lama."

"Hayden Sayles doesn't give a damn about the Tibetans. He just hates the Communists, and he blames the Dalai Lama for not having taken a more militaristic stand. Those original recordings were sent to Jigme and other fighters in the seventies—a desperate call to arms. Anyone who listens to that tape knows he's mad."

"But now, if the Tibetans believe that the Chinese are behind the shooting . . ." Anna took a deep breath. "It's insane!"

"Of course, it is," said Afridi, "but in Sayles's own paranoid logic, the plan makes sense. That's all that really matters. He's driven by a desire for revenge as much as by his conviction in a final futile scheme to create a revolution out of anarchy. It's him against the world. More than anything, Sayles wants to make one last nihilistic statement."

"Do you seriously think he'll try it?" Anna asked.

"I know he will," Afridi replied.

By this time they had come to a point on the Chukkar overlooking a broad panorama of foothills to the east, folds upon folds of darkened ranges, like an endless blue fabric of pleated shadows.

On one of the closest ridges, just beyond Landour, stood a ruined house. It was perched on an exposed spur with cliffs dropping away to the south, the main bungalow silhouetted against the mountains beyond. Even from this distance, it was obvious the house was abandoned. The roof sagged, and no lights were burning in the windows. There was forest on all sides, and a couple of dead trees grew in the overgrown yard, with skeletal branches reaching toward a vacant sky. Anna had noticed the ruined building several times already.

Afridi broke their silence. "They say that house is haunted."

Anna looked at him, distracted. "Is it?"

"Very likely. It's been deserted for years, ever since I can remember," Afridi said, "but I just learned that someone has been camping out there for the past few days."

"Sayles?" said Anna, startled out of her thoughts as the dog began to tug at the leash, wanting to turn back.

Afridi shrugged. "Either him or his ghost."

Thirty-Eight

The guards were barely able to open the gate in time before Anna's car came roaring out of the HRI, headlights blazing. Her hand moved from the gearshift to the seat beside her, making sure the pistol and headlamp were ready. The glow from the dashboard gave her face a blue complexion, while her eyes focused on the narrow road ahead. Anna had raised the canopy on the convertible, though the windows were down. By now it was completely dark, and the headlights flashed against *pushta* walls.

As she sped through Sisters' Bazaar, a street dog darted for cover. A. Prakash & Sons was just closing down. She saw the proprietor locking the shutters then shielding his eyes as the harsh glare of headlights blinded him for a moment. Seconds later, Anna's car had disappeared around the next corner, the sound of its engine swallowed up by the night.

Farther along the Chukkar, Karan was standing at the gate of Rokeby Manor. He shook hands with Renzin, who mounted his bike and drove away. Karan waited for a moment, wondering what to make of the visit. In the silence, he listened for the night sounds of Landour, which had now become familiar to him, the pulsing call of an owl and the distant barking of dogs far off in the valley. But at that moment there was nothing, a complete stillness to the night and a vast silence that seemed to obliterate any evidence of the world beyond the shadows in which he stood.

Then, suddenly, he heard a muffled rumble, somewhere in the distance but rapidly approaching. Karan couldn't tell which direction the car was coming from until the headlights swung around the corner, slicing through the darkness. The silence was torn apart by the engine's thunder, as the sports car raced past the gate. Karan recognized Anna behind the wheel, driving as if she were escaping from someone. But there was nobody behind her. Immediately, Karan sprinted back up to the portico of the hotel and jumped on the ATV. He gunned the engine as he raced to catch up with Anna.

Heading down the switchbacks, he could see her headlights flashing through the trees on the road below. At the bottom of the hill, the BMW turned left along Tehri Road. The car was moving faster than the ATV, and Karan wasn't sure he could keep her in sight. Each time he took a turn, he saw her tail lights vanishing around the next bend. The road was empty except for a couple of drunks sprawled on the ground beside a lamppost near the bus stand. Though he kept the throttle pushed to the maximum, Karan didn't want Anna to know he was following her.

The only vehicle he met over the next two miles was a jeep with a single headlight. Karan nearly collided with it as the driver swung around a corner and blew his horn. The wheels on the ATV brushed against the railing, but Karan was able to regain control and raced on in pursuit. No stars were visible overhead, only the waning moon, which cast enough light to etch the outline of a ruined house silhouetted against the night sky.

Several corners on ahead, Karan saw the sports car slowing down and pulling over to the side of the road. Easing back on the throttle, he switched off his lights. Parking along the shoulder, he approached on foot, taking his pistol out of the inner pocket of his jacket. Moving cautiously, Karan reached the BMW and saw that it was empty, the windows up. He hadn't brought a headlamp but carried a small penlight that he flashed inside, over the black leather seats. Glancing ahead, he saw the main road continuing through a cut in the ridge. An unpaved driveway turned off to the right. By now he knew where

Anna was headed. In his wanderings on the hillside, Karan had seen the ruined house, but only from a distance.

Keeping close to the hillside, he followed Anna. Just once did she switch on a light, a brief flash of her headlamp that illuminated the foliage along the edge of the path. She was about a hundred yards ahead, moving cautiously as she came in sight of the ruined bungalow. It appeared to be deserted, the verandah and windows dark and vacant. Anna could see where one section of the roof had collapsed and the crumbling terraces in front. There were two derelict buildings at the end of the driveway, outhouses that were nothing more than cracked walls without any rafters or roofs.

Anna was armed with a Belgian semi-automatic FN 57 loaded with steel-jacketed bullets that could pierce body armor. She was trained to use it and confident that she could hit a target at thirty meters, even in the dark. Coming to Mussoorie, the last thing on her mind had been that she would need to fire a weapon, but here she was, crouched against a tangled hedge of thorn bushes, preparing to ambush an assassin. If there had been a unit of the Rapid Action Force nearby, she might have let them handle this, but all of the employees at HRI were technicians and analysts, not soldiers. Even the guards were not trained for this kind of hostile encounter. Anna could already hear Manav scolding her when she got back to Delhi for taking a risk like this, but she was relieved to be finally able to do something, instead of just waiting around.

Staying low to the ground and taking cover behind the hedge, Anna moved forward quickly, her headlamp switched off. She reached the ruined house in fifteen seconds, kneeling at the edge of the verandah and listening for any sounds. On the ridges to the west, she could see the lights of Mussoorie and Landour, but here there was only darkness, no electricity, as if the air was ink, nothing but the faintest outlines visible. Creeping forward, she lifted herself onto the verandah and slid quietly toward a door that hung at a crooked angle from one hinge. The window next to it was broken and Anna's shoe crunched on fragments of glass. She froze and listened. Inside the bungalow she could hear a rustling sound, like a mouse or a snake burrowing into the walls. Through a gap in the doorway, Anna saw the faintest flicker of light, a candle or an oil lamp burning somewhere deep within.

Karan had seen Anna's shadow move across the open yard. He held back until she had positioned herself beside the door. Moving stealthily, he crept along the edge of a barbed wire fence, to the right of the building. He came to a gap, where one of the posts had fallen over and the wire had snapped. Stepping through, he crawled behind a low structure that looked like a garden shed, part of which had collapsed. As he made his way around the shed, he noticed a familiar shape in the darkness. The Royal Enfield motorcycle was parked against the wall, its front wheel turned to one side and only the blurred outline of its fuel tank and handlebars visible in the layered shadows. Until now, he hadn't been sure why Anna had come to the ruined house, but now he understood. Somewhere in the darkness ahead, the shooter was hiding. He could picture Sayles crouched inside the ruined house, alert but unaware of their presence, two figures stalking him from opposite directions. Karan couldn't help wondering if this was a trap, but now it was too late for him to turn back.

He circled the yard, to avoid being seen by Anna or anyone else who might be watching, past one of the dead trees, its branches clawing at the stars. Karan climbed a set of steps that led to the back of the ruins. Slipping forward onto an open porch, where a rain gutter was hanging from the eaves, he kneeled down and listened. It seemed as if the old house was so precariously balanced it would collapse if he touched anything at all; he was almost afraid to breathe for fear of blowing down the walls.

Inside was a light. Karan had spotted it, as he came up the steps at the back of the bungalow, a single flame glimmering within the extinguished heap of the ruined house. He could picture Sayle's face lit up by the flame, the flickering contrasts of light and shadow playing upon his aged features, the same face he had conjured up on the computer screen. As he flattened himself against the porch wall, Karan flicked off the Glock's safety catch and switched on the laser sight.

At the other side of the house, Anna knew if she pushed the door open, the hinges would shriek. The only other point of entry was the window, a rectangular maw of jagged glass. The air outside was cold and a breeze was blowing up from the valley that ruffled her hair. As she waited for her breathing to ease, her pistol ready to fire, she was aware of a presence inside the house. She saw a movement, a shadow within shadows, gliding across a wall. Anna wasn't sure if Sayles had sensed that she was stalking him, but she was conscious of a figure passing from one room to the next.

Somewhere to her left, she heard a clicking sound, like a latch being opened, followed by silence. Anna decided to risk the door, pulling it slowly toward her. The rusted hinge made less sound than she expected, an imperceptible squeak that could have been caused by the breeze. Once inside, she made her way around a pile of broken furniture. A wooden wardrobe lay face down, next to a chair with only two legs. Each obstacle required her to gauge every step, for fear of knocking something down. She kept her headlight off and felt her way past another door frame, into a larger inner room that had straw on the floor and smelled of goats. It felt as if she had entered a cave. Anna braced herself as she approached a hallway on ahead, no more than twenty feet from the candle flame reflecting off the blistered, peeling walls.

By this time Karan had also entered the house, the red bead of the laser sight tracing the cracks in the ceiling, as he held his Glock raised in both hands. Ahead of him was a closed door. He could see light coming through a cracked panel and under the sill. Karan had heard the same clicking sound thirty seconds earlier, as if a suitcase had been unlocked, or maybe a window opening onto the night outside. With the handgun firmly cradled between his palms and his finger on the trigger, he lowered his right shoulder and rammed the door.

It broke against his weight and fell inward, almost blowing out the burning candle which was fixed to the table with a congealed mound of wax. Beside it were the remains of a meal on the table, an empty packet of instant noodles, an apple core, and a small paraffin stove. All of this Karan saw in an instant, as the red bead of light swung across the peeling plaster on the walls and came to rest on Anna's forehead. She didn't flinch, for her pistol was raised as well, its snub-nosed barrel staring straight at him with blunt finality. She had stepped forward with the FN 57 ready to fire at exactly the same moment Karan had burst into the room. For several seconds, neither of them moved, their fingers prepared to squeeze off a shot even as the neural impulses in their minds processed this moment faster than any computer they might have used.

Before either of them could speak, they heard a noise outside the house. It sounded like a muttering grumble, as if some kind of mechanical beast was clearing its throat. Almost immediately, Karan realized it was the motorcycle.

Anna was the first to react, lowering her pistol and running back down the hall toward the broken door through which she'd come. The thumping sound of the bike's single piston could now be heard, as the driver accelerated away from the house. By the time she got outside, the motorcycle was gone, a guttering rumble receding into the hollow night. Only the moon seemed to smile, an upturned semicircle of reflected light.

"Shit!" Anna swore under her breath.

Turning back toward the house, she switched on her headlamp, catching Karan in the beam as he stepped outside. He still carried his pistol but slowly raised both arms in a pantomime of surrender and defeat.

Thirty-Nine

The phone call wasn't unexpected. In a subdued, discouraged voice, Anna reported that Sayles had escaped. Afridi wondered if he should have called in an anti-terrorism squad, but it would have taken him twenty-four hours at least to get the authorization. And if they had laid siege to the ruined house, as they were likely to do, Sayles certainly would have been spooked and disappeared. He was too clever to let himself get caught that easily, and he must have someone working with him who would alert him to a threat. Though he had got away this time, fortunately no shots had been fired, and he was likely to be holed up somewhere close by or already on his way to the Dzogchen Gompa.

At least Anna was safe. Afridi knew that she was capable of taking care of herself, but he felt a protective sense of responsibility. He wished that he didn't have to rely on her to carry out a task that should have been his alone. If only his legs allowed him to track down Sayles, he wouldn't have put anyone else at risk. He had chosen Anna because he knew that she was capable of carrying out a mission like this with calculated efficiency. When pursuing an adversary like Sayles, success depended on quick reflexes and an unflinching ability to use deadly force.

Afridi had studied Anna's file carefully before calling her to Mussoorie. There were several other agents he had considered, but she stood out among all of the candidates on his list, not only because of her experience in audio surveillance. The adjectives that her superiors had used in their assessment of her work ranged from superlatives to outright condemnation, though Afridi knew that these evaluations revealed less about Anna and more about the men who tried to manage a highly capable woman like her. "Independent," "Committed," "Brilliant," and "Exceptionally Talented" lay at one end of the spectrum, while in the other column she was described as "Stubborn," "Insubordinate," "Reckless," and "Unprofessional." Aside from the Rajdhani encounter, which had earned her admiration as well as disapproval, she was known to be outspoken, with a disregard for bureaucratic inertia within RAW and its affiliated agencies. There were very few women in the intelligence community, particularly in technical fields, and most of the senior officers were men, almost all of whom felt threatened by her.

Anna's file contained personal details as well. Her father's businesses had been scrutinized for any conflict of interest or security risks. Other than coming from a wealthy background, there was nothing significant about her family. She certainly didn't need the job and joined RAW out of a sense of duty as well as adventure. Anna was well educated and experienced. At the age of thirty-one, she was still single and her file contained only a couple of references to personal relationships, none of which had lasted more than six months. Clearly, her work was more important than her social life.

None of this had really mattered to Afridi. His main concern had been to find a young, resourceful agent whom he could trust. He didn't care whether she was a woman or a man, liked or disliked, single or married. All that he was interested in was finding someone who combined a mastery of technology with an ability to focus on a single objective, no matter how dangerous or elusive it might be. Anna had a sense of purpose and passion, which was rare to find. Though she had failed this time, Afridi knew that the next opportunity she got, Anna would carry out her mission with extreme resolve.

Pouring himself three fingers of Scotch, Afridi weighed his options carefully. At any point, he could pick up the phone and speak to the Home Secretary or the commanding officer of the Special Protection Group, which provided security for the Dalai Lama. He could just as easily call his contacts in the Tibetan government in exile and inform them of a potential threat to His Holiness. Either way, the Dalai Lama's visit to the Dzogchen Gompa would be canceled or postponed. At the same time, there was no need to hurry matters. Four days remained in which to try and flush Sayles out from hiding. Timing and secrecy were the crucial elements, and Afridi planned to monitor the situation carefully, keeping his own counsel until the moment was right. Even at the last minute, he could raise an alarm and the memorial ceremony would be called off. But it was better not to play that card right now.

So far, the police had made no headway in their investigation of the shootings. A senior CID inspector had been sent up to assist in the inquiry, but he was a man of little imagination and even less intelligence. Afridi hadn't expected the police to turn up any leads, though Fallows's and Jigme's deaths were obviously linked. The fire at the mission press and the dead body in the water tanks only added to the fear and confusion. The police seemed to be proceeding on the assumption that all of this was the work of Maoist insurgents who had come across the border from Nepal, armed with Chinese weapons. When the inspector had come to Afridi's office, he put forward this theory and Afridi made no effort to dissuade him. It was clear that the police hadn't connected the dots and weren't factoring the Dalai Lama's visit into the equation. The Dzogchen Monastery lay nine hours' drive from Mussoorie, in a different state, under separate police jurisdiction. While it was close enough for the killer to get there in a day, it was too far away for anyone to see a link with the shootings in Mussoorie.

His Holiness had several layers of protection. The Indian government treated him as an honored guest. Commandos from the Special Protection Group accompanied him wherever he traveled within the country. In addition to this, the Tibetan government in exile had recruited and trained an elite team of bodyguards who never left his side. Though he was a man of peace, there were multiple threats to the Dalai Lama's life, and he could not move about in public without elaborate security. Anyone might decide to do him harm or take his life, from Chinese agents to dissident monks or lunatics with unknown agendas. While the SPG commandoes provided the most visible form of vigilance with their bulletproof vehicles, black uniforms, and assault rifles, it was the Tibetan bodyguards who were probably the most effective deterrent. Each of them had sworn an oath of loyalty and were committed to sacrificing their lives for the safety of their spiritual leader. Afridi knew that they underwent rigorous courses in security protocols, martial arts, and weapons training at a Secret Service facility in the US as well as British military bases. All of them had passed the highest levels of background checks and psychological testing. Though they were plainclothes operatives and looked like low-level functionaries in the Dalai Lama's entourage, his personal bodyguards were armed with a sophisticated array of communications devices and lethal weapons. They were far removed from the ragtag band of freedom fighters who had protected him in 1959, when he had escaped into India.

As his mind returned to the present, Afridi opened and closed his sore fingers, stretching the cramped muscles and joints. He examined the abrasions on his right hand, where the knuckles were grazed and raw. The inside of his thumb was blistered and one of his nails had broken; he could see where the blood had seeped underneath. The pain was inconsequential but he found that as he grew older, minor injuries and bruises took longer to heal.

Earlier that afternoon, he had climbed a new route on the wall.

His shoulders ached from the exertion. Unlike the rhythmic action of propelling his wheelchair around the Chukkar, climbing the wall put unusual strain on his arms and back. Though he was restricted in how high he could climb, Afridi set himself challenges on the wall that would have tested any ordinary man. With only his arms to haul him up, it was twice as difficult, if not impossible. Two of the analysts at the HRI were climbers, and they helped him set the route, moving handholds as he instructed them. They also belayed Afridi, as he made his way up the thirty feet of artificial rock in his gym. He would start from his wheelchair and pull himself up, like an injured spider on a thread. The strength in his arms compensated for the loss of his legs, and he was able to wedge his hips against the wall to get some purchase as he climbed, a slow, agonizing ascent that left him breathless before he was halfway to the top.

He'd fallen several times today, exceeding his reach and losing his grip, swinging free on the rope. Afridi would shout with frustration and anger when the belay broke his fall and he was lowered back into the wheelchair. After resting for a few minutes and catching his breath, he tried again, refusing to give up. Today the route had been complicated by a bulge in the wall, not quite an overhang but enough to make it necessary for him to throw his arm up and over the obstruction.

Powdering his hands with chalk, he had tried again. This time, he'd figured out his moves and made it up the first twenty feet with relative ease until he came to the bulge. Here he paused a moment to steady himself, but not too long, for the muscles in his arms were already trembling. He counted silently to three, then blindly reached up over the convex surface, knowing there was a handhold some-where above. This time, his fingers caught it, holding on in desper-ation as the other arm went up to the left. His climbing partners encouraged him from below: "Well done, sir! Well done!" and then, with an effort that seemed almost superhuman, Afridi pulled his shattered body to the top of the wall, wedging his fingers into a gap and thrusting himself upward against the force of gravity.

As his free hand brushed the ceiling, he let out a defiant cry, before looking down at the empty wheelchair below.

Tomorrow, he would set another route.

Raising his glass toward the fireplace, where a stack of oak logs were burning brightly, Afridi drank to Jigme's memory. The alcohol burned and soothed his throat. He wished his old friend and companion was here to share it with him. *They say you shouldn't drink alone*, he thought, but Afridi had always found that good whiskey was something best savored in private. Though he'd always been happy to drink a couple of pegs at an officer's mess or in the company of a close friend or colleague, the true pleasure of Scotch lay in the solace it gave to a solitary man, alone with his thoughts.

Forty

"If you're a software engineer, then I'm a ballerina." Anna spoke with frank insistence, her hands folded on the table in front of her.

Karan smiled. They both knew the rules of this game. Neither of them was going to tell the other any more than he or she already knew. They had guessed each other's identity, of course, but now it was a matter of selective denial.

"Let's agree," he said. "No personal questions."

The two of them were seated at a table in Doma's Inn, each with a bottle of Kingfisher beer and a plate of finger chips between them. Nobody else was in the restaurant except for a waiter and the receptionist, who were watching a television set in the corner, which was playing old Hindi film songs with the volume turned down.

"Okay . . . so, why were you at the ruined house?" Anna asked.

Seeing him up close, in the light, she focused on the cut of his sideburns and the windblown curls of his hair, tousled from riding the ATV. He was an attractive man but not her type, too self-confident and aggressive. She still had trouble matching the face to his voice, the Boston accent.

"I was following you."

"What for?"

Karan met her eyes with his. "You're a beautiful woman."

His gaze moved down the smooth curve of her throat, to where it disappeared into the V-neck of a dark gray sweater. Anna's hair was pulled back from her face and her clothes fit her so that he could see the strength in her arms and the athletic firmness of her body. She was almost his height. Karan wondered where she carried her pistol, probably in the sweatshirt knotted at her waist.

"Cut the bullshit," Anna said, though she smiled when she spoke.

"Come on," said Karan. "We both know why we were there. The question is, how do we stop the shooter?"

"We don't even know who he is," said Anna.

"Do you have a theory?"

He could see the evasive hesitation in her glance. She was wearing no makeup, but her skin was perfect and her dark eyelashes needed no mascara. Half an hour ago, she had been creeping through shadows with a gun in her hand. The danger they had faced together added a seductive intimacy to their conversation. Though she was attractive, Karan had decided she was too focused and unemotional for him. He liked strong women, but they needed to have a sensitive side as well.

"We're looking into several possibilities, but none of them has been confirmed," Anna said. "The CIA must have its theories too. Otherwise, why would you be here?"

Karan shook his head. She certainly wasn't playing by the rules, giving him no slack. Both of them knew who the other worked for, yet Karan could not acknowledge that he was a spy. He spoke with guarded candor.

"The truth is, this man is not your standard terrorist. We've got more questions than answers," Karan said, swirling the beer in his glass and watching the bubbles rise to the surface. He paused and grinned. "By the way, I never said I work for the CIA."

Anna studied the image of a dragon painted on the wall, the contorted shape with a twisted tail and claws that looked as if they could rip open the sky. It was strange what fantasies were spawned by fear.

"So, you were born in America?" Anna asked, sipping her beer.

"Remember, no personal questions." Karan raised a finger in warning.

"Come on, this isn't some national secret." Anna laughed at him. "Did you emigrate? Green Card? Naturalization?"

Karan remembered how the muzzle of her pistol had been pointed at his chest, the semiautomatic held perfectly steady in her hands. The slightest pressure of her finger on the trigger and he would be dead. At the same time, Karan thought of the laser sight on his Glock tracing a line from her ear to her nose, how close he too had come to squeezing off a shot. His pistol was now safely put away in his jacket pocket.

"I was born in Boston. My parents moved there in 1974," Karan said.

Anna did a quick calculation. He had to be in his thirties, maybe thirty-five. She'd guessed as much.

"So, you're a native American?" she asked.

Karan began to laugh. "Not quite. But I'm not Indian, either."

"Of course you are," Anna insisted. "An NRI."

"Not Really Indian," he said. "Like you."

She frowned at him. "You don't think I'm Indian?"

"I don't know," he said. "Not the kind of *desi* girl my mother told me about. How many Indian women pack a Five-SeveN and chase assassins in the night?"

"You're right," she said with a laugh. "Your mother would never approve of me."

Another song came on the television, and Karan looked up with recognition. Across the room, he could see Dev Anand and Hema Malini flirting and dancing with each other as they sang on the screen. It was an old classic from the early seventies, before anyone had coined the expression "Bollywood."

Anna took another swallow of her beer and caught his eye with a questioning stare, noticing that Karan had recognized the song.

"*Johnny Mera Naam*," Karan said. "*Pal bhar key koi hame pyar kar le.*"

Laughing, Anna put a hand on his arm. "You see, you are an Indian. Playback singer *kaun tha?*" she asked.

He answered her in Hindi.

"Kishore Kumar. Usha Khanna. When I was small, my mother used to watch videos every night. I've seen all of Dev *Saab's* pictures."

Tapping his fingers on the table, Karan sang along with the lyrics. He hadn't consciously memorized them, but they were imprinted in his mind from childhood. As he did this, he cocked his head to one side, mimicking the way Dev Anand was gesturing on the screen.

"*Achcha, tera naam Johnny hai?*" Anna said. "So, your name's Johnny?"

"*Jasoosi mein koi naam nahin hote,*" he answered, as the song carried on. "In espionage there are no names."

"*Chuppa Rustom,*" Anna said. "Double Agent."

As the final refrain of the song trailed off, Karan looked suddenly serious.

"No," he answered, with conviction in his voice. "I only serve one country. The United States of America."

Anna was taken aback by the intensity in his words. It sounded almost like a warning. She turned away with a bemused expression and noticed a photograph on the wall, a portrait of the Dalai Lama, with a white scarf draped over the frame.

Forty-One

The gray Ambassador was the same color as the smoky dawn coming up out of the Gangetic plain, a sooty, nondescript vehicle that circled around the switchbacks as daylight began to filter across the foothills. The man who called himself Bogart had left Delhi around midnight, traveling in the dark. He was accustomed to overnight journeys. The name Bogart had been chosen from a dozen aliases he'd used in the past, pseudonyms he picked to suit the occasion—an expatriate with an unknown past. Nobody knew his real identity, not even his colleagues in the Commercial Section of the US embassy, where he had been posted for the past twelve years, longer than anyone else. Most of the time, he kept to himself. His desk was usually empty, and it was accepted practice that he worked from home. He had no family, though there were rumors that his ex-wife was from the Philippines and that they had a son in college, somewhere in Minnesota.

Within the embassy, he was simply known as "Management," a title he himself suggested, during a brief conversation with a couple of the Marine guards, drinking off duty at the American Club. He usually ate his dinners there alone and seldom mixed with the rest of the diplomatic community.

The name had stuck, and he didn't mind it. After all, spycraft these days was mostly a matter of effectively managing your assets while keeping an eye on the bottom line. He had a simple, entrepreneurial approach to intelligence gathering. You had products to deliver, which were information, perspective, and analysis, collected on a cost-effective basis. The days of reckless spending and unlimited expense accounts were over. "Management" liked to think of everything in terms of business plans and organizational charts, in which he occupied one of the anonymous boxes midway between the desk officers at Langley and the lower rungs of agents and contractors in the field. It was no different than running a company—*the* Company. You specified desired outcomes and deliverables, established your targets, calculated a budget, minimized risks, then set the whole strategy in motion, holding everyone accountable. That was what good management was all about.

The only difference was that "Management" himself operated outside the ordinary span of control; officially, he reported to nobody, and nobody reported to him. Though there were other spooks in the embassy, including the CIA station chief, "Management" had little to do with them. Some said he worked for the DEA, others had labeled him as Homeland Security, though nobody was really sure what role he played. Even the ambassador discreetly ignored his presence, except when they met for a briefing once a month in his private study at Roosevelt House in Delhi. Bogart's contacts lay outside the secured perimeter of the embassy compound, beyond the sandbags and police sentries of the diplomatic enclave in Chanakyapuri, within the markets and side-lanes of the city. He knew Delhi better than anyone, from the commercial clamor of Karol Bagh to the broad fairways and clipped greens of the Delhi Golf Club. Twice a week, he teed-off at 5:00 a.m. with three companions who were equally informed and unprepossessing as himself, a retired lieutenant general, the managing editor of a current events fortnightly, and an unofficial security advisor to the PM. Each of them understood the rules of the game, a genteel competition—eighteen holes. No secrets were betrayed, no hidden assets revealed, but if there was information that needed to be confirmed, it was discussed in oblique terms between sand traps and bogeys chipped out of the rough.

This morning, "Management" was missing his game of golf.

Through the tinted windows of the car, he watched the shadows form themselves into trees. Blurred ridgelines coalesced into distinct profiles. The driver still had the headlights on. As they came around a blind corner, a herd of cows were standing in the middle of the road. They slowed down, and the driver blew the horn as he eased his way through. Coming from the opposite direction, Bogart noticed a single headlight approaching. It was a motorcycle, an old Royal Enfield Bullet. He recognized the make and model as the helmeted driver edged his way between a cow and its calf, before hurtling on down the hill. There was nothing unusual about this encounter, and "Management" looked away as they carried on up the road to Mussoorie. A short while later, they rounded a bend where the town became visible, spread across the top of the hill where lights were still burning.

"Management" enjoyed Mussoorie, not for its mountain air or the dramatic panoramas, but for the anonymity it provided. He had come up here more than once to clear his head and spend a weekend composing quarterly reports he sent to Langley, which were known for their incisive perspective on South Asian politics as well as their poetic simplicity. The man who called himself Bogart was deliberate in whatever he wrote, whether it was a memo regarding an emerging threat from a splinter group of the Jaish-e-Mohammad or a position paper on the nuclear standoff between Pakistan and India. He had written several of his most eloquent communiqués (a word he preferred to memoranda or reports) here in Mussoorie, hidden away in a comfortable but understated hotel that was once the home of a minor maharajah.

On a couple of occasions in the past, he had visited Dexter Fallows but had found him difficult, high-strung, and self-righteous, not a good combination. In "Management's" opinion, Fallows had served his time and served his purpose. It was a shame he had been killed so near the date of his retirement, but in some ways "Management" thought of it as a brutal kindness, an act of mercy, which would, ultimately, save the agency thousands of dollars in benefit payments.

Better to be killed quickly and painlessly in the line of service than drift away into enfeebled retirement. He'd seen too many agents lose their dignity when they returned from the field. Life in Virginia or Maryland, or Illinois, was never as fulfilling as it was in India, Thailand, or the Middle East. But more than a change of scenery, it was the sense of being cut out of the loop that made things difficult, not knowing what was happening under the surface of the daily news.

His own retirement was coming up, in another three years, and hints had already been dropped that "Management" should consider making a transition back home from Delhi, a final promotion to the South Asia desk on his way out the door. They would miss his "Epistles to the Philistines," as he titled of them, the subtle, nuanced descriptions of ground realities that were eventually reduced to a line or two in security briefings for the president.

The last piece he had written from Mussoorie was an assessment of Dexter Fallows. It contained a paragraph in which he mused about the efficiency and ethics of employing missionaries as spies. "Though it's obviously in the interests of the agency to recruit a broad range of assets, there is a definite risk involved when it comes to missionaries. Intelligence gathering and evangelism don't always go hand in hand. It's possible that someone like Fallows may be a long-serving patriot in a far-flung land, but he has never really been tested and the question that remains unanswered is whether he would choose his God above his country. On the other hand, it's true that missionaries cost far less than journalists or agricultural experts. They seldom have serious addictions or predilections that might compromise their ability to collect and convey information. Dexter Fallows smokes but doesn't drink. Though his wife died ten years ago, he seems to sleep in a single bed with no pornography under his pillow. My only concern about a man like him is that he sees the world from his own narrow field of vision. Being here in Mussoorie, there is little to be gained from pious dispatches on the politics of Christian minorities in India or the logistics of smuggling Tibetan Bibles across the Himalayas. Fallows has served us moderately well for more than forty years, but the return on investment is rapidly diminishing. Nothing more can be gleaned from this man. The sooner he is retired and dispatched the better."

Bogart felt a twinge of guilt at his choice of words. He still couldn't understand the shooting, though the information he was carrying with him now provided more answers than before. As the gray Ambassador swung up the final switchbacks to Mussoorie, Bogart took out a stick of chewing gum. Unwrapping it carefully, he savored the artificial sweetness on his tongue.

~

Karan had been awake since 5:00 a.m., but this time it wasn't jet lag. His mind had been racing, trying to decide what his next move should be. At 6:00 a.m. he had got out of bed and changed into his running clothes, heading out of the hotel and circling the Chukkar in a clockwise direction. After a week in Mussoorie, he was finally getting used to the altitude, and his lungs didn't ache the minute he jogged up the slightest hill. Running alone, he saw the sun coming up beyond the snow peaks, their blue profiles silhouetted against a sky as glossy as mother of pearl. He was happy for the exercise after tossing about in his bed for the past hour, reminding himself how close they'd been to the shooter yet how easily Sayles had eluded them. Anna, too, was on his mind as he started his second lap.

A selection of R.E.M. and Nirvana was playing on his earphones. The steady beat and jangled harmonies gave Karan's stride an easy rhythm. Ten minutes later, as he circled around toward Char Dukan, he saw several women lining up to fill buckets of water at a roadside tap. A stray dog with yellow fur was sniffing at the benches in the park. On ahead, he saw a vehicle take the turn near St. Paul's Church, a gray Ambassador with tinted windows. His loping stride was interrupted as he recognized the car.

Unplugging his earphones, Karan slowed down to a walking pace as he approached the Ambassador, which had pulled over to the side of the road. The rear door swung open and Karan stepped inside, wiping sweat on his forearm. Bogart took off his dark glasses. The tired eyes that studied Karan were remorseless in their omniscience. Without any greeting, Bogart pressed the remote control buttons on the armrest, and the video monitor opened out of the back panel of the seat in front of them.

"Scratch what I told you earlier," Bogart began, without preliminaries. "Haji Yaqub was killed in a drone attack outside Muzzafarabad. . . . We've reassessed the situation. It's possible the shooter could be one of our own, a little history coming back to haunt us. Dirty linen from the agency's laundry basket."

Karan nodded. "I know about Hayden Sayles," he said. "There was a file in Fallows's safe. I broke into his house a couple of days ago."

Bogart ignored the comment and continued speaking. "Fallows was involved with the Tibetan resistance in the late sixties, though his contacts were limited. This was the height of the Cold War. After the Chinese marched into Lhasa. Long before you were born."

On the screen, Karan saw archival footage of Chinese troops marching in front of the Potala Palace. It was like a clumsy PowerPoint presentation of the agency's efforts to combat Communism, edited in a documentary style but without any transitions or narrative voiceovers, just images of Chinese soldiers roughing up a group of monks and a temple being ransacked, its library burning. Bogart provided the commentary in a few clipped phrases. Though the tinted windows filtered out some of the morning's brightness, Karan was interested to see Bogart in daylight. He looked like a man who stayed indoors after the sun came up, with a pale, unhealthy complexion. His dark glasses anchored his receding hairline, combed straight back and held in place with some kind of old fashioned pomade that had a faint scent of Bergamot, though the source of the fragrance could have been a discreet splash of 5711 cologne.

"The Dalai Lama escaped to India in 1959," Bogart recited the events. "Three years later, India and China fought a border war in the Himalayas . . . 1962."

The images were now of refugees flooding across the border, black-and-white scenes from a Lowell Thomas newsreel, though the sound was off. Karan recognized the Dalai Lama on horseback being greeted by Indian sentries.

"Meanwhile, we were fighting the Communists in Vietnam. The CIA saw this as an opportunity to distract the Chinese, divert their resources. Nobody seriously believed that we could drive the Chinese out of Tibet. We supported the Tibetan freedom fighters, even trained them in Colorado and Guam. It was cowboy stuff . . . a new frontier."

Bogart fell silent, unwrapping a stick of gum and chewing silently. On the screen were pictures of American officers teaching Tibetan recruits how to operate a radio and assemble an assault rifle.

"Those were the bad old days," Bogart said, as an abrupt jump cut took them on to a parachute drop over the Tibetan highlands, "when covert ops still meant something and the only computer we had was as big as a trailer home."

Karan noticed that the scenes had shifted to a mountaineering expedition, a line of men carrying backpacks up a steep trail. On either side were the rocky profiles of mountains that looked as if they had never been scaled. Bogart's monologue continued, though it didn't appear to have any relevance to the pictures that Karan was being shown—climbers on a glacier, hammering pitons into the ice.

"Everyone was worried about Lop Nor missile base, but by then the Chinese were shifting their nuclear bases to Nagchuka, 165 miles north of Lhasa. We'd monitored some of their tests, and it was clear the Chinese had some nasty hardware aimed at India."

There were faces now, a group of mountaineers standing together around a fire and drinking tea from enamel mugs. Indians and Americans, white features with stubble beards, someone lighting up a cigarette. A Tibetan man was laughing at the camera and holding up two fingers, a V for victory.

"That's when the agency came up with a plan to place listening devices in the Himalayas, an early warning system to track Chinese missiles and nuclear tests. Great idea but kinda risky. The first attempt on Nanda Devi failed because of bad weather. They got close to the top but then there was a major screw-up. The device had to be abandoned at twenty-four thousand feet. When they came back the next season it was gone . . . carried away by an avalanche into the glacier below, or so we were told."

The film clips had changed from black and white to color. Karan tried to focus on what Bogart was telling him, but he was distracted by what looked like a Tibetan Devil dance, monks wearing grotesque masks, circling around the courtyard of a monastery. There was still no sound.

"After Nanda Devi, a second expedition was authorized. Up a mountain called Rataban, an easier peak to climb. Hayden Sayles led that team. He'd been an Army Ranger in Vietnam, a specialist in long-range reconnaissance patrols. Helped train Tibetan fighters at Camp Hale in the heart of the Colorado Rockies."

Karan recognized a face in the clip, a grizzled man with a white beard and blue eyes that looked as if they could freeze you with his stare. Sayles was armed, and standing beside him were a dozen of his fighters, watching the monks perform their dance. The faces were as fierce as the masks.

"The Tibetan who was shot two days ago, Jigme Phuntsok, was on the Rataban expedition with Sayles, along with a man named Colonel Imtiaz Afridi, who runs the Himalayan Research Institute here in Mussoorie. Army intelligence . . . supposedly retired. All of them disappeared after planting the listening device on the summit. At first, it looked like an accident, then Afridi turned up alive but badly injured. Sayles crossed the border into Tibet."

"You think he's still alive?" Karan asked.

Bogart gestured toward the screen, on which a monk was whirling with his arms outstretched, wearing the mask of a horned eagle.

"This footage was taken five years ago at a monastery in Guge. Sayles disappeared in sixty-nine, hiding out in Western Tibet. We assumed he was dead, but he resurfaced a few years later. Though he cut his ties with the agency, he kept in touch with Fallows now and then, did some odd jobs for the Mossad and South Africans. He even signed up as a mercenary in Angola, killing Communists. As far as we know, he kept slipping back into Tibet . . . off and on. We've tracked some payments out of Johannesburg to a bank in Abu Dhabi but not enough to fund his militia. He seems to keep himself afloat by hunting Tibetan antelope and musk deer."

"Who took these pictures?" Karan asked.

"An Afghan journalist who worked as a stringer for a couple of European news agencies. He was following a story about an American aid worker in Gilgit and Hunza who was kidnapped in 2003. In those days, Sayles often crossed back and forth from Western Tibet into northern Pakistan and Afghanistan . . . operating in the Wakhan Corridor and some of the tribal borderlands in the Karakoram and Hindu Kush. Earlier, back in the eighties, when the Soviets were fighting in Afghanistan, Sayles joined forces with some of the mujahedin who were opposed to the Communists. He was involved in a couple of skirmishes but nothing serious. Turns out, his men were the ones who kidnapped the aid worker, who was eventually released and claimed to have met Sayles. The journalist who took this footage wasn't so lucky. He was killed on his way out of Tibet, though this cassette turned up in Peshawar."

The camera moved in close on Sayles's face, almost as if he were posing for the film clip. It was the same face Karan had created on his computer, except that his beard was longer and his gaunt features looked thinner, almost emaciated.

"A lone wolf," Karan said.

"Yeah, sort of," said Bogart. "Sayles is an old-school survivalist. Looks as if he's come out of hiding to fight the last battle of the Cold War. He's desperate and dangerous. Fallows refused to help him and took a bullet in the head."

"What did Sayles expect from Fallows?"

Bogart chewed in silence for thirty seconds, as if he were trying to decide whether Karan needed to know this information.

"A botched operation," he said, at last. "Sayles wanted us to divert a shipment of arms that were supposed to go to the Afghans.

RPGs, Stingers . . . the works. Fallows had negotiated this with us, but nobody was excited by the prospect, and in the end, the Pakistanis got into the act, and it was never delivered. Sayles blamed Fallows for the fuck-up, and it was only made worse because he'd sent a shipment of Bibles as a dry run, to make sure they could get across the border. That pissed Sayles off even more."

"There's no way to contact him?" Karan asked.

Bogart shook his head.

Just then, the film clip ended abruptly, as if the camera battery had suddenly died. As the screen went blank with static, Bogart turned to look at Karan, still chewing on his gum, the muscles in his jaw clenching and unclenching.

"Sayles is redundant. A corrupt asset who needs to be taken out."

Karan understood he was being given an order. He could feel the sweat drying on his skin, an uncomfortable chill that traced a path down his spine.

"One more thing," said Bogart. "Sayles grew up in Mussoorie, a former mish-kid. He knows these mountains like the back of his hand. Don't underestimate him."

Karan nodded, meeting Bogart's gaze.

"My cover's blown," he said. "I've made contact with Indian intelligence—"

"We know," said Bogart. "Annapurna Tagore. Nice piece of ass."

"She knows who I am."

"You want me to pull you out?" Bogart asked.

Karan saw himself reflected in the shades, two identical images of his face warped by the convex lenses, as if he were staring into a pair of blackened mirrors.

"No," he said. "It's okay, I'll finish this job."

Forty-Two

"We don't know if he's operating alone or who's supporting him." Afridi explained. "It's very likely that he's been in contact with a splinter group of the Norbulingka Brigade, a terrorist cell that shares his desire for vengeance."

"But I thought Manav said we'd arrested two of them," said Anna.

"Yes, but they're not cooperating, and who knows, there may be others. They've lain dormant for a while, but there's always the possibility of resurgence, especially if somebody supplies money and motivation. Sayles has been sending out word that he wants to revive his ties and lead a new campaign."

"But, how serious is the threat?"

This time, instead of tea, Afridi had offered sherry. When Anna asked if she could have a beer instead, there was brief look of disapproval in his eye before he fetched a bottle from the fridge. It was late afternoon, another hour to sunset.

"Even if there's one person who is determined to commit an act of violence, it means that others will join him, particularly if he succeeds," Afridi went on.

"Does he have any credibility, after all these years?"

"Even the most evil, desperate people live in hope."

"But, wouldn't the Norbulingka Brigade want to attack Chinese targets? Why would they kill Fallows and Jigme?"

"Terrorists create fear and confusion, that's the primary purpose behind their acts of violence," Afridi said. "They might claim to have higher goals—freedom, equality, defending their homeland or their faith—but in the end, it's nothing more than a brutal, cynical decision to destroy any semblance of security or peace. They might pretend to be acting upon moral imperatives, but in fact there isn't a shred of morality in their actions. For them, all that matters is that they take power into their own hands by causing chaos and uncertainty."

"How can that be something you believe in?" Anna asked.

"They convince themselves that they are fighting a righteous war in which everyone who opposes them is an enemy combatant." Afridi leaned forward in his wheelchair, his eyes full of intensity and conviction. "For a terrorist, innocent deaths are a necessary means of generating fear and panic."

"But Sayles doesn't sound like a terrorist. He seems more like a frustrated old man, acting out a grudge from years ago."

"The weaker someone is, the more dangerous they become," Afridi insisted.

"Why would he come to Mussoorie and kill his childhood friend, then burn down the mission press? He's crazy."

"Who knows what secrets he carries with him from his past? All of us have childhood fears and anger. Sayles grew up on this hill-side. This was his home, his community. Whatever he believes in was forged right here, in these old bungalows, along these paths. Whatever anger he harbors was ignited on this ridge. He's come back here seeking personal redemption, acting out whatever festering fantasies have eaten at his mind for all these years."

"You're saying he's mad, a lunatic?" Anna stood up, shaking her head.

"Yes, but not the debilitating kind of madness that drags you into despair or inertia." Anna had never heard Afridi talk with such animation, his hands held in front of him, as if he were strangling a ghost. His glass of sherry remained untouched on the table beside him. "This is a form of madness that focuses all of your thoughts and motivations on a single objective. Sayles may be irrational, but he is operating out of a personal logic that is, for him, irrefutable. He knows exactly what he's doing. There is a plan to his campaign, as carefully thought out as any military maneuver. He's killed twice already, and he's going to kill again. I know this man. I could write a book about him."

"But if his main objective is to assassinate the Dalai Lama, I don't understand why he would come here to Mussoorie and go on a shooting spree. Wouldn't it make more sense to just fire the one bullet that counts, rather than alerting everyone to his presence?"

"Yes, of course, but then he remains anonymous. He wants the Tibetans and most of the world to believe that the Chinese have killed His Holiness, but he also wants us to know it's really him. That's the paradox."

"I still don't get it." Anna took a swallow of beer and watched the bubbles rise along the edges of the glass.

"Think of him as an actor playing a role. Beneath the character's facade lies the actor's ego, which struggles for our attention even as he hides behind a mask."

Anna laughed. "You make it sound so dramatic!"

Afridi smiled and leaned back in his chair. "I'm not exaggerating," he said. "Believe me, the man we're dealing with is far more complicated than you think. On the surface, he's a right-wing fanatic, the kind of person for whom the world is black and white. And yet, within his soul, or whatever vestige of a soul remains, lies a very convoluted, twisted man. His hatreds and his fears, his passion and inadequacies are all tangled up like a climber's rope fastened to a precipice."

"But then, he must be acting alone. Nobody would share his delusions."

"Not necessarily. I imagine Sayles has his sympathizers. Those who will give him shelter and allow him to hide among us. Remember, even though Sayles has always been a loner, resisting authority, refusing to follow orders, he also depends on a network of contacts. When he worked for the South Africans and the Israelis, he knew how to collaborate and ally himself with those who shared his goals. He's a perpetual outsider, but at the same time Sayles understands the value of association. Within the Norbulingka Brigade, he was always a bit of a legend. They used to have a code name for him. They called him Chaco, after the renegade bandit from the Italian western *Four of the Apocalypse.*"

"I haven't seen it."

"You haven't missed anything. It was made before you were born," Afridi said, his lips forming something between a grimace and a smile. "Sayles was never really part of the Norbulingka Brigade, but he had ties with many of its members and they used him whenever they needed, mostly to raise money outside of India."

"Why would they revive their campaign now? They're not going to be able to hijack a plane." Anna sat down again, in a chair next to the fireplace. "They don't have the resources."

"No, but they have plenty of other targets, including Option Twelve."

Anna caught his eye. "What's that?"

"When we broke up the Norbulingka Brigade, we were able to get a lot of information on future operations. They had planned various attacks on Chinese diplomats and commercial interests, but they also believed that the Tibetan government in exile was too complacent. They wanted to destroy the sense of growing equanimity, which they believed was hindering the goal of freeing Tibet. They rejected the idea of passive resistance. They wanted Tibetan exiles to rise up in revolt. That was how Option Twelve was conceived. It was the most extreme action they could take, almost unthinkable. And yet, there were those who believed it was the final answer . . . the only solution."

"What about the other eleven options?" Anna said, skeptical.

On the other side of the house, she could hear the dog beginning to bark.

"There were no other options. Twelve refers to the Twelfth Dalai Lama, Trinley Gyatso, whom many believe was assassinated in 1874, either by his own advisors or the Chinese. His three predecessors also died under suspicious circumstances, and conspiracy theorists suggest that all of them were murdered to achieve political ends."

For a moment, Anna was silent, as she watched Afridi drumming his fingers on the armrests of his chair.

"So, that's what Sayles is planning to carry out? Option Twelve?"

"No Tibetan would ever want to fire that bullet," said Afridi finally picking up his glass and draining half the contents.

"But an American vigilante . . ." said Anna.

"Chaco," said Afridi.

By now, the barking of the dog had grown louder, and Afridi started to wheel himself across the room.

"What is it?" Anna asked. Outside the sky was darkening.

"Monkeys," said Afridi. "They must be raiding the garden."

Anna followed him through the hall, past his bedroom and into the gym. For the first time, she saw the climbing wall, amazed at Afridi's persistence and discipline. The dog was standing at the glass door that opened onto the garden. Outside, forty feet away, were a dozen langur monkeys feeding in the flower beds. Afridi slid the door open, and the old dog bounded across the slate patio and into the yard. Before he could reach them, the monkeys scattered and leapt into the nearby trees.

Afridi gave a hoarse shout to scare them off, which the monkeys ignored, watching him from the branches of the oaks and chestnuts that surrounded the house, their large silver bodies gracefully perched out of reach, tails hanging down.

Anna could see where the flower bed had been stripped. The garden was going to seed, but there were plenty of nasturtiums, which they had been feeding on, as well as a bed of marigolds, most of which were uprooted. The dog was circling slowly under the trees, growling and letting out frustrated barks. An evening glow touched the snow peaks toward the north, setting them alight with purple and amber hues. A stone birdbath stood in one corner of the garden alongside a wrought-iron bench. Anna could see that Afridi had carefully arranged this space, just as he had cultivated his life, despite his disabilities.

She watched him pause, reaching down to pick up one of the torn blossoms scattered on the ground. Looking up into the trees, he seemed to fix the monkeys with an angry stare. They watched him from above, dark faces peering through the leaves.

Moments later, there were three sharp reports, like someone snapping sticks of bamboo, followed by three distinct thuds. Anna heard the sound clearly and she knew it was a rifle, though it took her several seconds to react. Her first concern was Afridi, but he had already spun around and taken his pistol from the holster strapped to his chair. For a moment, she thought the shooter had missed his target. Anna was about to shout for Afridi to move back, but then she saw three bodies on the ground. They had fallen from the trees. Two had landed near the birdbath and the third on the wooded slope above the garden.

By this time, Afridi had reached the fence at the edge of the yard, staring down into the darkening forest beyond the Chukkar road that ran below his house. The shots had been fired from this direction, but there was nobody in sight. A guard came running up the ramp, his rifle ready. Briefly, Anna thought that maybe the guard had shot the monkeys, but he too was scanning the forested flanks of the hill from where the bullets had been fired. The shooter had vanished.

Cautiously, Anna stepped across to see if Afridi was all right.

"Were you hit?" she asked.

He shook his head.

"Sayles?"

Afridi nodded. "He wants me to know that he's still here."

Anna turned toward the dead langurs. She could see two of them sprawled in the grass. Both had been shot in the head. One of them lay on his back, furred legs outstretched with both of his forepaws folded across his chest, in a final gesture that was so completely human it made Anna wince.

Forty-Three

Renzin had carried a portion of his father's ashes to a hilltop at the eastern end of Mussoorie, a secluded place that overlooked the high Himalayas. It was a sacred spot, where people from the Tibetan community
came to tie prayer flags and leave votive offerings. Jigme had often come
up here to meditate, climbing the ridge and gazing out over the mountains that he once conquered. As he had grown older, no longer strong
enough to cross those high passes, his mind still carried him beyond the
snow peaks, returning to the land of his birth. Strings of colored flags
were tied to the trees, block-printed with emblems of wind horses and
conch shells. Several small chortens and prayer sites had been built on
the ridge but no larger structures. Mostly, there was forest, a dense jungle of oak and rhododendron trees, as well as pine and deodar. Renzin
had come here many times before, accompanying his father and helping him ascend the rocky trail as his legs grew weaker.

   Jigme's remains were contained in a copper urn, an antique vessel
that Renzin had chosen from the shop. He had filled it after the pyre
burned out. Some of the ashes and charred bits of wood had been
consigned to the stream, floating away on the current, but he had
wanted to scatter the rest in sight of the mountains that his father
climbed. Jigme had never told his son what ceremonies and rituals
he expected to help his soul pass through the portals of the afterlife.
But Renzin knew that he had an obligation to conduct some rite of

passage for his father. As he scattered the ashes on the breeze, he felt a sense of release and sadness. He didn't know any of the prayers he should say, but in silence he asked forgiveness for his father's soul, absolution for the bitterness and anger that Jigme had harbored, the men he'd killed—even if they were Chinese soldiers.

Emptying the urn, Renzin felt as if he had cast off a weight that he had carried all his life. His parents were both dead, and he had no brothers or sisters, no other family. Standing on the hill, he felt completely alone, bereft yet free. Placing the empty urn in a shallow depression between two rocks, he sat down and closed his eyes. Unconsciously, he emptied his mind, letting his memories drain away. After several minutes, the image of the sand mandala entered his thoughts, and he could picture it in detail, layer upon layer, ring upon ring, a circular rainbow of vivid colors. Each grain of sand glowed like burning coals, a fire of many hues, searing intricate patterns onto the surface of his mind. The vision startled Renzin, even as it held him in a hypnotic trance. He had never experienced anything like this before. Troubled yet fascinated, he felt as if he was traveling along the path of the mandala, which led him back into the mountains to a distant point of origin.

An hour might have gone by or only a few minutes. The wheel of time turned at its own pace, sometimes faster, sometimes slower, in rhythm with the pulsing of Renzin's heart. When he finally opened his eyes again, it wasn't like waking out of sleep, but instead a gradual fading of the mandala, its colors growing dull, and the patterns withering like petals on a dying flower. He had been aware of so much more in his trance, a world of mystery and magic. Returning to consciousness was like falling back into a disappointing dream.

What surprised him most, as he saw the fluttering prayer flags and clouds hovering above the Himalayas, was the warmth of the sun on his face. Seconds later, he became aware that someone was watching him. He turned to find Noya standing to his right, a little below him on the ridge. For a moment, he stared at her, as if she were a stranger. Neither of them spoke, at first. Renzin felt self-conscious as he got to his feet. She had caught him unaware in a private moment of grief and meditation.

They hadn't seen each other since the night they'd argued. When Noya didn't call him after that, Renzin was convinced he had offended her.

"What are you doing here?" he asked.

She shrugged. "I saw your motorcycle parked at the foot of the hill," Noya said.

He picked up his empty backpack, in which he'd carried the urn.

"I came to leave my father's ashes," he said.

Noya nodded as Renzin walked past her down the path, stopping at a rocky ledge, from where they had a clear view of the mountains to the north and the forested ridgeline of Landour to the west, the red rooftops of houses jutting through the trees.

"How did you get here?" he asked.

"I walked. It's not that far," said Noya.

"Why did you come?" Renzin asked again.

"I wanted to say goodbye," Noya replied. "I'm leaving tomorrow morning."

"Back to Israel?" Renzin asked.

She nodded. "I need to go home and get a job."

He smiled for the first time. "That's very practical of you."

Noya shrugged and fell silent for a few moments as they scrambled down a shortcut, following the crest of the ridge, while the main path circled back through the forest, descending gradually.

"I haven't seen you since your father died." Her voice carried a hint of sympathy, but she offered no words of condolence or comfort, almost as if she were indifferent to his death.

Rejoining the wider path, they walked side by side. Few people came up here. The shadows darkened as they descended through a stand of pine trees, dry cones, and needles scattered on the ground.

"My father had been planning to visit the Dzogchen Gompa. He wanted to be there for the memorial ceremonies. There were only three survivors left."

"Did he ever talk about Paryang?" Noya asked.

"Only when he'd been drinking, then he'd tell me how the Chinese jets swooped in and strafed them. He said the bullets fell like hailstones of lead, and the bombs were like a year of thunder compressed into a single reverberation."

The mandala had vanished from his mind, but he was aware of its absence. Renzin now lit a cigarette, squinting into the smoke. Noya began to speak, her voice distracted, as if she was talking to someone else.

"You're fortunate to have had so many years with him," she said. "My father left us before I was born. My mother raised me on her own. We didn't talk about him. He was a secret we couldn't share. I knew he was alive, but I didn't know where to find him. After my mother died, I realized how little I understood about myself. I began to search for my father."

"Did you ever find him?" Renzin asked.

"Yes," said Noya. "But he didn't believe I was his daughter. He didn't even know that I existed."

"Were you able to convince him?"

"After a while he accepted me," Noya said, "but I'm still trying to prove it to myself . . ."

Her voice was subdued.

"How did your mother die?" Renzin asked.

"Cancer . . . a slow, painful death."

There was no grief in her voice, as if she were reciting facts.

"My mother died when I was six," Renzin said, exhaling a cloud of smoke from his lungs. "She killed herself."

"Why?" Noya asked. There was no emotion in her eyes. They were talking to each other, though it felt as if nothing remained between them, only words.

"I don't know . . ." Renzin flicked the ash off his cigarette. "She didn't give a reason. Maybe she was just tired of living with my father's demons."

For the first time, Noya reacted to what he'd said. Reaching out, she brushed her hand against his shoulder.

"Shit!" she said. "Parents have a way of fucking us up."

They had reached the motor road, and Renzin stopped to look back up at the ridge above, the crooked spine of rocks and trees. He had fulfilled his obligations to his father, but Renzin felt, somehow, there was more to be done, a final act of closure. As he mounted the bike, Noya waited for a moment and then climbed on behind him.

Forty-Four

Anna felt as if she'd seen this man before, though she was looking at the face for the first time. Displayed on the screen of Karan's laptop was the computer-generated image of Sayles, aged to seventy, with cropped white hair and beard. He looked like a minor Hollywood actor whose name she couldn't remember, one of those supporting characters who routinely appear in detective films, familiar but difficult to place. His hair had receded into a widow's peak. His skin was blemished and wrinkled, deep lines on his forehead and under his eyes. All of the details appeared in 3D, giving the image depth and proportion. The face was turned slightly to the right, as if he were peering out of a window. The image was cut off at the shoulders—it was like a sculpted bust of Caesar or Napoleon. The frozen features could have been a death mask, fixed in a final scowl, rigid and unresponsive except for his eyes. They stared straight out of the screen and seemed to follow Anna as she circled behind Karan to the other side of the desk.

"Are you sure that's what he looks like?" she asked, leaning closer to study the digital portrait. The two of them were in Karan's room at Rokeby Manor. Though he hadn't told Anna about Bogart's visit, Karan shared with her whatever he knew about Sayles.

"It's a cloned image, constructed out of several different photographs and adjusted to approximate his age. Of course, we don't know if he has a beard or how he cuts his hair, or whether he wears glasses or not, but other than that it's accurate enough to put his face on a wanted poster."

As he spoke, Karan typed a command, and the head turned slowly to the left and the lips began to move, as if the death mask had come to life. Sayles was talking, but there were no words, like a newsreader with the volume turned off.

"Hang on," said Anna, reaching into her pocket and taking out a flash drive.

As Karan paused the image, she plugged the flash drive into one of the ports on his laptop, then showed him the file she wanted to open. It took a minute, but when Karan pressed the Play button, Sayles began to speak in an angry, belligerent voice.

"We should have dropped a fucking atom bomb on the Red Chinese," he said with a menacing snarl.

Though the movement of his lips and the words were not in synch, the effect was convincing, and Anna felt the hairs rise on her neck. She looked at Karan, who seemed hypnotized by the image. The voice matched the face completely, the angry rant reflecting the venom in his eyes. Karan turned up the volume until it sounded as if Sayles was shouting, like someone abusing them from a distance.

"Instead, we let them march into Lhasa . . ." Anna could see the hatred in his glare. "Tibetans have always been fearless—they're fighters, bandits, and warriors. All of this non-violent Buddhist crap is a fucking lie!"

He was like a vicious oracle possessed by a demonic spirit, prophesying doom and destruction. The face actually seemed to lean forward as if the three dimensional image was going to burst out of the flat surface of the screen. Karan moved back in his chair. Sayles could have been speaking to them directly, giving a brutal harangue.

". . . The Nobel Peace Prize! Shit! It's more of a consolation prize!"

After this, Sayles began to speak in Tibetan. Neither Karan nor Anna could understand what he was saying, but the message was obviously the same, wild promises, accusations, and threats. He was clearly fluent in the language, and the guttural sounds and chopped syllables only added to the hostile intensity of his speech, as if he were cursing them directly, blaming Karan and Anna for the failure of his deranged plans.

Switching back to English, he blurted out another string of obscenities, then broke into Hindi. It was like listening to a short-wave radio that kept switching frequencies, moving between one language and another.

"Bastards! *Bhainchod!* All of you are fucking cowards . . . scared of your own goddamn shadows. I don't need you. . . . I don't need your money. I don't need to hear excuses. It's gonna happen, whether you like it or not. We're gonna do it. We're going to set the Himalayas on fire! Blow them up and start again. . . ."

The rant went on for several minutes, until the recording finally ended. Karan paused the image again, and the features froze, lips opening in a vindictive sneer over a line of crooked teeth. Anna could imagine a weapon in Sayles's hands, his eyes lining up the sights on a rifle that was pointed directly at her.

"Now, there's a patriotic American!" she said, under her breath.

"More like a nut case," said Karan.

"Do you really think Sayles is the shooter?" she asked.

"Who else could it be?"

Anna reached over and removed the flash drive. The sniper's eyes seemed to track every move she made, even though the image was still. The penetrating stare and aged face bore a look of demented madness.

"This recording matches his voice signature," she said. "All of it points toward one man, except we don't have any proof." Anna gestured toward the screen.

Karan finished her thought: "We've brought him back to life, but how do we know, for sure, if he really exists?"

Forty-Five

The anger in Sayles's voice was nothing compared to Afridi's rage.

Rather than taking Karan to the Himalayan Research Institute, Anna had brought him with her to Ivanhoe. The minute she explained who he was, Afridi exploded.

"Who the hell do you think you are? I'll have you arrested and thrown in jail!" His voice was full of indignation.

Karan watched as Afridi's fingers gripped the armrest of his wheelchair, knuckles clenched. If he'd been able to stand, Afridi probably would have come right up to him and grabbed him by the collar. Instead, there was a suppressed hostility to his gestures, the way his right hand broke free of the chair and his arm swung out in a broad arc, as if he were brandishing a sword.

"This isn't some bloody Northwest Frontier Province"—Afridi was almost shouting now, and there was no way to turn the volume down—"where you can play cowboys and Afghans. In India, we hang people for espionage!"

Anna looked across at Karan. She knew that Afridi hated Americans, but she hadn't expected him to blow up like this.

Karan answered in a quiet voice, trying to calm the situation, though Anna could see his temper rising.

"Sir. I'm not here to spy on your country."

"Then what the hell are you doing?" Afridi shot back.

Anna wasn't sure if he was angry simply because Karan worked for the CIA, or whether it was the fact that she hadn't told him until now. Afridi stared at her with scorn, as if she had betrayed his trust.

"I've been sent to locate a corrupt asset," Karan said in an even tone. At first, he had looked alarmed by Afridi's outburst, but now he stood his ground.

The wheelchair rotated as Afridi turned toward the fireplace, where two logs were burning slowly. Suddenly, a flame shot up, as if ignited by the tension in the air, throwing sparks on the slate hearthstones.

"A corrupt asset?" Afridi's voice dropped to a whisper. The angry scowl broke into a cynical, humorless smile. "Don't you speak English in America?" he said, his eyes now fixed on the fire, as if he were speaking to Sayles's face reflected in the flames.

Karan answered. "Yes, sir. I've been authorized to terminate this asset."

Anna wanted to sit down, but she dared not move. The hostility between the two men was almost unbearable, and she was worried that Karan would lose his temper. She wished she hadn't brought him to the cottage, but there had been no other choice. Karan himself had insisted that they meet Afridi.

"Very good! And how do you propose to do this?" Afridi asked. "Are you going to press the delete button on your computer?"

The sarcasm in his voice was full of confrontation, as if he wanted to provoke Karan. Anna could see the pistol in its holster, strapped to the side of the wheelchair. Afridi hadn't touched it yet, but she knew his fingers could pull it out in a second, if Karan gave him any cause to use it. She met Karan's eyes and tried to warn him.

"We almost had him," Karan said, lowering his voice.

Afridi glanced at Anna, his eyes full of contempt.

"I know," he said. "Brilliantly executed! You let a seventy-year-old man outrun you. Two against one. He made an ass out of you. Well done! I'm sure your handlers must be very proud of you both."

Anna could see Karan stiffen. She interrupted, quickly.

"Sir . . . We know his next target. That gives us an advantage."

Afridi spun his wheelchair toward her, advancing several feet, until she was forced to step back.

"Tell me one thing, Miss Tagore," he said. "Why should I trust this man?"

Though she had no answer, Anna began to speak, stammering at first, but it was Karan who replied, moving between her and Afridi.

"Because I have nothing to gain by lying to you," he said.

Afridi's arm swung up again, a wild, dismissive gesture.

"I've learned the hard way," he said. "Never take Americans at their word."

"Sir . . ." Anna tried to speak again, but Afridi ignored her.

With an abrupt thrust of both arms, he pushed himself past Anna and Karan, making his way to a coffee table at the opposite end of the room. Both of them moved aside to let him through. Picking up a mobile phone, Afridi prepared to make a call, then stopped and stared hard at Karan, as if deciding his fate.

"You have twenty-four hours to get out of this country." Afridi's anger seemed to have turned to disdain. "If you don't leave now, you'll never go home again."

"But what about Sayles?" said Anna.

Afridi began to press buttons on his phone, searching for a number.

"I'll inform the Tibetan Government in Exile," he said. "There's a threat to the Dalai Lama's life. They'll cancel his visit."

"You can't do that," Karan protested.

Afridi looked up as if he were about to explode again, but Karan clenched his fists in a persuasive, placating gesture.

"Colonel Afridi . . . sir," he spoke respectfully. "This is the best chance we'll ever have. Sayles doesn't know that we've identified his target. If we can figure out exactly when he plans to strike, then we can be there to stop him. If we don't, he'll find another time and place . . . and we won't know when or where that will be."

Afridi hadn't moved, his fingers still poised over the keys on his mobile phone. Anna thought she saw his eyes waver, just for an instant.

"You're asking me to risk the life of a man who is revered by millions of people around the world"—Afridi's voice was measured now, as if he weighed each word on his tongue before it was uttered—"just because you want to eliminate a raving lunatic?"

"Sayles is a terrorist, sir. Like any other." Karan's shoulders relaxed, and he opened his fists as if to prove he had nothing in his hands. "Just because he was one of ours, doesn't make him any different."

"American justice, is that what it's called?" Afridi looked as if he wanted to spit. "I wish I believed you."

Karan took a step backwards now and turned toward the framed photographs on the wall. Only one lamp was burning in the room, but the glimmering firelight was reflected off the glass on the pictures. Karan reached up, as if to take the photograph off the wall. His fingers brushed the frame. As young men, Afridi and Jigme were smiling for the camera. Trishul. 1968. Then he moved his hand toward the picture of Sayles and Afridi standing on the summit of Rataban, each of them holding his country's flag. Anna could see that Afridi was studying him intently now, as if following the line of his thoughts.

Karan let his hand drop to his side and turned back to meet Afridi's gaze.

"Sir," he said, after a brief pause. "If you had only one chance to kill Hayden Sayles, wouldn't you take that risk?"

Afridi stared back at him, then slowly put his phone aside. The atmosphere in the room was still charged with tension, but Anna felt as if she could finally breathe again. Afridi turned back to face the fire.

Forty-Six

On the large screens of the HRI's surveillance monitors, the Dzog-chen Monastery and surrounding ridges stood out in precise detail. Every tree and rock, every prayer flag and chorten was visible, as if seen through picture windows flung open on a clear, bright day. The high-resolution images provided a three-dimensional, bird's-eye view of the terrain with roads and paths marked out. Karan and Anna could see the martyr's memorial and the eternal frame, as well as the brightly painted balconies of the temple, the giant prayer wheels turning in unison, as supplicants completed their circumambulation. Using a remote control, Anna was able to zoom in on two of the monks seated in the sun, telling their prayer beads as they chatted on mobile phones. A second screen displayed the ridge above the monastery, every contour and feature distinctly rendered. While the monastery was 230 kilometers away, Anna and Karan might as well have been there on the ground to study the topography, even if the images were being relayed to them from satellites 35,000 kilometers above the earth.

Karan asked one of the technicians to zoom out on a separate screen, revealing a map of the region, with motor roads winding through the hills.

"The Dalai Lama will arrive by helicopter. There's an Indo-Ti-betan Border Police helipad about fifteen kilometers from the monastery," Anna explained as she came over to study the map with Karan, leaning over his shoulder.

The main surveillance room of the HRI was deserted, except for two technicians assigned to assist them. After finally reconciling himself to working with an American, Afridi had reluctantly authorized Karan's security clearance and given orders that only essential personnel should be admitted while he and Anna set to work, plotting the assassin's next move, trying to second-guess his strategy. They were all aware of the stakes.

"Should anything go wrong," Afridi had said, "anything at all, I'll warn the Tibetans, even at the last minute."

The road from the helipad to the monastery passed through villages and forest, with terraced fields and open pastures scattered among the trees, a vertical, precipitous landscape observed from above.

"A motorcade will take him from the helipad to the monastery. They're scheduled to arrive at 17:00 hours. It's about a fifty-minute drive at the most. They'll reach the gate of the complex at 5:20 p.m."

Anna's finger traced the motor road on the screen, as it wound its way up and down the ridges, looping in and out like yarn unspooling from a ball of wool.

"Sayles could be hiding anywhere along this route," she said.

"The helipad is going to be heavily guarded," said Karan, "inside a military installation. He won't try anything there."

"But once the motorcade sets out, it's an open road. He'll have plenty of places to ambush them along the way," Anna added.

"Not likely," said Karan. "Especially, if he's working alone. An ambush doesn't make sense. The Dalai Lama will have several vehicles, and Sayles won't know which car he's in. He'll wait until he has a clear shot. That's how he targeted his other two victims. Confirmed visual. One bullet. That's all he needs."

Taking the controller, Karan panned across the ridge and zoomed in on the final approach to the monastery. Two hairpin bends marked the descent to a point where the road crossed over from the south face of the ridge. After that, a level stretch ran through the forest, extending along the north side of the hill for a half mile. Eventually, the road climbed up to the crest of the ridge and then dropped down in front of the monastery gate. From there it continued back into the mountains, one of several arteries connecting with border roads and remote villages in the Himalayas. Karan pointed to the inner gate of the monastery.

"I think he's going to try to get a shot right here, when the Dalai Lama steps out of the vehicle. The cars can only drive up to this point. After that, they'll climb these steps and enter the main court-yard. It's about a hundred meters from the gate to the temple. They'll take their time getting inside, unless it's raining. Sayles will have at least seven or eight minutes to get off a shot, maybe longer."

"I've checked the weather reports," said Anna. "There's a storm passing through tomorrow, but it will clear up by the day of the ceremony."

"I'm guessing Sayles is going to be somewhere on this ridge, opposite the gate," said Karan. "It will give him an unobstructed shot as soon as the motorcade pulls up."

Anna went back to the larger screen and rotated the image, so that they were looking down at the monastery from the east.

"Remember, it's going to be late afternoon," she said. "If he's anywhere on that ridge, facing in this direction, the sun will be in his eyes."

It was like a game of chess on a three-dimensional board, where the crucial pieces could be a thousand feet above or below each other and the terrain couldn't be divided into neatly ordered squares of black and white. Instead there were cliffs and forest, high ground and low ground, jungle and gorges. None of the paths or roads followed a straight line.

They had decided to use satellite imagery to plot their moves, instead of visiting the monastery itself. Aside from saving time, it allowed them to study the topography unobserved. If Sayles got any hint that someone was on his trail, he was likely to vanish.

Shifting from live imagery to computer animation, they mapped the area using a simulation program that made it look like an elaborate video game, a multifractal landscape, reproduced through environmental modeling graphics, accurate to half a centimeter. Instead of looking down on the monastery complex and the motor road, they were able to explore this space virtually. First of all, they surveyed it as if from a helicopter, hovering and swooping down over the ridges, gauging the elevation and obstacles that lay between each location the shooter might select. A scene graph program calculated the time of day and the angle of the light, so they could see exactly how the shadows fell and where the glare of the setting sun might blind the assassin. Distances and estimated times between two points appeared on the screen. While the margin for error was infinitesimal, to Karan's eye, the whole thing still seemed uncertain and imprecise.

As the computers began to recalibrate the program, Karan threw himself back in his chair and looked around the room. The two technicians had stepped outside for a tea break, so they could speak freely.

"I never guessed you had this capability here," he said.

"Neither did I," Anna said. "I'd always heard that Afridi had an unlimited budget, but I didn't know it was quite this generous."

"Now that I've seen what's here, I'm sure he'll have me eliminated once the operation is over," Karan said with a guarded laugh.

"I don't know. He wouldn't let you in here if he didn't think he could trust you," she said, "even if you are an American."

"It's not a matter of trust," said Karan. "It's a matter of expediency. That's the thing about intelligence. You can't let emotions intrude. You have to reduce the human factor as much as possible. Someday, we won't need spies anymore, just rooms full of technology that spits out answers. Sooner or later all of this will be reduced to an app on your phone."

"I'm not sure," said Anna. "I don't think technology can replace everything. Look at Sayles and Afridi. There's no way a computer could ever completely predict their thoughts or actions."

"Maybe. But their time is over," said Karan. "Both of them are redundant, obsolete assets who need to be retired."

Anna shook her head in disagreement.

"No, we're always going to need human beings on the ground, observing, making decisions, understanding what isn't there." As the technicians returned, the image coalesced in front of them. This time, they could see the road from the perspective of the motorcade. Nine vehicles were driving along the winding route through a simulated environment, two pilot cars with flashing lights and four SUVs with tinted windows, followed by a couple of police jeeps and an ambulance. In the parallel rendering, they could see a police checkpoint on ahead, a makeshift barrier with old barrels and a battered sign that signaled for them to stop. None of the vehicles slowed down, passing through the checkpoint at forty kilometers an hour.

"Let's see what it looks like from the ridge above the monastery." Karan gestured to the technician, who fine-tuned the image.

Now they were directly over the gate but higher up, at an angle of almost ninety degrees. The motorcade was approaching the monastery, about to take the final turn. Anna asked the technician to pause the action and the vehicles on the screen stopped abruptly.

"Show me all of the potential locations for a shooter," she said.

Ten seconds later, half a dozen icons appeared on the screen, the crouching profile of a man aiming a rifle. Each of them blinked on and off, including two figures directly above the monastery and temple complex. Realigning the screen so that she could study these positions, Anna got out of her chair.

"What do you think?" she asked, looking over at Karan.

"I'd put my money on the upper one. There's better cover, and it would be easier to get in position without being seen. He'll have a clear shot from there, either at the gate or when they cross the courtyard."

"Four hundred and thirty meters," said Anna, checking the distance. "It's out of range."

"Not for Sayles," said Karan. "He can probably hit a target at twice that distance."

"What about those rocks below the tree? It's closer," said Anna.

"Maybe." Karan was on his feet as well, the two of them standing side by side. "It's possible, but he'd have to cross through those buildings to get there, too much of a risk of being seen."

At a signal, the technician restarted the program and they watched the motorcade approaching the monastery gate. They were now locked into the perspective of a shooter on the hill above. As the vehicles swung into view from behind a forested bend in the road, crosshairs appeared on the screen, inside a moving circle that tracked the motorcade as it pulled up next to the gate. The red lights on the pilot cars were oscillating, but there was no sound. Yet the whole thing seemed to be happening in front of them. The animated imagery had a stylized, cartoon-like simplicity, though it seemed completely real. The colors were flat, with little contrast and no gray tones, but they suggested photographic details, creating an optical reality for the human eye. The car doors opened. Security guards got out. A crowd of monks was waiting at the gate. None of the faces were visible, just figures outlined on the screen but each of them looked as if they were alive.

Anna held her breath as the door on one of the SUVs opened. Despite the animation and computer modeling, there was something undeniably authentic about the imagery. Instantly, the crosshairs settled on the figure who emerged. Everything seemed to be moving in slow motion, though the seconds were ticking steadily in one corner of the screen, marking real time. It was like watching a disaster unfold on television, the same footage shown again and again, until you knew exactly what happened next, but there was nothing anyone could do to stop it. Karan felt his mouth going dry.

A moment later, they saw a flash on the screen. The rifle made no sound, and the crosshairs remained absolutely still, fixing their target in a lethal gaze. The scene froze as the figure went down.

Forty-Seven

Renzin had kept the shop locked after his father's death, though he knew that sooner or later he would have to open up again and carry on with the business. For the past eight years, since finishing college, he had helped Jigme run Potala Antiques, buying and selling the merchandise that filled their shelves. As he looked around the shop, it reminded him of a tomb cluttered with objects preserved for the afterlife. There was a depressing stillness to the windowless room, with all of those images gazing down at him. The devil masks, with their contorted features, glowered in the shadows, bulging eyeballs and menacing scowls.

More than the masks, it was the bodhisattvas that unsettled Renzin, dozens of them in all sizes and postures, molded out of brass and copper, bronze and steel. Their calm, implacable demeanor suggested an indifference to suffering, no empathy for his loss. He wished the Buddha figures showed some expression, grief or humor, anger or fear, instead of their unresponsive metallic gaze. All of the statuary had a sameness, more artifice than divinity. It was as if the myths and magic had been melted out of them. Renzin had bought these idols by weight from wholesalers in Delhi and Moradabad who amalgamated religious icons, using cheap alloys and hollow molds. Even the *thanka* paintings were replicas of older icons, with their detailed ornamentation and copied brushstrokes, figures of saints and guardian deities, Tibetan symbols with untold stories lost in translation. Surrounded by all of these figures, even the tantric couples in the throes of coital ecstasy, an orgy of faith and sexuality, mythology and passion, Renzin felt an overwhelming sense of isolation. In his mind, he could still see faint shapes of the sand mandala, like the flickering residue of a hallucination or a migraine that was slowly dissolving in his brain.

Switching off the bulb and stepping into the back room of the shop, he found it was raining outside. The windowpanes were beaded with moisture, and water was streaming off the corrugated roof. This room had been his father's private sanctuary. Though they owned a small apartment on the other side of town, this was where Jigme often slept after locking up the shop. It was a rectangular space, with a low roof, facing the hillside. There was no view, but light came in from above, and it offered the kind of privacy his father craved. The room was shabby, the walls cracked and unpainted, a stained carpet on the floor. The only furniture was a couch-like bed and a small table and chair that looked as if it might have belonged to an English magistrate a century ago. The cane seat was broken, but Jigme had fixed it with a piece of plywood. On the wall was a calendar from 1988, with pictures of mountains. It had been given to Jigme by one of his climbing friends. None of the peaks were ones that he had scaled himself, but summits in Europe, North America, and the Andes. He had liked the pictures nevertheless.

This room was where his father drank. Against one wall stood a wooden cabinet with a bent metal hasp. Renzin chose a key from the ring his father always kept hidden under the sink in the bathroom. The first key didn't work, but the second opened the lock, and the panel on the left swung open. The sound of rain on the tin roof was comforting—a muted chatter. Outside the window, he could see the rough stones dripping like a waterfall.

Inside the cabinet, on one of the upper shelves, sat a bottle of rum. Three quarters of it had been finished. Jigme bought his liquor from the military canteen and the label was stamped "For Defence

Services Only." Renzin took it out and held the bottle up, the dark caramel color catching the opaque light from the window.

Two glasses sat inside the cupboard, as if Jigme was prepared to share a peg with a friend, though he usually drank alone. Renzin poured himself an inch of rum and sat down in the magistrate's chair. Taking out his cigarettes, he lit one carefully. The neat rum scorched his throat and he set it aside, wondering for a moment where Noya might be. He had dropped her at the guest house. She hadn't suggested that he stay with her, and Renzin wanted to be alone. Whatever they had shared between them was over now. He had called the hotel this afternoon, and they confirmed that Noya had checked out.

The second sip of rum went down more easily than the first, quenching a deep thirst within him.

Renzin's cigarette burned slowly toward his fingers. He felt less lonely now that he had escaped the collective gaze of the Buddha images in the shop. The prattle of the rain on the roof erased all other sounds. It was October, though the calendar on the wall displayed the month of June with a photograph of Mount McKinley. The caption was printed below, but it could have been any snow peak in the world as far as Renzin was concerned, the Himalayas just as easily as Alaska. He had never been interested in mountaineering—too dangerous, too cold.

From the cabinet, he took out the copper cylinder and laid it on the table. Opening it carefully, he unscrolled the *thanka* painting that Jigme had brought from Tibet many years ago. In the dim light, the shapes and images were barely visible, though Renzin knew every figure and episode it contained. He could hear his father's voice telling him the stories of the great Bonpo shamans and oracles, how they predicted future events with uncanny accuracy—spiritual journeys, kings enthroned and deposed, battles, invasions, and exile. He could see the mountain god riding his yak around the sacred snow peak, Mount Tise, a pure white pyramid that stood at the heart of this country, a homeland reclaimed in the imagination of the artist and the priests who committed these stories to heart. For all his doubts and uncertainties, Renzin knew it was his duty to preserve this *thanka* and return it someday to the temples across the mountains. With care and reverence, he rolled the painting up and slid it back into the cylinder, which he replaced in the cabinet.

Draining the glass of rum and stubbing out his cigarette in a copper bowl that served as an ashtray, Renzin got up and went back to the cabinet. He picked up the bottle as if to pour himself another drink, but put it down almost immediately. Opening the second panel, he could see a set of drawers. The cabinet had been built to contain crockery, perhaps the dishes off which the unknown magistrate dined long ago in some colonial time.

Renzin opened the uppermost drawer. It contained only papers, his father's documents and accounts, a lease agreement for the shop, which would have to be renewed next month, receipts for shipments of merchandise, electric bills. The responsibilities he had inherited seemed overwhelming.

The second drawer was filled with broken objects, a cracked vase glued back together unsuccessfully, the handle from a copper teapot, even the knob from a faucet in the bathroom, as well as several adapter plugs and other electrical fittings that could never be used again. Jigme refused to throw anything out, as if he believed that by keeping something long enough it might gain value over time.

But it was in the third drawer that Renzin discovered what he was looking for. Behind a box full of glass beads and buttons, he found a bundle that he recognized by touch, wrapped in layers of silk brocade. Taking it out, he felt the weight in his hand, heavier than any of the hollow Buddhas. For a moment, he almost put the bundle back but then carried it to the table, where he unswaddled it slowly, deliberately, removing the layers of silk, canvas, and leather. When it was finally unwrapped, Renzin picked up Jigme's service revolver. It was a Webley Mk IV .38, manufactured by the Indian Army's ordnance factory, a heavy, old-fashioned weapon, but deadly nonetheless. Renzin flipped the cylinder open. The revolver was loaded with six rounds.

Forty-Eight

Rain continued all day, a sullen October squall that drew gray curtains across the ridges, blowing westward over the lower Himalayas. The tea shops at Char Dukan, which usually had tables set up outdoors or in the small park across the street, seemed to have shrunk into themselves, half-shuttered and lit from within by naked bulbs. A few language school students were eating a late breakfast under dripping awnings, wrapped up in sweaters and shawls. Their classes had moved indoors and the bright sunshine of the past few weeks had suddenly vanished into gloomy dampness. Mussoorie was a town of changeable moods.

Karan had borrowed an umbrella from the front desk at Rokeby and walked down in the rain. Huddled inside the telephone booth, he listened to the crackling dial tone and punched in a number. He could have called from the hotel but it was safer here, where the connection would be harder to trace.

Outside the booth, he saw a car drive past, spraying water from under its tires. The walnut tree in the park had lost most of its leaves, and the weather reminded him of late fall in Massachusetts. When he had left Cambridge, ten days ago, the foliage was still gold and orange, but he knew that by the time he got back, the autumn leaves would be gone, soggy heaps raked up along the curb, blown off their limbs by an early Nor'easter.

The ringing on the other end of the line was persistent and prob-
ing as a dentist's drill. He glanced at his watch and tried to calculate
the time difference, knowing Ivana would be asleep. After the sixth
or seventh ring, she finally woke up. Karan could picture her loft
apartment off Central Square. He wondered if she was alone in bed
or whether his place had been taken by one of her other lovers. For a
brief moment, he felt jealous but didn't really care.

"Hello . . ." She sounded drugged.

"It's me," he said. "Sorry."

"Jesus . . . Karan! It's two in the morning. Where are you?"

He didn't tell her, though nobody was listening. This was her
sister's old phone, a number Ivana had given him to avoid detection.
As coworkers, they weren't permitted a personal relationship, which
only made it more likely that they would end up together in bed.

Quickly, Karan told her what he wanted, spelling out the names
and repeating the dates so that she could write them down. By now
Ivana was fully awake, and he could visualize the goose-necked lamp
beside her bed and her long blonde hair pulled back in a tangled
braid. She was probably wearing one of his T-shirts, left behind as
carelessly as he treated their relationship. For both of them, it was
more a matter of convenience than commitment, though they liked
each other well enough—friends first and lovers second.

"Where are you?" she asked again, her Russian accent garbling
the words as much as the static on the phone. "You left without saying anything."

"I'll be back soon," Karan said. "I just need your help. Please."

"Okay . . . I'll check it out and email you."

"No. Don't email. I'll call you back tomorrow, a little earlier than
this."

"Okay . . . Sure." She understood the secrecy of his call, the need
to limit their exchange to the barest details.

Ivana could access the servers without raising an alarm; she had a
security clearance that allowed her to research the agency's archives.
Eventually, someone might discover what she was looking for, but

none of the information Karan needed was likely to raise a red flag. He had thought of asking Bogart, but he had no way of getting in touch. Though he knew he was putting Ivana at risk, she could always plead ignorance, an innocent favor for a colleague. Besides, the whole thing would be over soon enough, before anyone cared to investigate their indiscretions.

As he hung up the phone, Karan realized the windows of the booth had steamed up. He wiped the condensation off the glass enough to see the weather outside. Earlier, there had been lightning and thunder, but now it was silent except for the whisper of rain on concrete. Someone was standing next to the booth, smoking a cigarette. As Karan pushed open the door, he thought the man might have been listening, but he was simply taking shelter from the storm.

The phone booth was part of a small cybercafé and photocopying center. The owner also made omelets and toast for those who wanted to check their email over breakfast. Two language students were seated in front of glowing screens. Karan paid for the call and shook open his umbrella. He was glad for the rain and mist. It seemed easier not to be noticed when the weather turned bad.

Forty-Nine

Ten kilometers to the east of Mussoorie, rain was falling with the same intensity along the outer margins of the storm. A steady stream of drops ran down the rough-hewn rafters under rotting layers of thatch and fell with a hiss in the open hearth. A handful of burning twigs gave off more smoke than warmth or light. A wet smell of damp straw and manure filled the darkness of the *chaan*, where a figure sat on the floor, leaning against the wall. A hand reached over and added another stick to the fire.

The cowshed had been abandoned for the past two seasons, though it still smelled of cattle and wood smoke. A low, temporary structure with mud walls and a thatched roof, the *chaan* looked as if it had started to collapse from the minute it was built. The single pine beam sagged in the middle, and the doors were barely high enough to admit the buffaloes once stabled here. Terraced fields covered the slope above the *chaan*, but these had remained uncultivated for more than two summers. A few amaranth bushes had survived from earlier plantings, their crowns turning a rusty red with the October chill. Most of the fields were overgrown with nettles and other weeds. A pile of dung and dry leaves lay to one side of the *chaan*, composting slowly into the earth. Cucumber and pumpkin vines clambered up a section of the roof, but these had been raided and stripped by monkeys while they were still in flower.

Ordinarily, dairymen from a village in the valley would have occupied the *chaan*, but the owner of this land had abandoned his cowshed this season and the last, letting it go to ruin. The monkeys had destroyed a section of the roof, tearing the thatch in their eagerness to devour the cucumber blossoms. They had uprooted the few potato plants that survived. Mice had colonized the thatch as well as insects, beetles and ants, fleas and ticks.

Rain beat down on the surrounding forest with a steady thrumming sound, as if all of the leaves were vibrating as one. Overhead, the clouds were the color and texture of cold oatmeal. The monsoon had ended more than a month ago, and this was the first rain since then. A dirt path that led up through the fields was awash with mud. No footprints appeared on this trail. Only deer and wild boar had left their impressions in the soil. Porcupines had dug up the earth in places, but the cold rain seemed to cast a lifeless spell over the *chaan* and its fields, shadows of emptiness and decay.

Another hour and it would be dark, though inside the *chaan* it seemed as if the rain and smoke had brought an early end to the day. A pale shaft of light entered through the collapsed roof, and a red battery light glowed in the shadows.

"*Om mani padme hum!*" the voice intoned. "*Om mani padme hum!*"

A beetle crawled across the patch of light on the damp earth floor. Its legs moved slowly, like a windup toy. The brittle carapace over its wings had an iridescent sheen.

"Death is only an awakening." The words were slurred. The recording clicked and paused, as if rewinding. "*Om mani padme hum!* The bullet that kills us is the sacred jewel within the lotus, a precious nugget of lead."

Silence for a moment and the sound of uneven breathing, a cough suppressed.

"The wheel of Dharma never stops. It crushes those who stand in its way. We must do our duty. We must fight the enemies of truth and freedom. We must avenge their evil ways."

The battery light was extinguished as the recording device switched off. Seconds later, the figure arose, stooping to avoid the sloping rafters and the low doorframe. The fire had all but gone out as the boots left crude impressions in the ash, then stepped on the beetle, crushing it deliberately under their tread.

Fifty

Building a good fire is a practiced art. Afridi took pleasure in tearing and crumpling yesterday's newspaper to use as tinder, misleading headlines and pompous, ill-informed editorials that would soon be reduced to ash. On top of this he placed three pine cones, then splinters of kindling, arranged in a pyramid. After that he stacked the logs, choosing them carefully from the metal bin beside the fireplace. Two pieces were banj oak, the best wood for burning, giving off a steady flame. The other two logs were split deodar, which caught first and burned faster. It was important to prop them against each other, so they didn't smother the tinder and kindling, but ignited easily, with an even conflagration. Twenty years ago, when he'd bought Ivanhoe, one of the first things Afridi had done was to rebuild the fireplace and chimney. Originally, it had a shallow, poorly designed grate and a flue that sent smoke back into the house and carried all of the heat up the chimney. Afridi had personally supervised the masons. He would have laid the bricks himself, if he'd been able.

When the logs were properly stacked, he took out a matchbox from his pocket and paused a moment before striking. He prided himself on using only one match. Most people in Mussoorie poured kerosene over the wood, so that the fire blazed up in a sudden burst of flames. He preferred to watch it grow from the flickering orange tongue on the matchstick to the quick and restless burn of the news-

269

print and then the true point of combustion, when the pine cones caught, their resin spitting sparks on the hearthstone. After that, the chimney began to draw and the fire reached a climax, blue and saffron flames sucking oxygen into a whorl of heat and light.

Dusting off his hands and putting the matchbox back in his pocket, Afridi wheeled himself across to the bar. He had to circle around the dog, who had already claimed his spot on the carpet in front of the fire and lay there with the flames glimmering in his moist old eyes. A music system was discreetly positioned beside the bar, with four speakers at each corner of the room. Afridi had already chosen the CD—*ghazals* sung by a *Qawwali* troupe from Hyderabad. His taste in music ran from Hindustani classical to Puccini to Edith Piaf, but today he wanted something to match the sound of the rain outside, the flutter of fingers on a tabla, the wheezing notes of a harmonium, like restless wind blowing through the trees. In Farsi and Urdu, the word *ghazal* suggested the wounded cry of a gazelle, its heart pierced by a hunter's arrow.

It was already dark, and the storm had built to a crescendo with a drum roll of thunder and blanched streaks of lightning. The gutters outside the window were overflowing, and the line of flowerpots was hammered by gusts of wind that spattered raindrops against the glass. Inside, it was dry and warm, but outside the weather had grown ugly, one of those vindictive October storms that seemed almost spiteful after weeks of clear, bright weather.

The lead vocalist eased into his *alaap*, calm authority in his voice, exploring the notes without any lyrics, his throat a well-tuned instrument of the soul.

Opening the bar, Afridi took out a tumbler—Polish crystal, the perfect weight. You could feel the lead in the glass. His servant had placed the ice bucket within reach, and he chose three cubes with the tongs, then reached for the decanter and poured himself a generous peg. The whiskey he drank was blended. He found single malts overrated, most of them undrinkable. A splash of soda, and Afridi was ready to raise his glass to the fire. As he did this, the cut patterns in the crystal seemed to ignite, and the amber spirits glowed with liquid warmth.

Until now, Afridi had avoided thinking about the consequences of his decision. He knew that he should have had the American agent arrested and shipped home before the embassy or the press knew what was happening. Now, there was a danger that Karan would be exposed while working with Anna. Plenty of people within the intelligence community would have gladly used this breach of security against Afridi, allowing a foreign operative inside the HRI, breaking every rule and compromising national interests. The fact that Karan was Indian by ancestry meant that his identity would not become immediately apparent, but sooner or later, somebody was going to find out. Though he still felt a stab of anger at the Americans for interfering, he had reconciled himself to Karan's presence. Despite misgivings, Afridi was convinced the risks were worth taking. They had less than twenty-four hours. By this time tomorrow, either Sayles would be dead, or the Dalai Lama's visit would have been canceled.

He had calculated his moves deliberately. Now, there was nothing to do but wait. Like a falconer who releases his hawk, Afridi no longer had control over predator or prey. That was the ultimate challenge of the hunt, the unpredictable calculus of the game. *Blood sport.* Afridi had often reflected on that expression, considering the violent nuances of his profession. He had waited a long time for this moment. He had been inordinately patient. Another sip of whiskey eased his prickling nerves.

At that moment, the singer launched into the first verse of the *ghazal,* echoing the anguished cry of a dying gazelle. Afridi knew the etymology, its roots in Farsi, but the poetry and music seemed to erase his thoughts, taking him somewhere he had never been before, beyond the boundaries of imagining, beyond pain and loneliness. The lyrics and melody spoke of suffering and loss, but to Afridi they promised fulfillment.

ᔧ

If there was a path, it was hidden beneath the weeds, though the figure moved with surety in the semidarkness, a watery shadow that was barely visible as it passed beneath the darkening trees. A mix of oak and cedar, maple and pine covered the steep slopes, though the foliage was indistinguishable, branches entwined in the rain. Only when the lightning flashed were the distinct shapes of wet leaves apparent in the canopy overhead. Covered in a dripping poncho, the hunter climbed the slope with determination and stealth, as if following the spoor of wounded prey, tracking an injured animal to its death. The figure carried no light, and after the thunder had rolled back into darkness, it was impossible to make out a human shape within the swirling mist.

The rain had conjured up a vaporous phantom, a spirit of the storm who roamed the mountains under cover of fog and clouds. Leaving the forest, the predator climbed to the exposed nape of the ridge, descended through thickets of dwarf bamboo, and appeared once more, briefly crossing a rocky crag before merging into the jungle again.

Nobody was watching the hunter's progress or the direction in which this spirit moved. The only hint of human presence was the alarm call of a barking deer, a sharp, shrill cry, like a strangled yelp of warning. No other creatures made a sound in the storm.

The anonymous figure could easily have been a ghost, one of the *devtas* or *prets* that haunted these hills, a tormented spirit, whose shrines were hidden in forest glades and attracted the rituals and worship of those who feared its dark mischief.

Only the rough tread of heavy boots left evidence of the hunter's passage, biting into the mud and mulch. Within minutes, though, even these traces had been washed away by the steady cannonade of rain.

~

No storm appeared in the simulation. The same scenario had been displayed again and again, more than a hundred times, plotting the movements and location of the shooter, who appeared as a crouching icon with a rifle pressed to one shoulder. Karan and Anna had sent the technicians home. Since late afternoon, they had been alone. It was a waiting game. They dared not act too soon for fear of alerting the killer. As the program recalculated each option, it adjusted the images on the screen, mapping different angles of the ridge and each approach, from above, behind, and below. The forest was a pointillist's canvas, pixilated by dots of light and shade, colors that replicated the foliage and rocks, the chorten and other funerary shrines as well as the underlying contours of the ridge, the inner structure of the mountain.

As Karan studied the computer-generated cartography, he wondered if there was any chance of finding the assassin through this digitized landscape. He knew that the technology was accurate, but he also understood that what they were observing could never fully replicate the ground realities of this terrain.

Anna shifted the sniper's icon farther up the ridge, her eyes intent on every variable she could observe. Their faces were only inches apart. Karan remembered when he was a boy, how he and his friends used to focus for hours on video games, like hunchbacked gnomes manipulating their controllers as Nintendo figures jumped and jinxed through different levels of complexity, challenge, and accomplishment. Whenever a screen lit up, he still felt that same excitement he experienced as a child, playing Mario Bros. and Battletoads. Glancing across at Anna, he recalled how many hours he'd sat huddled together with silent companions trying to get a perfect score and defeat whatever villains and obstacles lay in their path.

"There are only three possibilities," Anna said, leaning back in her chair. "The saddle of the ridge, the knoll below the tree . . . or those rocks over there."

As she pointed at the screen, her arm brushed against Karan. They sat side by side, as if the restricted dimensions of the laptop had pulled them together. The simulation had been downloaded from the servers so they could carry it with them.

Karan rolled his chair back and glanced around the empty room. The bluish-white glow of halogen bulbs and the ambient colors emanating from the banks of monitors made it feel as if he was in some kind of spacecraft far away from Earth, one of those orbiting satellites that beamed these images onto their screen.

Anna turned to look at him, dazed by hours of concentration.

"Let's take a break," he said. "We've got it worked out as close as possible. Now it's just a matter of picking the most likely option."

Glancing at her phone, Anna laughed. "God . . . it's past eleven."

Karan pushed himself out of his chair.

"I need to get back to the hotel," he said.

Anna nodded as she saved the most recent scenario and shut down the program.

"We'll have to get an early start."

She was about to say something more, when Karan slid open the door at the far end of the room and a burst of lightning flashed outside, followed, two seconds later, by a crash of thunder. Beyond the verandah, rain was pouring down with gusts of wind. Inside the surveillance center they had been completely unaware of weather or time, locked into the virtual world of their computers. As they stepped out into the darkness, the reality they confronted was completely different from the pastel hues of simulated mountains and the easily manipulated positions on the ridge.

Anna pulled the door shut behind them as the rain blew in at an angle under the eaves of the metal roof. She and Karan stood there for a minute, mesmerized by the dramatic intensity of the storm. Unlike the images on the laptop screen, the lightning and thunder consumed the sky. They felt small and exposed, no longer players controlling a miniaturized scenario but tiny figures dwarfed by the enormous forces of the night. No keyboards, controllers, or commands could manipulate these elements of nature. As Karan turned toward Anna, she moved closer. Another gust of rain swept over them, and they raised their arms to protect themselves, laughing at the sudden violence of the storm. Until now, it had been just a game.

Fifty-One

By the time the predator reached the cemetery on the north side of Landour ridge, the storm was beginning to subside. Rain had turned to mist. Gauzy veils of moisture were draped from the trees and enveloped the tombstones. Between shifting layers of clouds, the moon spilled its light over the ridges, appearing and reappearing like a celestial beacon. The mist captured its illumination, diffusing the pale aura across the forested slope, seeping into crevices between rocks and roots, filtering the shadows. The dark profile of the hunter climbed the terraces marked by graves, moving at a steady, relentless pace.

Ascending to the Chukkar and scaling the parapet wall, the predator slipped off the poncho and shook it out, before folding it away in a backpack. Boots grated on the concrete surface of the road, but the figure vanished, as the moon was swallowed by clouds. Water dripped from bark on the trees, through moss-covered stones, trickling into the earth, where the moldering bones of the dead bore mute witness in the soil.

Four hundred meters on ahead stood Afridi's cottage. Ivanhoe—a heroic name chosen more than a century before. A single lamp was burning outside, surrounded by a pale nimbus of glowing moisture. In the guardhouse, a lone sentry had fallen asleep at his post. The sharp blade of a commando knife reflected the light for a moment before it slit the guard's throat.

Without making a sound, he died in his dreams.

༄

On the other side of the hill, where the moon had emerged from the clouds to cast its milky eye over checkered panes of glass, two lovers were entwined in a knot of passion, their limbs cinched together, tangling and untangling.

Less than an hour ago, they had run through the rain. Their clothes were drenched. Entering her room, Anna had found the windows wide open and the curtains billowing in the breeze. She had forgotten to secure the latch this morning. Before switching on the light, she hurried across to shut the windows. Water had pooled on the terrazzo floor, reflecting the lightning that flashed outside. When Anna pulled back the curtains, they were as wet as her clothes. Karan stepped behind her, his hand stroking the soaked fabric of her sleeve as she turned toward him. Anna's fingers brushed the damp strands of hair that fell across his forehead, while Karan leaned down to kiss her on the mouth.

They made love hurriedly at first, undressing each other with impatience and throwing their wet clothes on the floor before falling naked upon the bed. The storm muffled the sound of their pleasure, and the darkness cloaked them in furtive shadows. Only they could see or hear each other, so close together it seemed as if they'd never been apart. They needed no computers to simulate their voices or reveal their features, mapping intimate terrain. Each of them explored the other's body with an eager, ardent touch.

Everything was forgotten in those first few minutes. Nothing stood between them any more—no sense of duty, no hidden identities, no official secrets or fatal truths. Karan whispered Anna's name, though it sounded more like an incoherent sigh. Immediately, she answered him with a quick intake of her breath, hands gripping his shoulders. They moved together in a rhythm that was as natural as the wind and rain outside, wild yet gentle, full of strength though almost weightless. His hand slid down the arched contours of Anna's back and lifted her, as if they could, impossibly, draw any nearer to one another. Their breathing was synchronized, each of them inhaling the other's scent, the earthy odor of rain moistening the earth. Their nerves were twisted into a tourniquet that grew tighter the more they struggled.

In those first few moments, they had surprised each other, but once they discovered a conspiracy of shared desires, each knew exactly what the other wanted. As their passion built to a climax, murmurs became cries, moans erupted into shouts of pleasure, which even the storm could not subdue. If there had been music playing it would have reached its crescendo, a raucous cacophony of notes. *Yes. Anna.* He repeated her name. *Karan.* They remembered nothing in those heaving moments, nothing of the past, no intimation of the future. *Now!* Only the present mattered, each throbbing second erasing the ones before, and the ones beyond, as their bodies shook together with a shared orgasm. It felt as if they had exchanged, in a single instant, every sensation they had ever known, entering and receiving every impulse, knowing exactly what their lover experienced beneath the urgent friction of their skin.

Afterwards, when she had drawn the covers over them and lay against his arm, Anna asked Karan if he had guessed that this would happen.

"From the first moment I saw you in your car," he said.

"Liar!"

He laughed, then asked her, "What about you? Did you ever think that we might end up making love?"

"Of course not. I thought you were a creep."

"So much for first impressions."

"Sure," she said. "You know when I first thought of it?"

"When?"

"The other night at the ruined house," said Anna. "When I had my pistol pointed at your heart. I almost pulled the trigger."

"That's very romantic," he said. "But I don't believe you."

She pressed her finger to his chest.

"Right here. I was going to put a bullet between your ribs."

"And I was aiming for this spot," he said, touching her forehead lightly.

"Would you have shot me?"

He fell silent for a moment.

"Maybe."

"Did you really think we'd ever end up in bed?"

He frowned at her.

"Remember," Karan said. "No personal questions."

Within a few minutes they began to make love again, but this time it was slower, unhurried, as eager as before, yet driven by languor instead of lust. The rain had grown calm outside and the moon and mist peered into the darkened room through warped panes of wet glass. They talked to each other as their bodies responded to unspoken inquiries, fingers curling into question marks, the subtle punctuation of a tongue, a kiss where none had gone till now. Neither of them spoke about tomorrow, as if those events, inevitable and yet unknown, could wait a few hours more. The killer and his target remained distant and detached from the peaceful expectations of the present. Anna touched Karan's chest again, but this time with her lips, then pressed her ear against his breast, to hear the pounding heartbeat caged within his ribs.

෴

Alone in bed, Afridi put aside the novel he had been trying to read before switching off the bedside lamp. Sleep remained impossible. He lay awake in the darkness, his eyes barely able to trace the converging lines of walls and ceiling. A faint sheen of moonlight, filtered by clouds and mist, entered through a crease between the curtains. Inside the cottage, the only illumination came from the open doorway to the living room, where the faint electric glimmer of the music system smoldered like a dying cinder.

Having eaten a simple dinner by candlelight after the electricity went off during the storm, Afridi had locked the house when his servant left. He had washed up in the bathroom, then come to bed, where bars were fixed to the walls, allowing him to get in and out of his wheelchair without assistance. This was a regular routine that he performed each night, an act of independence, self-reliance, and determination.

When the electricity came back on, he tried to watch the news on television, but his mind was distracted. There had been another bombing in Afghanistan and demonstrations in Cairo, economic crises in Europe and a hostage standoff in Lagos. The world beyond Mussoorie seemed a dangerous, unsettled place. He switched channels, picking up fragments of the news from different reports but barely listening to the coverage. His mind remained focused on tomorrow's events. Earlier in the day, he had spoken with Anna and Karan, who briefed him on their strategy. Sayles was likely to position himself on a ridge above the monastery. If all went well, the two agents would take him by surprise. When Afridi made a caustic remark about how they'd let him get away from them before, Anna assured him that this time they were prepared to take him down. Despite their confidence, the potential for miscalculation was always there. Afridi had arranged to monitor the Dalai Lama's visit on the screens at HRI. He would be watching every move they made. If anything seemed to be amiss, he would phone the Tibetans and call off the ceremony.

Lying in the dark, his mind raced through the various possibilities for disaster. Weather reports predicted that the storm system was moving quickly to the west. It would pass over the Dzogchen Monastery tomorrow morning, with bright skies in the afternoon. His technicians had assured him that they would have clear satellite images, no cloud cover in the region. Without alerting the police, he had received a full report on security arrangements for the Dalai Lama's visit, a minute-by-minute schedule for the ceremony. Neither CID nor the local police seemed to have sensed a threat. All of the newspaper reports and TV stories about the shootings in Mussoorie had focused on suspected Kashmiri terrorists or Maoist insurgents. Afridi himself had contributed to these theories through his media contacts. He had meticulously laid the trap for Sayles but wondered if there was anything he had overlooked, a careless detail that might make the whole operation fall apart, an unpredictable element that could jeopardize success.

Forty years was a long time to wait for his revenge, but Afridi felt it would be worth it in the end, if he could finally look Sayles in the eye and lock him up for the rest of his life. That was the only justice and satisfaction he craved. Afridi had instructed Anna and Karan to take Sayles alive, if possible, though they were authorized to use whatever force was required. If he refused to surrender or fired at them, they could shoot to kill.

The silence of the night was broken by the faintest sound of water dripping onto the roof. Afridi shifted his head on the pillow and used his hands to adjust the position of his crippled legs. There was no feeling in them, only the withered weight of atrophied flesh and bone. The nerves were dead and useless, one foot amputated at the ankle because of frostbite, the other minus all its toes. Occasionally, he felt sensations, but these were only muscle memories, the vague stirrings of phantom limbs. At times like this, he almost wished there was some lingering pain to prove his legs were there, instead of the limp absence of feeling and the clumsy weight, as if his pajamas were filled with sticks of firewood dangling from his waist.

Just then, he heard the dog begin to growl from the living room, a low rumble followed by a hoarse bark. For a moment, he thought the old Bhotia was chasing monkeys in his dreams, but then he heard him growl again. Quietly, Afridi removed the covers from his legs and slid across the bed. He stopped and listened, but there was no sound. His hands reached up to grab the bars above him. With agile strength, he hoisted himself into the wheelchair, which was positioned by his bed. Moving as quickly as possible but in silence, he fastened the straps that held his legs in place, then released the brake. As he rolled himself backward in the dark, one of the wheels scraped against a corner of the bed. He waited, holding his breath, but even the dog had fallen silent. It could have been a false alarm, but Afridi reached down to unsnap the cover on the holster strapped to the chair, running his fingers over the textured pistol grip. He was armed with a Smith & Wesson 40VE, more than enough to stop a predator in its tracks.

Wheeling himself forward, he slid open the door between his bedroom and the gym. Every sound seemed to betray his movements. When he listened for other noises, however, there was nothing. All of his five senses were alert, but it was his sixth sense that he trusted most of all, an innate feeling of being stalked, the twitch of fear that crept along his neck.

The gym lay in darkness. Afridi had to feel his way past the climbing wall, his hands brushing the harness hanging from a rope, the first few handholds that he recognized by touch. He rolled himself past a rack of dumbbells and behind a weight machine, customized for his use. Working the wheelchair into position, he turned so that he was facing the open doorway into his bedroom, shielded partially by the steel frame of the exercise machine.

Again, the dog began to bark. Afridi took the pistol out of its holster and released the safety catch. The decisive click was answered by a similar sound of metal scraping against metal.

A shadow had fallen across the flowerpots near the cottage door, where the bulb from the outside lamp cast a semicircle of yellow light. As the dog began barking again, a pair of hands picked the lock, working swiftly in the darkness. It took only seconds for the tumblers to fall in place, but the door was secured by a barrel bolt at the top. An elbow shattered the glass. Silence no longer mattered.

As the front door opened, the old dog charged at the intruder. But before he could carry through with his attack, there was the dull thud of a pistol being fired. Its silencer reduced the report, but it was loud enough for Afridi to hear the gunshot in the other room. No sound came from the dog as muddy boots stepped over his lifeless form, dripping water on the floor.

Afridi held one hand on the wheel of his chair. In the other, his pistol was ready. Silence followed for several minutes. A shadow moved, but it was much too quick for Afridi to risk a shot and give away his position. He would have a clearer line of fire as the intruder came out of the hallway, unless he stayed low and used the bed for cover. Suddenly, the darkness seemed more complete than ever before. Afridi's eyes strained to spot any trace of movement, calculating invisible shapes in the room. He heard the approaching tread of footsteps but couldn't locate the sound precisely in the darkness.

The intruder crept forward, flat against the wall and brushing one of the framed pictures that hung near the bedroom door. With a crash, it fell to the ground. Immediately, Afridi fired at the sound of shattering glass. His pistol had no silencer and the explosion boomed within the cottage walls. There was a pause, after which two bullets erupted from the intruder's gun. The muffled sound was like someone punching a balloon. One of the slugs ricocheted off the weight machine with a ringing whine. Afridi aimed toward the muzzle flash and fired again, his wrist jerking with the recoil. The mirror on his dressing table shattered. An instant later, both weapons were fired again, followed by a silence so complete and final it seemed to echo the infinite emptiness of eternity.

Fifty-Two

Daylight pried its way between the ridges. At first, the dull patina of a false dawn seemed to outline the mountains without erasing the darkness. Half an hour later the black sky began to dissipate into shades of charcoal, ash, and tarnished silver. Finally, a russet glow emerged above the farthest peaks while the nearer slopes still showed no definition. Birdsongs began long before the sun came up, pheasant calling on grass-covered slopes, green pigeons and hill partridges, scimitar babblers and laughing thrushes all joining in a rousing chorus.

The storm was over.

Karan opened his eyes when the first glint of sunlight touched the window panes. For a second or two he couldn't remember where he was until Anna moved beside him. He closed his eyes again and lay there for a minute, replaying their lovemaking in his mind, like a dream he didn't want to forget.

She nudged him, and he turned to look at her.

"Come on," said Anna. "You better get up. If Afridi finds me in bed with an American, we'll both go to jail for treason."

Karan rolled toward her and put his hand on her hip. Anna pulled back and shook her head.

"Save it for later," she said. "Not now."

As the sheet fell away from Karan's shoulder, she noticed the scar and reached over to touch it with her finger.

"What's this?"

Karan sat up and faced the window for a moment, before picking up his jeans.

"A memento from Afghanistan," he said, then glanced at her with a cynical smile. "Friendly fire."

Anna was about to ask him for an explanation when she heard him curse.

"Goddamn it!"

"What's wrong?"

"The only thing worse than getting into wet jeans is putting on wet boxers, and then wet jeans."

Anna laughed. "I'd loan you some clothes, but they wouldn't fit."

Karan struggled to dress himself and tie his shoes, shivering and swearing. He took his Glock from the inside pocket of his jacket and checked to see that it was dry. Anna watched him with amusement, but after he kissed her she could see the serious look in his eyes.

"I'll be back in an hour," he said. "We need to reach the monastery before noon."

"Sure. There's plenty of time," Anna said, picking up her watch. She lifted herself out of bed and headed toward the bathroom as Karan shut the front door behind him.

The air outside was clear after the rain. Leaves and twigs had fallen from the trees. Karan walked quickly toward the gate, past Anna's car, which was shrouded under a waterproof cover. The gardens in front of the institute had been battered by the rain, though now the air was perfectly still. Far off, to the north, the snow peaks had a fresh coating of white. As he approached the gate, Karan could hear a phone begin to ring. One of the security guards picked it up. Reaching the gate, Karan saw the sudden look of alarm in the sentry's eyes. Seconds later, there was a shout of panic and the sound of someone running.

⌒

Anna kept her foot on the accelerator as she maneuvered around the corners of the Chukkar. Karan watched the language school and the gate of the cemetery fly past. By the time Anna hit the brakes, he was already opening his door. The two of them ran to the guardhouse at the foot of the ramp. A rivulet of blood spilled into the gutter. The sentry lay slumped against the door, his neck turned to one side, a yawning wound across his throat.

Without stopping, they reached the main entrance to the cottage, which was partly open. The door scraped against shattered glass, as Karan pushed it inward. The lights were off, but Anna could see the furred shape of the dog lying beside a chair. He looked as if he were asleep, except for the crooked angle of his paws and the stillness of his form.

Both of them had their weapons ready. Karan covered Anna as she moved down the hallway toward Afridi's bedroom. A picture frame lay on the floor, its glass broken. The sheets on the bed were rumpled, as if someone had just risen from sleep. Anna held her pistol steady as Karan moved past her into the room. The shattered mirror on the dressing table reflected shards of light coming through a window where the curtains had fallen down. A novel lay on the bedside table, a bookmark tucked between its pages. Afridi's clothes were neatly folded at the foot of the bed, where he had laid them out with care the night before. Through the sliding doorway into the gym, Anna caught sight of dumbbells strewn across the floor beside the climbing wall.

The bathroom door was closed. Karan covered Anna as she pushed it open, but there was no one inside, except their own reflections in the mirror above the sink.

As Karan followed Anna to the other side of the bedroom they could see no sign of Afridi or his attacker, despite the obvious evidence of a struggle. The doors into the gym hung open and as they stepped inside, Karan glanced up at the climbing wall, as if he expected to find someone hanging from the rope and harness overhead.

"Here," said Anna, softly.

Just inside the gym, near the toppled rack of dumbbells, lay a body, hunched into a fetal crouch. The first thing Karan noticed was the boots, their soles caked with mud. Then his eyes moved over the camouflage trousers and jacket. Three dark ribbons of blood spilled out from beneath one arm, unraveling across the floor. One hand lay open, its upturned palm as pale as wax, and beside it a pistol with a silencer.

Anna could see that the outer door of the gym was open, leading to the terrace and the garden, but there was nobody in sight. She kneeled down quickly and rolled the body over, startled to see it was a woman with ginger blonde hair, hidden partly beneath a camouflaged hood. Her gray-blue eyes stared up at the ceiling and her colorless lips were open. She had been dead for several hours.

ᴄᴏ

The wheelchair stood beside a marble birdbath, next to a bed of orange and yellow nasturtiums creeping up a wire-mesh fence. The grass was still wet from the storm. Afridi sat with his back to the house, shoulders slumped but his head raised, as if staring out at the mountains, which were barely visible through the trees. When Anna and Karan rushed across the lawn, he turned to look at them with an expression of exhaustion and sadness. He was still wearing his nightclothes and holding his pistol in one hand, though it was pointed at the ground.

Afridi looked older, almost defeated.

"I thought it was Sayles," he said, looking up at Anna.

"Are you hurt?" Karan asked.

"No." Afridi shook his head, turning toward the house.

"Who is she?" Anna asked, following his gaze.

"Her name is Noya Feldman," Afridi said. "Sayles's daughter."

Anna looked at Karan, confused.

"It's true," he said. "I've checked our files on Sayles."

"Her mother was Isabella Feldman, now deceased." Afridi spoke softly, almost a whisper. "She was a case officer for the Mossad. During the seventies, a few years after Rataban, Sayles resurfaced but kept his identity hidden. He worked freelance for the Israelis and

286

the South Africans, fighting Communists in Angola, Palestinians on the West Bank, Hezbollah in Lebanon. In 1981, when Sayles was in Israel, he and Isabella had a brief affair and she got pregnant. After that, they never saw each other again, because Sayles went back to Tibet. He didn't know he had fathered a child."

Slowly, deliberately, Afridi put his pistol back in the holster, closing it with a decisive snap.

"It was only later that Noya contacted him," Afridi continued, "after her mother's death. It must have been difficult to find him . . . and even more difficult to convince Sayles that she was his daughter, though Noya inherited his survival skills, as well as his perseverance. She was trained as a commando in the Israeli Army."

"How do you know all this?" said Anna.

"Through contacts in Tel Aviv," said Afridi. "None of this was particularly sensitive information and the Israelis were willing to share it with us, just as they shared it with the CIA."

He gestured toward Karan and then continued.

"After leaving the army, Noya became interested in the Tibetan cause . . . took part in protests, was arrested several times for demonstrating at the Chinese embassy in Israel. Eventually, she got involved with radical elements, members of the Norbulingka Brigade. They were the ones who probably helped Noya find her father."

"Was she the shooter?" Anna asked. "Did she kill Fallows and Jigme?"

"No," said Afridi. "She helped Sayles and gave him information, served as his eyes and ears, supplied him with food and cash while he was hiding, but he's the one who pulled the trigger."

"It's complete madness. What made her do it?" Anna's voice was full of disbelief.

"Sayles couldn't do it by himself," said Karan. "He needed her. . . . He may have been a paranoid, delusional man, but he was her father. . . . She believed in him, and he used her without any hesitation."

"But last night?" Anna asked. "Why didn't Sayles come here, himself?"

Afridi answered her. "Because he's already left Mussoorie. By now, Sayles must be at the Dzogchen Monastery, preparing for his final victim."

Fifty-Three

Butter lamps burned with greasy flames, black smoke oiling its way toward the ceiling of the temple. The placid features of the Future Buddha, Maitreya, observed the preparations with perpetual detachment. The goddess Tara, who sat beside him in the glass-fronted shrine, seemed equally removed from the present, though the amber glow emanating from the lamps set her gilded features and naked breasts alight. Dozens of images filled the temple like a celestial conclave—Bodhisattvas of all ranks and description, female consorts, both demure and dangerous, fierce guardians and supernatural creatures, sylphlike nymphs, and brooding saints. But in the midst of all these figures, myths, and symbols, the face that stood out most clearly was a black-and-white photograph in a dark, unornamented frame.

Surrounded by the panoply and pomp of the temple, the photograph conveyed an austere dignity, as if the Dalai Lama's exile had revoked the exotic mysteries and marvels of Tibetan heritage to reveal a singular man, without a country, who understood and taught the most basic, elemental truths. Even the white scarf, draped over the picture frame, had a bleached purity that suggested a need to slough off the ephemeral decorations and gaudy colors of illusion, as well as the trappings of identity and selfhood, to attain the ultimate transcendence of nirvana.

Before entering the main sanctuary of the temple, Renzin had gone to see the sand mandala, which was now complete. He remembered how clearly it had appeared in his mind, after he had scattered his father's ashes. Having driven all the way from Mussoorie, he was exhausted, but his thoughts were focused. Four monks were seated in meditation on opposite sides of the mandala. Once the ceremonies were finished, the colored grains of sand would be swept up and collected in an urn, just like the ashes of the dead, to be scattered on the wind or poured into the swift-moving current of a stream, borne away into nothingness. Renzin understood the meaning of these rituals, though he found the fatalism disturbing, believing there should be more to life and death than hollow vessels filled with ash or sand.

He lit a butter lamp in front of the Maitreya Buddha and placed it amid the shimmering multitude of flames that rustled like fiery petals. Renzin stood alone, though dozens of others were inside the temple, monks engaged in final preparations for the ceremonies, arranging and rearranging the throne-like chair, selecting scriptures from the library shelves, polishing the accoutrements of worship, gilded thunderbolts and yak-tail whisks with silver handles. Ignoring all of this, Renzin lowered himself to the floor, folding his knees beneath him and extending his body forward so that his arms were outstretched, flat against the ground, in an attitude of reverence and abnegation. His prayer was silent, his eyes closed, his forehead pressed to the polished floor.

Fifty-Four

The helicopter flew parallel to the snow peaks, heading west across the Yamuna river, over Chakrata, and into the Rohru valley. There was only enough room in the cramped cabin for the pilot and two passengers. Strapped into the jump seat at the back, Anna could see the storm advancing ahead of them, a dark tide of clouds that swallowed up the ridges beyond. The weather reports indicated that most of the rain would have blown past Dzogchen Monastery by the time they got there, though it looked as if they were about to fly straight into the eye of the storm. The chopper rocked and swayed on the air currents, tossed about like a bottle thrown into the sea. Several times, they dropped suddenly, a sickening emptiness beneath their seats, as if they were going to crash into the ridges below.

Though he had warned them of a rough flight, the pilot confidently maneuvered the helicopter through the wake of the storm, as if it were a speedboat riding the waves. Several times, Karan looked back and grinned at Anna, then rolled his eyes. Fortunately, the flight was less than fifty minutes, and as they approached the monastery, Anna caught sight of the yellow rooftops silhouetted against the bruised shadows of the sky. The area was similar to Mussoorie, about the same altitude, with dense forests covering precipitous slopes. For a moment, the sun broke through the edge of the clouds and a rainbow arched over the temple complex. To the north stood the snow peaks bordering Tibet, stark white pinnacles rising out of a roiling mass of thunderheads.

As the pilot circled the gompa in his final approach to the helipad, both Karan and Anna surveyed the contours below, which they had studied on the computer simulation. For a few minutes, they forgot about the turbulence that shook the chopper as they got their first view of familiar terrain. While they recognized all of the features, it looked much more rugged and unpredictable than the images they had observed on the screens at HRI.

A light sprinkling of rain speckled the glass cabin of the helicopter as the pilot brought them in to land, skimming treetops and fences, then hovering for a few seconds before descending abruptly to the ground. The wind from the rotor blades rippled pools of rainwater, which had collected on the tarmac. When they finally touched the ground, it was a relief to feel the earth beneath their feet as they stepped out onto the helipad. Afridi had arranged for them to be met by one of the ITBP officers, who led them across to the gate of the complex where a jeep was waiting. The officer handed Anna the keys and within minutes, they were on their way.

While he was relieved to be out of the helicopter and driving along a well-paved road, Karan knew that far greater dangers lay ahead. Approaching the monastery from the west, they came to a makeshift checkpoint, manned by two policemen. The dented barrels and a temporary sign, with the word STOP painted in uneven letters on a rusting piece of tin, hardly seemed a deterrent for even the most incompetent assailant.

As Anna slowed down to weave between the barrels, the constables waved her past with a casual gesture of their hands. Both of them were lounging on the parapet wall, smoking bidis and leaning on their rifles, old .303s, a weapon that had first seen service in World War I almost a century ago. Afridi had told them that security would be lax, but Karan eyed the policemen with dismay. No effort had been made to secure the route of the motorcade, and there were at least a dozen points where the shooter could easily position himself, close enough to fire into a passing vehicle.

After another two bends in the road, they came to the outer gate of the monastery, which was open and unguarded except by a dozen monks who were putting the final touches on a floral arch. Anna steered the jeep underneath and headed up the winding driveway, toward the inner gate. Here were a couple more policemen in disheveled khaki uniforms, rifles dangling from their shoulders. None of them paid any attention to the jeep as it pulled up in the parking area, opposite the main courtyard of the temple. Several vehicles stood nearby, a couple of taxis, two jeeps, and a police van that leaned to one side on broken springs. The battered vehicle looked as if someone would have to push it to get it started.

Anna had a copy of the program in her hand, which Afridi had given her, listing the schedule of events.

"The motorcade will stop here," she said, turning her attention to the steep ridge above the monastery and shading her eyes. "It's an awkward angle from the upper position above that pine tree."

"It looks closer, doesn't it?" said Karan. "Less than four hundred meters."

"Hard to say. I'm sure the maps are accurate." Anna studied the schedule. "They'll stop for about five minutes here, as His Holiness is received by the Rimpoche and his monks. Then he and the others will cross the courtyard to the temple."

"I think Sayles will definitely take up his position behind those rocks, near the ruined chorten," Karan said. "The sun will be over there, going down behind that ridge."

Without the digital simplicity of computer-generated graphics, the landscape looked much less predictable. Each tree provided cover for a sniper, every rock and contour of the ridge could shield the killer. There was no defensible perimeter to the monastery, which had buildings constructed at different levels and nothing more than a sagging barbed wire fence to keep stray cattle off the grounds.

"For all we know, the shooter could be inside any one of these buildings," Karan said, pointing to the lines of windows, where monks were housed.

"Not likely," said Anna. "Sayles isn't going to take that chance."

"You never know. He's capable of anything."

"Come on," said Anna, heading up the steps to the courtyard. A couple of young boys were playing cricket, but an older lama shooed them off as Karan and Anna followed the route of the entourage. Within the courtyard, the sightlines became more restricted and only sections of the ridge above were visible. The most likely location would be when the target stepped out of his vehicle near the gate. The only other place that afforded a clear line of fire was the memorial to the martyrs of Paryang. According to the schedule, His Holiness would stop here for several minutes to pay his respects before entering the temple. Later, he would return to conduct official prayers and ceremonies. For the first time, Anna began to doubt the simulation, wondering if maybe this might be the intended site for the assassination. Someone like Sayles would appreciate the symbolism of killing a man of peace at a shrine dedicated to warriors who had sacrificed their lives for his cause.

A group of men were hurriedly spreading carpets on the ground, and a small stage had been erected in front of the memorial. The storm had delayed preparations and they were now rushing to get ready for the Dalai Lama's arrival.

Anna looked at Karan, who was scanning the slope of the ridge, as if trying to spot a figure moving through the trees, the glint of sunlight off a rifle scope. Two hours remained until the motorcade was expected. After the attack on Afridi, Anna's first instinct had been to alert the police and cancel the ceremony. But Afridi had insisted that they continue with their plan. Stopping now only meant that Sayles would wait until he got another chance, when nobody could predict his presence or his actions.

"Do you think he might take his shot right here?" Anna asked.

Karan's eyes followed the invisible geometry that linked separate points on the ridge with the memorial. As he did this, the men who were preparing the stage unfurled an orange and yellow canopy and began to position bamboo poles.

"All of this will be covered," he said. "They'll have a *shamiana* on top. You won't be able to see anything from above."

There were many things that the computer simulation could never predict.

A few minutes later, they entered the temple where His Holiness would conduct the first sequence of prayers. From here they passed into an adjacent room, where a group of monks was seated on the floor around the sand mandala. The room was smaller than the other chambers of the temple, with narrow windows at shoulder height. As the light entered this space, it seemed to fall directly on the colored patterns of the mandala, as if the sun's rays were passing through a prism and casting a rainbow on the ground.

Karan and Anna circled clockwise around the room, between the monks and the painted walls. The abstract designs of the mandala created a complex symmetry that folded in upon itself while opening outward in concentric layers, like the circles formed by a pebble tossed into a reflecting pool. The mandala had a center and an outermost ring of sand, but it appeared infinite, with no single point of origin or culmination. As Karan stepped slowly forward, he felt as if he had entered this hypnotic maze, searching for someone who kept eluding him within the spiral walls of time. The pursuit went on forever. Nearing the door through which they had entered, Anna took his hand in hers as they completed the circumambulation. She didn't need to remind him that they had several deaths to avenge and yet another to avert.

Fifty-Five

The plan was simple. Instead of climbing uphill from the monastery toward the shooter's position, they would come down the ridge from above and take Sayles by surprise, before he was able to fire a shot. Everything had been worked out in detail. They had identified an old forest road that circled above the monastery. From there, several trails descended to the rocky outcropping and ruined chorten, four hundred meters above the gate. On the satellite maps, everything appeared to be clear and logical, but now that they were ready to put their plan into action, both Karan and Anna began to have doubts. There was no room for miscalculation. Though the two of them had examined the terrain for several days, memorizing every feature on the slope, they knew the sniper must have explored the ridge himself and studied every option on the ground. One of the main reasons they had used the simulation was to avoid being seen and alerting Sayles, but this was now a disadvantage, for they were setting foot on the hill for the first time and trusting a computer simulation to guide them down the ridge.

As Anna drove past the checkpoint once again, heading up the road, the policemen didn't even bother to wave them through. There was now more traffic on this route, vehicles arriving for the ceremony. They passed several buses full of Tibetan monks on their way to the monastery. Some of them waved and called out as the jeep raced by.

Two kilometers farther on, the motor road looped back across the ridge. On their way down from the helipad, Anna had already spotted the forest road, where it passed through a stand of pines. She swung the jeep up a sharp turn, wheels skidding as they left the paved surface of the main road before gaining traction on the loose gravel. No signs were posted, but they knew that the unpaved road led around the ridge to the south side of the mountain where there was a Forest Department nursery and plantation.

Neither of them had spoken since they'd left the monastery, each playing out potential scenarios in their minds. It was all a gamble, Anna thought. They still didn't know for sure if Sayles existed, though everything that had occurred so far confirmed his presence. Still, there was no proof. Karan was more anxious about the endgame, whether they would actually be able to ambush the shooter before he carried out his assassination. Their plan depended on an element of surprise, having plotted the shooter's moves without his knowledge. He wondered how Sayles would react when they confronted him. More than likely, they would have to take him down. He wouldn't surrender without a fight.

"Maybe we should just pull the plug and warn them," Anna said, as she shifted gears to take a corner. The open forest of pine was now behind them, and they had entered a thicker growth of oak and rhododendron, branches reaching over the forest track and casting more shadows than there was light.

"Sayles is here," said Karan with conviction, his eyes fixed on the dense foliage. "Close by. I know it."

He glanced at his watch. They had an hour to go before the motorcade arrived. Anna checked her mobile phone to make sure there was a signal. She had arranged to call Afridi as soon as they were in position. In case anything went wrong, Anna also had a number for the Dalai Lama's chief of staff, as well as the senior superintendant of police who was responsible for security at the venue.

"If we don't find him in half an hour, I'll call it off," she said.

Karan didn't reply as they made their way slowly up the road. The rutted track was narrower now, and rocks had fallen from above so that Anna had to navigate carefully. At most, there was another kilometer before they reached a point directly above the monastery. They recognized each twist and turn of the forest road, which was mapped out in their minds. But as they came around a tight corner, Anna was forced to brake abruptly. A section of the road had washed away, after the storm the night before. She edged the jeep forward cautiously and was able to squeeze past, tires clinging to the crumbling margin of the road.

Accelerating, she took the next corner and headed down a steep incline. Less than a hundred meters on ahead, however, lay another obstacle that the simulation had not predicted. A tall deodar tree had fallen across the road, uprooted by the storm and lying at an angle from the slope above. As soon as Anna stopped, Karan got out and shook his head. There was no possibility of the jeep passing underneath the toppled tree. Its branches blocked the road completely.

"Let's go," Anna said, jumping out of the vehicle, her pistol ready in one hand. "It's only another five hundred meters from here, before the trail drops down the ridge."

"Maybe Afridi was right, in the first place," said Karan. "There's too much at stake."

"Afridi approved this plan," said Anna, moving past him.

"What if we're wrong?" Karan said, stooping under the fallen tree to follow her. "Sayles could be anywhere."

"Shit!" Anna swore as she looked at her phone. "I've lost the signal."

Hesitating for a second, she waved her pistol impatiently.

The two of them began to jog along the road, which leveled out as it passed a clearing where two cows were grazing on the slope above. The bells around their necks made a gentle, plaintive sound. Nobody seemed to be tending them. Karan kept his eyes on the unpaved road, trying to see if there were any tracks, but the rough surface was mostly gravel and shale.

As they rounded the next bend, both of them broke stride immediately, coming to a sudden halt. Parked in front of them, twenty meters on ahead, was the Royal Enfield motorcycle. It was leaning on its side stand. The shooter had made no effort to conceal the bike. As they reached it, they could see their warped reflections in the headlamp. The motorcycle looked as if it had been parked out in the rain, and the wheels were coated with mud. Oil was leaking from the gaskets and the old bike was battered and abused, though sinister, as well, confirming that all of their suspicions were real. Sayles could only be nearby.

Just then, they heard the sudden, thumping sound of an engine. Karan took a moment to recognize the grating roar of a helicopter overhead as it came in sight, flying well above the trees. As Anna looked up, she saw the Dalai Lama's chopper circling the monastery, then turning back toward the helipad at the top of the hill.

Karan checked his watch. "Fifteen minutes early!"

უა

Seen from above, the mountains looked less steep, flattened out by the perspective of a satellite camera. The helicopter slipped over the green folds of the ridges, its rotors whirling silently as it glided over a rumpled expanse of foliage.

Afridi checked his watch, then gestured to the technician, signaling for him to pull back so they had a complete image of the Dzogchen Gompa and the ridge above. *A bird's-eye view,* he thought to himself, like a falcon hovering above its prey. He could see the floral arch at the outer entrance to the monastery and the crowd of monks waiting farther on, in front of the temple complex. Leaning back in his wheelchair, his eyes traced the curving line of the forest road, threading its way through a canopy of trees. Beneath a webbing of branches, he could just make out where Anna and Karan had left the jeep. Seconds later, he spotted them standing a short distance on ahead, two figures seen from above, so that they looked like insects crawling between the trees. Impatiently, Afridi picked up his phone and rang Anna's number. She was supposed to have called. After a moment or two, the message came through telling him that she was "out of coverage area."

The silence was unnerving, to see everything in detail but not to hear a sound.

"Go down the ridge, to the shooter's position," Afridi said, his voice calm, though his fingers were drumming on the padded armrest of his chair.

It took several seconds for the image to reconfigure, zooming in and panning down the slope, until they could see the rocky outcropping and the chorten. Nothing moved, except for a string of faded prayer flags waving in the breeze. There was no sign of Sayles, though Afridi knew he must be there, camouflaged within the trees and rocks, hidden somewhere within the myriad pixels on the screen.

～

Anna and Karan scrambled down a trail that branched off the forest road. They knew exactly where it led and understood that the shooter would be waiting somewhere below. More than likely, he was already in position and must have watched the helicopter pass above the ridge, while the crowd of monks waved from below.

Moving as quietly as they could, Anna and Karan negotiated the slope. At places they could see where the shooter's boots had left skid marks in the mud and leaves. Because of the recent rain, they were able to move silently, for the leaf litter on the ground was damp and didn't rustle underfoot. Time was running out, but they wanted to be sure that Sayles was unaware of their approach, so they could take him by surprise. Most of their doubts had been swept away, but there were still too many things that could go wrong.

As they came to a fork in the trail, Anna motioned for Karan to go to the right, while she took the other route on the left. They knew that the paths converged again on the ridge, four hundred meters lower down, near the ruined chorten just above the rocks. If they approached from either side, it would block any chance of escape. The monastery was still not visible because of the angle of the ridge and the trees. While Anna descended cautiously, she caught glimpses of the motor road. Another ten minutes, and the Dalai Lama would reach the gate. It wasn't too late to warn him off, but there was still no signal on her phone.

Karan could see the yellow roofs of the monastery below as he slid down a steep section of the path, his Glock ready to fire with the safety off. The sun was just beginning to go down behind the mountains to the west, and the burnished colors of late afternoon were deceptively calm. A few clouds covered the snow peaks to the north, but the rest of the sky was clear. The storm had passed out of sight to the west. Karan could hear voices coming from the monastery, excited cheers and laughter, as the monks gathered to receive their spiritual leader. On all sides, the forest seemed peaceful, though eerily silent, as if the birds had sensed danger lurking within.

All of the elements of their strategy were falling in place, almost exactly as they had planned and predicted. It seemed as if their movements had been choreographed by computers, blocking out the action on a virtual stage and then projecting it into reality. Anna crept forward, keeping low so as not to be seen, as she came around the shoulder of the ridge. She kneeled and listened, then crawled ahead until she could see the crumbling chorten and the gate of the monastery below, swarming with monks holding white scarves. There must have been three hundred people, maybe more, a boisterous, festive crowd.

Seconds later, Karan saw the flashing lights of the motorcade as the pilot cars came down the switchbacks on the opposite ridge. He calculated another three minutes at most, before they reached the monastery gate. Slipping forward, he had no choice but to cross an open clearing. As he reached the trees on the other side, he crouched down to study what lay ahead. The path had disappeared, and all he could see was a tangle of underbrush and ferns. Beyond this lay the stand of pines and the rocks below, where Sayles was likely to be hiding. Realizing he had no other option, he pushed his way through the thorny scrub.

From her position, Anna heard the sounds that Karan made and spotted a sudden movement amongst the rocks below. The shooter was there, exactly at the spot where they had placed him, camouflaged within the bushes and boulders. Breaking cover, Karan emerged from the edge of the forest and ducked behind one of the pines, its branches draped with prayer flags. Before Anna could warn him, there was a shot and the bullet smashed through the soft bark of the pine, just above his head.

At the same moment, the pilot vehicles of the motorcade pulled up in front of the gate. Instantly, the camouflaged shooter turned back toward the target, aligning his scope as doors began to open. Security guards had taken up position, but the crowd pressed in from all sides, eager to catch a first glimpse of the Dalai Lama. Anna raised herself, releasing the safety catch on her pistol. The shooter was hardly thirty feet away but obscured from view. With the arrival of the motorcade, nobody at the monastery seemed to have heard the gunshot. As she stepped forward, Anna's foot brushed against a pine cone that went rolling down the slope, bouncing over the rocks. By this time, Karan was also on his feet and both of them stepped out from cover, handguns aimed at the figure crouched among the rocks.

"Put down your weapon. Now!" Anna yelled.

The shooter spun around. As he did, the hood on his jacket fell back, revealing a shock of white hair and bearded face, set in an expression of defiance and hostility. The killer's eyes showed no sign of fear as he swung his rifle 180 degrees to point at Karan, the barrel level with his chest.

"Hayden Sayles. We know who you are!" Karan shouted.

Anna's pistol remained fixed on the sniper. Below them, the crowd had fallen silent, as bodyguards stepped forward to shield the figure emerging from the car. Out of the corner of her eye, Anna could see an elderly man step out, wearing maroon and ochre robes. He raised one hand in greeting. She could see Sayles hesitate, knowing his only chance was about to pass.

Karan lowered his voice. "I'm with the CIA. If you surrender, I can guarantee your safety."

Anna could see no change of expression on Sayles's face. He looked almost exactly as they had pictured him, though his hair was longer and disheveled. He was wearing the same kind of camouflage jacket and trousers that Noya had worn, and his rifle was wrapped in shredded canvas to hide its outline.

Without moving his weapon, Sayles glanced back at the gate of the monastery. His target had disappeared within the milling crowd, dozens of monks wearing the same color robes, a swarm of maroon and yellow fabric, their heads all shaved. From this distance, it was impossible to tell them apart.

"Your daughter's dead," Karan said. "Afridi killed her."

Sayles looked back at him, but with no remorse in his eyes.

"It's over," Anna said. "Put down the rifle."

For several seconds the three of them remained motionless, as if waiting for someone to fire first.

"Give it up, Sayles!" Karan said. "We'll get you out of here."

"Fuck you!" Sayles spoke. "Nobody's going nowhere."

Anna recognized the voice immediately, the American accent laced with bile and phlegm. His aging features were familiar, framed by a white, whiskery beard. The eyes were unmistakable, cruel and full of loathing, exactly the same face that appeared on the laptop screen.

At that moment, Anna saw Karan begin to move, taking a step forward. Her finger tightened on the trigger, but before she could fire, a single shot rang out. She expected Karan to fall, but he remained on his feet. After two or three seconds, Sayles fired his rifle but the bullets hit the ground, harmlessly kicking up dust and grass. He stumbled backwards, lurching with the recoil and struggling to stay upright. Anna couldn't understand what was happening until she saw blood coming out of his mouth. He coughed—a rattling, hollow sound.

Karan fired twice and Sayles crumpled, losing a grip on his weapon as he toppled into the grass, folding over onto his face.

Instantly, both Anna and Karan pivoted, trying and locate where the first shot had come from. As they did, another figure appeared in their field of vision, standing in a clearing opposite the rocks. Renzin lowered his revolver but stood his ground. He had fired only once; the bullet that caught Sayles in the throat.

Taking his eyes off Renzin, Karan stepped over to check on Sayles. Holding his pistol ready, he rolled him over with his shoe. The body felt lighter than he expected, as if there was nothing but bones beneath the loose camouflage clothing. Sayles was dead. His lifeless features seemed to have aged another ten years.

～

As he watched the scene play out in front of him, on the high-definition screen, Afridi's face revealed little emotion. But his fists were clenched, and he leaned forward in his wheelchair. Unlike Anna and Karan, he had seen Renzin step out into the clearing and watched him fire, thinking how much he looked like his father as a young man. They had spoken only an hour ago, by phone, when Afridi had told Renzin that Noya was dead. There was no change of plan. Renzin had his orders. He knew what had to be done.

Afridi felt a muted sense of satisfaction, as if his precautions had been vindicated. But, at this moment, the only thing that mattered was the motionless body sprawled in the grass, a twisted form in camouflage, a man he'd known in another life.

Fifty-Six

The somber chanting of monks fills the sanctuary, a hollow, resonant sound that seems to have traveled over centuries and crossed the farthest boundaries of existence.

A low, guttural incantation answers them, words of peace and absolution.

Drums and cymbals punctuate the liturgy.

His Holiness sits upon a ceremonial throne, wearing an abbot's yellow cap on his head and holding a sheaf of scriptures in his hands. Facing him is a congregation of several hundred monks and other followers, gazing up in reverence and devotion. They listen to the sacred teachings that have been handed down from one generation to the next. Yet, the meaning of these chanted words seems less important than the cadence, the rhythmic intake of the singer's breath, his exhalations, agitating the air and fluttering the moth-like flames of the butter lamps.

Beneath the golden membrane of his skin, the Maitreya Buddha waits impassively for the future, a promise of better lives to come, a release from sin and suffering as well as the ultimate ecstasy of annihilation.

In a room next door, four monks are kneeling at the cardinal points of the mandala, echoing in unison the chanting from the temple. The light that enters through the window is flecked with floating motes of dust, like miniatures galaxies.

When the ceremony in the temple ends, His Holiness rises to his feet and enters the room where the mandala has been constructed. In extended silence, he meditates upon the colorful symmetry of the design—cosmic patterns of time and space. Slowly, he reaches out and brushes the sand with his fingers, gently but deliberately erasing the lines. The monks who have created the mandala follow his lead, sweeping the colored sand aside with their hands, destroying the delicate patterns.

As chanting voices invoke the mysteries of faith and renounce the false promises of illusion, the monks scoop up the sand in their palms and pour it into a copper urn, carefully collecting every granule, until the wheel has vanished and there is nothing left of time.

References

The Himalayan proverb that appears at the beginning of this book is taken from E. Sherman Oakley's *Holy Himalaya* (Nainital: Gyanodaya Prakashan, 1905, reprinted 1990). Details regarding Tibetan culture and history were taken from Charles Allen's *The Search for Shangri-La* (London: Abacus, 2007) and John F. Avedon's *In Exile From the Land of the Snows* (New York: Vintage, 1979) as well as Samten G. Karmay and Jeff Watt's *Bon: The Magic Word* (New York: Rubin Museum of Art, 2007). W. Y. Evans-Wentz's *The Tibetan Book of the Dead* (London: Oxford, 1960, 178–79) is quoted at the end of chapter eleven.

Glossary

aap: polite form of "you"

arrey: exclamation, similar to "hey"

besharam: shameless

Bhotia: Tibetan

bidi: small, inexpensive cheroot

Boditsattvas: incarnations of the Buddha

Bon: ancient shamanistic religion of Tibet

Bournvita: malted chocolate drink

bugiyal: high meadows above the tree line in the Himalayas

chaat wallah: vendor selling fried snacks

chaan: thatched cowshed

chiru: Tibetan antelope

chinar: Himalayan plane tree, found mostly in Kashmir

chowkidar: watchman

chukkar: circuit (In Landour the Chukkar road circles the top of the hill.)

dargah: shrine at a Muslim grave

desi: Indian or literally, "of the country"

dhyana mudra: meditation pose

ghazal: vocal music, with the lyrics usually sung in Farsi or Urdu

gompa: Tibetan monastery and temple complex

gurdwara: Sikh temple

havaghar: open-air pavilion, literally "breeze house"

Haryana: an Indian state, near Delhi

keema: ground meat

khadi kurta: handspun cotton tunic

khud: steep hillside or ravine

kya patta?: Who knows?

lungi: unstitched cloth worn as a lower garment

madamji: slang for "madam"; "ji" adds politeness

mallu: slang for "Malayali" (person from Kerala)

mandala: sacred diagram of the cosmos, used in meditation by Tibetan monks

mazaar: Muslim gravesite shrine

momo: dumpling usually filled with meat

namaskar: polite greeting in Hindi usually accompanied by a gesture of folded hands

nimboo pani: lemonade

om mani padme hum: Hail the jewel in the lotus

paan: betel leaf confection eaten as a digestif

parantha: fried flatbread

pushta: retaining wall made of stone

qawali: choral group of male vocalists singing in Farsi, Urdu, or Punjabi

salwar: loose drawstring pantaloons

shahtoosh: underlayer of wool from a Tibetan antelope

shikar: hunting

tabla: a pair of drums played with the fingers

terma: buried relics or teachings

thana: police station

thanka: Tibetan painting, usually on a cloth scroll

yungdrung: swastika, symbolizing good luck and auspiciousness in Tibet